T0348656

BOOKS BY K. R. BLAIR

THE HAUNT FOR JACKALS
The Hushed

THE BECKONING SHADOW
The Beckoning Shadow

STANDALONE
Unchosen

NONFICTION
The Busy Writer's Guide to the Business of Writing

THE HUSHED

K. R. BLAIR

**BLACK
STONE**
PUBLISHING

Printed in the United States of America

First edition: 2024
ISBN 979-8-212-56456-4
Fiction / Thrillers / Suspense

Version 1

Blackstone Publishing
31 Mistletoe Rd.
Ashland, OR 97520

www.BlackstonePublishing.com

For Ash, who keeps all the good fires burning.

For as sure as God made black and white,
what's done in the dark will be brought to the light.
    —Johnny Cash, "God's Gonna Cut You Down"

ONE

I knew Sarah would die.

I saw it in her eyes the moment she arrived at the Boneyard. I could see it in the way she talked and the way she pulled at the sleeves of her government-issued windbreaker jacket.

She smiled too much. Tucked the dark hair behind her ear and tilted her head, like if she tried hard enough, the world would forget she wasn't human. But I knew that underneath all her warmth, it had already started. She wanted to tell . . . to utter the words that would erase her from the world. We're secrets wound into human skin, after all. Telling secrets is what we were created to do. Once the thought starts, it grows. A sickness of syllables that plants an itch somewhere deep in the chest. From the tightness on her face, I could see that the sentence was starting to spin together like a ball of sparks in her mouth.

But even knowing what would happen didn't make me ready for it. I'm never ready for it. And I sure as hell didn't want it to happen. I liked Sarah.

There was a sense of inevitability about it that coated my lungs with a thick, inky dread. It lessened over those six months she stayed at the Boneyard. Six months of the sound of her hairdryer in the bathroom at five in the morning. Of her singing while waiting for the toaster.

But for some reason, I wasn't thinking about it when it happened. Maybe it was because it was one of the first cold nights after a long North Carolina summer, and she was so excited to be able to wear the chunky gray scarf we found on sale at Target.

Maybe it was because there hadn't been a Haunt attack for a month, so we were able to avoid the bad publicity those brought on. It had been a while since we'd needed to cover over spray-painted skulls and crossbones on our front porch—the ones we could always expect as re-taliation for some shit the Haunt pulled.

Or maybe it's just because you never really expect someone to die in the middle of a homecoming game.

❧

The bass was deep, rattling the aluminum of the bleachers as I tugged at my jacket and looked around. The field below was drenched in flood-lights, and the bleachers on both sides were filling up.

It was a fall night, the kind that follows a day that still held onto summer but carried a chill on its edges. And it was windier at the top of the bleachers than I'd expected.

"I hate this," I whispered.

"I told you to bring a bigger jacket," Rory replied, unwrapping a piece of gum.

"I'm not even cold," I grumbled back. There were too many faces around us—too many new people. "I hate being trapped in the middle of a row. This is going to be a nightmare if I have to pee."

Rory popped the gum in her mouth. "Do you have to pee?"

I was still for a second as I considered. "I don't know."

"You don't know if you have to pee?" she asked.

"Jury's still out," I replied. Rory gave me a sideways glance, a smile playing on her lips. "Come on. This is good ol' American fun. Nostal-gia. Crosstown rivalries."

"It can't be called nostalgia if we've never done it before," I corrected her quietly. She rolled her eyes at me.

"No one else knows that," she whispered back flippantly. Almost hopefully. By the time she finished the sentence, I could tell she didn't believe it any more than I did. We looked over our shoulders, a habit that felt like breathing.

We were Hushed. We looked human, but we weren't, and all it took was one human with a sharp eye to recognize us from the registration office or Gravedigger databases. Our presence among the regular womb-comers was unwelcome at best, and things could quickly get ugly.

A blip of color flashed in the corner of my eye, and I turned just in time to see Sarah on the edge of the field, her emerald ribbon whipping around under the lights. She did that often, appearing just when I felt like the panic I kept even-keeled in my chest was about to start sloshing over. She was the reason Rory and I were there, two ancient anomalies tucked away at a high school football game.

She was one of us, but when the Haunt got the government to agree to let our kind play school sports with regular humans, she was ready. She wanted to be a cheerleader—to fly and smile and tell others they should *be aggressive be be aggressive.*

We could all tell that the cheer coach didn't want to let her try out last month. It was one thing to let us register for school, but letting a Hushed be a cheerleader seemed a special kind of insult. As much as they might have wanted to, they weren't going to tell her no. The Haunt for Jackals was an ever-present threat. They couldn't be everywhere, but it *felt* like they were. Any given act against Hushed could be the catalyst for retaliation. They'd found out about discrimination toward Hushed that happened on oil rigs in the middle of oceans. They'd avenged a Hushed that was killed on a wilderness retreat in the middle of Tongass National Forest. The Haunt for Jackals could be watching, always looking for unlikely people to make examples of. So, Sarah got to cheer. Still. It didn't mean the team was happy about it.

I watched as Sarah practiced along the sideline, hyping herself up for her first game. A girl with dark skin and a french braid tied with the same ribbon joined her, but the other girls pretended she didn't even exist. I smiled and waved at her, scooting closer to the railing as

I surveyed the almost-full bleachers. "I'm so glad we didn't stir at high school age. This is brutal," Rory said quietly.

"I think I do have to pee," I whispered.

"You do not."

"Oh, good. Never mind, then," I shot back.

Rory smirked, and I felt myself smiling too. Rory was my best friend . . . one of the only people who could make me feel safe about going out among the humans. She was easy with them. Even the ones who knew what we were almost seemed to forget when she ran a hand through her hair and laughed like she'd been a kid once. Like she didn't wake up naked in the dirt a few years ago like the rest of us.

Someone below laughed. It was more like a cackle, which broke off into a stifled snort. I looked down over the left side of the bleachers. Jason Bell stood below me near the fence that led to the parking lot, wearing his black Gravedigger jacket. I shouldn't have been surprised that he was there. He graduated three years prior, but everyone was at the homecoming game. Rearden Falls was that type of town. Even if it wasn't, though, Jason Bell was still the kind of creep would have nothing better to do on a Friday night than lurk around the high school where he peaked. My eyes fixed on the Gravedigger insignia on his jacket—the one that was supposed to be illegal. They'd been labeled as a domestic terror organization by the Department of Justice the year before, when several chapters in major cities couldn't hide the blood on their hands anymore. Not like Gravediggers were ever really trying to pretend that they didn't have one goal: they liked to kill Hushed. They saw it as righting some sort of cosmic wrong—putting secrets back in the grave where they belonged. And they had more sympathizers than anyone wanted to admit. They were allowed to be blatant about their desire to snuff us out . . . as long as no one could prove they actually did it.

Jason cackled, and I bristled at the sound. I knew him, and his brother Marcus—they were well-known in Rearden Falls, and they made sure to know the specifics of every registered Hushed in the area. I peered down at them through the metal posts of the bleachers, a sort of morbid fascination pulling me to watch as he slung his arm around

Tansy O'Mare, his twentysomething girlfriend. She was from South Rearden, the part of town where syringes washed up when it rained and most of the houses could be put on wheels. Lucky for her, she was pretty enough for Jason to overlook that. Her bleached hair fell in thick waves down her shoulders, and she teetered slightly on her black leather ankle-breakers. There was another kid with them. He had a bowl cut and a Gravedigger insignia—a skull and crossbones—on his backpack. *Bury the Bones*, it said underneath. And that was the ironic truth that no Gravedigger wanted to really think about: the Gravediggers only exist because we do. We gave them purpose. I stared at the words until they went blurry. *Bury the Bones.*

"Nice," I muttered, finally nudging Rory and motioning to the scene below. I needed to let her know they were there. We were already watching our backs, but now the threat was more specific.

"Well, if you do have to pee, I vote you just do it over the railing, and make sure to get them in the splash zone," she mused.

"How long do you think we'd have if we pissed on the president of the Gravediggers's little brother?"

"'It's not about the number of breaths you take, but the moments that take your breath away,' isn't that the saying?" Rory said softly.

"I'm deleting Instagram off your phone."

I watched them, feeling strangely detached as Rory turned back to the field. Jason had a scab on his cheekbone. I'm sure he wanted people to think it was from a fight, but my money was on it being from him picking at his cystic acne. The tag on Tansy's T-shirt was hanging out.

"I should have used the extra-hold hair spray on Sarah," Rory said, more to herself than to me. "It looks like her bangs are already starting to fall."

"She looks great," I said as I turned back to Sarah, and I meant it. She looked happy, and I smiled as I looked at her. She wanted to be a cheerleader, and she was one. Sometimes, joy seemed simple.

The lights dimmed, and there was a deafening roar as a senior cheerleader with legs longer than my entire body jumped onto the center of the small, scaffolded stage situated at the fifty-yard line and grabbed the mic, squinting into the spotlight.

"Welcome to the homecoming game!" the girl shouted into the mic, doubling over in exaggerated giggles and *oh stop it*s when her friends erupted in shouts of "GO TARA!"

Rory mimed tossing her hair over her shoulder as she waved to imaginary fans, and I joined her, doing a fake queen's wave.

I couldn't tell if we were petty for picking on a high schooler while being semi-functional pseudo-adults—it's not like stirring as a twenty-year-old was that different than stirring as a seventeen-year-old, despite the cultural gulf between high school and college—or totally within our rights as we were both technically only three years old.

"Okay. So, as we all know, we lost Coach Lahey last spring." The girl's smile faded into a caricature of somber respect, and the whole field quieted.

"He was the pioneer of the football program here at Rearden Falls High, and all of us in the athletic department spent the summer re-painting the locker rooms in his honor. We had this made"—the girl gestured to two quarterbacks in silver and green jerseys as they walked out onto the field, carrying a wooden plaque between them—"and his wife, Marian Lahey, has flown out from South Beach, Florida, to be here as we dedicate this field to his memory!"

No. No, no, no.

"Eerie," Rory breathed, and her voice sounded very far away.

The whole stadium erupted into applause and the spotlight swiveled to the eastern side of the field. An older woman in a silver jumpsuit covered in emerald ribbons walked onto the grass, flanked by football players.

I braced my hands on the metal railing next to me and swung my legs over as Rory scrambled to her feet, straining to keep her eyes on Sarah through the crowd.

Sarah was standing on the opposite side of the field with the other cheerleaders, next to a table with an orange Gatorade jug and some paper cups. I saw her lean on it, her thin fingers gripping the edge. She looked up into the bleachers, her eyes narrowed against the light. She was looking for us.

Marian Lahey moved slowly through the crowd, stopping to give kisses and shake hands.

I saw Sarah's lips move as she searched for me in the crowd. *Eerie*, she mouthed my name. Her eyes were wide and terrified.

Rory started shoving her way down the bleachers, but I knew she'd never make it in time. With one movement, I loosened my grip on the metal and slid down the supporting beam.

I crashed into the concrete harder than I thought I would, and pricks of pain shot up my legs.

"Shit," I whispered, shoving off the rail and turning, readying myself for a full sprint.

Instead, I found myself staring at Jason, Tansy, and the other wannabe Gravedigger, who were all staring at me with wide, amused expressions as I muttered *shit shit shit* over and over and tried to regain the feeling in my shins.

"Oh, hey, Boney," Jason said, turning to fully block my path toward the field. *Boney* was their clever name for us since we were the skeletons in their closets. "Where you headed?"

Over his shoulder, I saw Sarah take another step. Then another. She was walking toward the stage.

I didn't have time for a fight. I ran forward, shoving past Jason. He didn't stop me, but Tansy's boot caught my foot and sent me sprawling to the ground. A sharp ache shot up my wrist, and I gasped.

I rolled over and scuttled back just as Tansy leaned down.

"Sorry. I didn't see you there. Maybe it's because you're not supposed to exist?" She might be white trash, but she knew she could bully me anyway. She straightened, and Jason let out another cackling laugh as his hand snaked around her waist. I knew I should be more afraid of them, but I could only think of Sarah.

I shoved myself up to my knees and sprinted into the thick ocean of bodies, the soles of my shoes sticking on spilled soda.

I couldn't see Marian through the crowd, but I saw Sarah, her eyes fixed forward as she took the stairs to the stage. The crowd was still applauding and cheering, and my voice was lost, a whisper against the din.

My shoulders barely made a dent as I shoved as hard as I could, ducking under elbows as I went.

My terror roiled and bubbled, the adrenaline in me burning hotter with every second. I willed it to make me sharper, to turn me into something that would draw blood. I begged my lungs to turn that fear into something useful, but it died somewhere on the back of my tongue and crawled past my lips as nothing but a limp plea.

The closer I got to the stage, the more the crowd thickened. Yearbook photographers stood with their cameras up as they tried to get the perfect shot.

I clawed through, pulling at shirt collars and not caring if I raked over skin. Panic bit at my chest.

"What the hell?" a lacrosse player yelled as I shoved the side of her face, positioning my body between her and a basketball player. Finally, my voice caught the breath in my chest, flaring up like a spark meeting a gas leak.

"SARAH! NO!" I screamed. I screamed so hard I thought I might turn inside out. I screamed until I felt something pop behind my eyeball.

The cheerleader holding the microphone looked confused when Sarah reached for it.

"*MOVE!*" I screamed. "SARAH!"

I heard Sarah's breath over the PA. Her breathing was ragged, and the *whoosh whoosh* came harsh through the speakers. The spotlight tilted, illuminating her as she stood, the mic in her shaking hand.

"Coach Lahey didn't love you, Marian. You were right that he was having an affair with Nancy."

I stopped as the words fell over the crowd. Marian turned, looking up, her pale blue eyes narrowing and then widening as she found Sarah on the stage. A heavy silence fell over the field.

I shoved hard, one more time, pushing through the last line of still bodies.

"In your husband's email, you'll find the login information for two secret bank accounts. He never wanted you to find them."

I reached the top of the stairs just as she finished. She turned to me, swaying on her feet, her expression elated. The floodlights caught the shine of the glitter on her eyelids. It had been ninety-nine cents on an endcap at the pharmacy.

"It doesn't hurt anymore," she whispered after she'd let the microphone drop from her hand.

Then she crumpled to the stage, and I lunged forward to catch her. My small frame was no match for the weight of sudden death, and we both went down. I barely managed to keep her head from smashing against the edge of the metal, like it mattered. My leg twisted beneath me at a strange angle.

I put my hand to her cheek. In my mind, I said her name over and over like they do in the movies, like this was a mistake I could reverse for her. Like dying was a hallway and she could look over her shoulder and change her mind if only she heard me.

Not today. It didn't make sense. She was supposed to dance to some awful techno mash-up and make right angles with her arms and wink at the crowd and tell them to *be aggressive be be aggressive*. She wasn't supposed to be here, looking up and seeing nothing.

The collar of her cheerleading outfit was high, but I could still see the black tendrils that spread upward under the skin of her neck, the smudged ink at the end of the last sentence she'd ever say. A Hushed that does its job falls back into darkness. You tell your secret to your Wounded—the person that needs to hear it most—and then you stop breathing. I've seen it before. I've seen it dozens of times.

Rory careened up the opposite stairs, sliding on her knees.

"No," she cried, running her hand over Sarah's forehead.

I don't know when I realized the sound had stopped and that a deep and unnatural silence had made something out of nothing around us. But I know when I looked up, I saw a thousand faces staring at us from the darkness. Their expressions were tight with fury and horror and everything in between.

The crowd parted, and Marian walked through, her bright eyes fixed on Sarah's form. She came up to the front of the stage, and some heavy floral perfume wafted up with her. The spotlight made a halo of her white hair.

"A Hushed," Marian whispered, sniffing and wiping her nose with the back of her hand.

I nodded. Sirens sounded from somewhere behind me.

"My husband swore I was just imagining things," Marian said, shifting slightly and tilting her head like she wanted to look at Sarah from a different angle.

Sarah's head felt heavy against my forearm and my leg was falling asleep, but I didn't move.

"He died six months ago," Marian said, examining the body. It was quiet then, and I could almost hear the realizations clicking into place one by one, like heavy metal cogs in a clock. "The Hushed are supposed to tell their secrets. What took this one so long?" she asked, her voice exposing the sharp edge of her pain.

"Her name was Sarah," I said.

Marian's expression darkened as the sirens grew louder. They were on the street behind the gym.

"Hushed don't have names," Marian said, turning away.

One basketball player put an arm around her shoulders and led her through the crowd.

Voices started again, an angry rumble.

Rory met my eyes over Sarah's body as the paramedics came in through the space between the bleachers. They ambled, there was no rush.

They lifted her from me, and I watched her head flop back. Her hair smelled like Aqua Net. The black had worked its way over her jawline. One of the silver ribbons from her ponytail stayed tangled in my fingers, coming undone. I clenched it in my fist as Rory and I followed the paramedics out. They didn't cover her up, and it felt like everyone was taking a piece of her as they watched—a detail for a story they'd tell later but would never think of again after that. Rory and I walked behind them, even though we knew what would happen. They'd take her back to the lab, where they'd confirm that she was a Hushed. They'd make a note for Internment statistics, and then we'd never see her body again.

Behind us, the boom of the speakers squeaked back to life as Tara the cheerleader took the mic again and explained that they'd need to reschedule the game. Sarah was an unexpected rain out; Sarah was a bout of the flu taking out half the team. Sarah was a shrug and a *what are you gonna do?* Things like Sarah happened.

We watched the ambulance roll away, its lights flashing soundlessly. The wind whipped against the three impressive thirty-foot emerald-and-silver balloon arches that led to the stadium.

As Rory and I walked under them toward the parking lot on our way home, we cut all of them loose.

TWO

I stood in the middle of the forest behind the Boneyard, looking up at
the giant spruce tree above me, its dark branches stark against the white
sky. A necklace was twisted in a branch. That had belonged to Silas.
There was a piece of twine at eye level—Amy—and then a silver key
tied with lace a little lower down. Margo.

It had been six weeks since Sarah died, though humans don't call it
that. They prefer "expired," as though we've simply reached the extent
of our shelf life. It was the first snow of the season, and I'd waited until
today because I knew she would've loved it. She'd been so excited that
she'd spent half her paycheck on a pair of snow boots.

I pulled Sarah's ribbon from my pocket. It still looked pristine, with
pressed edges like it had been ironed. I wanted it to look tattered, like
she'd put up a fight. I leaned into the tree, tying it tight around a thick
branch near Silas's medallion necklace.

This was the worst part. Hanging it up like there was some sort of
point to it. Like I could tether her memory to this tree, and it wouldn't
follow me home. But there wasn't a real body to bury, and it's not like
real human cemeteries would take Hushed, anyway. This was my grave-
yard. My monument to the ones we'd lost.

If this were a real funeral instead of a Boney funeral, a priest who didn't really know Sarah would say comforting words. And then we'd throw dirt on the tree and go eat turkey wraps from Costco wearing all black.

I never invited Fabian to this part. He knew about it, but he didn't ask to come. And I never invited any of the others either . . . I knew they wouldn't want to go. It is too much of a reminder of what we are. I liked that they thought I was braver than them for doing this, being strong enough to face down our fate.

The wind brushed over my ankles, and I looked down. The trinkets in the tree bumped the bark. Maybe it would be better if Fabian came—he was the only one who'd ever been to a human funeral. I was just going off of what I'd seen on TV.

The way back was quick, quiet, and colorless. Black trees, white snow, gray sky. The nearby mountains stretched up into the sky, their tops hidden by the low clouds. It was beautiful, but I wasn't in the mood for beautiful things, so I looked down. One crunchy step in front of the other, trying not to think about the way Sarah's hand had flopped over the side of the cart when the paramedics rolled her out. Or the way a kid in pink jelly sandals stepped on Margo's arm at the mall as her mom tried to guide her around the body, leaving a checked sole imprint over the black stretching tendrils by Margo's shoulder. Or how Fabian had tried to cover Silas's mouth when he saw his Wounded at the grocery store, and how Silas had still spoken the words that would kill him through my brother's fingers. No one was around when Amy died. She was on a walk, and we found her hours later.

Soon I could see the slanted rooftop of the Boneyard, our little manor-for-misfits. It was the place where the Internment put every registered Hushed within thirty miles. There were only six of us now. That's because the volunteer registration rate was always low. Not many signed up unless they had no other choice. Fabian and I were in that "no other choice" category, but it made me angry to think about it, so I tried not to.

Footsteps sounded in the snow behind me, and my hand went to my jacket pocket, wrapping around the 9mm Beretta Storm I always carried when I went into the woods alone. I'd bought the gun in a pawn shop in Texas, no questions asked.

I'm sentimental, not dumb.

As the sound grew louder behind me, I pulled it out of my pocket and spun around, aiming the barrel at the center of my brother's wide chest.

"Eerie-girl, it's me," Fabian said, his hands raised in the air. His dark scarf blended with his black coat, and his eyes followed the gun as I lowered it to my side.

I exhaled sharply, breath leaving my body in a white puff. My nerves vibrated as I shook my head at him.

"Since when have you started lurking through the woods so early?" I asked.

"Since you didn't show up for breakfast," he countered.

He looked down at me—he was over six feet tall; he was always looking down at me—his amber eyes nothing like my blue ones.

Probably because we weren't actually brother and sister in a biological sense. We just stirred at the same place on the same bloody night and had been together ever since.

No one asked me where I'd been when we walked in, a small mercy I was thankful for, though I could tell from the thick silence that everyone already knew.

"Fabian! Waffles or pancakes?" Eva called over her shoulder as she stood over the stove.

Seph sat on the counter nearby, stirring the batter.

"Um. Waffles, I guess, thanks. I'm going to go put on some dry socks," Fabian said before disappearing up the stairs, three at a time.

"Eerie! How was your walk?" she asked, though her gaze lingered just a moment too long, and I knew what she was really asking. *Are you okay?*

When I first arrived at the Boneyard, I hated it. I didn't want her checking on if I was warm enough or asking how I liked my eggs. I didn't know what caring looked like, so I mistook it for pity. But she wanted to take care of us, and the Internment needed a point person—someone to hold the lease and send our mail to. That's Eva. She didn't look that much older than me—her body was no older than thirty—but she stirred in the 1950s, and that's what made me finally realize she had what it took to watch over us. She'd avoided the Pull for over fifty years. That commanded our respect, even if nothing else did. So, I let her show me where the extra towels were kept, and I now know I like my eggs poached.

"Fine," I said, adding a smile for good measure.

I peeled one boot off with the toe of my other foot, and then stepped out of the other. The kitchen looked like it always did. High, domed ceilings and open curtains to let in the cold morning light. Eva and Seph stained all the wood in the place after watching some do-it-yourself online video, so it looked better than any kitchen in a hundred-year-old foreclosure had any dream of looking.

They'd taken Sarah's chair from the table the day she died and spaced all the rest around it to look as though she'd never even been there. It was against the wall, now, waiting for the next Hushed the Internment dumped at our door in a flurry of paperwork and static walkie-talkies. I tried not to look at it.

Seph dipped her finger in the batter, and Eva smacked her with the spatula. If Eva loved being the mother figure, then Seph loved being the rebellious teenage daughter. And they both loved making breakfast for all of us. Pancakes and waffles. Orange juice in a pitcher. Plates in a circle, utensils laid out. I think she saw it in a movie, once, and assumed that eating a family breakfast could help make you feel like a real family.

Reed lounged on the other end of the table, flipping through the newspaper. He held it up higher as I walked by, and the thick, black headline ran across my eye level.

"One of Our Own: Trial of Ironbark Prison Guard Leonard Mark Begins the Defense Testimony." I stopped when I saw it, realizing too late that I'd given Reed the exact reaction he'd wanted. He smiled up at me, his gray eyes lighter than usual.

"Put it away," I hissed, shooting a glance at the stairwell as I reached out to snatch the paper.

He was too quick, holding it just out of my reach and turning the story toward me. I'd had enough. I didn't need Fabian seeing anything else about that stupid trial.

Reed's curling smirk deepened. "I'm learning about your culture, Eerie-girl."

"Do not call me that."

He smiled, satisfied at the growl in my voice.

Reed never read the paper. He got his news from ads on YouTube. I knew he probably saw the paper on Mr. Cauly's driveway when he walked out to scrape his truck's windshield. I wish I were more shocked that one of my housemates stole a newspaper from the veteran next door who could barely make it down his steps, but I wasn't.

I didn't want to look at the picture stamped on the page, but my eyes drifted anyway.

Leonard Mark looked up at me from the paper, his mug shot expression carefully blank. I'd seen that picture a thousand times, but it never failed to make my gut twist with sickness.

"You're an ass." It was all I could muster. Fabian's footsteps were heavy as he came down the stairs.

"Want to read it when I'm done?" Reed fake whispered. Fabian returned to the kitchen then and snatched the newspaper from Reed as he walked by.

"Hey, I said *when I was done*," he snarled, but Fabian ignored him as he took his seat.

I watched Fabian, the same way I always watched him when this happened. I knew the lines on his face, every movement of his thick eyebrows and the scar above his top lip.

Ironbark Prison was a federal women's prison less than a mile outside Rearden Falls, North Carolina. Three years before, it burned down. Everyone inside died, including several death row inmates, three guards, and a few staff members. The fire spread through the forest, leaving a blaze that jumped and shifted for almost a month. Leonard Mark was the man in charge of the prison, which meant he had to answer for the fire. The official statement was simple: there had been slippage in the upkeep due to reduced budgets, and an electrical fire had broken out. He was being tried for negligent homicide, along with lesser charges. But Leonard Mark had spent his whole career in government and had the support of everyone in the state that had an official motorcade. I don't think anyone really expected real justice, anymore, but people showed up on the courthouse steps every day, anyway. Fabian had gone the first couple of days and sat with some protesters from the local university, but even he understood that it was too risky for a Hushed to look too interested in a trial.

Especially us. Especially this trial.

Fabian and I stirred in the middle of the Ironbark fire, but no one knew that. The only official survivor was Leonard Mark, and we could never let anyone know any different.

I watched Fabian as his eyes raked over the page. I knew what he'd see. Several photos that had run alongside every article about Ironbark . . . the charred skeleton of the building in between the trees, mug shots of the inmates that had died. *Madeline Winspeare, 42. Susan Ainsley, 51. Monique Cavers, 24.*

I didn't have to ask if he recognized anything. I could see the vague, practiced disappointment slip over his expression: his shoulders fell, slightly, and he blinked more as he got to the end of the article. Nothing. He handed it back to Reed and reached for his coffee mug, and I felt the muscles in my chest relax.

We'd had years without any answers. Fabian had really hoped that the trial would spark something, but it had been going on for almost three weeks. Nothing.

"Fabe?" I asked, lifting the coffeepot as I sat opposite him, trying to use anything I could to pull him back to the kitchen—to me, to this life we've carved out of slippery rock.

Fabian nodded at me, smiling softly—a small concession. He reached back to snag the calendar section out from under Reed's elbow.

More footsteps sounded on the stairs, but they were quicker and lighter than Fabian's. Rory held on to the edge of the banister as she swung into the kitchen, her backpack slipping down her arm and taking half of her red cardigan with it.

"Morning all," she said, barely looking up as she dropped her backpack to the floor with a *thunk*. Several strands of hair had worked their way out of the bun twisted at the back of her head. She pulled a notebook out of her backpack and tossed it onto the table.

"Morning," I replied, keeping my eyes on Fabian. He straightened when she came into the room. He looked over at me, and I smirked. He gently put his foot over mine under the table.

"Get enough studying done?" Eva asked, handing Rory a plate.

"Never," Rory said. She slid into her seat and tucked her hair behind her ears. Her necklace was crooked, and I reached out and fixed it. She took a bite of the waffles, her eyes still holding the faraway look I'd grown to expect on exam days. She looked down at her notes.

Silence covered the table. They all knew where I'd been, but it felt like talking about it broke some sort of unspoken truce.

"This is weird," Seph proclaimed as she jumped off the counter. She was short and looked fifteen, at most. "I have an idea. Let's play 'marry, fuck, kill.'"

Eva almost dropped the plate of waffles.

"Josephine!" she said, her eyes wide as she looked over her shoulder.

Seph shrugged and sat in her seat at the table. She tried to act confident in the way she used the swear word, but I saw the pink in her cheeks and knew it probably took her ten minutes to find the courage to say that in front of Eva.

"It was Sarah's favorite game, and since Eerie just got back from her Boney funeral, I think it's only fitting."

Seph cocked an eyebrow at me. I couldn't help the smirk that pulled at my mouth as I looked at her. None of us choose the body we show up in—but the way Seph wore being a manic pixie dream girl with a literal pixie cut made me believe that whatever force created us got her just right.

Rory looked up, confused. Her eyes shifted past my shoulder, seeing the light drizzle of snow drifting down from the sky. Then she understood.

"Sarah called it 'marry, kiss, and extradite,'" Fabian amended, not looking up from the paper.

Eva set the plate of waffles down harder than she needed to. "You know I don't like that word," she said.

Seph bit a ragged fingernail. "What, 'fuck'? Well, I don't like being called *Josephine*."

Eva turned back to the refrigerator.

"She meant 'Boney,' you obtuse twit," Reed said to Seph, finally looking up from his paper.

"Hey," Fabian shot at Reed, who blinked and slid his eyes over to Fabian with an exaggerated slowness.

"I wasn't talking to you," Reed replied through gritted teeth.

"Stop," Rory said, looking from Fabian to Reed. "She hated when we fought."

Reed opened his mouth and then shut it, but only because it was Rory who asked.

Rory looked back to her notes, and I stuck my fork into the waffles Eva had handed me, watching the syrup pool into the divots.

Seph's voice broke the calm.

"Eerie: Jason Bell, Cole Madison, and . . ." she stopped, leaning over the table to tilt the newspaper closer. "Logan Winspeare. M-F-K." She laughed and brought her tea up to her lips, while Eva muttered something about the death of propriety and set the orange juice on the table. I watched the pulp swirl against the glass.

"Seph, that's gross. The poor guy's mother died in that fire," Rory said without looking up from her notes.

Seph looked down at the picture of Logan on the back of the paper. His pictures were always the same. Tie loose and crooked, his hand out, blocking the shot as he walked up the courthouse steps. He was the media darling of this whole trial: the tragic boy whose mother was a murderer. The press had followed him since he was a kid, and the cops arrested his mother at one of his soccer games. The picture of him trying to shove the cops off his mom in his cleats and jersey became a national story. He wasn't a kid anymore, but the press still loved that picture. The way he carried a disdain in his eyes for every lens pointed to his face told me that he hated it.

I chanced a look at Fabian, but he said nothing.

"Well, his life can't suck that bad. *Look* at him," Seph said, holding the newspaper up. Her dark purple nail polish did little to hide the fact that her nails were bit down to nubs.

"I can't see much, seeing as he is holding his hand in front of the camera," I contested, though I knew what he looked like. Fabian had a complete file on everyone having anything to do with Ironbark.

"*Psh.* Ain't no hiding that jawline," Seph said, setting the newspaper back down. Her dark eyes glittered.

"Seph, he's way too old for you," Eva chided from the counter, and Seph rolled her eyes.

Reed ran his knuckles over the jet-black scruff that covered the sharp hollows of his cheek. "Okay. This is fun. Answer the question, Eerie. Who'd you *F*?" he asked, pulling out a cigarette and sticking it between his teeth.

Eva walked by and, without skipping a beat, pulled it from his lips and sat it back on the table. He rolled his shoulders but didn't fight her.

"Too bad you're not in the mix, Reed, because then I know who I'd kill," I said, twirling a fork in my hand.

He waggled his eyebrows at me. "You sure about that?"

"I will literally kill you," Fabian offered lightly, pouring more coffee into his favorite chipped mug. He raised his eyebrows at Reed.

Reed leaned back, his eyes glinting. He hadn't been alive as long as Eva, but he'd been at the Boneyard the longest of all of us. When the Internment dropped him off, the house had been a crumbling mess. He'd slept on a bare mattress in one of the smaller bedrooms and littered the house with cigarette butts. It wasn't until Eva arrived and Seph shortly after that the place started looking something like a house. I'm sure Eva thought she was saving him, just like she saves everyone . . . but something told me that Reed didn't mind living in filth like a rat. He ran a hand through his wavy hair and stuck his cigarette behind his ear.

Eva watched us as she stood behind the island, drinking her coffee. She tried not to look out the window at the cold, but I caught her doing it once or twice. Sarah's excitement had seeped into everything. We had all been waiting for the first snow whether we realized it or not.

Rory noticed the time and shot up from her seat.

"Eerie! You didn't tell me it was seven fifteen!" She practically tripped on her own ankle boots as she jumped from the table and stuffed her notebook into the backpack. Fabian kept his head down, but his gaze followed her until it landed on me, and I met his eyes.

He looked down at his phone.

Typical. My brother, who once distracted an entire bar by doing overly emotional Taylor Swift karaoke so I could pick pockets, was afraid to tell Rory how he felt about her.

"Go to school, Eerie," he said, pushing himself out of his seat.

Seph walked over to get her toast out of the toaster and stopped to rub Reed's shoulders. "It's going to be a good day, okay?"

He didn't smack her hand, but I saw him clench his jaw.

Seph held her hand out as I passed, and I gave it a little squeeze. Eva told us to have good days and to be good, as if any of that would make a difference.

I took the newspaper, rolled it, and put it back into the plastic. I walked carefully on the ice back to Mr. Cauly's house and set the paper on his stoop, right on top of his threadbare welcome mat that read *One Old Buzzard Lives Here (With One Cute Chick!)*. His wife died fifteen years earlier, so I knew the mat must have been there for a long time. I slipped back down the driveway, past his rusting Ford F-150. The horn played "La Cucaracha." Knowing Mr. Cauly, he probably bought the truck from a scrapyard and just never got around to changing it.

I looked around as I jogged back to the car. All the houses around the Boneyard were kind of like Mr. Cauly's—run-down and unkempt. But there was a certain warmth in the way everything seemed held together by bungee cords and duct tape. I liked it this way. If it was a nicer neighborhood, the Boneyard would stick out like a sore thumb, and we didn't need any more attention. All the kids already avoided our house on Halloween, and we never got a chance to order Girl Scout Cookies. I knew humans were afraid of us, all together in one house like some creepy fairytale. I wondered how people would feel if they could see what we were really like. Half-eaten waffles. The bouquet at the center of the table that Eva had picked up from the grocery store when she'd gone to get more dish soap and decided to splurge a little. I think they'd be disappointed.

But even as I jumped into the car with Rory and she pulled out of our overgrown driveway, I wondered how long we could play pretend before everything caught up to us.

I checked the date on my phone. I only needed 173 more days.

THREE

I've heard a thousand different theories on how the Hushed came to be.

A cashier in Gideon, Missouri, told Fabian that she thought we were a side effect of Wi-Fi.

A gas station attendant just outside of Tulsa told me he thought we were aliens.

They didn't know, of course, that they'd been talking to Hushed at the time. We hadn't been caught yet. Since we hadn't been caught, we weren't in the system. We looked like two regular people. I didn't hold it against them. Honestly, it made me more uncomfortable when they assumed Fabian and I were married than when they assumed we were human.

I never argue. I don't know why we're here. I just know we're nothing new.

I first heard a glimpse of our origin story three days after I stirred, when Fabian and I slipped into a bar to steal nuts from happy hour. Six drunk sorority girls in matching pink "If you're not dating an Alpha Phi, raise your hand and then your standards" sweatshirts were playing "Hush-a-Bye" at the bar, chanting as they filled up a line of shot glasses.

In the darkness, there were three.
Stone and dust let blood run free.

Born of whispers, raised by death,
They were eager daggers, breath to breath.
But creatures are as creatures do—
Then there was one where once were few.

I already knew the words. I knew it like I knew how to breathe, like they were etched on my bones. So did Fabian. It turns out that every Hushed knows it when they stir. It's like a shitty factory setting that we all have. It's been found written on walls in caves alongside thirteenth-century artifacts. It's been etched into trees in old forests and scrawled on bathroom walls. We don't know where it comes from, but the fact that we all know it instinctively tells us it's important. The only piece of history we actually have as our own, and it's not much. Once upon a time, there were three of us. Then there was one. We've been around ever since, though no one realized it for hundreds of years.

The point of the game, we later realized, was to see who could drink the most while still remembering the chant after every shot. Loser had to tell a secret. From the way the girls were all sobbing and screeching an hour later, it was pretty obvious that they had secrets to spare.

I learned the rest of the murky history about a year later when I slipped into the back row of a history class at a local college when we were killing time passing through another nowhere town. The professor told the tale like he was explaining how a horrible venereal disease managed to spread across continents.

There are stories of the Renaissance Era when a painter died and, the next day, a mysterious traveler showed up at one of his posthumous exhibits and announced to everyone that the painter had been stealing art from his apprentice and passing it off as his own—before dying himself with black ink spreading across his chest. At first, people thought we were just truth-tellers who had been poisoned—hence the dark spread that starts in the chest and eventually covers the entire body. But no one could name the poison, replicate it, or find it, even as it dotted the histories of almost every culture in the world.

They called it the "Teller's Fever." For a time, it was amusing. A strange conspiracy theory or riddle for historians and anthropologists to play with over drinks.

But then, somewhere around 1943, it spread. Unexplainably. Quickly. Within a decade, people were dropping dead daily. Mass pandemonium. Millions of dollars went into trying to find out the cause of Teller's Fever. The World Health Organization put together a global task force that tried to get ahead of the disease—there were PSAs that ran every hour. *If you come across a victim of TF, do not touch the corpse and contact your local authorities.*

Everything changed when they realized the dead weren't the victims of TF.

They *were* the disease.

We are embodied secrets that wake up the moment our human dies. The more secrets you have, the more Hushed wake up when you bite it. The bodies dropping like flies were Hushed that had given in to the Pull—the need to tell the secret.

There are a lot of terrible aspects of being a Hushed. But the Pull is the worst. It never goes away, even if our Wounded dies—it just gets transferred to the next living person affected by the secret. In theory, a Hushed could live long enough to get enough practice to resist the Pull. But even Eva had to move across the country to get away from her original Wounded's great-grandson, who was now her Wounded. I still sometimes found searches on the computer about Sacramento, California, and I knew Eva had spent a couple hours trying to track him down. Even over half a century isn't enough to make the Pull go away.

You'd think it would calm everyone down to realize that they weren't going to catch an accelerated version of the Black Death. I think the National Campaign to End TF thought they were announcing something to put everyone's minds at ease when they announced Teller's Fever wasn't a transmissible disease. They should've known that the truth really wasn't that much better than the panic: *Don't worry, you won't die from this. But when you do die, your secrets are going to come to life with the single purpose of exposing everything you tried to hide while you were alive.*

Maybe it wouldn't have mattered if it only affected the dead, but it didn't. The secrets that walked in during funerals or at birthday parties told secrets that ruined the living as well. If a man made his whole fortune through fraud and the Hushed exposed it, the man's family stood to lose everything. That's the thing about lies, I guess. They don't really care where they get tangled.

I didn't last long in that class. I started sweating as I watched the professor hit the eraser against the whiteboard with what felt like exaggerated zeal that I could only read as anger. I left, but I've picked up bits and pieces since that day. Moments in public libraries or newspaper articles, glimpses of news reports in run-down diners that have a TV running behind the bar.

No one knows why we went from myth to epidemic in a few short years—there are no answers to that. The spread accelerated in the 1950s, steadily covering the globe. Eventually, I just chalked it up to one more unsolved riddle in this whole mess, one that didn't matter much in the face of what we all knew: the Hushed were here.

The Campaign to End TF gave way to the Internment, the federal body tasked with dealing with and monitoring Hushed activity. They were harmless for a while. Hushed lived and Hushed died—sometimes publicly, but sometimes all there was to show a Hushed had been there at all was a body in an alley that the trash pickup scooped up like roadkill. The Internment had one major challenge—Hushed looked human.

Then, ten years ago, Connelly Stewart, the head of the Internment, made an announcement at the National Mall: they'd discovered a way to identify Hushed.

I don't remember this, obviously. I stirred seven years later. But I'd seen the footage. Connelly, in a stark black suit that contrasted with his golden hair, holding his hand up like a prophet.

That's when the Internment became dangerous to us: the second they had a sure way to identify us.

Honestly, the Internment's official offer sounded nice enough: Hushed could go to the recruiting station, prove they were Hushed, and get registered. Then, they'd take care of us. House us. Clothe us. It sounded innocuous, but not many Hushed were trusting or desperate enough to believe it. Most were caught against our will, like Fabian and me.

They gave the two of us a choice: go to school or work at the lock factory. Which is why I was in the car, headed to the local community college, where I was working to get my associate's degree in veterinary sciences. Fabian wanted the factory; he said he wanted to work with his hands. But I knew the real reason was because he never intended on leaving Rearden Falls. There was something that felt less permanent about school—something transient. Fabian made himself essential at the factory. I don't think anyone in my classes knew my name. I liked it that way, though I knew that my loose grip on our lives here didn't matter much when Fabian held on so tightly. I could get my degree and have a reason to move on. But Fabian could work here for as long as he wanted. He wanted answers . . . answers I knew he'd never find.

But there was a part of me, a part that could never quite catch its breath when the name "Ironbark" popped up on the TV or in newspapers, that whispered: *What if he does find answers? What if it kills him?*

That thought was a brittle scratch down my spine that reminded me of why I needed to find us a way out of this place. Even if I didn't think anything could ever be unearthed—I needed to get him away from the place where he could dig.

That's what I thought about as we headed down Cross Road, the main street that cut through town. I looked out the window. It was cold, but not "fuck that, I'm calling an Uber" cold yet. Two girls with long earrings and hip-looking beanies walked arm-in-arm, their breath coming out in bursts of little clouds of steam as they laughed at something. A tattooed man carried his small dog under his arm, and an elderly couple power walked in the bike lane. Rearden Falls was a strange melting pot of rural sensibilities and artistic expression. Galleries sat crammed next to flooring depots, and you were just as likely to find a place to get your hunting knives sharpened as you were to find a cup of artisanal coffee. There wasn't one "type" of person, here, which made it easier for Hushed to slip in and out as we pleased. That was the one upside to this place, though I'd never admit that to Fabian.

Rory drove us past the courthouse. I narrowed my eyes through the glass, forcing myself to look at it, even as adrenaline spun up my neck, locking my jaw into place. The fear was more out of habit than anything else, because I knew I would probably feel nothing.

I didn't feel the Pull . . . I never had.

"Still nothing?" Rory asked, splitting her gaze between the frosty windshield and me.

I shook my head.

Nothing.

Rory didn't come to us through the Internment. A group of campers found her in the woods in Carrier, the next town over. She'd made it on her own for a while before catching a ride to our doorstep just two weeks after Fabian and I showed up. She heard that the Boneyard was where the Hushed were, and she also knew Hushed didn't last long on their own.

I'd been a small little bramble of anger then, content to curl up in the corner of my assigned room and disappear. At the end of each day, I'd realize I hadn't even opened my mouth. My lips almost fused together when I went to brush my teeth, and it hurt a little to pull them apart.

Rory wasn't Sarah. She didn't show up with smiles and fill our kitchen with sugar clouds. But she did ask me which bed was mine and when I ignored her, she asked again.

I pointed to my bed beneath the window, hoping she'd get the point.

But then she sat next to me at breakfast the next day and asked why I wasn't eating. She asked where Fabian and I came from. She asked about what classes I was taking at Rearden Community and the scar on my shoulder.

She broke against me like a wave and wound herself into me like a vine. She wore me down until one day, while we were peeling carrots in the sink for Eva, I snapped at her and asked her if she ever shut up.

Without skipping a beat, she turned the sink nozzle on me, soaking me in seconds despite my shrieks.

"We've got too many enemies to treat each other like shit," she explained, pulling the sink cord as far as it would go. Eva and Seph stood behind her, shocked, but neither moved to stop her. "You don't have to like me, but I'm not the one looking to put a bullet in your skull. I'm your ally, and I deserve better than your scraps of melodrama."

Then she put the nozzle down and went back to peeling carrots, leaving me drenched on our kitchen floor.

She was right, and I could tell by the way neither Seph nor Eva protested that maybe the message was long overdue. We needed each other—our survival depended on it.

Hushed can tell other Hushed their secret without dying. It doesn't get rid of the Pull. But it eases the ache, even for just a moment. And sometimes that's all you can do to make the difference. I don't need that, because I don't feel the Pull. But I know how badly the rest of us do. Now that I've seen Hushed give in to the Pull, I'm surprised Rory didn't do something more drastic than spray me with the nozzle.

The next day, Rory asked if she could borrow one of my shirts. I said yes. Then we were friends.

We stopped at a stoplight.

"What is it?" she asked. She always knew when my thoughts were getting too deep, when they were turning from musings to obsessions.

"I hate it when he looks at me like that."

"Like what?" Rory asked, rubbing her hands over the steering wheel. She knew I was talking about Fabian.

"Like he's disappointed we've survived this long."

Rory shook her head. "He's not disappointed you've survived."

"He's disappointed that we're freaks."

"Well. We're all freaks."

"What kind of Hushed can't remember a damn thing? Who they came from? What they're supposed to know? Who their Wounded is?"

Rory got quiet, then, and I could feel her chewing on her answer for a moment, rolling it around in her mouth like she was deciding whether or not she should spit it out.

"The kind that don't have to worry about winding up like Sarah," she said finally.

Her words sunk into my chest, and I sat deeper into my seat. It's true. No Wounded, no Pull. I can't tell a secret I don't remember.

Rory tapped her fingers on the wheel. "And what about the other thing? Are those drifts getting better?"

We turned the corner, and I leaned my shoulder into the seatbelt buckle until it hurt.

That's another reason I've always preferred traveling with Fabian, eating lukewarm hot dogs and staying on the fringes of whatever town we were in: drifting.

Hushed can still dream like humans, but drifting is something different . . . almost like a communal consciousness that links us when we fall asleep within a certain distance of other Hushed. It's just a mess of bits of memory, pieces of our human's secret, snapshots of their lives.

Strange little slivers and tastes that we all experience, a weird, shared homeland we all wandered toward once slumber found us. There were nights when we didn't drift and just dreamed, like normal humans with normal minds. But I could usually tell the difference, and my dreams weren't often a nice change of pace. Lots of blood and snow . . . ash on my tongue.

We knew everyone's drifts; we were used to each other. When a new Hushed passed through town, we'd see new things. The year before, we'd seen the inside of a WWII submarine for a week straight. At first, I thought it would be fun, because *WWII* felt exciting to me in the way that war always seems exciting to people who've never been in it. But I quickly realized that I was claustrophobic, and that submarines suck. Every night, we'd drift into a tiny, locked box full of panicked people who were on the edge of death. We were all really glad when that Hushed left town.

Some of my drifts were different, though. I was the only one seeing them.

One minute I'd been sleeping, and the next I was in a domed stone room, with the shafts cut into the roof spilling thick moonlight onto the floor in puddles. I was watching three figures stir on the dirt floor. They happen just like all of us happened . . . they weren't there, and then they were. A muscled man with a jagged, puckered scar cut on his neck; a girl with dark hair, olive skin, and bright green eyes; and a thin, pale girl with bright red lips.

"You still can't see faces?" Rory asked, turning her blinker on.

"No. I'd think it was just a dream, but I've seen the same thing four times. Different angles, but never in any detail." The rest was smudged watercolor and the only parts of them that stayed intact were the man's scar, one girl's red lips, and the other girl's green eyes.

Night after night, I stood in the haze of the drift, watching as these three Hushed stirred around me in the stone room.

"And nothing new happens after they wake up?"

I shook my head. "Nope. Scar and Green Eyes are trying to get their bearings . . . they're scared. Red Lips just stretches. It's weird . . . like she woke up from a nap, or something."

Rory narrowed her eyes through the windshield.

"He has a scar?" she asked, squinting like she was trying to picture it.

"Yeah," I said, looking at Rory. "Which makes no sense, because where would a Hushed get a scar?"

"It's too early for philosophical musings, Eerie," Rory warned playfully, and I shook my head. She was right—and there wasn't an answer. We knew how Hushed worked . . . we knew our rules and limits. But the *why?* It was a mystery. And the *what*—*what* we were . . . that was a mystery too. I didn't know why I had freckles from sun damage on my nose, or why Rory's knee clicked when she stretched. We hadn't *lived*, but it was as though our bodies had. I didn't know why certain secrets came into older or younger bodies—why Sarah was in high school or we were in college—or why some came into male bodies or female bodies. There wasn't a clearly obvious design to us, and it all seemed random. I just knew we woke up when our human died, and we didn't age.

Sarah believed we were taken from somewhere else . . . that we were misplaced in time and given a new purpose. She was like Fabian in that way. She thought we were part of some bigger plan.

And look where that got her, I thought.

"Do they say anything?" Rory asked, and I blinked, coming back to the conversation. I took a deep breath. I shook my head.

"A little? But I feel like I can hear some of what they say, even though I can only catch glimpses of what the words. You know, in dreams, how sometimes you just *know* things, but you don't know how? Like you know someone is good, and another person is bad, but you don't know where you made the distinction?"

"You think one of them is bad?"

"No. Not like that. I just . . . I have a feel for them. Like they've imprinted in my mind."

"Okay. I take it back. You are a freak," Rory said, a smile on the edge of her lips. I knew she was joking to give me a way out, a chance to back away slowly from something that scared me. I appreciated it.

We kept driving, and Rory sighed. "It's probably nothing serious, but it's clearly bothering you. You should let me try again to teach you how to restrict your drifts."

I shook my head. Rory had learned how to control her drifts, more or less. She'd tried to show me how, but it never worked for me.

"I don't have it in me to fail at that again."

The window steamed up, and I ran my sleeve across the glass. I didn't know why I was the only one drifting with whatever new Hushed was around, but I hoped they moved on, soon.

We pulled up to a red light next to a local coffee shop that was partially covered by a canopy of trees. Three figures walked out, hoods pulled tight against the cold. Jason Bell froze as he saw me through the glass. Bloodred letters splashed across the sweatshirt stretched over his broad chest: *Choose Freedom—Bury the Bones.*

He met my eyes through the smudged glass, and he smiled. It was a sick smile, like he'd been looking to run into a Hushed and I just granted his wish.

We pulled into the parking lot of Rearden Community College. Rory stopped to let a woman in scrubs pass in front of us, and she gave us a quick wave between deep drags of her cigarette.

We parked, and I turned the visor down and looked at myself in the mirror. My blond hair stuck out in odd angles, and the remnants from the previous day's mascara still shadowed beneath my bottom lashes. I spent the first two years of my life giving myself impromptu showers in gas station bathrooms, so I had a pretty high tolerance for how awful I could look, but I winced. My blue-gray eyes looked milky, somehow. Bloodshot and tired.

Rory reached into the center console and pulled out a makeup wipe, handing it to me without taking her eyes off the road.

"Someone could've told me I looked like this," I said, wiping the black from under my eyes.

"I thought you were trying something," she said.

"Whatever I was trying, it didn't work," I countered, and she snorted.

We walked through the parking lot without saying a word, and I looked up as we climbed the front steps. The building looked so much bigger up close. I hated how small it made me feel.

⸙

One hour into class, and I knew it was one of those days I should have faked sick and taken the hit when the Internment called to check where I was.

There was really no rhyme or reason to the classes I took. I just had to be enrolled in a certain number of credits, per my agreement with the Internment. My registration process tended to amount to running my eyes down the list of classes and hitting "enroll" on any reasonable-sounding class that was open.

In my biochem lab, we wound up talking about the bioluminescent amino acids in Hushed DNA, the ones that give us away when you stick us under a special black light. I spent the entire class period glaring at the professor, daring her to call me up to the front of the classroom for a demonstration. She didn't. I wouldn't have done it, and it wouldn't have worked, anyway.

I fell asleep in my Brit Lit Survey course and managed to blend into the last row of the lecture hall in my business admin course.

Rory and I always met for lunch, but she texted me that she'd be a couple minutes late. I hung back, leaning against the hallway just beyond the wide double doors of the mess hall.

My phone buzzed.

I looked down and froze. It was from Fabian.

Haunt attack at the capital. Get home.

My fingers moved before my mind caught up—a skill I learned from Fabian and honed in countless moments of blind panic. I forced myself to steady my breathing as I tried to call Rory.

She didn't pick up.

We didn't have much time.

It wasn't thirty seconds before I heard someone yelling the jarring melody. It was off-key and stilted, more a shout than a song. My blood spun with thick chunks of ice as I flattened my back against the wall and stared down the empty, echoing hallway.

> *What's in a man should stay with him*
> *What's his should never walk*
> *No deed or look should crawl back up*
> *And sure as hell should never talk*
> *We're digging deep back in the earth*
> *And let our voices sound*
> *We'll fight these Boneys day and night*
> *'Til they're all back in the ground.*

It's the anthem of the Gravediggers, their response to the "Hush-a-Bye" rhyme. They were always writing the lyrics on the marquee outside the Yard, the Gravedigger bar just outside of town. If today were a regular day, some administrator would've strolled out and told them to shut up—even if he gave them a "rules are rules" kind of wink as he walked away. But if everyone was just hearing news about the Haunt attack, then the anger was fresh. That tended to make even the most sympathetic blind to things like this.

I stared down the hallway as the noise grew louder. A couple more voices joined in.

I wasn't afraid of Jason Bell or any of the other Gravediggers—not in the real sense of the word. Just an idiot with too much Internet access and the carefully curated outrage that can only be generated by men who think that the life they feel entitled to is somehow being taken from them. For Jason and his kind, we were the ones to blame. Gravedigging was the answer to the rage they all felt, a way to not be helpless. Bashing my skull in would do nothing for his cause, but he'd do it just to see what color my blood was. My fingers flexed against the hard metal of my phone. I'd never let him, of course. But fighting back would come at a cost—attention I didn't want and could not afford. I needed to play nice for just 173 more days.

I turned as the noise got louder. I was about to go hide in the bathroom when one of the classroom doors to my right opened suddenly, and a dark-skinned girl with wide, searching eyes met my gaze. It was the cheerleader who had been nice to Sarah.

"Come in here," she said, looking past my shoulder and down the hallway. Jason yelled the last line of the song again and was met with dozens of peals of laughter. Tansy's voice was somewhere in the din, too.

I hesitated, and the girl reached over and yanked me inside, closing the door behind her. There was already a group of about a dozen people inside—a woman holding a baby, and two older men sitting next to two teenaged boys. The girl flipped the lights off and locked the door.

"What is this?" I asked, standing close to the door even when the girl motioned for me to take a seat.

"Missions. We're from the church down the street."

Of course. Some local charities had their chapter meetings in this building during the week.

"I don't need your help," I said. I meant to sound sharper, but my voice came out soft.

"Didn't say you did, but it's better to avoid those guys," she said simply as she leaned against the desk.

The song got louder—the group was only a few feet away now. I stepped to the side of the door so that no one could see my silhouette against the frosted glass. I hated that my heart rate was spiking.

Someone in the hall kicked the door and I jumped, swallowing the sound that flew up my throat. They were just passing through; I could hear them kicking trash cans as they walked away.

The girl stepped forward, her hands extended like I was a wounded animal.

"Are you okay?"

I didn't move, and she pulled out her cell phone and hit the screen twice. A news article appeared on her screen.

The Haunt for Jackals Attacks Washington, DC: Top aide revealed as Hushed, exposes backdoor deals on Senate floor. I only saw the screen for a minute, but that's all I needed. It was one good thing my human left me: a near-photographic memory. Almost perfect.

The girl's eyes were hard as they met mine. The light from the pixelated words felt burned into me, like I could read them against my eyelids if I shut them. They reminded the humans of this world that they were no longer alone. I wondered what she was thinking. If the starkness of the word—*attack*—made her rethink her kindness.

I'd stopped trying to explain long ago that I had no control over the Haunt—that none of us did. We didn't ask them to fight for us. In fact, if I could have, I would've told them that their attacks were the opposite of help. How things could be good sometimes, almost peaceful, until the Haunt launched one of their attacks on the humans.

I started to turn away, but she held her phone out to me.

"Do you need to use this?" she gestured to her phone.

The girl's voice was soft. Concerned, almost. The words got stuck in my mind, tripping over what I expected her to say. Not that.

"What?"

"Does your family know what's happened?" she asked slowly, reading my confusion.

Family. I felt a bitter sting in the back of my throat as I realized—she knew that Sarah and the rest of them were family.

"I can use my own phone," I said. Her face fell, but I didn't do anything to soften my tone as she tucked her phone back in her pocket.

Fabian was at the factory, around bars of metal, heat and edges. It was moments like that when I was glad Reed was with him. Should anything happen, Reed's rage might keep them safe. Seph was at the trade school three blocks over, studying cosmetology. Eva would be going to get her. Rory was upstairs. Everyone I cared about—this little ecosystem I'd let myself become part of—was all scattered, exposed to a world that was just given an incentive to bite.

I yanked the door open but stopped for half a second to look back at the girl. She picked at a hangnail as she stared at me. She knew Sarah, but I wasn't Sarah. Still, I swallowed, my tongue dry and scratchy as I searched for words.

"Thank you," I whispered.

She blinked too many times. "Do you need help getting out?"

Rory and I had a plan for moments like this. With any luck, she'd be at the car already.

"No." I hoped I was right.

I stared down the emptying hallway, ignoring how I could hear the Gravedigger anthem still bouncing off the tiles like a rubber ball.

I threw my hood over my head and did what I did best.

I ran.

FOUR

Rory was already waiting in the car with the engine running.

"Fucking Haunt," I said, slamming the car door. Rory peeled out and reached for the radio dial.

"Don't," I said. "I don't want to hear his voice."

Rory merged with traffic on the main street and pulled her hand back to the wheel.

I hadn't said his name, but it was like I had. The thought of him felt like a tangible thing, a presence in the car we needed to make room for. Railius.

He was the leader of the Haunt for Jackals. We never saw his face, but his voice was the one that took over the radio after an attack. Especially one where one of the Haunt revealed a huge, geopolitical secret that ignited a 24-7 news coverage upheaval.

Our bones can break yours. It will be easier for us to bury you than the other way around.

I could conjure the voice in my memory, a thick, living thing, cutting syllables on the edge of threats. I looked out the window. The snow had slowly turned to a slushy drizzle, and I drew my knees up to my chest.

He says he fights for us. He says they all do. The Haunt—a secret society made up of Hushed born of the world's most famous and most powerful humans—who have united and become exactly what the humans fear we all are: their reckoning. The biggest, darkest secrets, all ready to give in to their Pull at the right moment; ready to destroy treaties, peace talks, trade deals. With only a few words, a Hushed could shred a reputation. The humans call the Haunt's tactics terrorism, and I don't disagree. The entire human world is a carefully constructed tower of lies that survives because of ambition and mutually assured destruction. So, to them, transparency is destruction.

I've seen renderings of what the humans think the Haunt looks like: figures in black robes, sitting in some stone throne room, their index fingers pressed together under pensive faces, planning surgical destruction. That could be how they are—I don't know. None of us do. The Haunt is everywhere and nowhere all at once. They are a force that works from the shadows, and when humans push, the Haunt pushes back, always using the most powerful weapon: secrets.

The day Connelly Stewart announced the ability to identify Hushed and implied that compulsory mass registration was something being "considered," three Hushed born of assassinated dignitaries took the floor at the UN and revealed secrets of six top officials who were negotiating nuclear deals. The deals all fell apart.

Connelly Stewart backed off the next day on the morning show circuit, insisting that the Internment would only forcibly identify Hushed if necessary, like if you were running from the Internment, or if you were arrested. As a result of the compromise brokered by Railius and the rest of the Haunt, we've wound up with a life that's neither terrible nor great. We're rather like humans in that respect, I suppose.

But the ground was always shifting beneath our feet. The push and pull between the human governments and the Haunt for Jackals was constant. Humans would kill a Hushed in Portland, Oregon, leaving a skull and crossbones etched in his chest. The Haunt would crash the Campfire Boys induction ceremony and expose enough tax fraud to shut down the whole organization, leaving the Haunt's emblem—a skeleton with clenched fists raised with crossed arms above its head—spray-painted on the hood of the director's car.

And whenever the Haunt pushed back, the hatred around us amplified.

"Silver lining? Mal texted me and told us not to come to work today," Rory said, pulling me out of my thoughts as she switched lanes.

"Good call. He already gets enough grief for hiring us. He doesn't need protesters today."

Rory put the car into third gear and climbed the onramp up to the tree-lined highway. The rain blurred the windshield, and red taillights shone like fuzzy Christmas lights.

"That's weird. What time is it?"

"Too early for this kind of traffic," I said, stretching myself as far forward as I could.

Up ahead, I saw the reason for the holdup. Police cars sat at awkward angles on the side of the road. A bashed-up pickup truck hung from the back of a tow truck, and a white sports car with a dented fender slowly made its way back onto the highway.

"Accident. It's clearing up," I said.

A couple officers stood on the side of the road, wearing cheap plastic ponchos. They waved cars past the scene of the accident, then stopped us as the tow truck pulled out onto the wet asphalt. We were next, and the closer officer motioned for us to drive. The tow truck beeped, then, and the officer motioned for us to stop as he walked up to Rory's window.

"Sit back," Rory said as we pulled forward.

The cop knocked on the glass twice. Rory lowered the window, wincing as rain splashed inside. It was just on the edge of freezing, and I shivered as wind gusted inside.

I recognized the sharp angles of his face and the way his ears stuck out awkwardly from under his plastic-lined police cap. It was Kevin Allinson, a regular at the diner where we worked. He reacted slightly when he saw Rory, then looked back to an officer standing about ten feet down the road. The wind shifted, and I twisted the heater up to full blast. It did nothing against the brutal cold, so I leaned forward and pressed my fingers to the vent. It was too hot, but I didn't move.

Everyone always said that Fabian and I were lucky to have survived as long as we did out in the world, especially since killing an unregistered Hushed was easy. Maybe part of it was luck, but there was more to it. I learned to listen to that prickle at the back of my neck that told me *look around. Something isn't right.* As I looked at the other officer, his silhouette smudged by the soaked window, I knew something wasn't right.

But as I glanced in the mirror at the cars lined behind us, I realized there was nothing we could do. We were trapped.

"What's the problem, Officer?" Rory asked. She knew just how to pitch her voice in these kinds of situations so that it sounded a half-octave higher and a tad slower. She tilted her shoulder upward. Rory always knew how to talk to humans, and she had a knack for charming them so completely that they tended to forget what she was. Officer Allinson leaned against the windowsill. At the diner, he was all smiles and "yes, ma'am" and sly grins and leaning on the counter. But this was different. He looked down, shuffled his feet. Glanced over his shoulder, like he was hoping the other officer wouldn't look our way. My fingers felt like they were on fire against the heating vent, but I didn't move them.

"We just need to give the tow truck a minute," he explained as the truck beeped. Metal clanged as the gears shifted, and Allinson looked down at us. "What are you girls doing here?" He looked at his watch. His eyes shifted as he adjusted his stance.

"Class ended early for us," she said smoothly, sensing the way his hands flexed at his side.

"You should've taken the surface streets," he said quietly, shooting a careful look sideways at the other officer. I looked through the windshield just as his partner took notice of our car. Our wipers bumped uselessly against the ice gathering on our windshield as he walked closer, a dark blur through the hunks of sleet. But even through the distortion, I could see that there was a hunger in the way he was walking, like he was a coil ready to spring.

"Problem, Allinson?" he barked as he reached our window and peered inside. He was older, probably in his midforties. I squinted at the name on his chest. *Officer Durham.*

"No, sir. I was just about to wave them through."

While Durham's body looked soft underneath the poncho, his eyes were like flint as he met Rory's gaze.

"License and registration, please," he said through a forced smile.

"What for?" she asked, her voice taking on an edge that made Allinson close his eyes. I popped the glove compartment and thrust the registration at her. She passed it over with her license to Durham as she threw a look at me. Whatever she read on my face, it was enough to make her clamp her jaw shut. Officer Durham regarded me from under the brim of his soaking hat. I turned and stared out of the windshield, though I couldn't see out of it anymore. Durham let out a breath, and I don't know if it was a sigh or a laugh. Either way, it was a cruel sound.

"What for? Miss, you're already being cited for driving with an unbuckled passenger in the front seat. Would you like to add an aggravation charge to that?"

Rory looked at me. I was braced forward, my hands on the dashboard, but the seatbelt was obviously buckled. She slid her eyes up to mine. I shook my head, just slight enough for her to see.

Durham turned his flashlight on and held Rory's license up in front of him, making a show of inspecting it. I knew what he'd see: the little red line across the top that indicated that she was registered with the Internment.

"Pull forward and onto the shoulder," he said.

"Sir," Allinson started, but Durham shined his light directly in Allinson's face.

"Last time I checked, Allinson, I was your superior. So shut up."

Rory eased off the brakes and let the car roll forward, turning the wheel slightly to the right and onto the muddy shoulder of the highway.

"We'll be fine, Rory," I said, though my voice sounded uncertain to my own ears. I looked over my shoulder. People were opening their car doors. Sticking their heads out to brave the freezing rain for a moment before slipping back inside.

"He's a prick," Rory said, her jaw chattering.

"Yes. And we need this prick to get bored with us. So just do what he says," I hissed through my teeth.

I shot off a quick text to Fabian.

Highway 57. Exit 217. Thoroughfare.

"Did you text Fabe?" she asked. Her voice was tight.

"Yeah," I said, looking down at the phone. Little ellipses appeared on Fabian's end of the conversation, but I didn't have time to see what he was saying.

Then Durham was opening Rory's door.

"Step out of the vehicle," Durham said. It sounded formal. Official. Allinson walked around to my side. He pulled open my door, and I shivered as the wind blew chunks of ice onto my cheek. The rain was thick and heavy, splashing up from the slushy snow at the turnout. Rory reached in for her coat in the backseat. The movement was slow and smooth but didn't stop Durham from yanking the gun from his holster and pointing it at Rory.

"Hands in the air! Do not reach back into your vehicle!" he shouted.

Rory raised her hands above her head, her eyes wide as she stared at the wheel in front of her, her gaze avoiding the barrel. "I was just reaching for my coat!"

Allinson held up his hands. "Mike! Mike, she's fine! She was just—"

"She doesn't *breathe* unless I say so! Up against the fence! Get the other one."

Durham grabbed Rory's arm, and then everything seemed to happen at once. My fingers curled into claws as Allinson reached for me, and he stepped back, startled. I jumped out of the passenger seat as Durham yanked Rory from the car.

"Don't touch her!" I screamed as I slipped in a puddle of icy slush. The rain bit through my clothes in seconds, I barely caught myself on the open car door, and my knees landed painfully on the frigid road. I found my footing and fought back the racking shivers that overtook my body.

"I'm fine!" Rory called to me as Durham shoved her forward toward the thin chain-link fence at the edge of the turnout. Allinson's voice was low over my shoulder. "Just keep calm, okay? He's not going to hurt her," he said as he grabbed my arm and walked me over to the fence. Beyond the fence, a sea of black pine trees swayed in the wind. I could hear tires crunching on ice, rubber splashing through puddles, and I knew that the road was clearing. People were leaving.

"He already *has* hurt her," I hissed.

Allinson leaned down so he was closer to my ear.

"I cannot help you if you don't keep your mouth shut," he warned.

I clenched my jaw so tight that I was afraid I'd crack my teeth. I didn't want his help, and I hated that I needed it. I looked over at Rory. She was only wearing a thin sweater, and she was soaked down to the bone.

You okay? I mouthed.

Someone drove by, and I heard the familiar twang of a country song blasting in the muffled cab as they passed. I tried to imagine what it would be like to be the person who was simply seeing an odd moment in an otherwise regular day. Wondering, briefly, what was going on. And driving on, not worrying that it could ever happen to them.

A horn blared from somewhere a few hundred feet away. A tan truck further down the line flashed its lights a couple times and pressed on the horn. The drivers in front of it braved the cold to give one-fingered salutes out their windows.

"Please let my friend get her jacket. Or let her take mine. Please," I said, looking over my shoulder at Durham. Behind him, cars moved on.

"Eerie, I'm fine," Rory said through clenched teeth.

I heard Durham get closer. The crunch of muddy ice under his rubber boots, the clinking of the keys on his belt. I looked up at him, though it hurt to keep my eyes open.

Allinson tightened his grip lightly on my shoulder, as if to warn me to look away.

But I needed him to see me. I needed him to see the veins in my eyes and the mascara running down my cheeks. I don't know why I cared, why I thought that maybe he'd have a brief moment of guilt where he realized I looked like his daughter or the neighbor who walks his dogs when he's out of town or the girl who made his coffee this morning. I guess I wanted him to see how human I looked. How scared, how cold, how tired. How human.

"What are you worried about, Allinson? You think these things get sick?" Durham asked, his voice taking on a lilt that sounded like a sneer. Allinson didn't answer, and Durham pulled his hat lower over his ears.

The horn behind us got louder.

"Even if they do . . . they'll go to the hospital and we'll foot the bill, won't we? We let you go to our schools, pay for your housing. We live under the threat of those fucking Boneys, and what do they do when we do one thing they disagree with? They throw a tantrum and screw everything up. If that's how you want to play, then I'm afraid you're going to be a little inconvenienced, fuckers."

It hurt to breathe. I looked over at Rory. Her head hung between her arms, her eyes closed against the cold.

"We don't have any say about what they do," I said, hoping my voice was loud enough for him to hear. My fingers felt like they were freezing against the fence. I couldn't take it anymore. I turned around.

"Back against the fence," Durham said. His hand twitched against his gun holster.

"We have nothing to do with the Haunt. We had nothing to do with what happened today," I said, though it came out more like a plea.

The truck pulled up behind Rory's car and let out one last honk.

Durham and Allinson turned, and Durham shielded his eyes against the bright headlights.

The driver's-side door opened, and a figure jumped out into the rain without even bothering to kill the engine.

A sharp gust of wind careened across the highway, and Rory slipped to her knees.

Allinson rushed to her side, taking his coat off and throwing it over her shoulders.

"What the hell is this?" a male voice asked from beyond the headlights.

"Police business, sir. Get back in your vehicle and be on your way," Durham shot back.

The figure kept walking, and when he passed the front headlights, I saw his face.

A man with green eyes looked up at me, and then to Rory.

Logan Winspeare, my nearly frozen mind registered.

"It's the policy of the Rearden Falls Police Department to keep two civilians outside in freezing rain?" he asked, his expression tight with fury.

"We're fine," I called, my voice strangled with cold. Something about the expression on his face told me that he was only going to make things worse.

"You heard the girl. Back off. This ain't your problem," Durham warned, his professional tone slipping enough to show the edges of his rage.

Allinson helped Rory to her feet, and Durham turned.

"Back against the fence," he spat, but Allinson just shook his head. "Mike. She can't."

Logan looked back to me and took off his jacket. I was so cold it felt like everything was happening in slow motion. He took one step toward me, but Durham stepped in his way.

"Go back to your car, son," he said. "That's a direct order."

Logan looked at me through the haze of ice.

"I don't take orders from cops who are one complaint away from a three-month suspension, *Officer* Durham."

Logan stepped closer to Durham and sniffed the air. "Especially one who spent his lunch break drinking at O'Flannagan's." He rocked up on his toes and sunk his hands deeper in his jeans pockets. His eyes were lit up with a challenge. Almost like this was a game to him, and he was winning.

Durham's lips curled.

"We know all about you, Winspeare. You might've come back here with some bullshit axe to grind about your dead mommy, but you've got no power here, you understand? Go back to your car."

I shook my head and took a step toward both of them.

"It's okay. We're *okay*. We were just finishing up here, weren't we, Officer?" I asked.

Out of the cover of my eye, I saw Allinson putting Rory in the passenger seat of his squad car.

Durham sneered and shook his head. He was losing his footing in the situation, and it just made him angrier.

"This is over when I say it's over, bitch," he seethed.

Logan tried to sidestep Durham once more, but Durham reached over and shoved him back. Logan slid in the snow, dropping his jacket.

Durham whipped around and grabbed me roughly by the elbow.

"Mike!" Allinson yelled, but Durham didn't listen. I heard the faint crackle of the radio mixed with Allinson's frantic voice. Rory called my name.

Everything after that happened so fast. Logan rushed Durham, ripping him off me and shoving him back. I lost my balance and caught myself on the fence, the skin on my fingers tearing as all my weight pressed my flesh against the thin metal rings.

When I looked over my shoulder, Durham was raising his gun toward Logan. I didn't think—I rushed at Logan, throwing all my weight forward. We crashed to the frosty ground, and his elbow hit me straight in the temple.

Rory's screams were the last thing I heard before everything went black.

⌘

My first breath was louder than I meant it to be.

It's funny how I knew that, even then. How I immediately clamped my lips over the scream that coiled up my throat.

Most Hushed know where they are when they first open their eyes, but I was drenched in a sort of blank fear. Stirring is our first moment of consciousness. I lay under a chrome desk. The buzz of the fluorescent lights sounded odd in contrast to the ragged, panicked screams coming from the hallways.

My cheek was pressed to the cold tile under the desk, my fingers curled against the scuffed, unforgiving surface where someone's feet were meant to rest. The smell of smoke assaulted my senses, stinging my eyes and nose.

Get out.

The world tilted and bucked as I shoved myself up to my hands and knees, my skin freezing against the ground. Hair fell into my eyes as I struggled to take an even breath.

That's when I heard my heart for the first time. There, under that desk, I felt my epicenter. Blood pumping in and out, thrumming past my ears and making my limbs sing with burning adrenaline.

Even in a panic, I waited for the moment when the blank pages in my mind filled up. There was this breath, this expectation, like I was hovering too near a blaze and waiting for it to reach out and grab me. Hushed talked about the moment when they remember everything about their secret—it usually happens right when they stir. But not for me.

Nothing came. No memories, no purpose. Somehow, I knew that, even then. Naked and newborn and reeking of ash . . . I still knew something deeper was wrong. But I couldn't figure out what.

Get out.

I was about to make a run for it when the door opened. Rubber-soled boots squeaked against the tile. I pressed myself tight against the back of the desk.

Drawers slammed. A quiet voice cursed. Male. Then female. There were two.

Somehow, I knew if they found me, they'd put a bullet in my skull.

I heard them walking around, getting closer to where I was hiding. I shifted further under the desk, the balls of my bare feet screaming in protest as I rested my full weight on them and turned.

That's when I saw the lab coat, folded and resting on a pair of size-six rain boots next to the desk.

"Lab is empty. Clear the rest," the male voice said.

They left the room. I slid the boots on my feet, wrapped the coat around my shoulders, and sprinted out of the room.

Everything roared to life.

They called the Ironbark Prison tragedy "Lit November" because it took a full month to contain the massive forest fire that it sparked. But it all started as a single night.

The lights went out, and the whole place was illuminated by flames. I saw the outline of people, unmoving, splayed against the floor, and

I knelt to check a guard I nearly stepped on. She was dead, her eyes glassy and empty.

I couldn't tell if I was choking on smoke or my fear, but I stumbled forward, screams echoing off the walls. I didn't stop. I couldn't stop. Down the hall, to the left. Straight ahead. The lit, green sign on the wall read 3B. The rest of the escape was a fiery blur.

Then it was dark and cold, and I was running through the trees and tripping over vines. *Out. I'm out.* But there was no relief. The sky exhaled a soft drizzle that soaked my thin coat.

It could have been hours before I collapsed, or maybe just minutes. I don't know.

I crawled when I couldn't walk anymore, spurred on by the prodding fear that came from the harsh cry of fire trucks.

With the screams still rocketing off the inside of my skull, I fell to my stomach on the wet forest floor. I was alive, and they weren't. Every person inside was dead.

Fabian found me curled up next to the trunk of a sweetgum tree and told me we needed to run. I thrashed when he tried to touch me. He had two lab coats tied around his waist and was smudged with smoke and ash. He grabbed my face. *We need to go*, he said. I didn't know him, but I knew that he was like me, and I knew he was safe. When I looked up at him, my face covered in dirt and streaked with tears, arms shaking from fear and cold, he picked me up and tucked me up against his chest. He was warm, and I let him.

And then we ran as far away as we could.

But it wasn't far enough.

❧

I took a sharp breath, and the panic bells rang off inside my head. Pine-scented cleaning solution invaded my sinuses, and bright fluorescent lights glowed red behind closed eyelids. Iron bars were the first things I saw when I opened my eyes. I recognized those bars. Silver, with a blue-green tint. I'd seen them before.

I can't be back here. I can't.

I shut my eyes tight, and it was like I was falling and being yanked upward by the spine at the same time.

I got my bearings. I was on a cot against the wall, and I shoved myself up. It was a stupid move, since the blinding, pulsing headache caught up to me, a deep throb right at my temple. I swayed on the spot. My fingers were wrapped in a bandage, and they pulsed with pain when I moved them.

"Easy, you're okay," a male voice said as hands grabbed my arms to steady me.

I blinked twice, forcing myself to focus on the figure kneeling next to the cot.

Logan Winspeare. Madeline Winspeare's son. The boy from the newspaper this morning. Though he wasn't a boy anymore. He was somewhere in his twenties . . . I was bad with placing human age. It never really made sense.

I looked around wildly. I was in a cell. I was in a cell in Ironbark Prison.

How is this possible?

I shoved backward, and Logan held his hands up, as if to show me that he wasn't dangerous. Please. He was the last thing I was afraid of.

"Where are we?" Everything around us looked like where I stirred, but we couldn't be there. Ironbark was a gutted shell. *I can't be in Ironbark.*

"The holding cell at the station. Next to the courthouse?" He talked slowly and kept his hands up.

Of course. I looked back at the bars. They were probably built at the same time. Same manufacturers, same design. The fear licked at the bottom of my ribs, and I took a deep breath, hoping to extinguish it.

I shut my eyes against the glare of the overhead lights, and I spoke just to keep my voice louder than my thoughts.

"Where's Rory?"

"She's in the waiting room. She wasn't arrested, but she wouldn't leave without you," Logan answered.

My back hit the white-painted brick of the cell wall, and I forced myself to take deep, steadying breaths as I remembered what happened.

It went wrong, and now I'm in a cage.

A cage.

Then, I felt the pull of my loose thread. Once it started, it was hard to stop. I felt like I was falling.

You're locked in a cage. You're going to die here.

Panic was a knot, a hot piece of coal stuck in my throat, searing a scream deep inside of me as my chest moved, fighting for breath. I was on fire—every part of me burned as I fought to grab hold of any scrap of a thought that I could cling to in order to stop the freefall of panic. *You're in Ironbark. You're locked in the place that holds the key to your death. You're going to die, Eerie.* The panic was real, a weight wrapping around my ankles and pulling me down. My mind spun as the lights got louder. They hummed, the pitch seeming to rise with the temperature of my blood. *I can't be here.* The tile looked the same. It smelled the same.

Even with these thoughts, even as my fingers twitched against the fabric beneath me and I shook with terror, I was still keenly aware that I was being watched. There was still something latent, a voice far away but loud enough to remind me of the importance of not making a scene. I bit down hard on my lip and put my head in my hands, tangling my fingers in my hair to remind myself that I still had hair. I was still sitting in the cell. I wasn't spinning off into nothing. I wasn't unraveling.

"Hey. You okay?"

Logan's voice was far and warped as he leaned down in front of me. He reached out for me, and I dug my fingers into his forearm, pressing my flesh against the leather of his jacket as hard as I could. He was warm. I felt his bones, radius and ulna, concrete and real.

"No. No, I'm not," I said. My voice sounded strangled and weak, full of breath but not enough air. I didn't feel like I could breathe.

He put his hand over mine. It was warm, his skin rough. He pressed my palm into his forearm, like he knew it was an anchor. I wanted more than anything to pull back. He was connected to Ironbark, which meant there was a chance he was just as dangerous as Ironbark itself. I knew

I should pull back, to scream at him not to touch me, but instead I clutched at his shoulder with my other hand. He was steady, the only steady thing I could hold.

I was falling into the nothingness below, and I didn't know if I'd ever find my way back. I always do. There's always a way back, and I'm always surprised when I find it yet again.

"Want me to get someone?" he whispered. His voice was deep and hoarse, his tone low. He had shifted so that I couldn't be seen by anyone walking by. He was shielding me from sight.

All I could do was breathe and shake my head a little.

You're still alive.

I found purchase on that thought, and I caught just enough of it to slow my freefall for a moment: *You're not dying. You're still alive.* One moment of relief gave way to the next, finding each other in the dark and lighting up one by one: *Here. Here. Here. Here.* As quickly as the panic came, it ebbed. Once I caught my breath, I felt my head lighten. Oxygen let me string thoughts together again, letting the ground come together under me. *You're not dying. You're alive. You're still breathing, you've got a fighting chance.* The panic attack passed. Every muscle in my body quivered and shook. I let go of Logan's arm, and he didn't move, like he wasn't sure if I'd need it again. I scooted back, burning from embarrassment instead of panic.

"Thank you," I said quickly. Tersely, like he'd held a door open for me instead of helped me stay tethered to reality.

Logan sat back, nodding as he inched away from me.

There was another person in the cell with us—a man with a grizzled beard who was fast asleep on a bench opposite me. He let out a strangled snore and turned over.

Logan looked at me for a minute.

"We're in a holding cell," I repeated to myself. *Not in Ironbark.*

"We weren't booked on any charges because there aren't *any charges to hold us on,*" Logan called over his shoulder as he pushed himself to his feet. I could see the officer at the front desk, a woman in her early forties, shake her head at the sound of his voice.

I tried to remember what I'd said in the height of panic . . . had I said anything? I hated the aftermath of panic attacks, when I realized how turned inside out I was. How complete strangers could see my gaping wounds and watch me struggle to stay alive. It felt like a violation. Something intensely intimate that is wrenched from me with no warning.

He turned and met my eyes.

"I told them to take you to a hospital, but they had a medic look you over and then brought you here because they're assholes. Did they at least pretend they had a reason for pulling you over?"

He doesn't know. He doesn't know I'm a Hushed.

I opened my mouth to tell him, but as I took a breath, I watched him, the way his eyes searched my face, dropping down to the hands on my lap, roving over my soaked, ripped jeans. He wasn't looking for the other half of my existence. He wasn't looking for my *why*. He thought I was a person. He thought I was a *who*.

I clamped my jaw shut. I didn't know why I felt like I was doing something illicit . . . I'd pretended to be a human thousands of times.

The feeling that I was holding something back churned in my gut, and I didn't like it. Like I was trying on a warm jacket that I could never own. Like I was being secretive, somehow, by keeping something that was wholly and completely mine. *Fuck that*, I reminded myself. I didn't owe him anything.

"They pulled us over, but they arrested us . . ."

Slowly, the images came back to me. Officer Durham and his sneer. Officer Allinson helping Rory back to the car. Logan fighting with Durham—

"Because of you," I said, sliding forward on the rubber mattress until my boots touched the cell floor. I gathered every bit of nerve I had and looked over his shoulder and down the gray, empty hallway. No Pull. With every glance around the cell that didn't kill me, I felt bolder.

I didn't ask him to help us on the side of the highway, and I didn't ask him to help me through the panic. I didn't ask him to look at me like I was human and treat me differently because of it. I needed to get out of the cell. I needed to be alone.

He raised his eyebrow. There was a cut and a bruise over his right eye, and his lip was swollen in the bottom left corner.

"You think we're in here because of me?" he asked, smiling at me with a grin that didn't reach his eyes as he waited for the rest of my sentence.

"Yes," I said through clenched teeth. He'd seen me at my worst, and I wanted him to bleed for it.

He turned, unfazed. "Nope, but we'll get out because of me."

He grabbed the bars with both hands and looked like he was about to shout, but I shoved forward and spun him around with both hands gripping his jacket.

His eyes were wide as he looked down at me, but there was an infuriating amusement in them. We could have been killed. *He* could have been shot, and I was in a cell. Because of *him*.

"You aren't going to do anything. You've *helped* enough," I hissed.

He reached down and pulled my hands off his jacket, keeping his fingers locked around my wrists.

"They're holding us unlawfully, you know that? And that's not even mentioning the bullshit they pulled on the road—"

"We were *fine*, until you showed up with your misplaced hero complex and shot it all to hell."

He let go of my wrists, and the humor slipped from his expression.

"Really? Funny you can remember that well, considering you were half-frozen to death."

"Pretty sure it was the completely unnecessary blow to the head that would've jostled my memory."

Logan rolled his eyes and turned back around.

He sat down on the edge of the opposite bench, careful to avoid the sleeping inmate, and leaned against the wall.

I slid down to the floor with my back against the bars. I shivered slightly and tucked my forehead against my curled-up knees.

Suddenly, I was covered in warmth, and the smell of salt and the heady bite of leather filled my nose. I looked up and saw Logan walking back to his spot on the bench. He'd put his jacket over my shoulders. I stood up and pulled the jacket off. *This guy.*

"I'm fine, thanks though," I said, holding it out to him. I didn't want any more help. I didn't need to be covered.

He sat with his back against the wall, one arm draped over his raised knee. His eyes were closed.

"You're shivering."

"I'm not cold."

"You're scared, then? First time in a holding cell?"

Irritation rose in my gut, and I tossed the jacket back to him.

"I'm not scared. I'm not cold. I'm *fine*."

He opened his eyes as the jacket landed in his lap. My body let out another uncontrollable shiver, and that irritating smile slid up his lips once more. I turned away and rested my face against the cool bars.

"Damn. Sure is hard to find a good damsel these days, isn't it?"

I looked over my shoulder at him. His eyes glittered, and I knew he was kidding—but I was in no mood.

"Don't kid yourself in thinking that what you did out there was about me. Or helping me. Or rescuing me. That was about you."

Logan stood, his green eyes bright as he threw the jacket onto the bench. A muscle in his jaw twitched as he glared at me. The bearded man beside him rolled onto it, still snoring.

"Oh, well you just have me all figured out, don't you, Miss—"

"Eerie. My name is Eerie. And yes, Logan Winspeare, you're not a hard code to crack. You get off on pissing people off and you can't understand why *maybe* the consequences of your actions don't have me stumbling over myself with gratitude—"

He threw his head back and looked up at the stained, cracked ceiling before rubbing a hand down his face.

"—oh my *God*." He looked past me and called to the woman at the desk. "Ma'am? I'll confess to whatever. I'll take lockup." He looked back down at me. "I don't get why you're pissed at *me* when we should *both* be concentrating on becoming very methodical pains in Officer Asshole's . . . ass." He stopped as he realized how strange the words sounded when they were strung together like that.

"I don't want to be a pain in anyone's ass! I just want to go home!"
I shrieked, fighting the urge to shove him square in the chest.

A buzzing noise rang out above our heads, accompanying the click
of the large metal door at the far end of the hallway.

Eva walked down the corridor, escorted by Allinson.

"Eerie! Are you okay?" Eva whispered loudly as she came up on the
other side of the bars.

"I'm fine," I said once the door had opened to let us out, giving her
my best reassuring smile. She always looked older in moments like these,
when the worry creased her smooth skin and darkened her sea-foam-
colored eyes.

Allinson jerked his head at Logan, who followed us out of the cell. It
was silent as we walked down the sterile, metal hallway. I met Allinson's
gaze, and he looked like he might say something. Apologize. I looked
away. He didn't deserve to apologize.

Rory and Fabian were waiting for us in the waiting area, and Rory
threw herself on me the moment I was clear of the door. She'd been crying.

"It's okay." I squeezed her hand three times, and she squeezed back
four. I don't remember when we started doing it, but it had become
our thing. Our way of signaling to the other that everything was fine.

Fabian came up behind us and tucked his hand under my jaw, tilting my head to inspect the wound. He shook his head. For a moment,
it looked like he was going to turn around and say something to Logan,
but I put my hand over his.

"Don't."

Fabian stopped and looked down at me. He nodded and pulled me to
him, engulfing me in a tight hug. I watched from under his arm as Logan
walked out the automated front door, his shoulders high around his ears.

"Ms.—" Allinson started, looking down at the paperwork.

"Ashwood," I answered, filling in the last name Fabian had made up
for us. The ones we put down on all Internment forms.

"Officer Waybourne would like to see you."

I knew the name. The new head of Internment Relations for Rearden
Falls.

I nodded at Fabian before following Allinson behind the desk and into a back room.

Officer Waybourne's office was at the back of the building. She was a small woman, smaller than I expected. Younger, too. Her mousey hair was in a low, sensible bun. Her makeup was minimal, though her shade of lipstick might be what Seph would call "playful." Her eyes moved from her computer as the guard ushered me inside.

"900628?" she asked, using my Hushed ID number.

"Eerie Ashwood," I replied. She took it as a confirmation and motioned for me to take a seat.

Behind her, the Internment's mission statement sat encased in a black frame: *Recover and Rehabilitate*. Other than that, the room bordered on sterile, except for the two pictures that faced her on her desk.

I stared at the word. *Rehabilitate*. I couldn't tell if that was something they really believed, or if it was a nice-sounding buzzword that allowed for more funding, but the idea of a Hushed being "rehabilitated" was an empty promise. There were once whispers of a pilot program that helped a Hushed stay far away from their Wounded— one that would relocate a Hushed to make it harder to give into the Pull. But that meant disclosing where their Wounded lived, which was more information than most Hushed were willing to give to humans, so that idea fizzled.

She clicked around on her computer for thirty more seconds. I recognized the power play, and I leaned back in the seat. It was one of those awful ones with a completely straight back, and I couldn't get comfortable.

It took all my self-control to stay silent. I couldn't afford to be in more trouble than I was already in. But when the panic receded like a low tide, it always left rage in its place. Like my body was trying to coat my open, shameful cracks in liquid metal.

Click. Click.

She finally looked at me and pursed her lips together. The dark pink gloss was smudged on one side.

"We've been alerted about today's incident. I've been told that there will be no charges filed. There usually aren't in misunderstandings like these."

Misunderstandings. Right.

I looked at my lap. She didn't care about what really happened. She just wanted me to know that I was being watched.

That's what the Internment does best.

"So, we're done, then?" I asked, setting my hands on the arms of the chair.

"Not quite," she said. She leaned forward and laced her fingers together. Her expression was pinched. "You're aware of the provision of your registration that forbids you from engaging in illegal activity?"

"No charges were filed," I said, an edge creeping into my voice.

"Which is why this is just a warning. I thought you should also know that there is a provision against *associating* with anyone who has a criminal record. That, unfortunately, includes your friend, Mr. Winspeare."

She winced at the word *friend*.

I smiled, but I knew it looked more like baring my teeth.

"I wasn't made aware of that. Then again, we didn't have much time to go over details before I signed the forms."

She could read my record. She knew what I was talking about.

Officer Waybourne's face broke into a tight smile.

"Well. Let me enlighten you. Any further illegal actions or associations with people in possession of criminal records could result in the termination of your stipend and revocation of your work permit."

My mouth dropped open.

"What?"

She looked at me and then turned to the computer. "Also, you could be in danger of losing your chance to apply for the transfer next year, if that is something you are interested in doing."

"Today was not my fault," I said through clenched teeth.

"It's just a warning, Eerie. There is no need to get upset."

She said it lightly, like she knew she enjoyed putting the tip of her knife against my most exposed vein.

She leaned onto her desk a little further.

"I know it must be a shock to hear, but you don't run this show. We do."

I curled my toes in my still-soaked shoes and nodded.

"Contrary to what others might tell you," she added as she sat back.

I stopped, and a smile slipped up my lips as the exhaustion that I'd been wearing all day finally hit bone.

Her veneer had cracked, even if just a little. This was about the Haunt. She'd wanted to seem so diplomatic, so poised. She'd wanted to know that all those years in whatever the hell prim and proper sorority house she spent her time in had shaped her well. She wanted me to play the part of the criminal. But she'd shown that she hated us as much as we hated her.

She was no better than me. My smile widened, becoming genuine as it spread across my face.

She leaned back, unnerved at the sight of my glee, and motioned that I was dismissed. I kept nodding as I walked toward the door. I turned at the doorway.

"Oh, by the way. Your lipstick is smudged."

FIVE

The street was quiet as we pulled through toward the Boneyard, almost like we were rolling through a minefield, our tires crunching over the blanket of ice.

Our headlights roved over an older man in a thick plaid coat on the sidewalk near our driveway, his veteran's cap pulled low over his eyes. Fabian slowed as we rolled up next to him.

"Mr. Cauly," Fabian called as he lowered the window.

Mr. Cauly walked up to the window, hobbling slightly. His doctor told him that if he didn't walk twice a day, his knees would turn on him. He took the advice seriously, even when it was below zero outside.

"Big van full of those punks pulled by here about an hour ago, Fabian," Mr. Cauly said, his voice wheezy. He adjusted the rim of his hat higher on his eyes. Gravediggers. He hated them, too. He hated them in the way older people hated young, disrespectful kids, but we didn't really care about the *why*. We just needed him to hate them more than he hated us.

"Mr. Cauly, can I walk you to your door?" Rory piped up from the back, leaning in between the two front seats to look at our neighbor.

"Listen to me! I don't need lookin' after, sweetheart—it's you lot that needs to be careful, ya hear? Get inside. Lock the doors."

"Thank you, Mr. Cauly," Eva said from the front seat, and Mr. Cauly waved her off, pinching his lips together and pursing them out as he looked up and down our dark street.

$$\backsim\!\infty\!\sim$$

Eva asked if I wanted her to bring some dinner up, but I said I wasn't hungry.

I showered, though the water never got hot enough to make me feel like I was clean.

The room I shared with Seph and Rory was empty, but I wasn't tired just yet. Or maybe I was too tired. I couldn't tell. I paced near my bed.

One hundred and seventy-three days left, and it could all be taken away by a few words. The thought was a rolling boil in my stomach.

I walked to the dresser and knelt before the bottom drawer that used to be Sarah's. Her clothes were still there. I shoved aside her sweaters and socks, reaching for the back paneling of the drawer. The smell of her Lilu perfume still lingered on the soft cotton, and I shut my eyes tight against it. I hit the wood paneling with the heel of my palm, and it came loose. I pulled it forward and reached around until my fingers brushed up against a paper bag stuffed in the empty space behind the drawer.

It's where I kept all my cashed paychecks from the diner. We gave our stipend to Eva, who kept careful records and receipts of everything bought for the Boneyard. But this money was mine.

The Internment allowed a request for location transfer two years after the initial registration date, and that day, for us, was 173 days away. Everything had to be ready by then.

I'd been working on this plan since the week we arrived here. Fabian had only been able to find one slip pill, which is why we were in this mess. There was only one and he'd given it to me. I decided I was going to find a slip pill for him.

I started slow. I scoured the Internet, going on all sorts of sketchy chat rooms and websites—though I had to keep that to a minimum because there was always a chance that the Internment was keeping tabs on our search histories. I knew I had to take a different approach, so I started offering to run errands for Eva. Before I went to the store, I'd head to the outskirts of Rearden Falls, where the mountain roads started curving steeply upward. I'd spend as much time as I could manage walking around the gas stations and fast-food joints, looking for someone who could help me. I'd been able to spot those kinds of people when Fabian and I were on the road—people who knew how to get antibiotics without a prescription or, more often, something stronger. They knew where to take shelter on a rainy night . . . people like that were always around if you knew where to look. Human or Hushed, I didn't care, as long as they could help me. I had rules: I never went out on the same day of the week twice in a row. I varied where I went and at what time of day. I made sure to look busy while inside a store or gas station.

For months, there was nothing.

Then one day as I was sitting in a plastic booth at a Stop & Shop and scanning the parking lot beyond the smudged window, someone slid in across the table. He had dark skin and inky black curls that just barely brushed the shoulders of his green canvas jacket.

"Sitting alone in a gas station. You're either desperately in love or looking to kill someone. Which is it?" he asked. His voice had a lilt to it, like the words danced off his tongue.

I was used to creeps trying to talk to me, so I just sat back and narrowed my eyes. "Either way, you're sitting across from the wrong person, don't you think? Either my lover will end you or I will."

The man smiled and reached across the table, wrapping his hands around my lukewarm cup of coffee. He took a sip and grimaced.

"Tastes like the piss of someone dying of kidney failure," he murmured, drawing the back of his hand across his mouth and setting the cup down.

"If this is how you always hit on girls, then I'm not surprised you've resorted to gas stations."

"Oh, you flatter yourself, my dear. I'm not flirting, I'm answering your cry for help."

I reached for the coffee cup, readying myself to throw the mud-water in his smug face. But his next words stopped me cold.

"You're looking for a slip pill, are you not? You've been looking for someone like me for months."

I froze. There was a chance he was a cop, or an undercover Internment officer. Even more likely, he was some pervert looking to chuck me into his van. It seemed too easy, and the hairs on the back of my neck tingled. I thought I'd been careful, but the thought that he'd been watching me made me sick.

But there was also a chance he was telling the truth, and that he had a slip pill. After months of nothing, I was willing to take that chance.

"If I am?" I asked.

He smiled, then, and told me his name was Ajit. He worked with a network based out of Omaha that ran slip pills. All it would cost me was a thousand bucks.

"Oh, that's all?" I quipped, feeling my stomach plummet. It would take months to come up with that kind of cash, and that was if I could pull extra shifts. "I don't have that kind of money."

He leaned forward on his elbows. "I think we'll be able to work something out."

"And how do I know you're not lying?"

He pulled a little plastic envelope from his pocket and set it on the table. Inside was a little pink pill with a smudged, iridescent center. I'd seen one like it before, in Fabian's wet, outstretched palm. A slip pill.

❦

We agreed that I would pay three hundred dollars every three months. I made the first payment in late August, following his instructions to the letter because he said if I messed them up, the deal was off. I put the money in a manila envelope, folded it in half, and wrapped it with three rubber bands. *The thick kind*, he'd said. *The kind that really hurt when you snap them against skin.* I went to four different office supply stores to find them, which was a pain in the ass. Then, after a late shift at Mal's, I walked over and dropped it in the US mail drop box on Carmody Avenue. It didn't have an address on it, so I knew that it wasn't actually being mailed. Somehow, Ajit found it. I just never knew how.

How will I know you got it? I'd asked.

You'll know, he'd said through a smile.

The next day at work, Rory walked back into the kitchen and waved a red rose in my face. "Someone left this for you on a table," she sang.

I snatched it from her. "Who?" I asked.

"Didn't see him. But look! Starbucks gift card!" she gestured to the dark green envelope tied to the stem that had *Eerie* written in big black letters. "You've got a secret admirer," she called over her shoulder as she walked over to pick up a plate of fries.

I opened the card.

Well done. Now get yourself some non-piss coffee. See you in November.

Part of me was creeped out that Ajit had managed to slip into the diner undetected, but I was also relieved that he had received the payment.

I looked down at the cash in my hands as I stood in front of the dresser. I needed to see it now, to feel the crinkly package in my fingers. It was November, and time for another payment.

I was going to request the transfer for Fabian and me next year. I'd have the slip pill by then, and somewhere on the road from Rearden Falls to Boston . . . we would escape. We'd make our way across the Atlantic, somehow. We'd disappear. The plan was a mess, and I knew that. But it's all I had. Fabian and I had defied the odds once—we'd lived for two years without the Internment catching us. We could do it again. We could do it better.

I pushed the bag deep into the dresser once more, and then put the back paneling in place. I closed the dresser drawer slowly, feeling the resistance of the bag at the last inch of the runner.

I stood, my bones feeling stronger already.

I may be a Hushed, but I had secrets of my own. The thought gave me comfort.

Reed was watching a movie downstairs. I could hear it as I walked down the hallway. I also heard the slight *pop* and *hiss* of a beer bottle opening, and Seph's soft, warning voice. I couldn't make out her words or his gruff reply, but I knew what was going on. She was asking him to take it easy on the drinking, and he was telling her to back off.

Fabian's light was on, though his door was closed.

I knocked twice and opened the door, but I stopped short when I walked inside.

Rory sat on his bed. Fabian sat beside her. His arm was up, his fingers almost touching her face. It dropped when he saw me.

"Um. I'm sorry. I just . . . um . . ." I stopped.

"I should get to bed," Rory said. I chanced a glance at her. Her cheeks were red, but she didn't avoid my eyes. Rory gently pulled the door closed as she left. Fabian moved to the chair in front of his desk.

"What. Was. *That*?!" I whispered, crossing the room in three strides and throwing myself on the bed.

Fabian scooted his chair in closer to his desk, but he couldn't hide the red flush that crept over the collar of his plaid shirt.

"I will get more and more annoying every time I have to ask you this question," I warned, smiling as I reached over and pulled on his earlobe.

He pulled himself away from his desk to look at me, a slight smile playing on his lips.

"Are you okay?" he asked, reaching and brushing a finger gently over the bruise near my eye.

I pulled back sharply. "Totally fine."

He didn't look like he believed me.

"Stop stalling," I grinned, motioning to the door with my head.

"There's nothing going on. Besides. The last thing I need right now is a distraction. You know that." My grin faded as the smile slipped from his voice.

He gestured to his desk. I pushed myself up to my elbows and looked, though I knew what I'd see.

Floor plans of Ironbark Prison covered the left side of his desk. On the right side, in the direct light of his black metal desk lamp, sat profiles he'd made of each of the victims. He spent at least two hours every night going over every detail he could find about the night we stirred.

I sat up, the cords of my heart tingling unpleasantly.

"Maybe a distraction is exactly what you need. This *Suck* cannot be healthy," I said. I knew if he and Rory became a thing, it could complicate my plan to leave. But I also knew that the less time Fabian sat staring at his desk, the better. Maybe he'd see some of the other things life could offer. That would be worth it, no matter what complications came from it. We could always save up and get another pill for Rory, and then send for her to join us. It would give Fabian something else to obsess over, and I knew Rory would agree with me. He needed to get away from this. If anything, she'd be the one who would help me convince him to leave when it was finally time.

Fabian looked over at me, his eyes narrowed with the focus that came whenever we talked about Ironbark. It made my stomach clench.

"I hate it when you call it the Suck."

I shrugged. "Well, it's not the Pull. But you're drawn to it, and it sucks. It works on so many levels."

Fabian sighed. "What are you so afraid of?" he asked. Like he hadn't asked a thousand times before. Like my answer had ever been different.

I was afraid of the Pull. I'd been afraid of it even before Sarah died in front of me, but it had gotten worse. Sarah loved this world more than anyone I'd ever known. She would catch raindrops on her tongue and sit too close to the fireplace because she loved the feel of it on her skin. She wanted to live, but the Pull was stronger than her. I didn't want to know what it was like to come up against something that powerful. Fabian and I had been spared that—we were the only Hushed I knew of that had that freedom. It was a blessing, but for some reason Fabian treated it like a curse.

"I'm not. I just think there is more to life than this stupid trial," I said finally.

"If you knew half as much as you think you do, you wouldn't be calling it stupid."

I bristled. "I know just as much as you, Fabian. Just because I'm not obsessive doesn't mean I'm naive."

Fabian pursed his lips and held up a mug shot. A woman with short brown hair and deep-set eyes stared back at me.

"Who is this?" he asked, and I gave him a look.

"Your memory is so good that I know you wouldn't forget, so that must mean that you weren't listening the first time," Fabian said.

I rolled my eyes. Fine.

"Monique Cavers. First-degree murder and three counts of attempted murder. Died in cell A1."

Fabian set the picture down and picked up the next one. She had bleached blond hair and black roots.

"Lila Evans. Two counts of second-degree murder with three counts of bribery and two counts of tampering with evidence. Died in cell B3."

Next one. The redhead was almost smirking in her mug shot.

"Reva O'Brien. First-degree murder. Cell B4."

Next one.

"Chin Lee Ro. First-degree murder and several drug charges including intent to distribute. Cell E5."

He did three more in rapid succession.

Heather Mora. Dee Riles. Stephanie Montier. C2. C3. D1.

I stopped before he announced the last one.

A woman with blond hair and striking green eyes stared into the camera. Her gaze was searching, like the hope was still stirring in her, refusing to lie down and give up. I'd seen those same green eyes a few hours before.

"Madeline Winspeare," I said. Fabian was about to set the picture down but stopped at the sound of my voice. "Convicted of the first-degree murder of Stephen Winspeare. Died in the stairwell between levels one and two."

He showed me a couple of pictures of guards, and I named them as well.

Tate Givens. No smile, all business.

Rudy Sugita. A candid photo of him fishing.

I looked at the last one. The man had a kind-looking face, the kind of face you'd look for if you were scared in a crowd.

He smiled in his official photo. *Sam MacDonald*, I knew. He was one of the guards.

Fabian lowered the pictures. I looked up at him, trying to hide the way my chest tightened. He flipped through them once more, and then stopped.

"Well done," he conceded. He set the picture of Madeline down on his desk, and I looked over his shoulder despite myself. There were more, but he didn't quiz me on the rest. He got the point. In total, there were eight guards. One custodian. One doctor. All floors, from the basement to the top fourth floor, were gutted. That's how I knew my memory of that night wasn't completely foolproof. 2B was the lowest level on the plans. In my memories I always saw a level marked "3B," but according to the official info, that floor didn't exist.

Everything was fine at 11:06, the last logged check-in.

Then by 12:03, everything was in flames.

I ran my eyes over their faces. They were so static in my mind—a piece of history I was more than happy to forget. Fabian didn't think like that. When he looked at the pictures, he saw them move. He thought of the families who never saw their loved ones come home again. He imagined tears and laughter on faces that showed mostly blank stares.

I lay down on his pillow, bunching it up under my head for more support. Fabian didn't like pillows. He had always slept upright, with his head leaning against a wall. He only kept his pillow because he said the bed looked weird without it.

I looked up. Handwritten scriptures were tacked above his desk and bed.

I never understood how he could've stirred with so much faith when I had so little. None.

"I didn't want this life for you, you know," he said finally, as he rubbed his hand over his face.

Anger looked like a stone striking against my rib cage, sparking and illuminating memories I wanted to leave in the dark.

I was still, my chest rising and falling as I let my eyes shift to him.

It had been over a year, and I was still pissed. He was, too. I'd screwed up his plan, after all.

Because I didn't leave him, bleeding out in an overturned car in the middle of the soaked woods. Because I didn't abandon him when he screamed at me to go. He'd told me he'd taken his slip pill, that we were in it together, instead of being honest that he'd only been able to find one, the one he gave to me. He didn't understand that there was no version of freedom for me that didn't involve freedom for him. We were family, and I wasn't leaving him. It was selfless, sure. But he lied to me, and that was hard to forget.

"I don't want to hear your self-sacrificial bullshit right now."

"Everything that's not running for your life sounds like self-sacrificial bullshit to you, Eerie," he said.

I shoved myself off the bed and spun, taking two steps toward his door.

"At least I'm not so scared of living that I hole up in a room, piecing together a puzzle that will *never* be solved."

I jabbed at the ground so hard that my elbow over-extended.

He leaned back in his chair, looking at me with heavy eyes.

"Scared is *all* you are, Eerie."

I leaned back, reeling as his words hit me in the gut, knocking all the air from my lungs. Fabian stood when he saw me take a staggered step back, and his eyes widened slightly. It was like the words had surprised him, too. I knew he regretted them.

Fabian was closer than my own skin. He always had been. His words slipped like a razor between my bones, hitting the soft parts. He knew the real reason I went out to bury Sarah by myself. He'd been there the first time when I'd had the panic attack—he'd held me until it passed. I went out to that tree to prove to myself I could lay my friends to rest without losing my mind, and I'd succeeded. But in the cell, I was untethered. At the slightest push, all my strength had amounted to nothing. I was still always one thought away from coming undone.

"Eerie," he said, like he wanted to try and put me together with his soft voice.

My nostrils flared, lit by the heat in my breath.

"Go to hell, Fabian," I said, fumbling for the doorknob behind me.

I ripped into the hallway, hatred writhing in my chest.

Not for Fabian. I couldn't hate him if I tried.

Not even for the words he'd said.

But for the way the words sunk into my chest and felt at home.

I hated that they were true.

SIX

The drift started like all the others, like a stream of water running down a painter's palette. One color ran into the next, one sound wove into the spaces between a different memory. Almost like a dream, but not quite.

I saw men sitting around a campfire, their eyes lit by whiskey and flame.

This was Rory's drift. Her memory. When the men spoke, their words were muffled, like they were coming through water.

I never heard what they said, because she never let her drift show for long.

I saw ripples of other images. Eva's was of a couple entwined on a beach—an affair. Seph's was a crumpled piece of paper—a daughter's suicide note that was thrown in the trash instead of given to her parents.

I didn't know why we were all connected like this. Why some things spilled into the center when we slept near each other. I didn't realize it until we came to the Boneyard. I'd only ever been around Fabian, and we didn't share anything but ash-filled nightmares that could have belonged to either one of us, so we never noticed the overlap. With the others, sometimes it was a memory, sometimes a glimpse of their secret. Sometimes it was through our own eyes, like watching a movie, and sometimes it was through the eyes of the Hushed. Or the human the Hushed belonged to. Sometimes it was nice. When we slept, we all shared each other's burdens.

Sometimes it was not nice.

I tried to pull out because I could feel the sinking, cold, brittle fingers of something I didn't want to face. I smelled smoke. Not woodsmoke, but cigarette smoke. The image of concrete walls fluttered up around me, then sharpened. Dull gray light filtered in through the one window on the left side of the basement, and a desk lamp sat on a workbench under the stairs.

This one was always vivid. This one, the one I was thrashing against, felt like oil-covered vines slipping up my calves. It was Reed's.

I saw it through the eyes of a child; I could tell by the small hand that gripped the comic book in front of my vision and the thin legs that stuck out from the beanbag chair. For a moment, everything was still. Then, the door above the stairs opened, and a jagged silhouette spread down the sparse concrete stairs. Fear was like static in the air. My hands started to shake as they lowered the comic book. I pulled back from this as hard as I could. A man's work boot appeared on one of the highest stairs, and then the basement was gone.

I was yanked upward, my head a flurry of echoes and whispers. But there, in the swirl of color and chaos, something stopped me. A face caught my eyes, and everything slowed down. I was suspended, there in the soft mist of sleeping and waking, and a little boy I'd never seen before smiled at me. It was an easy smile, with missing teeth and a scrunched-up nose. Peanut butter on his chin, something like paint on his cheekbone. It felt personal, like it was just for me. His dark blond hair was messy, and he crossed his arms across his chest as he sat on a window ledge. The ocean sprawled out across the horizon behind him. I saw it for no longer than a space of a breath before I fell hard and fast, waking up in my bed with a jolt.

I was dripping sweat, and I looked over at Seph. She was sitting up in her bed across the room, her short black hair sticking out around her head. It was still dark outside. My clock read 2:15.

"Reed's?" she asked, putting a hand over her heart.

"Yeah," I said absently, running a hand through my hair.

"I told him to lighten up. He had like three beers tonight. He always drifts more when he's been drinking, and I *told him* I don't want to see that shit!"

I was trying to call the image of the little boy in the window back to my mind. I thought about saying something to Seph, or even running to Fabian's room and shaking him awake.

I remember something.

The thought pounded against my chest like a second heartbeat.

I think I remember something.

Did they see it, too? It happened right as I was waking up, but maybe one of the others caught a glimpse of it.

I expected terror, or something. I expected fear. Blood. Darkness. Something bad. The little boy's face was still lit up behind my eyes.

"Did you . . . did you wake up right after? Did you see anything else?" I asked, tentatively.

Seph shuddered. "I saw that man's face as he got to the bottom of the stairs. Then I pulled out," she said. She slipped her socks on and walked to the door.

"Did you see something else?" she added as an afterthought at the doorway.

"No," I lied. My feet found the cold floor, and I felt the lie sit heavy on my tongue.

⚬⚭⚬

"Don't even start with me," Reed paced in front of the fireplace, his sweats hanging low on his lean, bare torso. Fabian stood opposite him, his hands braced against the back of the couch.

We'd all drifted with Reed before, but some nights were worse than others. The clearer the memory, the angrier Reed got.

It wasn't as bad as it could have been. Once, after Reed mixed some muscle relaxants with gin, we saw it all. We watched what happened when the man in the work boots came down the stairs. We heard the man tell the boy that if he told anyone, especially the boy's mother, the man would kill her in her sleep.

The man in that memory died seven years ago, and Reed woke up in that basement. He belonged to a child molester, and he lived and breathed hatred because of it. When I remembered that, I hated Reed a little less. He could tell, too, and that made him hate me even more.

"All of you need to get the fuck out of my face," he seethed.

"We can't do that," Rory said, stepping around the side of the couch and walking toward Reed with an outstretched hand.

Reed stopped pacing as Rory came closer. He looked at her tentatively, like he couldn't stand the fact that she could make him stand still.

"We can't leave you alone," Rory repeated, stopping when she was just a foot in front of Reed.

A year ago, Reed took too many of those muscle relaxers on purpose. It was only because Seph came home early from school that she found him in time. The Internment launched a full-scale investigation as to how Reed got the pills, and it almost cost us the Boneyard.

"We know how you feel," Rory said lowly. "That's what this place is all about. That's why Hushed stick together."

Reed laughed, a derisive, cutting sound. "Know how I feel? Like hell you do. Yeah, your secret is bad, but at least you keep it on a leash. And you?" He pointed at Eva. "An affair? All you have to live with is a fun little voyeuristic fantasy?"

Seph took a step forward, and he held his hand out, gesturing for her to stop.

"Your human found the note his twin sister left when she committed suicide, a note that would've destroyed their parents' lives, and he never told them. That's nothing, so stop trying to act like keeping the secret is hard for you—"

"No one is trying to compare, Reed," Fabian said.

Reed eyed Fabian. A smile slunk up the side of his mouth, like he was grateful someone finally pulled the trigger on his rage.

"You," Reed whispered, looking from Fabian and then to me. "And you. Both of you can get off your high horse and shove this *sticking together* thing up your asses. Because you have no clue," Reed hissed, looking back at Fabian. "You're a freak of nature, and you don't belong here any more than you belong in your precious church."

"That's enough, Reed," Eva said, her voice wavering with emotion as she looked to Fabian, who went stock-still. His knuckles were white as he grasped the back of the couch.

"Reed." Rory's voice cut through the thick silence.

"Why do you even care, *Fabe*? Why do you care if I swallowed six different bottles of pills? Won't I just . . . *come back*, somehow? Don't you believe in second chances?"

Eva ushered Seph out of the room, and Seph reluctantly let her.

"Exhumed are a myth, Reed. And even if they weren't . . . that's not how it works," Rory said. Reed looked down, turning his smirk slightly more in the direction of her voice.

"Why don't we talk, just you and me?" Rory asked.

Reed turned at her words. He searched her face, his hateful expression yielding ever so slightly as his eyes took in the sight of her. He blinked as he swallowed hard, like she was a voice calling him out of a bad dream. For a second, it looked like he'd follow her.

Then, Rory glanced at Fabian. It was a quick look that lasted a fraction of a second, but the spell was broken. I saw the rage pool back inside him like a backdraft, and I braced for it.

Reed sneered and wrapped his hands around Rory's throat, every muscle in his back tightening with the tension.

"You think I don't know what you're doing?" he cried.

Rory's hands reached up and wrapped around Reed's arm.

I didn't even have time to scream before Fabian launched himself over the couch and tackled Reed to the ground, freeing Rory from his grip. I ran to help her up.

Reed rolled, flipping Fabian onto the corner of the fireplace. I heard the sickening *thud* of flesh on brick, but Fabian recovered quickly, turning Reed on his back and then wrapping his arms around Reed's, pinning them to his side in a bear hug as he pulled them both to their feet.

"Let me *go!*" Reed screeched.

"You need to take a deep breath," Fabian said calmly, putting his face over Reed's shoulder.

Reed threw his head back, trying to hit Fabian, but Fabian leaned away, tightening his grip.

Reed laughed as sweat dripped down his forehead.

"Well, well. Little preacher man, getting into a death match over a piece of ass," Reed choked out.

Fabian clenched his jaw but didn't say anything.

Rory stepped back from me. "I'm fine," she whispered, though I could see her hands shaking as she tied the band back into her hair. She left the room, and Reed's gaze followed her, a trace of sorrow gathering between his eyebrows as he frowned. He took a sharp breath through his teeth and yanked away from Fabian, who let go.

Reed ran a hand through his hair and looked to Fabian, his chest heaving.

"Don't fucking touch me again," he said.

"Then don't touch her again," Fabian said quietly.

Reed stalked back to his room, and no one followed him. Voices rose from the kitchen—Seph and Rory talking quietly as Seph made tea.

I found Fabian by the stairs, but he snatched his coat from the hanger by the door and stormed out into the night before I could talk to him.

My chest thrummed, the adrenaline in my chest slowly seeping out of me. I slipped up the steps, making sure to be soundless as I dipped back into my dark room.

I didn't have the strength to do anything but slide back in between my sheets, listening to the electricity crackle under my skin, slipping between all my thoughts.

Don't you believe in second chances? Reed's words raced through my mind.

I don't think any of us believed in Exhumed. Not even Fabian, who had more faith than anyone I knew. It was a myth, the thought that if the exact same secret happens twice, the exact same Hushed comes back to carry it. This was not the same as multiple Hushed coming from the same shared secret—two people having different Hushed about the same affair was common, but they had two different experiences, two different perspectives, and two different Wounded. Exhumed were a myth because the idea was rooted in the belief that Hushed made sense, and we didn't. There was no rhyme or reason to which Hushed carried which secret. But if you believed that there was a design to it, then I guess the logic worked.

Sarah used to tell me it would be like an explorer discovering a lost kingdom and then dying before they told anyone. A Hushed would carry that. Then, if something happened to that Hushed (killing Hushed has always been a human-favored pastime), the secret would be loose, like all others. Then, let's say . . . *centuries* later, another explorer found the same lost kingdom and then kept it a secret. When that explorer died . . . the same Hushed would return. They would be an Exhumed.

It made no less sense than us existing, I guess. But I didn't buy it, and I knew Reed didn't either. We'd never heard of it actually happening.

I shut my eyes, and the image of the little boy was there.

Three years of nothing, and then, there it was. I was too stunned to panic. Too stunned to do anything but look up at my ceiling.

I remember something.

I think I remember something.

SEVEN

Rory and I went to Mal's. She didn't say a word about the night before, and I didn't either. Fabian left before I came downstairs, though he did text me to ask how I was doing before my shift. I didn't reply. He was always first to reach out after a fight. But this time, I didn't really want to reconcile. His words still spun around in my head like a curse.

Rory reached into the glove compartment and handed me my wrinkled ball of an apron. Hers, of course, was perfectly folded. As she slipped hers on, I opened my backpack just enough to check on the rubber band–wrapped manila envelope stuck in my notebook. I zipped up my bag and threw my apron over my shoulder.

Mal's was one of the oldest diners in Rearden Falls, and I'm pretty sure it's smelled like the same strong coffee since it first opened in 1987.

"Hey, Dee," Rory called as we both punched in on the back wall.

Dee, whose papery eyelids were covered in bright pink eye shadow, waved back at us.

I leaned through the order-up window and looked over at Mal as he sliced bread in the kitchen. He was old enough to be my dad, if I had one. He wore a blue baseball cap and his sleeves were rolled up enough to reveal the "Semper Fi" tattoo on his weathered skin.

"Does this taste dry to you?" he asked, pulling a piece off a slice and tossing it to me. I caught it midair and popped it into my mouth. It was moist, like it had already been coated with butter.

"Nope. Perfect," I said, holding up my hand for another piece. Mal tossed me one.

"Dee says my taste buds are going."

"She's right," I replied, throwing the other piece of bread up and catching it on my tongue.

"Thanks," he said sarcastically, wiping the knife on his apron and setting it down on the sink. "You both did okay yesterday, then?" he asked over his shoulder as he washed his hands.

"Yup," I lied so easily that, for a minute, I almost believed it.

"Good. Cause I heard about a holdup on the Thoroughfare exit last night. Just good to know it wasn't you." He shot me a look over his shoulder, and I swallowed the mouthful of bread. He knew.

Mal was one of the only business owners in town that would hire Hushed, even though the official law prohibited discrimination. He'd been our safe haven for years. I asked him about it once, but he just said he'd seen enough bullshit in his life and didn't need to see anymore. Something about his tone made me leave it at that.

The bell on the door rang out, and I turned. Two men and a woman in suits walked in. Next, a woman on her cell phone entered, followed by a man carrying a video camera. Three more suits walked in. Mal's was next to an antique store and a vape shop—in other words, there weren't many people in suits who wandered in. But the courthouse was two blocks down, and Mal's was the best place to eat within walking distance. They were all probably coming from there. I looked across the Formica countertop to Rory. The trial must have just taken a recess.

Mal let out a low whistle and jerked his head, motioning for me to come.

"Hey," he said when I was close enough, "so, there's a trash bag near the back door that I need you to take out."

I looked up at him, but his eyes were fixed on the people coming in over my shoulder.

"Um. Okay," I said, confused.

"Don't use our dumpster. I need you to take it a few blocks away. Come back when this place is a little more cleared out. Understand?"

He set a salad on the pickup bar and dinged the bell.

Rory grabbed it.

I don't know how he knew that the people from the courthouse made me nervous. Maybe it was just intuition from working with Hushed for years. Either way, I was grateful. I slipped the envelope in my jacket as I walked through the back door.

I turned left toward Carmody Avenue, the old center of downtown that was deemed too decrepit and run-down to be rehabbed, which had since then been recreated on Main Street. Trees, surrounded by piles of dirty snow, lined the outer rim of the sidewalk, protecting the walkway from the frosty drizzle that had started to fall. Even with that slight reprieve, there weren't many people out. A girl vaped on a corner as she talked on the phone, and a guy with huge gauges locked his bike on a parking meter before disappearing into a shop. Neither of them looked twice at me, and I was grateful for that.

Thoughts started to bubble to the top of my mind, but I sucked in a deep breath and shoved them down. The air was cold and felt like it scrubbed my throat raw. I didn't want to think of Officer Waybourne's threats or Fabian's biting words or whatever weirdness was happening between him and Rory. I didn't want to wonder if the fragment of memory that surfaced was the first of many.

Whatever it was inside of me that was starting to spin, whatever I was feeling . . . it reeked of fear. And powerlessness. Fabian had called me scared, and he was right. I battled my own mind enough as it was with run-of-the-mill panic, and I'd seen what the Pull could do to someone. I'd watched countless Hushed lose the battle. I didn't want to know what could happen when panic and Pull came together in my chest. I often wondered if they were the same thing—if the panic attacks were just a part of the Pull, and vice versa. But the more I see the Pull in action, the more I think that my Wounded just left me with a fucked-up fight-or-flight response. Which simply meant that I had even more liability than a normal Hushed. I wanted to believe I was strong enough to learn the truth and make a choice, but the harsh reality was that I probably wouldn't even remember saying the words that would kill me. That was the bundled, black razor wire I wore deep in my chest, the fear that fed all other fears. I didn't know if I was strong enough to survive knowing what I didn't already know.

I reached the mailbox, which was rusty on top and slightly dented on the side, and fought the urge to look over my shoulder. Was Ajit watching right now? With one quick movement, I dropped the envelope inside and closed the trapdoor with a *thunk*. It was done, and I was another step closer to getting Fabian away from here.

I passed a Chinese restaurant, a leather repair shop, and a nail salon, looking at the people inside as I walked by. People laughing and talking, picking up their orders or on their phones. People living normal, non-Hushed lives. At least, I assumed they were all human. I knew there was at least one unknown Hushed within drifting distance around here, given the weird shit I'd been seeing at night. I kept walking, breathing into my hands to warm them up.

Had I not seen the words etched on the glass window, I would've missed it. It was a small shop, wedged between a barber and an hourly-rate chiropractor. The glass paint was faded, and it was clear from the outlines of letters above it that there had been several different businesses there before it, but it was still legible: *Karenina Harborers*.

I stopped for just a moment, and only because I had never noticed it. Maybe it was the way the light was hitting the glass or something.

When the Teller's Fever started in the 1940s, everyone was confused. Then, they were panicked. Panic gave way to industriousness, and then industriousness dissolved into hatred. But somewhere in there, years ago, humans thought there might be a way to solve the problem.

Harborers were secret-keepers. The idea started with priests and psychologists—the traditional secret-keepers of the world. Humans flocked to them in a desperate flurry, knowing that the only way to not have Hushed was to have no secrets when you die. There was a serious supply and demand problem, so people started setting up shop and calling themselves Harborers. They would keep your secrets for a fee.

A couple of years after that, a Harborer named Moira in Granite Bay, California, retired and moved to Florida to spend her retirement on the edge of the Everglades. After six years, she died in a hospital outside of Tampa.

Seven thousand Hushed appeared near her body. In the halls, in her room. In the parking garage and even on the main street outside. They were the remnants of her life's work.

That's when humans realized that the Whisper Epidemic wasn't so easily fixed. Nothing gets rid of a Hushed, not really, not fully—except telling the secret to a person who really matters. Telling a Harborer doesn't change the fact that you have a Hushed. It just changes where the Hushed stirs. Instead of a lover's bedroom, a bank, a playground, or wherever else, Moira's clients' Hushed all appeared at her bedside, linked to her through the act of telling. They still walked off in the same direction they would have before, drawn to their Wounded like all Hushed are. When a Harborer is used, the place they stir is altered—but the Pull remains.

By now, almost all Harborers had gone out of business.

I stared into the dark building, looking at the empty, broken-down couches that lined the wall and the dusty floors.

It was a vain hope, to think that Hushed could be so easily avoided. But even during their heyday, I don't think Harborers were the answer for everyone, because the people with the darkest secrets, the ones most desperate to find relief from them, knew the truth: everyone has a price. Everyone has a limit. The Harborers would listen to secrets of affairs and theft and hatred . . . but they could always be bought. The only foolproof way to avoid having a Hushed was to tell the secret.

I circled the block one more time before heading back to Mal's. I was turning back onto Carmody Street when I saw him across the street on the opposite corner.

I froze.

Logan was wearing the leather jacket he'd tried to give me in the cell over a thin hoodie, his hands tucked in his pockets as he sidestepped a woman with a bright purple umbrella.

Don't see me. Don't see me. Don't—

He looked up, like he could hear my thoughts.

The drizzle had wet his hair, and it looked as though he hadn't shaved in a day. He looked tired, and for a moment, I stared. I'd only seen him in strange settings: the roadside, the cell. Pictures in newspapers. But seeing him right in front of me, walking like he was lost in his thoughts . . . it was different.

Look away, turn away. He's going to look—

And then he did.

We locked eyes, and I didn't wait long enough to see if there was recognition there.

He has to get to the courthouse. That's the other way.

I hurried back to Mal's. I needed to be busy.

Three minutes later, I was putting my apron on in the kitchen. I pushed the double doors aside and stepped out, stopping short when I saw the figure sitting in a booth next to the window. Logan sat on the cracked red vinyl seat. His eyes panned across the diner, stopping when he saw me. His mouth opened slightly, and his brow furrowed. Then, he looked down at the table, cracking his knuckles. Whatever he was doing, he didn't seem certain about it either.

But he was in my section, and we'd have to interact at some point. I could always ask Dee or Rory to take him, but they'd already been covering for me as I hid from the courtroom crowd. I didn't want to ask them to do it again. And truly, whatever he wanted to say to me, maybe it would be good if we got it over with. I grabbed a pot of coffee and walked around the counter, trying hard not to wince as the pot handle yanked on the bandage around my fingers. He wore the shiner above his eye as though it wasn't his first. He was avoiding the gaze of the people that walked past his booth. He pulled his sleeves low, trying to hide his still-bloody knuckles. I took a deep breath and walked over to him. A weird, panicky thought bloomed at the base of my skull: *What if he knows? What if he's here because he figured out that I stirred at Ironbark?*

The thought was enough to stop me in my tracks, but I took a deep breath and pushed forward, sticking my hand in my apron pocket just to make it look like I was checking that I didn't forget my order pad.

"What can I get for you?" I asked as I reached the table. I lifted my eyes to his, praying to Fabian's God that the practiced look of gradual, vague recognition slipped over my expression like I wanted it to. If it ever got back to Officer Waybourne that we had spoken, it would look like nothing more than a normal professional interaction.

The collar of his sweatshirt was stretched, and he had dark circles under his eyes. He sat up straighter as he looked at me, and then glanced back down at the menu like he was searching for words. He glanced around the diner before blowing out an uncomfortable breath. "Um. Hold on." He looked back down at the menu.

I stood there for a second longer, letting the awkward pause stretch to its limit.

"I swear I'm not following you," he said finally, his eyes still on the menu. "I get that it might seem like that, since I—"

"—you followed me in here," I finished for him.

He nodded, finally looking up at me. His eyes met mine, and he didn't smirk or scowl. He picked up the cup and looked at it. "I'm not great with apologies," he said finally, looking down.

I don't know what I expected, but it wasn't that. He'd been so sure of himself on the roadside, and in the cell, he'd been kind of a prick. But now, he wore a look of regret.

"Well. I don't need one," I said softly, remembering how he'd held my hand when I was panicking and looking for anything to keep me grounded. Heat flushed the back of my neck as I imagined how I had probably looked to him.

He set the mug down and looked up at me.

"I know. But I need to give one. I made things worse," he said quietly. "I'm sorry."

I didn't know what to say. My fingers played with the edge of the order pad as I ran my tongue over my top teeth.

"Lots of cars drove by," I said finally, looking around to make sure other people weren't listening. The diner was mostly empty. "No one else stopped. So."

Logan considered the words, and he seemed to relax a bit. His shoulders dropped and he studied me, narrowing his eyes. It was true. He'd tried. That was more than most people could say.

"Eerie. That's your name?"

I nodded, not knowing what to do with the weird hitch in my breath that happened when he said my name like that.

I poured coffee in his cup, even though he hadn't asked for it. I had to do something with my hands.

"Logan," I said, and he nodded.

The bell jingled on the door, and I looked over my shoulder. It was the local historical society—they came in weekly for pie and coffee after their meeting.

"Can I get you anything else?" I asked. I had to go serve them, but something made me want to stand there a little longer. It was surreal, seeing someone in pictures for so long and then having them in front of you as a living, breathing thing. He'd always just been a frozen image in a newspaper, and now the words that I said were making him smile a bit. He licked his bottom lip absently as he wrapped his hand around the mug.

"I'm good now, Eerie. Thank you."

There it was, again . . . this strange ache in my chest. I turned to leave, but I stopped when I saw a group of people outside. From their attire and the way they carried cameras, I knew they were press. I spun to look at Logan, who had already noticed them. He pulled his hood over his head.

If they noticed him, they wouldn't care that he was alone. That he looked tired and weary. They'd want a photo of the boy with the beautiful, dead mother.

"Come on," I whispered, putting my free hand out.

Logan looked confused but took my hand anyway. He followed me out of the booth as I led him to one of the farthest alcoves—one that we used on breaks because it was close to the kitchen. It was secluded enough that no one would see him.

His hand was warm and rough in mine, and I dropped it as we reached the table.

"Here. Stay as long as you want," I whispered, looking up at him.

In that moment, I realized I'd never fully understood what Seph was talking about when she talked about Logan being attractive. I'd never really let myself think that about *anyone* in real life, really. I'd just always been more focused on survival. Since I stirred, I was running, hiding, or working on a plan to escape. But this . . . this stopped me in my tracks.

Logan Winspeare was beautiful, and the way he peered down at me with confusion and gratitude made my breath feel too shallow.

"Thank you," he said, and I knew he meant it. He slid into the booth just as the door jingled and the press walked in. I turned around, making a beeline back to the counter.

"See? That's the kind of hustle I like to see," Mal joked as he set a fresh rack of clean, steaming dishes on the far side of the stove.

I put in an order for a sandwich, even though he hadn't ordered it. I just needed to look as though we'd been talking for a reason. A better reason than the truth.

I took a deep breath and looked down at my hands. They were shaking, and for the first time in my short life, it wasn't because of blind terror. I felt all lopsided, like I'd been taken apart and put together wrong. When Mal finished the sandwich and put it on the bar, I delivered it to Logan. He was reading a rolled-up book, one that looked like it'd been in his pocket.

"On the house," I whispered, and then took off again. I didn't want to talk to him. I didn't want whatever this feeling in my chest was to grow any bigger.

I let the clean plates burn the pads of my fingers as I worked, and the world felt more solid under my feet by the time I finished the third load.

He was connected to Ironbark. His mother died there, and something about that night was buried deep in my skull. For all I knew, somewhere in my subconscious I knew who set the fire. I was a missing puzzle piece in the whole weird story of his life. Getting close was a terrible idea. *Talking* to him was a terrible idea. What if he caused more memories to surface? I needed to stay away from him.

Even if there was a new feeling inside of me, sprouting up like a sapling through dirt: *I didn't want to.*

He sat there for the next two hours, reading his book. The reporters ordered a few rounds of coffee, but they didn't see him. I liked knowing that he was hidden from them, and that I had been the one to hide him. As I was setting a plate of pasta down at the booth next to his, I looked over to find him looking at me. I looked away, and when I glanced back, he was smiling as he read.

When I made my way back to the counter, Rory was leaning on her elbows, her eyes narrowed.

"Explain," she said softly as I came around the counter with a fresh rack of dishes.

"Explain what?" I asked, though I knew playing dumb was worthless around Rory.

"Winspeare. In the break booth."

I pulled a clean dish from the rack. "He was apologizing, and then the vultures showed up."

Rory cocked her eyebrow as she studied Logan from across the room. "Right. And that's it, then? Nothing more?"

I ducked down, putting more mugs away, trying to steady my hands as I slid each ceramic piece into place.

"He was being nice. I was being nice. That's it," I said, holding onto the cabinet in front of me. Rory knelt beside me.

"Babe, I think you have a crush. A legit, real, human crush."

I looked at her, eyes wide. "I don't want that," I said, shaking my head.

Rory laughed and then sat next to me on the tile floor. She wrapped her fingers in mine, and I closed my eyes tight.

We'd talked about it—relationships and everything that came with them. I'd read the books that talked about star-crossed lovers and melding kisses and twisted bedsheets and shared secrets. And I'd been perfectly content to watch it unfold elsewhere. All of the stories—even the good ones—all just seemed to end in a tangled mess with no way to extract yourself—no way to come out without being altered in some way. I couldn't afford that. No Hushed really could. I knew that if I managed to live long enough, I would probably stumble into attraction of some kind. I just didn't think it would happen so soon, and I certainly didn't think it would be with someone like Logan Winspeare.

Humans and Hushed . . . it wasn't unheard of, but it was not something that ever ended well. Best-case scenario, the Hushed lives without aging, and the human gets old and dies. But I don't think any Hushed has lived long enough for that to happen. What really happens mostly is that the Hushed goes mad trying to suppress the Pull, and eventually gives in, leaving their human lover alone. There was no happy ending for a romance like that.

"He thinks I'm human," I whispered to Rory, and I shook my head as the total and complete absurdity of what I was thinking washed over me. My mind recalled the curve of his full lips as he smiled, the way his broad shoulders hunched in the booth like we were in on a secret together.

"I wouldn't know the first thing about . . . *anything*," I breathed, putting a hand to my head. My stomach fluttered. The feeling was similar to the unpleasant burn of adrenaline, but just different enough that I didn't want it to fade entirely.

"It's easy, Eerie. It's the easiest thing in the world, falling in love," Rory said wistfully.

"Who said anything about love? I literally just brought him a sandwich, Rory," I shot back, and she cocked an eyebrow.

"Fine. No love. But I'll be honest, you don't strike me as the casual encounter kind of gal," she joked, and my eyes widened at the thought. My face got hot as my stomach flipped again.

"Let's just say I figured out how to appreciate the male form in close proximity. So we know I like green eyes and he smells good. I'd say that's a good first lesson. I'll try again in a few decades," I replied.

I started to stand up, but Rory grabbed my arm and playfully yanked me back down.

"It's worth it, I promise," she said. I looked at her, and she bit her lip, because she knew I knew who she was talking about. Fabian. But this wasn't falling in love with my kind. This was different.

"I'm Hushed," I whispered.

"So?" she countered.

"I'm an *Ironbark* Hushed, Rory," I said, lowering my voice even more.

She shrugged. "Despite that, I promise the rest of you is in good working order," she joked, and I shook my head.

"Keep it simple. Do you like him?" she asked.

"What? Do I *like* him? How old am I?" I moaned, covering my face with my hands.

"Three. Answer the question, Eerie," she said, pulling my hand from my face.

I paused, and Rory put her hand on the side of my face. "Close your eyes."

I did.

"When you saw him sit down, did you feel it here?"

Rory pushed her hand to my chest, and I put mine on top of it.

"You make it sound so dramatic," I whispered.

"Answer the question," she demanded, and I sighed and nodded. "And here?"

She put her hand over my stomach, right over my belly button. I gasped and opened my eyes. She looked at me expectantly, and I nodded reluctantly.

"Yeah." I slapped her hand away, and she smirked.

"You're assuming he's interested in me. Doesn't a crush have to go both ways for it to become something else?" I asked, and Rory leaned up to look over the edge of the counter.

"He's been on the same page for two hours," she said, settling back down as Mal walked in with more dishes.

"He's hiding from the press. You know how they are," I whispered.

"There's a back exit two feet from him," Rory shot back.

"For fuck's sake, girls. Do you have to do that there?" Mal grumbled, stepping over us.

"Almost done, Mal!" Rory chirped, and then turned back to me.

"You want him. And he wants you," she said. "You're stronger than you think, Eerie. Don't be so scared of dying that you don't live."

"I'm fucking deleting Instagram off your phone when the shift is over, this is getting out of control," I said.

She peered over the top of the counter. "He's still here."

She stood and helped me up, and I started wiping the counter down.

"You can't get him if you don't talk to him," Rory said from behind me.

"You keep saying that and I don't even know what *get him* means," I whispered, turning away in frustration. Rory wiped her forehead with the back of her hand.

"Refill his cup, leave your number, and tell him to text you," Rory replied, like it was the most obvious thing in the world. "Or just go ask him to meet you out back. Either way works."

I could feel my heartbeat in my fingertips as I let my gaze wander back to his table. A joke bubbled up on the back of my tongue, and I grabbed it.

"Is that what you did with Fabe?" I asked.

Rory dropped a cup but managed to catch it. There was a moment as she looked over at me, like she couldn't believe I'd asked it.

"No. It didn't go that way," she said finally.

"But it did go *some* way," I clarified.

Rory opened her mouth slowly, laughing silently. She wiped the countertop. So, they were together, then. I watched her and felt myself smile. I'd been so worried about Fabian missing her that I didn't really let myself stop to realize how much I'd miss her. I shoved the thought down. I couldn't afford to think like that. It hurt too much.

"Do you want to know details?" she cracked, turning back to me.

"Gross. No. *Truce*," I said.

I looked over at Logan. He turned the page on his paper, and I wiped a nonexistent stain from the countertop.

EIGHT

Logan stayed until the reporters left, about an hour later.

I just swept floors and wiped down the counters, because as long as I was moving, I had a good reason to not think about what Rory had proposed. There was no world where I was actually going to do anything. But this strange holding pattern, this beautiful little waiting place where the possibility just rested, waiting to disappear, I wanted to keep it for a little longer.

At eight, Mal turned the "Open" sign to "Closed."

Mal and Dee stayed late to count the register, and Rory and I headed out the rear exit. The sky was a dark purple dome stretched across the black asphalt and white snow.

We hadn't taken three crunchy steps when Rory stopped suddenly.

"Forgot my phone," she said. "I'll be right back."

She ran back inside, and I looked up at the one floodlight above me that threw light across the whole wide parking lot. I exhaled and watched the white mist twist against the dark sky. Footsteps registered in my mind right as someone called my name.

"Eerie?"

I jumped and turned around. Logan put his hands up and stopped walking.

"Shit," I breathed, putting a hand to my chest.

"Sorry," he said. "I didn't mean to scare you."

I laughed, my heartbeat stuttering into a sprint.

He looked at me with this half-held breath, and I knew he was going to say something.

A figure toppled from the hedges on the far side of the parking lot.

"Fucking hell," the person mumbled, and everything in me sank because I recognized the voice.

"Reed?" I asked, knocking Logan's arm out of the way as I took a step forward. He was supposed to be at the factory with Fabian. I turned back to Logan.

"Look, I have to deal with this. I'll . . . see you around?" I asked, hoping the words sounded natural. I'd never said them before.

Reed's dark green down jacket was open, and his scarf hung loose from his neck. He lifted his head and squinted against the light, stumbling slightly as he held a hand up to shade his eyes.

"Eerie-girl?"

He'd been drinking.

The back door opened, and Rory walked out, her eyes on the screen of her phone.

"Eerie, Reed says he's going to need a lift home—" She stopped as she looked up and saw Reed taking stilted steps through the parking lot toward us.

She reached up and tightened her scarf around her neck. "And now I know why," she said. She started as she noticed Logan, still standing there. I could see her bite back a smile. "Do you need a ride, too?" she asked.

"I just wanted to talk to Eerie for a minute," he said. His voice sounded far away. He was distracted by Reed, who was taking exaggeratedly crisscrossed steps across the parking lot.

"I'll call Fabian," I said lowly, turning to her. "We don't have to take him home, Rory. You don't have to look at him if you don't want to."

"I'm fine," Rory said, pulling her eyes from Logan to look over at Reed. I still texted Fabian. It was quick, and I kept my phone in my pocket.

"Well, well, well," Reed said as he teetered his way over to us. "I recognize your pretty face from the news, don't I?" He looked Logan up and down. Reed turned back to me. "And from our rousing games of marry, fuck, kill," he slurred.

Heat shot up my neck. *Shut up. Shut up shut up shut up.* I knew saying the words out loud would be pointless. The more Reed realized this was making me uncomfortable, the more he would push it.

"Why don't I walk you to your car?" I asked Logan hurriedly. I had to get him out of there, or Reed was going to have a field day.

Logan narrowed his eyes as he looked from me to Reed, a question forming on his lips as Reed's smile widened. "Is this your . . ." Logan was looking for a word to describe what Reed could be.

"Boyfriend? Paramour? Fuck buddy? Nope. Eerie here wouldn't dream of slumming it like that. Too good, right, Eerie? You and Fabian both." Reed looked over at Rory. "But you're the worst," he spat at Rory, the smile slipping from his face.

"Reed. Come on," Rory reached out and tried to grab him, but he pulled away. It was a sharp movement, almost violent. Rory jumped back like she'd been burned. Her eyes hardened.

"Logan, we're fine. You should leave," I said, trying not to sound as urgent as I felt.

"I'll help you get him home," Logan offered, and I shook my head. I was about to say something when Reed's laugh interrupted me.

"Well, well. Maybe you can learn something from him, Eerie? He doesn't seem afraid to slum it." Reed leaned closer. "You ever fuck a Hushed, Winspeare?"

Logan stopped. I could feel him grow still behind me. I could feel everything clicking into place. I shut my eyes tight.

I brought my lower lip up between my teeth as I looked up at Reed.

Reed's face became a mask of mock surprise. "Oh, no. Did I ruin some sort of Shakespearean hidden-identity thing?"

I couldn't get mad. I couldn't scream at him. Not even later, when we were back at the Boneyard. I never had anything. I never *wanted* anything. It was a nice thought, a glimpse down a path that I was never allowed to walk down.

Headlights turned into the parking lot. It was the Jeep, with Fabian at the wheel. He slammed on the brakes and jumped out. Reed threw his hands up in the air and shouted, "Fabian! You marvelous, marvelous asshole. I'm *so glad* you're here, because I'm pretty sure Eerie wants you to beat the shit out of me for cock-blocking her."

Fabian grabbed Reed by the forearm. Rory joined him and helped get Reed in the car.

I shut my eyes tight before turning around, forcing a smile on my face.

"Sorry about that," I said, using the same voice I used when a customer complained that the soup was cold.

Logan's face was unreadable. He shoved his hands deep into his pockets.

"You're Hushed?" he asked. There's no way he could have asked that question without making me mad. But the way he said it—softly—with the care someone might use saying the name of a dead loved one, was the nudge I needed.

"Yeah. We all are."

My words were sharp.

"But . . . in the cell, they did a scan on you while you were unconscious. It didn't work. It said that you were human."

He sounded disappointed. The cold air bit my lungs as I inhaled. The slip pill nullified the ability to detect the biolumins in our blood.

"And now you, what? Regret helping?"

I saw the shift in his face. I'd nudged him too.

"Did I say that?" he asked, his teeth clipping the words.

"You didn't need to."

Reed shouted something from inside the car. I heard a thump, and the horn blared. Getting him buckled in was always difficult.

Logan stared at me. His eyes held mine.

"Look. You helped me, and I helped you. You don't need to find a graceful way out of this conversation now that you know what I am. Let's just call it even."

Logan narrowed his eyes. "Guess you really have me all figured out, then," he said sadly. He smiled, but there was no humor in it.

Behind me, the Jeep roared to life.

Fabian pulled up alongside me, with Rory in the car just behind.

I pulled my eyes from Logan's and walked around the hood. I got in the car and slammed the door.

"Drive," I said, barely moving my lips.

Rory pushed on the gas, following the view of Fabian's taillights through our frozen window.

I didn't want to look in the rearview mirror. I told myself not to.

But when I did, I saw that Logan was still standing there.

⌎⌇⌎

I didn't want dinner, but when I went downstairs to make tea, I found Seph sitting with Eva in the kitchen. My stomach plummeted as I saw the look on Seph's face. I knew what was happening. Seph had been feeling the Pull worse since Sarah died.

"Deep breaths," Eva said, putting her hand to Seph's forehead.

I grabbed some ice from the freezer and handed it to Eva, before backing up against the kitchen wall. I hated watching this. It was my worst fear playing out right in front of me. The only thing worse would be running away. At one point, I thought if I watched, it would become less scary. It never did.

Seph was hyperventilating, her hand rubbing the center of her chest. "It hurts," she whispered. Rory came downstairs, followed by Fabian.

"Tell me," Eva said, resting the ice on the back of Seph's neck.

"There was a suicide note. My human threw it out before anyone could read it."

"Good. Say it again," Eva said, hoping it would ease the pain a little to say the words.

Rory knelt and rubbed Seph's back, and Fabian took a step closer.

"You can fight through this, Seph," Fabian said. "You're more than this secret. Remember? That's what Sarah said. You're more than this."

"Don't tell her that shit," Reed's voice cut through the kitchen. He was standing against the doorway, his teeth tight around a hangnail on his thumb. He'd sobered up, at least enough that he wasn't slurring his words anymore.

"Not right now, Reed," Fabian warned.

Reed dropped his hand and looked from Fabian then back to me. "And what the fuck are you two doing here? You have no idea what the Pull feels like. All you can do is fill her head with lies about how we've got souls and shit, even though we don't."

Rory stood, ready for a fight, but Reed's words cut her off.

"That's why you have to fight, Seph. This is all we got. Fight for it."

Rory stilled. Whatever she expected him to say . . . it wasn't that. Reed knelt in front of Seph, peering at her as he put his hands on her knees. Seph's breathing slowed, and Reed nodded. "That's it, little one."

My heart thudded in my chest, and I slipped upstairs.

I sat on my bed, legs crossed underneath me. Snow fell hard outside, sending pale light into the darkened room.

Tears ripped down my cheeks, and I sucked in a wet, sticky breath. Fabian came in to talk, but I pretended to be asleep.

My shoulders shook, my chest seizing as I pressed my palms against my eyes.

I didn't even know why I was crying. Or maybe I did, and I knew that acknowledging that would make it so much worse. I liked the way I felt when I looked at Logan, but that was just another human feeling that wasn't really mine to experience. I felt silly for letting myself entertain that idea.

I didn't hear the door open. Rory sat on my bed. She said nothing, and she was still beside me for a long while. When she reached out and pulled me to her chest, I didn't fight her.

NINE

The drift pulled me in hard and fast.

I saw a dusty road. It was narrow, with high, slanting rock rising up on either side like a threat.

The three figures were not supposed to be there.

The one with red lips was leading, her fingertips brushing against the stone as she walked. The man with the scar on his neck and the girl with the green eyes walked behind her, talking. Their words were muffled, but it felt like I could hear them with something other than my ears. I could sense them, like they were a vibration my blood understood.

The Adrenian Pass was for royalty. Only those with permission from the emperor were ever to set foot on it.

The man with the scar stopped at the mouth of the road and looked up at the carved warning on the overpass. It was written in Latin, and the pale one with red lips dismissed it with a coy roll of her shoulder.

"We *are* royalty," she had said.

"That's not how this works," the scar said.

"And how would you know how it works? We've taken the same

amount of breath, last time I checked. We are born of the emperor, right? Then we're royalty."

"Humans are born. We are something else," the scar said tensely.

"Exactly. We're more than human," she said, looking over her shoulder at him. "So we shouldn't have to think twice about taking this road."

"Do you feel that strange weight in your chest? That *pain*? We're not more. We're just different."

"We are consequence. Retribution," Red Lips added, turning back forward. She said it like she'd said it before. She said it like she didn't expect to be questioned.

His shoulders were tight, his fingers twitching until he just rolled them into a ball. The girl with the green eyes reached over, her slender fingers wrapping over his fist.

"Stop it, both of you. You're missing the best part," she whispered.

He looked over at her as she looked up, squinting against the stream of bright sunlight that broke through the heavy clouds and hit the side of the ravine at an angle. She closed her eyes against the strong wind that whipped past them, smiling and lifting her arms. Dead leaves swirled around them, scratching against the rock and whipping her dark hair around her face. The roar of it was deafening.

She laughed, and the man with the scar let his head fall back. Even the girl with the red lips smiled and lifted her hand, twirling her wrist against the breeze.

They were alive. The air was sweet, filled with patches and gusts of the last warm breaths of summer. That's what the girl with the green eyes wanted them to feel. They were alive.

Two men turned the corner. Imperial guards, with their bedrolls tucked under the rucksacks they had over their shoulders. They stopped at the sight of the three, and the shorter of the two guards drew his sword.

The scar pulled the girl with the green eyes behind him and reached for the other, but Red Lips stepped forward, just out of his reach.

"This is the emperor's road," the guard said, his voice deep and slow.

The girl with the red lips smiled, pulling a curved dagger out of her long sleeve.

They didn't even have time to raise their own swords. The girl moved fast, like a snake striking an outstretched hand. Her blade flashed in the sunlight. Both guards were on the ground before the scarred man could utter a sound.

The green-eyed girl looked up, her mouth open and horrified.

"They would have told someone," Red Lips explained, wiping her blade on the black fabric that clung to her slender frame.

"You killed them," the scarred man said, rushing to her side and kneeling down to check if there was anything he could do. There wasn't. He touched the gashes in their throats, raw and open like silent screams. The girl with the green eyes knelt next to him. The scarred man's hands shook.

"That's what the emperor did. He murdered thousands when he bid with the darkness to create us. Throats like this . . . women and children alike. You tell me that we aren't evil but look how easy it was for you to do the same thing." He looked up at the girl with the red lips.

She didn't move her sandaled foot as the blood coiled through the dust and brushed up against her toes.

"If I'm so bad, where are my other nine hundred and ninety-eight victims? You talk of this unspeakable evil, but you forget that a *human* did it. The bloodshed was born in his heart. Carried out by human hands. *I* just dispatched a threat to us. Nothing more."

Red Lips looked at the girl with the green eyes.

"You going to swoon, bright eyes?"

The green-eyed girl shook her head and closed her mouth.

The scarred man ran a hand over his face as he stood, and the girl with the green eyes met his gaze.

"She is right. They would have killed us," the girl with the green eyes said carefully, looking at the bodies as she stepped around them.

"You're not as naive as you look." Red Lips smirked, pulling another knife from under her black dress. "Compassion just ends in sorrow, and you have to stamp it out before you can survive." She handed the knife to the green-eyed girl. "Next time, you can help."

The girl with the green eyes took the knife as the girl with the red lips strode past her, leading the way down the pass without a backward glance at the carnage.

The scarred man met the girl's eyes, and she looked down at the knife in her hands.

The wind blew, then, leaves sticking in the blood, skittering through the puddle and dragging the mess against the stone. The guards looked up, their eyes wide and blank.

The scarred man would have stared at the bodies for hours, but the girl with the green eyes reached out, turning her wrist and extending her hand. He wrapped his fingers around hers and stepped over the unmoving forms.

I woke up with a gasp and looked around my dark bedroom. Rory slept soundly in her bed, her hand dangling near the floor. I thought about waking her up and telling her that I'd seen more. I looked at the clock.

It was 5:56.

She had to wake up in half an hour, anyway. It could wait. It was just more weirdness I didn't understand, anyway.

I lay back down. My head hurt from crying.

I fell back asleep to the thought of the blood smearing on the rock.

TEN

I went to school and kept the hood of my jacket pulled over my head the whole time. I passed a pop quiz in biology just by glancing at the study guide right beforehand. I slept through Business Admin.

I saw Jason in the hall but looked down. The memory of Reed's drift was days old, but still felt fresh in my mind. It would be even harder if I let myself think about the fact that the boy in the basement was Jason. The last thing I wanted to do was sympathize with him.

I often wondered if Jason would be different if he could get help, but it didn't matter. Reed was the Hushed with that secret, and it was locked with him. As long as Reed stayed silent, no one would ever know what happened in the basement. Jason could tell, of course, and stop his own Hushed from ever stirring . . . but he never would. That was what his uncle was counting on. The wound was too deep—Jason wouldn't let anyone near it.

The after-school shift at Mal's was split strangely, so I was done an hour before Rory. I took a muffin from the glass bake case and headed down the street.

Three blocks later, I stopped.

Our Shepherd of the Faith Church was small, but in good repair. Unfortunately, in this town, that was a defining feature. Influencers liked to take pictures on the front steps, even though the older parishioners would tell them it was rude. I'd been inside a couple of times, and always because of Fabian. Which is why I stood on the front steps, a muffin in my pocket. The factory was just down the road, and he liked to take his breaks in the sanctuary. We hadn't talked since the fight, and everything about life felt slightly off-kilter after that. I told myself it was because of the fight. It wasn't because of anything else. It couldn't be because of anything else.

The doors were open. They always were. I walked in through the foyer, stopping just inside the sanctuary. The ceiling reached up impossibly far, disappearing into the rafters. There were a couple other people inside, but they were further up, with their heads bowed low. They didn't notice me when I walked in. Fabian was in here, somewhere. As I waited, I slipped into the last pew, my jeans sliding effortlessly against the polished wood. I pulled myself to the middle with the armrest, and then pushed off again, sliding a foot down the bench.

Someone coughed next to me, and I stopped, setting my hands in my lap before looking up.

Fabian stared down at me.

"Thou shalt not slip and slide in the sanctuary," he joked.

"Sorry."

He motioned for me to scoot over, and he sat down.

I pulled the muffin out of my pocket and leaned over.

"Is 'thou shalt not eat' a rule, too?" I whispered.

"Only if said food is secretly a vegetable in disguise," he whispered back, eyeing the muffin.

"I promise, this is not a carrot cake muffin."

There was a beat as he looked at me out of the corner of his eye.

"I'll allow it."

I handed him the muffin. He broke off the bottom and handed it to me. I hated the top; he loved it. Another way in which we seemed like two parts of a matching set.

I looked at him as he looked around. His light brown hair hung over his forehead. He needed a haircut, but I knew he would only go get one once Rory mentioned it. He had a scar above that eye from when he was jumped a couple months ago after a Haunt attack. It was healing nicely. It sliced through his eyebrow in a way that made him look more dashing. I was worried for about a week that he would wind up looking like a cartoon villain. His blue work shirt was open, revealing a white tank top. His cross necklace hung over the hem. I got it for him at a gas station in Tulsa. I finally followed his gaze and looked around the church.

It was beautiful. The light from the stained glass lit up the cavernous space, and the ceiling rounded off high above my head. On the far right stood three confessionals, so inconspicuous that you might miss them.

Some churches stopped providing confession years ago. It turned the priests into Harborers, and widows got sick of having thousands of naked people show up the moment their husbands died. I couldn't really blame them. Still, it was nice to see that some were still willing to try and help humans through their problems.

Fabian's knee was warm against mine.

"I'm sorry for telling you to go to hell," I said, finally.

"It's not really an insult if you don't believe in hell."

"Har-har," I said through a mouthful of muffin.

"I'm sorry for what I said, too. It was below the belt at best."

Scared is all you are, Eerie.

I swallowed and leaned against his arm. He grabbed my hand.

"It's not like it wasn't true," I said quietly.

"It's really not, Eerie. And I shouldn't have said that. I said it to hurt you. And that sucked, because everything I do is about protecting you."

I drew a slow breath.

"You can't protect me if you're dead," I whispered. It was a cheap shot, but I didn't care. I didn't need to be honorable. I just needed to be effective. If this was Fabian following his Pull, I could forgive him not letting it go. But this wasn't the Pull. This desire for answers was born from his own search for truth, and I hated it.

"Why does finding out the truth have to mean that I'm going to die?" he asked.

"You might not have a choice, Fabian. If you find what you're looking for, if you unearth it, you won't be able to undo it."

Fabian shook his head. "I'm doing all of this because I have a purpose, and I'm not living it. I'm here for a reason, and I have no idea what it is."

I shook my head. I came here to end a fight, not to start a whole new one. "You think your purpose is to tell a secret and die in the middle of the street?"

This was the problem. The wall we hit every time we tried to reason with each other. He believed we weren't an accident. We weren't a mutation, or a punishment, but a different type of child in the eyes of God. Strange, unwanted by the rest, but still a part of the plan.

"No. Not to die in the street. To know where I belong, Eerie."

"Some people believe you belong in the street. Dead."

Fabian looked up at the rafters.

"Something terrible happened at Ironbark."

"Yeah, I know."

"I mean even before the fire. Something wasn't right there."

I was quiet, then. I knew this was the moment I should tell him about what I saw between Reed's drift and waking up. I hadn't thought about it much since it happened, but every once in a while, the memory would float to the surface of my mind, unbidden. The little boy in the window, the one smiling at me. But I had a policy of not telling anything to Fabian, no matter how small. If there were anyone who might be able to use information from drifts—no matter how small or random—it would be Fabian.

It was on the tip of my tongue, ready to fall past my teeth. But I sucked it back in. I couldn't do it. He'd gone three weeks with no sign of remembering anything, despite the daily updates on Leonard Mark's trial. Whether or not he admitted it, he was starting to think we would never remember, and that's what I wanted. It would make it easier to convince him to leave when the time came.

He leaned down next to me, resting his elbows on his knees.

"I'm not asking you to do this with me. In fact, I'm glad you're not. I'm just asking you to understand why I need to do this. It's dangerous, but it isn't a suicide mission. There are pieces to the puzzle, parts of the police reports and court records that just don't add up. And I want to know why."

I looked down at my knees. My jeans were thinning. I'd have to patch them before the winter was over.

"You know what I'll say to that." My voice sounded small, and I coughed. I normally didn't care if I looked small in front of Fabian. He knew how small I was. He'd carried me out of the smoke, tucked against his chest. I was allowed to be small with him. But the tinge of pain from the words we threw at each other two nights earlier was still there, and I wasn't ready to give him another clean shot.

"Everything is going to be okay. You've got to trust."

I felt his chin lift, and I knew he was looking at the altar at the front. I kept my eyes on his hands and swallowed another fight before it started.

It's not that easy. You were born with faith. I wasn't. His human probably had faith, so did Fabian. It was that simple. Or maybe not. Maybe our beliefs were random, like how we look, or our gender and age. Either way, Fabian believed down to his bones, and he wanted that kind of faith for me.

I just wasn't buying it. I'd seen too many Gravediggers come out of this place, crossing themselves and asking for blessings on their hunts. I didn't understand asking for help from something that seemed to also be helping people like Jason Bell.

I checked my watch. It was almost time to meet Rory.

"So, you and Rory, huh?" I asked, grateful for any type of conversation that wasn't about that fucking prison.

Fabian cleared his throat and shifted in his seat. I sat up.

"You gonna be needing that confessional, dear brother of mine?" I teased.

His face flushed. Even though we weren't actually related, I loved seeing that he blushed as badly as I did.

"We're . . ." he stopped. "I don't know what we are."

"Making out?" I offered. "Hooking up?"

Fabian put his whole open palm on my face, and I shoved him off. An old woman in the front pew looked over her shoulder. I expected her to give us a stern look or *shhhh*, but instead she smiled and turned back around.

"And what about you? I saw you talking to Logan Winspeare last night."

I shook my head and let my smile slip. He was trying to make his tone as light as possible, but I could hear the tightness in it. If anyone were okay with the idea of human and Hushed being together, it would be Fabian. But even he wouldn't be able to deny the danger that I would be risking. There was worry underneath.

"Nothing. Nothing at all," I said.

"I hope not, because it's dangerous, Eerie. If you were to remember your secret around him, and if it had anything to do with him . . . the Pull is hard enough to adjust to with time and distance—"

"Nothing, Fabian," I said, sharper this time. I didn't go into how hypocritical he sounded. That never got us anywhere.

He relaxed against me.

"Good. 'Cause he's trouble."

"Fabe."

"Sorry."

ELEVEN

The drift was dark, enveloping me like black silk.

The three took shelter in a cave they found in the mountains.

Soon, in a local village, the stories started.

The humans called the girl with the red lips the Ghost of the Adrenian Pass, her auburn hair like burnished autumn leaves, her lips like the glint of a red apple in the sun. A ghost, perhaps. A siren come ashore, making her life in craggy mountain rocks instead of sea-foam. Some claimed to see her roaming the cliffs at night.

The killing started. It was slow, at first. The nephew of a farmer wandered up the trail near Palestrina one day and never came back.

A merchant, searching for rare gems in the mountainside.

Two travelers trying to save time by cutting over the mountain.

Every time the girl with the red lips came back to the cave, hands covered in blood, satchel full of bread and dried meat or whatever else she took off the body, the scarred man tried to look away.

He hunted, bringing in fresh meat.

The girl with the green eyes carried buckets of water up from the river in the middle of the valley.

The scarred man even stopped traders on roads far from their cave and bought soft fabrics and gold with ruby edging and necklaces made with onyx.

There's no need to kill, he pleaded with her. She always claimed she had no choice, that the humans were coming too close to the cave. She said she was protecting them.

But the scarred man and the girl with the green eyes started to see something . . . a darkness in the girl with the red lips. A hunger that only killing could sate.

The girl with the green eyes stopped Red Lips early one morning as she was leaving the cave.

"Please. Not today. Just stay off the road. This is too much," she whispered. The girl with the red lips kissed her on the forehead.

"I do what I have to do for us, bright eyes. You would do the same thing," she said, pulling her hand free and disappearing into the morning mist.

The drift smudged, and I fell, landing hard in a different memory. This one invaded my senses. I wasn't just watching. I was *there*. It was the most vivid drift I'd ever experienced.

The tiles were warm under my feet, swollen with the heat of the day, even though it was dark.

Firelight stained the shadow, blending and smearing across the shifting, uneven images ripping across my mind. A light rain fell.

There were people, but I couldn't see their faces as they walked through the outer courtyard. Music pulsed from one corner of the market, its melody interlaced with the soft tinging of bells and the bubbling sound of children's laughter.

The man with the scar walked along the narrow streets with the girl with the green eyes. Her hair was longer. It had been at her shoulders, but it was at her waist now. She pulled her brown cloak closer, though her green dress was still visible when she walked.

There was a pain in her chest that radiated from her. I buckled under it, like I could feel it myself. It was like a force was bending my ribs. The Pull. I'd always heard it described, but never felt it. It was different than anything I'd ever felt. Not as painful as a panic attack, but more urgent.

The scarred man pulled the hood of his purple cape over his head. The sound of metal rang out. Shouts.

He pulled her into the shadows, blocking her body with his. Protecting her from whatever entered the courtyard.

Don't move. We'll be fine.

His voice was deep, though there was a hint of playfulness in it, like they'd avoided capture before. The years must have changed him. He was anything but playful in the other drifts. Somehow, even in her fear, she knew she was safe.

He leaned in.

There was a kiss—his hand on her cheek, her hands at his chest.

The shouts got louder, and he pulled back to look out of the alleyway.

I could feel the mob before I saw the wash of torchlight ripping through the courtyard.

They ran.

The anger rippled behind them, like the heat of the fire. They were shouting.

The man with the scar and the girl with the green eyes tore down the narrow streets, and I followed them. His rough hand wrapped tightly around hers, his cloak pulling against the wind.

They reached the end of a narrow, high-walled corridor and looked down at a shallow staircase that spilled out into a crowded courtyard.

Hundreds of faces looked back at them, all filled with hatred and anger.

"*What happened?*" the girl with the green eyes screamed.

He turned as he reached up to lower his hood. I saw the dirt under his fingernails, the deep cuts on his knuckles.

The girl with the green eyes slipped on the step, and the man with the scar reached out to catch her.

The roar grew louder as the courtyard closed in, the roar rushing in my ears as the ground beneath me gave way.

TWELVE

My breathing woke me. It was heavy and thick with fear.

Things only got worse when I opened my eyes.

I stood in the forest, looking into a smudge of black and blue, the shadows stretching across every direction I spun. My breath slid from open lips, the twisting white clouds contrasting strangely against the jagged shadows.

Panic unwound in my chest, spiraling, bleaching sense from my thoughts.

I'd walked into the forest in my sleep.

How. My mind thundered with the word.

I was in the middle of the woods, wearing my pajama shirt. My legs were buried in mud that reached my anklebones, but it was almost like I could still feel the heat of the tile on my feet. I'd put on the mud boots I'd left outside, but the rest of my legs, and arms, for that matter, were open to the cold. It felt like thousands of slivers of glass were slowly inching their way through my skin. I was wearing what I wore to bed—a shirt and underwear.

I took three steps back, throwing my hand over my mouth as I searched for an explanation.

Think.

Think.

I had to stop the spiral before it started. I couldn't have a panic attack here. I breathed through my nose, forcing myself to take deep, steadying breaths.

I exhaled slowly. *Think.*

I needed to get out of here. Get to a pay phone, or something. Get help from Fabian or—

Think. The word was less panicky, now. The ground sloped downward to my right, so I turned left, assuming I was somewhere near Rearden's Pass—the ravine that cut into the mountain on the way out of town.

Slinking through the trees felt natural. I was sure-footed in the darkness, and my eyes adjusted to the shadows as I stepped over twisted roots and slick, frosty mud. The clouds above moved, letting moonlight slip through. From the moon's placement in the sky, I guessed it was a little past midnight.

Music wafted down from the top of the ravine, stopping me in my tracks. It wasn't just music. There was laughter, too. I'd hoped to find a still gas station or maybe a quiet restaurant. I thought about turning around, but the cold bit through my bare legs with every step. There was no way I was going to be able to walk back the entire way I came without collapsing, and there was no way I'd survive a night in these temperatures. On top of all that, as much as I didn't want to admit it—I had no idea where I was.

I crested the hill, careful to stay in the shadows. The red-and-pink fluorescent light beamed through the darkness, lighting up the bar's name. *The Yard.*

The Yard. The Gravediggers' bar.

It was one of the first things Eva warned Fabian and me about when we showed up at the Boneyard. *Stay away from that place. You'll see the odd Gravedigger around town, but they're bold when they're together.*

My knees slowly gave out as I lowered myself down next to a tree.

I looked out across the parking lot. In the far-left corner, closest to the street, I saw Jason's white truck. If he was there, then his friends were too. The further we got from the center of town, the more dangerous it got for Hushed. In town, friend and foe was a mixed bag, but out here . . . there was a reason the Yard was built on this stretch of highway.

I pushed myself up, bracing myself against the tree trunk.

I looked back into the darkness.

Die in the wilderness or at the hands of some smirking asshole who would probably record the whole thing and upload it to the web. It would take them weeks to find my body.

I shivered, though it came out more like a convulsion. My shirt could pass for a dress if I pulled it down far enough, and, hopefully, most people would be too wasted to notice.

The warmth promised by the bar was too much to pass up, despite the risks.

And at least I might get to finally hit one of them in the face.

⸙

I skirted the trees around the side, staying hidden until I was looking at the backside of the building. The kitchen door swung open, and a lanky man in a white T-shirt and with a dark orange ponytail threw a bag of trash at a dumpster. It missed, splitting the bag on the side of the metal, sending green cans and Styrofoam boxes skittering into the dirty snow. He looked at it for half a second, as if considering whether to pick it up. Then he shouted something over his shoulder and went back inside.

The door sounded heavy as it slammed behind him.

Get in. Find a phone. Hide somewhere warm. Get out without anyone noticing. Don't kill anyone. Don't get killed.

The wind whipped, kicking up snow. I shivered as the trash rolled across the back lot.

My eyes drifted back over to the dumpster. Up above, high up in the wood paneling—a small rectangular window. On the opposite side of the building, I saw the same kind of window.

Restrooms.

I took off through the trees, less because I had a plan and more because I knew if I didn't move, my legs would freeze together. I stopped, skidding behind the dumpster just as the same guy opened the back door again. Another bag of trash smashed against the dumpster, though it sounded like it made it inside this time.

When the heavy door closed once more, I hopped up onto the back of the dumpster, wincing as the frigid metal bit into my hands. Somewhere in the woods, the bandage had fallen off, exposing the dark scab across my fingers. It would have hurt if I'd been able to feel them. I balanced on the thin ledge as I peered inside.

At first, I couldn't see anything, and I wondered if the lights were off. Then I realized it *was* lit but by a black light. The walls were splashed with fluorescent paint that glowed pink and yellow, like someone had cracked open a glow stick and then thrown the entire thing at the brick. Only one thing looked intentional: the words scrawled over the tampon dispenser in bright purple. *Bury the Bones.*

The ceilings were lofted, sloping from the opposite side down to where I stood. The sinks, I could see when I craned my neck, were beneath me. Three stalls. No urinals. The music was loud, loud enough to practically rattle my teeth.

It was as good as this plan was going to get, and I was too cold to think of anything else. With a grunt, I shoved the glass forward, and it gave against the creaky metal hinges. I knocked out the screen with an elbow and then jumped, pulling myself inside and ignoring the sharp stabs of pain as the edges scraped against my sides. I was usually good at climbing things, but this window was smaller than most, and it took me a few moments longer than I'd thought. Anyone looking in from outside would have one hell of a view. I hooked my hands into the sill and brought my feet forward, slowly, until they were resting on the sink.

If someone comes in, act drunk, I told myself as I reached up to shut the window. I'd cry about my boyfriend being *such* a dick and tell whoever walked in that I loved them. Maybe then they wouldn't realize I was wearing a T-shirt and worn-out, faintly bloodstained bikini briefs.

But my luck held until I jumped off the sink. Then the bathroom door opened. I threw myself behind the last stall, across from the sinks. Heels struck on the tile, and then, because the night couldn't get any better, Tansy O'Mare turned the corner.

Her blond hair looked white in black light. The reflection of the glow revealed small spikes on the shoulders of her leather jacket that matched the studs on her boots. She wore silver metallic leggings under a snakeskin miniskirt. I held my breath, waiting for her to see me.

But she kept her eyes down as she pulled mascara from her pocket and untwisted the cap with a sucking sound. I watched her for a moment, just like I had at the game. Before the Hushed arrived, someone like Tansy would have been the outcast, and surely she knew that. In another world, that would make us allies.

Oh, my gosh. I'm so sorry. Didn't see you there. Maybe it's because you shouldn't exist. Her words from the day Sarah died flitted through my memory.

Tansy put the mascara away and pulled a tube of glitter eyeshadow out of her pocket. I froze. It was the same kind I'd used on Sarah, that night.

Maybe it's because you shouldn't exist.

It wasn't Tansy's fault that Sarah died. I knew that. But maybe I would have been at the stage sooner had she not tripped me. Maybe.

And that maybe was enough to stir up rage.

My heart slowed. I stood there, hunkered in the corner looking like a vision straight from a horror movie.

We weren't in the city anymore. There were no rules here.

The thought had scared me a few minutes before, but it thrilled me now.

My footsteps were soundless.

When she looked up into her reflection, I was right behind her.

Her eyes filled with shock, and I wrapped my arm over her throat before her lip could curl. She screamed, dropping her mascara with a clatter before I clapped my other hand over her mouth. I dragged her to the other side of the bathroom.

Tansy kicked, her ridiculous leggings reflecting the light of the words on the wall.

Three pressure points. That's what Fabian taught me, and I'd done it several times before. Sides of the neck, under the collarbone.

"You're right to fear us," I whispered in her ear.

I let go of my grip for just a moment, and then pressed my fingers to her throat. She went limp, and I caught her before she careened into the tile. Her perfume was like cupcakes dipped in cotton candy.

The music thumped through the wall. Its tempo seemed to rise with my heartbeat.

I dragged her to the handicapped stall and set her against the wall, leaning her upright. Her chest rose and fell slowly. She'd wake in a few minutes. Then all hell would break loose.

The tile was cold on my bare knees as my mind spun. That's as far as my plan went. *Think*, I told myself for the millionth time.

I looked down at Tansy's metallic legs, and then I got an idea.

It took me about three minutes to peel the leggings off her limp body, because the damned things were practically glued to her skin. I took the jacket, too, before adjusting her skirt low on her thighs and checking her pulse. I looked down at the tacky silver fabric and winced. I was actually glad for the black light. It was probably best that I didn't see much.

I stepped out of the stall. I looked ridiculous, standing there in a worn Iron Man T-shirt, my legs the color of chrome, a leather jacket that could've doubled as a torture device, and mud-caked boots.

After checking to make sure no one was standing in the hallway, I took off, not really sure where I was headed. The whole place was as well-lit as the bathroom—black lights illuminated glow paint smears on the walls of the narrow space. The air was like steam, heavy and thick, melting snow mixed with hot breath all swirling in the deep bass of the music. A woman with "The Yard" written on a black apron walked past me, and I grabbed her arm.

"There's a girl passed out in the bathroom. She needs some water."

The waitress didn't look surprised. She nodded, and I let her go.

Tansy was a snake, but I wouldn't have her on my conscience.

The hallway emptied out into a main room, its raftered roof peaking high over the heads of the dozens of writhing bodies below that were kicking up smoke from the industrial-grade machine under the bar. This used to be a mess hall or something. Now it was dark, lit like one of those bad haunted houses the high school put up every year at Halloween. A bar lined the left side—"Watering Hole" was written in lime green glow paint above the backlit shelf. An old laptop was hooked up to a speaker system in the corner, under a smeared, hot-pink rendering of a skull.

Fear slipped up like bile in the back of my throat. Most of the people in the room were Gravediggers. I watched a man with skull and cross-bones tattoos on the backs of his hands drop matching shot glasses into two pints of beer and drink them out of both sides of his mouth as his friends laughed and cheered.

If they realized I was standing in their midst, chasing me down and killing me would be the highlight of their night. They'd probably mount my head on the wall above the dartboards and sing songs about that one time a stupid Hushed walked into a bar.

I finally saw Jason in the far-left corner by the pool tables and ducked closer to the wall. I thought he'd be looking for Tansy, but he seemed perfectly content talking to some blue-haired girl in flannel and over-sized readers.

I took in the whole scene, my hands still shaking from my encounter with Tansy in the bathroom. I made myself take several deep breaths, letting the fear sink to the bottom of my rib cage as the anger raged in my veins. *Maybe it's because you shouldn't exist.* Tansy's words still rang in my mind. I hated the Gravediggers then more than I'd ever hated anyone. I hated every single person in that room.

I shook my head, bringing myself back into the moment. *Phone.*

I looked down at the pants and cursed myself. I took those from Tansy, but I couldn't have stolen her cell phone? I checked the pockets of the jacket, but no luck. She probably kept it in her bra. It was too late to go back now. I stayed close to the dark wood paneling as I circled closer to the bar.

There it was—a gray phone hanging just on the other side of an ice machine.

I snatched the receiver and punched in Fabian's number before pressing my back against the machine, praying no one would see me.

It rang twice before I heard Fabian's groggy voice.

"Hello?"

"Fabe? It's me." My voice locked up as I spoke. I hadn't really given thought to how I was going to explain this. I took a shaky breath.

"Eerie?" he said, alarm sounding in his tone. "Where are you?"

I heard a voice, a soft whisper. Rory was there. Great, I'd have to answer her questions, too. I rested my head back against the wall. "I'm . . . I'm going to need you to come get me," I whispered. I knew I didn't have that much time.

"It's midnight, Eerie. Why the hell are you out without letting someone know?" His anger was slipping through, now, and I clenched my jaw as tears pricked my eyes. I didn't realize how scared I was until I tried to speak. I wanted to tell him the truth—*I have no idea where I am. I have no idea how I got here. I'm scared, Fabian.*

"Give me the address," he said, and I looked around, trying to find it on a menu on the bulletin board near the phone. "This is so like you, Eerie," Fabian said, his voice low. It was a throwaway comment, but I froze.

"What does that mean?" I asked, gripping the phone so tight I thought it would crack.

"Taking chances like this. You lecture me about doing dangerous things and then you run out in the middle of the night. Give me the address."

He had some nerve, lecturing me about taking chances when he was constantly giving in to the Suck that could eventually kill him. I didn't choose to walk out into the woods in the middle of the night. I didn't choose any of this.

I remembered my reflection in the mirror. *You were right to fear us.* I wasn't helpless. Screwed? Sure. Helpless? No. And I was done letting Fabian talk to me like I was the loose cannon when everything I'd done was to protect him.

"You know? I'll find a ride," I shot back. My chest was on fire, and I wanted to breathe it at someone.

"Eerie." His voice was thick with warning.

"Nah. You know? I'm good. I think I saw a couple older bikers drinking out of brown paper bags a couple miles back. I'm sure I can get one of them to take me home."

"Eerie!" Fabian was yelling now. He'd probably woken up the whole house. But maybe now he'd get a taste of what it felt like to watch him try and remember more about Ironbark. It was petty, but I had just knocked Tansy O'Mare out in the bathroom and stolen her pants. Petty was the vibe.

"Night, Fabian." I hung up. I rubbed my hands down my face.

Stupid. That was stupid.

The full weight of what I'd just done settled on my shoulders, and I put my hand to my forehead.

Maybe I could hot-wire a car from the parking lot or something. But I knew I couldn't stand that close to the bar anymore. It was too risky. I stepped out from the shelter of the ice machine. If I could just get out without anyone seeing me—

I chanced a glance across the room, and my heart jumped into my throat.

He was sitting at one of the tables in between the dancing pit and the barstools.

Logan.

He was by himself, a baseball cap pulled low over his eyes, a pint of beer untouched in front of him.

And he was looking straight at me, his eyes wide. I moved quickly.

I was down the hallway before I even had time to exhale. He definitely recognized me. That wouldn't have made me panic, but the realization kept spinning in my mind. *He's having a beer at a Gravedigger bar.* Maybe that was why he was so disappointed when he realized I was a Hushed. Panic came quicker now. He knew I was a Hushed.

I ran faster, as fast as I could without drawing attention to myself.

I'd walk home. I'd crawl home. I'd freeze to death. Whatever. I just had to get out of there.

His voice was calling my name. Faintly, at first, and then it got louder.

I was past the kitchen when he grabbed me, stopping me from opening the back door and pulling me into the shadow against the wall. We probably looked like any regular couple, tucked away in the dark.

"Do you have a death wish?" he growled, his voice hot in my ear.

I shoved at him, but he didn't move.

"If I did, you'd pull the trigger, right?"

Logan worked his jaw from side to side. "You know? I'm getting kind of tired of you thinking you know me, Ashwood."

"I know you're in my way, Winspeare."

His nostrils flared as his eyes fixed on mine. The familiar fire flared up under my ribs. I was squarely stranded far up shit creek, but my body didn't seem to care, much.

"What, you're going to walk the six miles back to Rearden Falls? In the snow?"

Six miles? I walked six miles in the dark?

"And you suddenly care what happens to a Hushed?"

"What the fuck are you talking about?" he countered, narrowing his eyes.

"You're the one in a Gravedigger bar," I shot back.

"Yeah, well. So are you." His tongue ran over his top teeth as he smiled humorlessly down at me.

I stopped.

True.

"That's not the same thing at all. You were sitting down. Drinking a beer."

"Drinking a beer means I'm down to commit genocide?" There was a glint in his eyes.

"It means you're here for recreational purposes." The argument sounded weak, even to me. But I held my ground. Logan ran his eyes up and down my body.

"Really? 'Cause you're the one lookin' like you're ready for a party."

Though his tone was still drenched in anger, there was a hint of a smirk on his lips.

I ground my teeth together and raised my eyebrows, fighting every instinct in me that told me to make a break for it. *I shouldn't be standing here, waiting for an explanation.* Yet, I stood there, weight on my toes, ready to run, waiting for his explanation.

"I'm here because this is the one place in Rearden Falls the cops avoid."

"What?" It wasn't what I'd expected.

"I was meeting a friend. She didn't want to be seen by the cops. She told me that this is where people met if they wanted to stay under the radar. Legally speaking."

I eyed him warily. He hadn't called attention to me. If he were one of them, he would have. That was something, at least.

"Why are *you* here?" he asked me.

"None of your business," I snapped.

We glared at each other. His skin was pale in the fading black light. He took off his hat and handed it to me.

"Put your hair up under it. You're lucky no one recognized you yet."

I hesitated as I looked down at it, and then back up to him. His dark hair was pressed against his head, and his jaw and under-eyes were ringed with shadow.

A clock ticked in my mind. I only had so much time before my luck ran out.

I took the hat and twisted my hair into a knot, sticking it up inside.

"Thanks," I said, tucking stray strands behind my ears. I looked outside through the back door and zipped up the jacket.

"You can't get to the front parking lot through the back," he explained.

"So?"

He motioned for me to follow him, but I didn't move.

I looked outside. It was snowing again.

Six miles wasn't all *that* far. I'd survived worse.

"Eerie," Logan called my name.

I turned around.

"Let me take you home."

The clock sounded louder in my head. Not just the one that reminded me that I needed to move. The other one. The one that started ticking the moment I looked twice at him. The moment I saw him as *Logan* and not just some human. He might feel differently about me if he looked at my face and saw *Ironbark* instead of *Eerie*.

It was playing with fire. The one in my memory, and the one just at my fingertips, now, as I stared at him. Something new was taking root in my mind, a new desire that was unlike any other before it. I knew *run*, I knew *hide. Eat, drink, lie, steal. Smile. Pretend.* But this was new: *Touch.*

"I don't need you to save me," I said, softer than I wanted to.

"I'm giving you a ride, not battling a dragon."

I felt my shoulders drop. My palms turned upward, and I shrugged as the words I'd been thinking rushed from me. "I can't go home," I said finally, looking up at him and watching as realization slipped over his expression. His gaze filled with a question, but he seemed to know better than to ask it. Instead, he licked his bottom lip and looked down the hallway both ways before reaching for my hand.

"I know just the place."

THIRTEEN

"So. Are you going to explain the pants?" Logan asked as we rumbled down the highway. His headlights lit up the chunks of snow that fell into the road.

"I ran into an old friend at the bar and she . . ." I said, not sure how to finish the sentence.

". . . gave you her pants?" His voice rose with the question.

"Well. Not voluntarily."

Logan looked over at me, doing a double take before a grin slid up the side of his mouth.

He shifted gears, and we lurched forward. The whole cabin of the truck smelled like him. Like spice and earth and warmth, like forgotten coffee cups and the stale, faint memory of cigarettes, like the upholstery held onto a decades-old scent.

I looked over at him, the angles of his face in sharp relief in the shadows and brief shine from other headlights.

I felt my face flushing and looked down at my lap. I had to focus on the drifts . . . and why the hell I was sleepwalking now. I had too many other things to worry about to keep getting distracted by a man.

Maybe that's why being distracted feels so good. I thought back to the moment in the hallway of the Yard. It made sense. I was used to fear, used to vigilance. But this . . . looking over at a man in the dark, that was indulgent, it was a moment to catch my breath. It was nicer to wonder about the merits of man smell than to try and figure out how in the hell I sleepwalked myself out of town during a vivid drift.

I'd thought the drift was an anomaly. That maybe the Hushed it belonged to would move on, taking this weirdness with them.

But it seemed like they were only getting closer.

I shook my head. I couldn't think about that right now.

"Wait. Did you just stand someone up?" I asked, remembering what he'd said about meeting a friend.

"No. She canceled about a minute before I saw you."

I didn't know how to act. Suddenly I was so aware of everything. So aware of the stupid leggings that suctioned onto my legs like latex. No wonder Tansy was horrible. Half of her body was constantly in a state of suffocation. I pulled at the fabric, letting it snap soundlessly back into place over and over.

He was so *close*. He made the seat feel small. He was so . . . *there*.

"Why did you think I was disappointed that you were Hushed?" Logan asked finally.

I stopped fidgeting.

"You acted like it."

"I was just surprised."

"There you go. Surprised. Disappointed," I said.

"Those are not the same things at all," he countered.

"They are to me."

A thick, expectant silence filled the cab, like it was a void waiting for me to throw something into it. I twisted my hands in my lap.

"I wasn't disappointed," he clarified.

"Then what were you?"

He didn't skip a beat.

"Intrigued," he said, looking over at me.

A neutral word.

He was intrigued.

So was I.

"So why the name *Eerie*?" he asked after a beat.

Safe enough. I could answer that.

"My brother named me. It was raining a few days after we stirred, and he remembered some word for rain in a foreign language. *Sirimiri*. So that's what he called me. It got shortened to Eerie over the years. I saw 'Fabian' on a map at a rest stop in Missouri and named him the next day."

"Brother?"

"Well. We stirred at the same time. He found me. Saved me—"

Careful. Careful, here.

"—at the shipyard where we both stirred. In California."

Lying came easy, like muscle memory.

Logan nodded.

"So. We just called ourselves brother and sister. Easier than explaining."

"Are you guys still close?"

I nodded. Despite everything—his lies about the slip pill, the accident, and all our fights—the answer rang out of my chest, true and strong.

"Very."

The word pulled on my heart. It was my anchor, the thing that kept me from tipping too far either way.

"You have any brothers and sisters?" I asked.

"Nope. My dad died when I was seven, and my mom went to prison when I was eight. Though, with all the affairs he had, I sometimes wonder if I don't have a half-sibling or six running around."

His tone was the edge of ice, carved down like a razor. Stephen Winspeare was found poisoned in his house one evening in March, eleven years ago. I'd only ever seen his picture—the one his company used for their mailers—in old newspaper articles Fabian had saved on his computer. He'd been handsome, just like Logan. I'd never heard anything about affairs, just about his donations to school lunch programs and the number of new employees he'd hired. Maybe that's because no one wants to speak ill of the dead . . . especially now that those ills could speak for themselves.

The silence was back. But this time, it wasn't that it was uncomfortable.

What was uncomfortable was realizing that I enjoyed the sound of his voice more.

"I'm sorry. For everything. It must have been rough."

"Everyone has sad stories," he said.

His father was murdered, and then his mother was put away for life for the crime. She died in a fire seven years after that. That wasn't a sad story. That was sorrow beyond words.

A tragedy of which I am a piece.

He looked over at me again, quickly. Our eyes met. He looked away.

What am I doing here?

"Can I borrow your phone?" I asked. He handed it to me. I typed in Rory's number.

It's Eerie. I'm with Logan. Will explain
tomorrow.

I looked up. We'd gone higher into the mountains, and it was beautiful. The air was cold and clear, and the glass slowly steamed. I touched the condensation, looking out at the tall trees. The darkness around us should have felt menacing, but I felt nothing but peace.

Eventually, the truck slowed.

I looked up.

We pulled through a gate, following a thin dirt road as it veered sharply to the left. We drove through an area of dense woods, so thick it felt like we were in a tunnel. The trees cleared suddenly, and I finally realized how high up we were. The mountain gave way to a sharp drop to the right, and I gasped as I lifted myself in my seat to look over. Low clouds and moon-soaked mist lay thick over the glittering lights of the downtown area; only the occasional tree was tall enough to break through. The road forked again to the left as it wound further up the mountain, but we pulled straight ahead. Just in front of us, wedged between the steep incline of the mountain and the ledge, was a two-story A-frame cabin. String lights stretched from the front porch to the surrounding trees. Some bulbs were burned out, and a worn patio set of chairs and tables was covered in reddish-brown pine needles, but it looked well-loved.

"Where are we?" I breathed, even though I knew the general location of this place. We were near Ironbark Prison. Fabian had driven up here a few times, trying to get a glimpse of it from the road, knowing it wasn't smart for us to poke too close. He could never see it, and I was glad when he finally gave up. I took a deep, steadying breath and kept my eyes on the warm glow of the lights.

"My cabin. My aunt bought it when my mom started her sentence at Ironbark so she could be close. Now it's mine. The press hasn't found out about it yet. So we should be good."

I followed him to the door without a word. The wood steps creaked under our feet.

It was tidier than I thought it would be. I'd always thought men who lived alone must live like Reed. But his house was bright inside, with high ceilings and exposed wood beams. Tasteful dark green couches rested near the wall, and a warm salt lamp glowed on the end table. A winding staircase sat in the middle of the front room, leading upstairs, with two adjoining rooms breaking off on either side. I caught a glimpse of a kitchen toward the back.

A bright orange cat slinked down the staircase, meowing feverishly.

"I hear you, Watson, I hear you," Logan said, walking through the living room toward the kitchen. The cat followed, playfully swatting at the back of his legs.

"Just give me a second, yeah? This little guy will attack you next if I don't feed him. Come in."

I walked into Logan's house, breathing in the smell of cut pine and wet dirt. It was cold, and I shivered as Logan fed the cat, turning on lights as he went. The wide windows gave a clear view of the forest beyond. Moonlight cut through the trees, and my eyes slowly adjusted. I'd always approached this part of the mountains with a tight-fisted fear. I would practically hold my breath until Fabian was ready to turn around, so I'd never really taken a deep breath this high up. But once I did, I could see the beauty I'd missed every other time I'd been down this road. Behind me, Watson kept meowing, and Logan talked to him in a soft voice as he opened a can. I turned and froze.

The coffee table was covered in papers. Clippings of his mother's trial, charts, uncapped highlighters. The abandoned coffee cups and protein bar wrappers reminded me of Fabian's room. I took a step closer. I recognized some of the newspaper clippings—Fabian had the same ones.

Logan was knee-deep in Ironbark investigations, too.

They should compare notes, I thought. My heart hitched slightly as I remembered Fabian's warning. If my memories came back to me at once and they had anything to do with Madeline, it wouldn't be safe for me to be around Logan. The Pull was bad enough when there were miles between a Hushed and a Wounded, and when the Hushed had several months or years to get used to the urge. Fabian was right about this being dangerous.

I stared down at the papers and folders, my heart beating faster. My eyes roved over the words and pictures, trying to look at it all at once to get it over with.

Nothing.

Nothing happened. There was no sudden rush of realization or clarity. There was nothing in my memory except shadows and stains.

"Sorry. I would've cleaned up if I knew I was going to be having guests," he said as he walked back into the room. If he'd seen me looking at the papers, he wasn't mad.

He moved to the fireplace and kneeled, lighting a match. The room roared to life. I hadn't realized how cold I was until that moment. I stepped forward, letting the heat wash over me.

"Careful. Those look like they might melt and fuse to your legs," he said, looking up at me.

I stepped back, cursing.

"If I had known I would be wearing these all night, I would've just opted to run around naked." I pulled at the fabric once more. They stuck to my legs.

Logan let out a soft laugh. "Maybe it's your punishment for stealing them. They never want to leave you."

"You're hilarious."

Logan stood. "Hold on."

He ran upstairs, his footsteps sounding throughout the house.

Moments later, he came back down with his arms full of clothes. "I had some of my aunt's old stuff here. Here."

He pointed to the bathroom off the kitchen, and I slipped inside.

The leggings came off my legs like wallpaper. I sighed in relief as I pulled on the sweatpants and shirt. My hair was damp from the snow that had melted in it, and I wound it in a loose knot at the back of my neck.

Logan looked up at me as I walked back into the living room. I held the silver pants up.

"You got them off," he said, placing all the folders in the middle of the table. "Want to burn them?"

I looked at the leggings. "I don't think this stuff would even burn," I whispered, holding them up to inspect them. I balled them up, tossing them near my boots.

"And it's probably not good for your fireplace."

"Gross. Yes. Are your legs okay?"

"Yes, but I mean, do people really wear things like that? In that bar, do you see many girls wearing plastic pants? Is it a Gravedigger trend?"

"I don't know. That was my first time there."

"And your date didn't even show up," I joked, half kidding.

"It was a *friend*. An acquaintance, really," Logan corrected.

"Sounds like the beginning of a film noir. You meet in a dark bar. You barely know each other."

"The sounds of drunks screeching in the background, calling for the murder of innocent people," Logan mocked, looking up dreamily. "The perfect spot for romance, wasted, since I was just meeting a hacker I'd hired."

I stopped, knowing we were moving closer to real conversation. Serious was coming. I just didn't want it here yet.

"No, that sounds even more romantic. It's a dangerous job. One you're not sure you'll survive. The two of you, on the run from the law."

Logan shook his head as he stood. He'd taken off his jacket while I was in the bathroom and was wearing a dark gray long-sleeved shirt with buttons down the top. The first one was undone, and he'd rolled the sleeves up. I could see the outline of his shoulder muscles through the thin fabric. I looked away, taking a deep breath. Then I turned back. I looked, and I didn't squash the heat that stretched up under my ribs.

"I'm pretty sure this particular hacker had a partner. Does that kill the vibe?"

"Nope. You'll just fall in love along the way, and then she dumps them in the end and chooses you." Talking to Seph about her TV obsession was paying off.

"Well, I had no idea I was signing myself up for such an adventure."

"Really? Cause I'm pretty sure adventure is the subtext of the sentence, 'I hired a hacker.'"

His eyes glinted as he walked past me, and I realized I held my breath as he moved around me into the kitchen.

What are you doing?

I shoved the thought down, under the ugliest parts of me and to the left of *this is crazy this is dangerous.* I was living. I was doing something other than surviving, and it felt good. I wanted more.

I turned and watched as he pulled two mugs down from the cabinet.

"Can I ask you something? It's one of those things I've always been afraid to ask because I'm pretty sure it would be considered offensive."

"Well, when you start like that, how could a girl resist?"

He set the mugs down on the counter but kept his hands on them.

"How do you know what film noir is? I mean, not just that. How do you know anything? Like did someone have to teach you everything about the world?" I made a face, biting back a laugh at the thought.

Logan stopped, staring down at the mugs before turning them over. "See? That sounded offensive."

"No. It's not. I just have never had to explain before. We just . . . know. We call it periphery."

He stopped and turned his whole body toward me.

"I know what my human knew, kind of. I have a general

understanding of culture and history. Not everything. Dregs. Weird tidbits, or odds and ends that wound up with me. People we recognize from their lives. Old locker combinations. My brother remembers bits of foreign languages, and my best friend is good with directions. She can find anything or anyone. I hate seafood, and I have no idea why. I have a really good photographic memory. And I always just knew that those *hey, stranger*, black-and-white mystery films were called film noir."

And that's all I know.

"That makes sense, I guess." Logan put water into the coffee maker, though his face was darkened.

"What? Not the answer you were expecting?"

"No. I don't know what I was expecting. I just thought . . ."

He set the coffeepot into the machine.

"I guess I just thought you were your own people, you know? I never would have guessed that it worked like that. That you were partly someone else."

I was very still, and I saw his expression drop. "No, God, no, I didn't mean it like that—I'm such an idiot. I know you're a *person*—"

I shook my head and stepped into the kitchen.

"No, I know. It's not that. I . . . like the questions, and I don't blame you for not knowing everything about us." I meant that. "It's just . . . I had a friend who would have agreed with you. Sarah. She thought we were hijacked souls, or something. Pulled from our place in history and stuck here to fulfill a purpose. That it wasn't just periphery. That there was a bit of *us*, whatever that meant, in there, too."

Logan nodded. "Your friend was smart."

"She was. She always saw the best in bad situations."

The coffee maker beeped, and he poured scalding liquid into the cups.

"You don't agree with her?"

I sighed and watched him pour milk into the cups. He held up sugar, and I nodded.

"I don't know."

He held out my cup.

"Isn't it like . . . three in the morning?"

Logan nodded.

"It will warm you up. I'd offer you my jacket, but the last time I did that, you threw it back in my face."

I rolled my eyes, and he lifted the mug to his lips.

We walked back into the living room. Logan sat on the couch. Watson lay sleeping on the middle cushion. I took the opposite side.

Exhaustion hung on my bones, pulling me deep into the soft fabric. I tucked my legs against my chest.

"Why don't you want to go home?" Logan asked.

I considered what I could say, and what I couldn't. I was starting to see that the most important decisions rise at the most unassuming moments. Not at podiums or in front of thousands. Not when there's a weapon in your hand or a camera in your face. The biggest, most important moments were like this, tucked away in the silence in the space between the popping of the fire. It was in the breath I was taking, giving a moment to decide to tell the truth.

"My brother and I had a fight."

Logan set his mug on the arm of the couch and looked over at me. My heartbeat thundered in my chest.

"We spent a year or so after we stirred just traveling across the country. We lived on food from gas stations and hitched rides in the back of cargo trucks. Slept in people's garages. I know it sounds miserable, but it really wasn't. It was just Fabian and me. Even when we could only afford toast and one black coffee to split in the grossest diner possible in the middle of Kentucky backwoods . . . it was us. But with the Internment trying to track Hushed, it became more and more dangerous. Any state trooper could have the enhanced black light scanner."

"The one that detected the biolumins in your blood?"

I nodded.

"I thought they said Hushed registration would be voluntary?" Logan asked.

"It always starts that way, doesn't it?" I countered.

He looked down and nodded.

"We even saw a convenience store clerk with one, once. He held it out over customers' hands before doing business with them. So, our only chance was finding slip pills."

Logan didn't look confused.

"You've heard of slip pills?" I asked.

"The ones that suppress the biolumins and pass you off as human?"

I was impressed.

Logan smiled and pointed to himself.

"Felony record, remember?"

"Yeah. Well. One night, Fabian said he'd found pills for us. The effects only last a couple of years, but that's more than enough time to disappear. Start over. Play human long enough so people thought we were."

My voice slowed as the thick memories came back all at once. It was hard to parse them out. The way I'd sat looking at the rain through the window of my booth beside the empty Pizza Hut in the Love's truck stop, waiting for him.

The crushing fear when he was five minutes late.

The way I'd almost cried when he showed up soaked to the bone, a pink pill in his hand.

He didn't tell me that the deal he'd been working on for a month fell apart and that the guy only managed to get one. He lied and told me he'd taken his already.

I thought everything was fine. It was, until later that night, when the car we'd hot-wired flipped once. Twice. Three times, stopping only when it hit the base of a tree.

The paramedics pulled me out and lay me across the grass. I stared up into the purple clouds—a typical New Orleans summer storm—as they ran the detector across the inside of my forearm. Clear.

I turned, fighting the paramedic's orders to *stay still, ma'am*, just in time to see them do the same to Fabian as they strapped him into a gurney. His eyes were shut. He wasn't moving.

It's an unregistered Boney, someone said.

And I realized what he'd done.

For two days, the Internment thought I was human, sitting there at his bedside. They had no way to prove otherwise. They probably thought I was too lovestruck to leave him, that Fabian and I were running away together, and something went wrong.

It would've been hilarious, the kind of thing Fabian would've laughed at, had he not been dying from complications of a collapsed lung and internal bleeding. We don't get sick, or at least, nothing serious. I've had colds and the stomach flu, but nothing life-threatening. Something about being a Hushed protects us from chronic illness as well as aging. But we're not indestructible. The Pull, knives, guns, car accidents—we didn't die easy, but we were easily killed.

Somehow, the Internment figured it out. Maybe it was how I looked at them like I hated them, or maybe it was because, despite my DNA telling them I wasn't a Hushed, there was no record of my existence.

They waited three days. Three days of me sitting next to an unconscious Fabian, listening to him struggle for breath, watching his body lurch and buck. Then they offered me a deal.

Admit I was Hushed. Register Fabian and myself with the Internment. In return, they would save his life. I'll never forget how cold the woman's voice was, and how even she kept it when she had to speak louder over Fabian's gasping.

There wasn't a choice.

I leaped out of my chair, yanked the pen from her hand, scrawled our names across the dotted line, and screamed for them to *do it*.

Thank you for your cooperation, they said as they wheeled him toward surgery.

I blinked, letting the warmth of the fire bring me back to the moment.

A single tear slipped down my cheek, and I brushed it away. I looked back at Logan. He hadn't moved through the entire story.

"So you both wound up here?" he asked quietly. "How?"

I'd left out the part where Fabian told me—through wet breath still in the car as we were trapped upside down, as we heard the sirens wailing—that he'd arranged for me to go stay with a community of Hushed in Oregon. Once I was safe and away, he'd make his way to Rearden Falls. He knew that idea scared me.

He'd signed up for Rearden Falls as soon as he was well enough to hold a pen in his broken fingers, and I went with him.

"It's where Fabian wanted to be," I said. Which was true. "He'd heard about it from some other Hushed and thought it sounded peaceful." Which was decidedly not true.

"So you had a fight about that night?" Logan asked.

Yes and no.

"He wants to protect me. He thinks he needs to."

"Does he?" Logan asked.

I took a deep breath through my nose.

"Probably."

I looked over at Logan. He turned to face me and set his mug on the coffee table.

"Because you have a habit of winding up in holding cells with people like me?"

I laughed. "I wouldn't call it a habit. Predisposition, maybe."

"You didn't need anyone's protection, though," he said, joining in with a laugh of his own.

"Well. I needed yours," I said, quietly, thinking about how he'd kneeled by me in the cell. He looked over at me, the firelight dancing in his eyes.

"It was bad then, huh?" he asked. "The panic attack?"

"How did you know?"

He leaned forward. "My dad used to have them. They would get pretty bad sometimes. Do you think that's from your human too?"

I pressed my lips together and shrugged. "Maybe. But I'm pretty sure if there was anything in me that belonged to *me*, that would be it." I swallowed hard. The only thing worse than having a panic attack was talking about them, but it felt easy, with him.

Too easy.

It's the easiest thing in the world, Rory had said. I bit the inside of my cheek as I stared at him. He was so close, closer than I'd ever let a human before.

"Well. I guess you're glad you pulled over to help me, huh?" I joked, trying to lighten the mood as I looked up to meet his eyes.

He didn't laugh or look away. Instead, he looked down at his coffee and rubbed the back of his neck.

"People have been treating me like I was made of glass since I was eight. I was 'the boy with a dead dad and a murderer mother.' You're the first person in a long, long time to let me help them. Everyone thinks I'm too fragile. You didn't act like that." He looked up at me. "I'm very, very glad I pulled over."

I sipped the coffee, using the brief moment to gather my nerve. I didn't know what to say.

"Okay. Your turn."

I turned to face him, feeling bold. We were at the hard parts now. Pointing to scars and showing where the knives went in.

"What was the hacker for?"

The words came out strong, though I worried they would waver. Every time I stepped closer to Ironbark, I risked the point of no return. But there was something thrilling about uncharted territory too. I'd never been here before.

Logan narrowed his eyes at me.

"My mom was innocent."

I nodded.

"This is where people usually check out," he said, motioning to the front door with his head.

"I've heard stranger things," I replied.

His gaze was skeptical. He was quiet for a moment, almost like he was at the edge of something and trying to decide if he should jump.

"I knew she was innocent. I'd told you . . . there was a side to my father that no one in Rearden Falls wants to admit existed—a side you could only see if you lived with him and saw how my mom covered up bruises with three layers of makeup. I didn't want him dead, I should probably put that on record. But I saw the look on her face when the cops showed up at our doorstep and told her my dad was dead. I knew right then that she had nothing to do with his murder.

"So when I grew up, I got mad. I pushed and searched and was determined to get my mom out of prison, no matter how much she begged me to leave it alone. Her lawyer and I thought we had enough evidence for an appeal. And then one night, they showed up at my house."

My skin tingled. "Who?"

"I don't know, exactly. I just know there were five guys in suits standing in the kitchen. They beat the shit out of me. It took six weeks and two knee surgeries to even walk again."

I searched his face in the dim glow of the fire.

"How old were you?"

"Seventeen."

"Fuck. You were a kid," I bit out, and Logan shrugged.

"They told me that it was my last warning, and that I should've listened to my mom and backed off. And they told me that she would be next if I didn't drop it."

"What did you do?" I asked.

"I told the police I'd walked in on a robbery. And then I left it alone, because I couldn't bear the thought of something happening to her. But when she died, I had nothing to lose."

"Except your life?" I countered, even if I was in no position to be telling people off for putting themselves in life-threatening situations.

Logan smiled sadly. "Sure. You could say that."

"Is that where your felony record comes from?" I asked.

Logan smiled and shrugged. "Two counts of breaking and entering and one count of disorderly conduct. Worth it, in the end."

He leaned over and grabbed the folders from the coffee table. "I've managed to get what I could from different sources. Legal and, well, not legal."

He held them out to me, the weight pulling his wrist down slightly.

I opened the first. It was about Sam MacDonald, the guard with the kind face.

I flipped through the papers on the right, looking through the bits and pieces of Sam MacDonald's life.

Logan looked over.

"Sam MacDonald. He grew up in at least three different places before settling in West Virginia and going to high school," Logan recited, his voice soft.

"Do you remember him?" I asked, looking over at him.

Logan glanced down at the picture in my lap.

I clasped my hands together so he couldn't see the way they were shaking.

"He talked to me once. Just before those guys beat me up. I was at visiting hours, and my mom asked me to stop digging, to stop pushing. She cried and told me to leave everything alone, and then she left. I sat there, you know, because I didn't know what to do. I was sixteen." He laughed softly at the last word. "Anyway. Sam . . . Officer MacDonald talked to me for a moment before he followed her into the hallway."

"What did he say?"

Logan's eyes roved across the ceiling as the memory replayed across his mind. "He told me that she was dealing with a lot. And that she loved me. That she wanted more for me than what I was chasing."

"That's weird, isn't it?" I asked, flipping through the papers.

Logan nodded. "I knew a lot of prison guards. Seven years' worth. Not one of them ever did anything like that."

He opened another file.

The picture was of a younger man with floppy brown hair and a sweet smile. He didn't look like someone who would work in a prison—I always thought that when I looked at that same picture when Fabian was telling me about his research.

Dr. Walter Davie.

"He was the prison doctor," I said when I found my voice.

There were pages of information. Fabian hadn't been able to gather much on Walter Davie. Just the basics. Logan, it seemed, had been able to dig up more.

"Not just a doctor," he said, flipping through the file. "A geneticist, Eerie. He got his Ph.D. at MIT and went on to work for the defense department's anti-bioweapon task force. I'm talking DARPA, RAND Corps shit."

He showed a document verifying Dr. Davie's security clearance.

My heart pounded. This was new earth, pulled up and plowed over.

This is what I'd dreaded, and here I was, staring it in the face. Maybe Fabian was right. *Fabian is always right.* I waited for the panic, but it didn't come.

I could have told Logan to drive me home. He would have. I didn't have to look at this. But something deeper than fear kept my eyes on the page. I wanted to stare this down.

I wanted to know the worst it could do.

"None of this information was in the public record about Ironbark. You tell me why a woman's prison in North Carolina needs to have a world-class geneticist on staff, especially when he only came in once a month for their checkups."

"I don't know," I whispered.

Nothing. No triggers, no rushing realizations. My heart found its steady rhythm again.

"I don't have much, though. I've been digging for years now. Aunt Natalie was digging for even longer. No answers yet. But there will be."

"The hacker," I said, filling in the blanks.

Logan nodded.

"I'm pretty sure you're going to have to do better than meeting in a Gravedigger bar if you want to avoid prison time for hacking a federal database," I said.

Logan scratched Watson, who had wandered over. "It would be a small price to pay."

He said it so offhandedly, like he didn't think twice about saying it. "My mom always protected me when my dad came home looking for a fight. She fought for me—" His voice was full of restrained emotion.

Something in my chest twisted violently. I remembered the bodies I'd stepped over—the ones I'd tripped on the night I stirred—and wondered if one of them was Madeline.

He was right. There was something going on at Ironbark that was off the books. Something that wasn't right.

I couldn't tell him where I stirred. Even if I could, I couldn't tell him what I knew, because I had nothing to offer but slices of fire-drenched memories that were as helpful as bits of ash. But for the first time ever,

I felt an anger in my bones that wasn't brittle. I was angry with the people at Ironbark. They had gotten away with something dark, something evil. Fabian was right.

I closed my eyes, remembering the prison that night. The smell of the smoke and the sound of the fire alarm blaring so loud I thought my ears would bleed.

Madeline didn't deserve what happened to her. None of them did.

"Can I look through the rest?"

"You want to read these?" he asked. "Why?"

I stopped. I couldn't tell him the real reason. *Careful, here.*

"You saw how the cops treated Rory and me. Any chance to nail law enforcement—count me in." The lie rolled off my tongue easily.

"Fair enough," Logan said.

The slipshod knot came undone at the back of my head, and hair fell into my face.

Logan leaned forward. He didn't hesitate before brushing it out of my eyes. His thumb skimmed my cheekbone, and I shivered. I loved the way it felt, and I closed my eyes. From the thrum that was pulsing just under my skin, I felt like I understood why being a human, or something close, at least, could be something good.

It's the easiest thing in the world.

I wanted him to touch me. Then I pulled back slightly, terrified that he would, because I realized I would have no idea what to do if he did. The look in his eyes had changed. He looked at my face like he was trying to memorize it, like he was sure I'd disappear at any moment. I was sure I was looking at him the same way, and I knew I needed to tell him the truth. Once more, just to be sure he understood.

"I'm not human," I said.

He didn't skip a beat. "That's fine. I don't much care for humans."

His thumb brushed over my cheekbone. It was a slow movement, like he had all the time in the world and wasn't going to waste a second. His rough fingers singed my skin. I wanted to disappear into the sensation. I wanted to devour it and let it devour me, I wanted to understand it all and leave it a mystery—

Watson jumped up on the table, startling me. He sniffed the coffee cups, and then flopped down onto the files, stretching out.

Logan's hand dropped as he laughed, and I swallowed hard, trying to catch my breath.

"We're going to need more coffee. I think he got fur in yours," Logan said, standing and grabbing both cups before disappearing into the kitchen.

When he was safe in the kitchen, I flopped back against the couch. My chest was on fire.

I could still feel his fingers on my cheek, and I wanted to put my hand to my cheek and keep the memory of the touch against my skin. I wanted to cut out this night and set it away from everything so nothing could reach it and it couldn't reach anything else. But that's not how it worked. Everything was intertwined.

I was going to help Logan. That was more important than whatever I was feeling, and I couldn't afford to be distracted. And he knew I was Hushed, but he didn't know the real story.

He walked back in with my coffee and set it on the table. He sat down and rested his head on the back of the couch.

His shirt was pulled a little to the right, and I could see where his collarbone connected to his shoulder. His chest was a ridge of hollows and sinews. I drank in the sight as he opened a different folder.

It would be easy. I could feel it. I could drown in this feeling.

But I had a chance to do something good. How I was feeling about him could stay my secret. It was only right that I had one of my own.

※

Two hours later, I was still flipping through files.

Logan was asleep next to me, his chest rising and falling softly with every breath.

It made sense that Logan would think his mother was a saint, but it turned out he wasn't the only one who felt that way. Her pure heart was reflected in not just her own file, but in others as well. Two weeks after she first arrived, she stopped a fight between Bree Cavendish and Monique Cavers by jumping in front of Monique when Bree pulled a shank made out of a melted toothbrush.

She'd been written up twice for saving her rations and giving them to one of the pregnant inmates.

I turned the pages, comparing logs and shifts until everything blurred before my eyes.

A letter fell out.

I glanced at Logan asleep next to me. He'd said I could read everything. But this felt too personal.

I set it down, and then picked it up again and opened it before I could stop myself. It was addressed to Logan's Aunt Natalie and dated a few months before she died.

It's okay. I know it sounds terrible, but it's better that I don't go on like this for the next twenty years: giving everyone I love false hope. Logan can close that chapter of his life and move on. That is my greatest hope for him. To find a love to sink his roots into, to know that he fell in love with a woman who can bring light to his eyes.

There is not much of a silver lining. I'm not so much a naive dreamer to not recognize that. But I'm not alone in here. There are so many people here willing to shoulder the burden of the pain we all feel. I've been so blessed with this.

— M

I set it down.

Nothing.

No memories.

Still, something burned in me as I looked at the curving words on the paper.

My chest ached for him. His mother's words were so alive that it felt like I could almost hear her voice.

The fire was almost completely dead. Embers gave off a red glow, but the rest of the room was shrouded in shadow.

I gently set the files back down on the table. I'd read everything there was to read on Madeline Winspeare. I'd read six different reports of what may or may not have happened at Ironbark that night. And nothing came to get me. I wasn't the answer to what happened to Madeline, and I was relieved. It made me feel sick and glad at the same time, like when I'd realized that guard was dead the night I stirred. I was glad there was nothing I could do to help her. Still, I felt a weight on me, and I heard the echoes of screams in my memory. If I hadn't been so scared, I could've searched for a way to help them. Maybe I could've even helped her.

I felt a heaviness in my heart as I sat with the realization that Fabian had been carrying this feeling since we stirred. I still felt protective of him. I still wanted to get him out of Rearden Falls. But I knew now that it wasn't as simple as I had thought it was.

Logan shifted longwise across the couch. In the dim light, I caught a glimpse of metal I hadn't seen before. A crucifix slipped out from between the buttons on his shirt, its thin silver chain glinting in the last glow of the fire. The purple bruise on his eyebrow looked darker, and I reached out, pulling back slightly before recommitting. I wanted to touch him. So I did. I brushed my fingers over the bruise, then down the side of his face. Over his jawline.

He was beautiful. I felt a drop in my gut like I was plummeting, but at the same time it was like someone had hooked me behind the belly button and was lifting me up. I looked at him, *really* looked at him, just like I had with the view from the windows: his full lips, parted softly in sleep. The thick column of his exposed throat, the pulse jumping just under his skin. It was almost too much.

Rory's words came back to me. *Don't be so afraid that you don't live.*

I turned, curling my feet up under me as I looked down at Logan. I took a deep breath. I knew what I wanted to do, but I was scared. Not of dying. No, this fear was different and new.

I didn't know if he wanted me like I wanted him. This desire was new, so I assumed the pain of rejection would be its twin. If wanting him felt this good . . . him *not* wanting me would gut me. And that was possible. He could have just seen a girl in trouble and helped. But I knew how it felt when he touched my cheek, and how I felt in my gut where Rory said I would.

Go live.

Slowly, I laid myself carefully next to Logan. I wasn't sure if it was okay, but then he curled himself into me. His breath was soft on my neck, and I leaned back, closing my eyes and trying to sink into the moment as much as I could. I wanted it to leave a deep imprint in my mind, so when this was over, when it was done, I'd be able to recall this.

Logan's fingers moved on my skin, and I put my hand over his.

And I knew, in that moment, I'd become those stupid girls in the stories. The ones who didn't walk away. The ones who risked everything for a man they'd touched in the firelight.

FOURTEEN

The drift started slow, like a sunrise. Dawn was breaking over the hill when the girl with the green eyes walked down to gather water. Her bare feet were silent against the pressed earth, her dark hair twisted just behind her shoulders as she walked the mountain road.

She stopped when she reached the stream and found a young guard kneeling, cupping water and dropping it over the back of his neck.

His eyes were closed, and she stepped back silently.

She couldn't let him see her. She would come back later.

But a twig snapped under her heel, and he looked up.

The blade Red Lips had given her was tucked into her belt, but she didn't reach for it. Not even when the guard whispered about the Ghost of the Adrenian Pass. Not even when she saw that his sword lay several feet away, and she realized killing him before he reached it would be easy.

Instead, she took another step back. "Leave here, now. Run and do not stop running until you're far from this road."

He did.

The girl with the green eyes released the twine handle of the bucket and looked down at her hands. The hands that couldn't do what the girl with the red lips asked of her. The hands that couldn't kill, and may have just cost them their lives.

She turned around, and her eyes were drawn up the side of the cliff face by the movement of a black cloak.

The man with the scar watched her from a ledge.

He'd seen everything.

The drift shifted and changed.

The fire was bright on their faces. They sat in their cave, and the flames hissed and popped in the darkness as they roasted a pigeon on a spit.

The girl with the green eyes sat with her back toward a log that rested against the low, slanting wall. The girl with the red lips sat opposite, and the man with the scar sat with his back against the cave's opening, exposed to the chill night. He twirled the tip of his blade against the pad of his thumb.

"Well, we can't just sit here, holed up in the mountains," he said finally.

The girl with the red lips gently poked the meat with a stick.

"Not now that this one let that guard go," she said. "He'll be here by tomorrow, make no mistake. And he'll bring an entire hoard with him, looking for vengeance."

"And where does the fault lie for that? You killed their people needlessly. They think we're monsters," the man with the scar said.

The girl with the red lips stabbed the meat through. "You both think you're so much better than me, don't you? That somehow we weren't made by the same shadow. Just because I can do what needs to be done—"

"Please," the girl with the green eyes begged. The other two stopped. "This is my fault. I know. But we need to figure out what we will do."

The man with the scar spun the knife over the back of his wrist. "I know where the darkness resides. That's part of this awful feeling in my chest. It's a remote island to the south. We can find it, maybe. Reverse this."

The one with the red lips laughed. "That's your plan? We need to go on a suicide mission against a beast with no shape or name?"

The man with the scar raised his voice. "We need to make sure that this never happens again. That creatures like us are never made again. That no evil human can ever make a deal like that again. Every night, I see the great halls where the emperor resided and I feel a pull to it, like it's calling me. I want to find my way there and tell them all how to do what he did, and that cannot happen."

"That *will not* happen, because we aren't going to Rome. And we are not going to chase down the darkness, either. Both will end with you dead," the girl with the green eyes said, matching his volume. "You need to think clearly. You carry the weight of death with you, and I know it isn't easy. But you have to realize that what is done is done, and you're here now. We all are. Hating that will change nothing."

The man with the scar spun his blade silently, clenching his jaw.

The girl with the red lips smiled. "Well said."

Green Eyes looked at Red Lips over the fire. "We cannot do what you want to do, either. If we find more of our kind—if there are more than the three of us—then we will talk about what to do next. But war on the humans is as insane an idea as his," she said.

Red Lips rolled her eyes. "Then what would you suggest? We join a traveling bard and juggle for stale bread?"

The girl with the green eyes swallowed hard. "We know things, right? I mean, I don't know about you two, since I only see strange fragments in the dreams we share, but I think you do, too. Trade routes. Schedules. Secret deals that no one else on this whole peninsula knows of."

The man with the scar stopped spinning the knife.

"There are evil humans. There are good humans. We have that same choice. We should use it, and all the knowledge at our disposal," the girl with the green eyes said.

The girl with the red lips looked up. The thought intrigued her. "We could be raiders. Take our retribution."

"No, we will wield justice and mercy. Provide a place for refuge for those who need it. I . . ." the girl with green eyes said, looking at the man with the scar. He stared at her over the flame, the edge of the blade against the palm of his open hand.

"What would we call this refuge? This justice?" he asked, and the girl with the green eyes smiled. If he was asking, then he didn't hate the idea.

The green-eyed girl bit her lip.

"I remember this script, written on a piece of paper. It's one of the emperor's memories, I think. A warning from one of the old prophecies he feared. It was something like . . . *the land of wicked will become a haunt for jackals, an everlasting waste; no man shall dwell there; no man shall sojourn in her.* Let that be our threat to those who seek to harm innocents—humans and our kind alike. We know where the truth is buried. We know about secrets that humans want to keep hidden. We're not monsters, we're the jackals that seek the bones that evil wants left alone. And those who profit off of the truth should fear us."

"So . . . we're the everlasting waste?" the red-lipped girl teased.

Green Eyes smiled wider. "No. A Haunt for Jackals."

❧

I fell off the couch, catching my breath on all fours. It was still dark outside. I'd had two drifts in one night before. But these were different—more intense, and they took place years apart.

A Haunt for Jackals.

It had been so clear. I still hadn't seen faces, but I heard their voices.

A Haunt for Jackals.

Did I just see the beginning of the Haunt for Jackals?

It couldn't have been just a dream. It was a drift. It felt like a drift. I walked over to the window and looked out at the moonlit forest. If I walked out into the melting snow, would I find to whom this drift belonged?

Would I want to find them?

I looked out over the moonlit pines.

I did. At least, part of me did.

I looked over at Logan, and a thought sank down across my shoulders. The entire time I'd known him, I'd wondered if Logan was a danger to me.

For the first time, I realized that it could be the other way around.

FIFTEEN

When I woke on Logan's couch in the morning, he was gone, and the smell of something burning was wafting in from the kitchen. I sat up suddenly. My head spun as I looked at my watch—it was eleven thirty.

I fell asleep on him. I fell asleep with him.

Logan stuck his head in from the kitchen, and I jumped as I heard his voice. "So. Breakfast round one was a charred failure. Breakfast round two is looking about the same."

He was wearing the suit he wore to court, and his hair was brushed out of his eyes. I pushed my hair out of my face and ran a finger under my eyes as I turned to put my feet on the ground. He disappeared again.

"I was thinking we should hit Mal's, because it's good to know when you're beat," he called from the kitchen.

The memories from the night before came rushing back. "Oh, crap. It's Thursday, isn't it?"

Logan nodded and disappeared into the kitchen. I pulled my boots on and followed him.

"Bree Cavendish is on the stand this morning," he said.

She was the inmate who had been at the local hospital at the time of the fire because her heart murmur was acting up. It saved her life.

"Aren't you late?" I asked.

"Yes. But I've heard her testimony a couple of times before. She's in the defense's pocket." His tone darkened. "She insists that Ironbark was 'a credit to the federal institution.' I don't want to sit through that. There is one interesting bit of news, though. Connelly Stewart will be testifying as a witness for the defense later in the trial."

My nerves snapped to attention. "What does Connelly have to do with it?"

It was the first sign that the Internment had something to do with Ironbark.

"He knew Leonard when he was working for the defense department. Old buddies."

I calmed down, a bit. *It's a personal connection. Connelly Stewart and Leonard Mark are friends.* Then my stomach churned.

Connelly Stewart would be in our town. The head of the organization that hunted my brother and I like animals.

"Connelly Stewart," I said before I could stop myself.

"I met him, once."

My eyes shot up to Logan's. "You did? Why?"

"I was at the courthouse with my aunt during one of my mom's appeals and he was in the building. He'd seen that damned picture of me—the one on the soccer field when I was a kid. He held out his hand for this sick photo op and told me he was sorry about my father. I didn't shake it; I knew it was only for the cameras."

"What did he do?"

"He smiled in the way politicians do and walked on. I spent some time looking into him, after that."

"What did you find?"

Logan looked at me. "That was the strange part. Nothing. There isn't anything on him at all. No traffic tickets or complaints from staff. He's squeaky clean. Which, of course, only means one thing."

I cocked an eyebrow.

"That man has more reason to fear your kind than anyone else. I'll bet everything I own that he's hiding some dark shit." Logan shook his head like he was trying to dislodge a thought. "But that's in a couple of days. Today is Bree Cavendish. I've read her deposition. I wouldn't mind missing that sideshow to get some breakfast with you if you want."

At that moment, a shadow walked across the window over Logan's shoulder.

I pointed behind him. With one swift movement, he reached into the drawer of one of the end tables and pulled out a gun before putting a finger to his lips. I moved closer, slowly, trying not to make any noise. I ducked, standing on the opposite side of the window.

Logan's body was as tense as a live wire as he pointed the muzzle at the glass, waiting for the shadow to appear. For a moment, I wondered if I'd imagined it. Then the sound of rapid footsteps on the ground ripped through the morning air.

Logan bolted, yanking the back kitchen door open as I pulled two long steak knives from a knife block on the counter. Logan jumped off the back porch in pursuit of a figure in a navy hoodie.

Spinning the knives so that the blades were facing outward against my forearms, I followed.

"Stop!" Logan shouted. The figure took a hard right turn toward the ravine.

"Logan," I shouted, but my breathless voice didn't carry enough to reach him. My heart felt like it was going to explode in my chest and my feet slipped in the muddy slush, but the adrenaline made it impossible for me to stop and catch my breath.

The figure disappeared down the incline, and Logan followed.

Whoever it was, they were running straight for Ironbark. I reached the edge of the ravine and skidded to a messy stop, my feet slipping on the bed of wet leaves and slush. I caught myself on a tree and looked out, aware that with every second I hesitated, Logan was farther away, closer to the hooded figure.

My heartbeat was like a war drum, sending waves of fear through my blood.

Ironbark.

Ironbark.

What was left of it was below, a stone husk cut out into a hillside. The windowsills were still marked with smears of ash. Three levels of chain-link fence surrounded it. Construction vehicles sat just past the perimeter.

"Logan!" I shouted.

I shoved off the tree and broke into a sprint, jumping onto the incline. I moved as quickly as I could to keep my feet beneath me, hurdling over a fallen tree that lay at the bottom before sprinting onward.

Logan ran into my line of sight from the left, almost running into me.

I swore, stumbling as I stopped.

"He's gone," Logan said as he gasped for air. His face was covered in sweat and dirt.

"He?" I asked, resting my hands on my knees.

"Well. I assumed it was a he. But you're right. Could've been anyone."

I looked up and jumped at how close we were to Ironbark. The fence was only about twenty feet away, and the hulking northern face of the building loomed just fifty feet past it. I put both blades in my left hand, squeezing the plastic handles tight as I pushed the hair out of my eyes.

"Where did you get a gun?" I breathed.

"You think I'm digging through my mother's case without a gun nearby?" he said, his hands on his knees. It was a fair point.

A soft *beep* called out from Logan's pocket, and he pulled out his phone. His face tightened as he read the screen.

"What?" I said, trying to stay as quiet as I could.

"Bree Cavendish was shot while testifying," he said, tucking the phone back in his pocket. "Her victim's son killed her."

Footsteps crunched behind us.

We whirled, Logan raising his gun as I gripped my knives.

The rustling sound happened again, and I tensed.

The sound of soft, jagged gasps came out from behind the thick branches. It almost sounded like crying.

"Who's there?" Logan called softly.

Logan moved closer to me, stepping in front of me slightly as he raised his gun higher.

A naked girl who looked about my age stepped through the underbrush. She didn't bother to try and cover herself as she took halted, unsure steps. She kept her dark eyes on us. Her chin-length, jet-black hair shone in the morning light, and her dark, mahogany skin was free of cuts, scrapes, or even dirt, and I felt a sinking feeling slip down my spine. Her bare feet crunched against the forest floor.

She hadn't walked here.

She'd appeared here.

She was a Hushed who had just stirred.

I took a step toward her, and she held her hands up.

"I know," she said shakily, her eyes filling with tears.

"Listen to me," I said, chancing another step forward. She flinched as I got closer but didn't stop. "Listen. I know this is scary—look at me—I know this is scary, but you have to come with me. I know a place where you'll be safe."

The girl's lip quivered as her gaze bounced from Logan back to me. "I *know*," she whispered again. The tortured sound of it grated on my heart like nails on a chalkboard, and tears tore down her cheeks. She put her hands to her chest, lip quivering.

"Whatever you know," I said, taking another step toward her as I slid my jacket off my shoulders. One more step and I could take her hand. "Keep it to yourself. Don't say anything, okay?"

Her eyes turned back to Logan, who stood, unmoving, behind me. "You're Logan," she whispered.

Slippery panic slid over my tongue, and I shook my head, unable to find words. She recognized him. That wasn't a good sign.

I closed the distance between us and set my jacket over her shoulders.

"We're going to get you out of here," I said mechanically. *Move. Get her out of here. Get her to Eva, she'll know what to do—*

"They were using them," the girl said, blinking tears over the edge of her thick brown eyelashes.

I lifted my hands from her shoulders like I'd been burned and took a step back.

She had the same peaceful look on her face that Sarah had, and she actually smiled as she looked back at Logan. "The Internment was using them as Harborers." She pointed to Ironbark behind Logan's shoulder.

"What?" Logan whispered.

I felt as though a white-hot poker had just been shoved through my chest. I spun, looking at Logan. Horror and understanding washed over his face.

"They were going to die anyway. All the secrets were locked in, then," the girl said softly. She swayed on the spot, and a dark, inky mark started in the center of her chest, twisting and curling its way up to her collarbone.

Logan moved to grab her, but a shot rang through the air.

A bullet ripped through the girl's chest, right in the center of the ink, knocking her body backward onto the forest floor.

It took a moment for us to register what had happened, but we both turned to look at Ironbark as the second bullet whizzed through the air and struck a tree near Logan's head. I dropped my knives.

Ironbark wasn't abandoned.

Logan swooped down, picking the girl's lifeless body off the floor with one clean movement as he ran.

We sprinted deeper into the thicket of trees the girl had stepped out of. Dozens of bullets peppered the woods around us, kicking up dirt and skimming trees as they searched for our flesh.

Logan jumped over a fallen tree, and I followed. He lay the Hushed's body down next to us, his hands shaking. "I couldn't just leave her there," he said, his voice wavering. He looked down at his hands, which were covered in thick, sticky blood. Even then, it startled me how human it looked. Logan wiped his mouth with the back of his hand as he took a deep, unsteady breath. He looked over his shoulder.

"Those bullets are coming from inside the prison," Logan rasped. Logan pulled his gun from his waistband, but we both knew that trying to fight would be pointless at best and suicide at worst.

"What are we going to do?" he asked, looking around for an escape route. The thicket had saved us from the immediate danger, but I realized our mistake as I peered ahead, where the brambles got so thick we'd never be able to push through without making enough noise to alert the whole forest to our whereabouts.

The sound of diesel engines roared through the woods, and I sat up, trying to peer through the dense curtain of leaves to my right. The gunfire came in short bursts every couple of seconds, but whoever was shooting had clearly lost sight of us, because they were hitting a copse of trees thirty feet away.

Black off-roaders appeared above us, stopping just short of the lip of the ravine. Figures in black fatigues jumped out, their semi-autos at the ready as they sidestepped down the incline. The Internment.

I turned to Logan. Why would the Internment send their agents out here? If someone had called about the gunfire, the police would've responded.

"Oh shit," I breathed, realization washing over me in a wave of nausea. I turned to Logan. "They came for her."

Logan's face fell as he looked at the girl's motionless form, and then back to me.

"When Bree died . . ." he whispered, piecing it together. "Her Hushed appeared where it was made."

"They knew a Hushed would appear here, where the secret was made," I said. That's why there were still forces in Ironbark. To keep watch for Hushed.

"The courtroom must be a madhouse right now," I whispered, looking over my shoulder again. This Hushed was Bree's and Bree's alone, so it appeared where it was created. But the ones that she took on as a Harborer would appear where she died. No doubt the Internment was handling that. I shuddered at the thought.

He closed his eyes. That was the secret his mother wouldn't tell him. It was the reason she begged him to let it go. She knew that an appeal wouldn't have made a difference. They were never going to let any of the prisoners leave there alive.

The shouts of the Internment grew louder.

They would look for the girl until they found her. And they'd know, from the dark spread on her chest, that she told her secret before she died.

The only way out was through the far-left side, where the branches were thin enough to slip through. Even then, we wouldn't be able to double back toward the cabin. We'd just have to run.

It was the only plan I had, so it would have to work.

The crunch of boots on leaves brought me back to the moment, and Logan opened his eyes, though his gaze seemed far away. Ten years of looking for answers, and here they were, worse than he ever could have imagined.

I put both hands on his face.

"Logan," I whispered, shifting so I was sitting in front of him. He looked into my eyes, but his eyes were full of a sadness that I could not fathom.

"That's why Connelly is coming to the trial. That's why he is supporting Leonard Mark. The Internment was involved in the whole thing," he breathed, his brows furrowing as he pieced everything together.

"Logan, I need you here," I whispered.

He shook his head.

I shifted so I was looking at him. "We have to get out of here, and I can't do it on my own, okay?"

He put his hand over mine and shut his eyes tight.

"If we don't get out of here, the secret will die with us. That's what they want, Logan."

He nodded, looking away. I bent lower to meet his eyes, desperate to have him back. I needed him to come back.

"I'm scared, okay?" I admitted, running a thumb over the raspy stubble on his cheek. "I need you. I need you to fight, right now, because I'm scared, and I can't get us out of here on my own."

He froze as my words hit him.

It was like someone turned the light on in his eyes, shook the smoke from his vision. He blinked, his clarity coming back in to focus.

He raised a hand to my neck and nodded, the last of whatever had been clinging to his mind slipping back into the corners.

The footsteps were getting closer.

An Internment officer stopped as her walkie-talkie buzzed out muffled words. She motioned a thumbs up to the prison, and then turned, narrowing her eyes at the thicket of trees.

The officer checked her gun before taking a step toward the shadows. We were still too deep inside to see, but that wouldn't last long.

I grabbed Logan's hand, ignoring the cold, sticky blood, and we ran.

We tore through the dark thickets, and I prayed, without even really knowing what I was praying to, that it was too dark for an accurate shot.

The Internment officer turned, and I heard her cock the gun. She fired once, missing and hitting the tree behind my calf. Logan pulled ahead, tugging my hand behind him.

We burst through the shadows and banked a hard right. We made it several dozen feet before the gunshots sounded again, and Logan pulled me behind a wide tree before chancing a look from behind the trunk.

Logan was turning back to look at me when two hands grabbed me from behind. One wrapped around my mouth while the other pressed a knife to my throat. The figure pulled me back, and Logan whipped around, pulling the gun from his pants and pointing it at the figure behind me.

His eyes shifted between my eyes and my captor's.

He raised the barrel over my shoulder.

"Oh, I wouldn't try it," said a soft female voice. It had an edge, though it was playful, somehow, with a thick Irish accent. It contrasted strangely with the way she pressed the blade to my throat as we backed up, which felt anything but playful. The gunshots peeled through the air, but we were blocked by the wide trunk. For the moment.

The woman continued to pull me backward, and Logan advanced with each step.

"I do not care if you're an Internment officer," Logan hissed. "I will bury a bullet in your head."

"I don't doubt it," she said, laughing. Her breath tickled my ear. "But your enthusiasm is misplaced. I'm not the Internment."

Doubt spread over Logan's features, but he didn't lower the gun.

I took a deep breath, the way I used to when Fabian and I were pulled over by police in a stolen car while living on the road. My thoughts sharpened. If she was with the Internment, why was she pulling me the opposite direction? I stopped fighting and loosened my grip on her forearm. Just enough for her to think I'd given up.

"Then let her go," Logan commanded.

I could see from the shadows that stretched in front of us that she'd backed us up against another tree.

I didn't wait to hear her next words. I tightened my hands around the arm with the knife and threw my weight forward. She wasn't expecting it, so it knocked her off balance. I twisted, aiming my elbow for her jaw. It connected with a horrible *thud*, but she was much more resilient than she looked and took a step back as she glared at me. She was slight, with bright red hair pulled back into a ponytail. It was the person in the hoodie—the one who had been spying on us. I was close enough to see the smattering of freckles across the bridge of her nose. The gunshots of the Internment were closer. I looked back at her, and she grinned in a tight grimace.

She kicked so quickly that it was almost like I felt the blow to my chest before I saw it. I flew backward, landing hard on the forest floor, writhing as I fought to breathe.

Logan skidded and closed the distance between us, kneeling next to me as I sucked in a deep gasp. He helped me to my feet as the young woman reached up, pressing her hand against the trunk of the tree. A blue line lit up on the bark beneath her flattened hand and quickly ran up and down the length of her palm before turning green.

The blood in her teeth from where I'd hit her was the last thing I saw before the ground beneath us gave way and we plunged into darkness.

SIXTEEN

My throat tightened, choking the scream off as we fell.

I kicked, my body thrashing in the hail of leaves and dirt that swirled around us, spinning and twirling as the ground slid closed above us.

There's no way we can survive this, I thought.

Then icy water engulfed me, feet first, swallowing me in one frigid gulp.

I should've been glad that it wasn't concrete, but the cold wiped my mind clean. My lungs contracted in my chest, and I opened my eyes, catching only bubbles and chaos in the blue light.

When I broke the surface, Logan was next to me. The fear slipped from his face as he saw me, and he nodded once, a question. I nodded back. I was fine.

We were in a circular cavern with metal walls, at least six stories high. A metal catwalk and railing lined the water's edge. The red-haired girl—she looked about seventeen—climbed up a rickety metal ladder.

"You can stay in there and get hypothermia," she said, reaching the catwalk and wringing water from her hair. "But I'd prefer you get out, because fishing bodies out of this thing is a bitch."

The dirt and leaves finally caught up to us, falling like rain on the water's surface. I blinked, trying to keep the dirt out of my eyes. "Where are we?" I asked, struggling to tread water with my sweats and shoes weighing me down.

The girl turned. "An abandoned coal mine. Specifically, the reserve water tank designed to put out fires when said abandoned coal mine was in operation."

A door opened, and a man with dark skin walked in. I stopped treading water and slipped under the surface, coughing as I came back up.

It was Ajit, my mysterious slip pill dealer.

"Are you okay?" Logan whispered.

Ajit handed the girl a towel. "Looks like you might reconsider the 'I don't need backup,' attitude next time, Margaret?" he asked, turning to the girl.

"That's rich, considering I still have the three slugs I had to fish out of your thigh in Mombasa," she spat, drying herself off.

Ajit smiled, keeping his eyes trained on Logan and me. "Are you going to get out?" he asked, humor slipping into his words as he met my eyes. "I promise you, it only gets colder. And a hell of a lot harder to find your way around once we leave this room and turn off the light."

Logan and I looked at each other, knowing that we didn't really have a choice.

Ajit handed us towels as we climbed up the ladder, and I snatched mine from him.

"What is this? What are you doing here?" I asked.

Logan drew the towel down his face. "Wait. You know him?"

Ajit cocked an eyebrow. "Oh, we're old friends," he said, reaching out to inspect the welt I felt blooming above my right eyebrow.

"Answer the question, Ajit," I whispered. My mind was racing. Was this a drug-running base? I yanked my chin back, and he rolled his eyes before looking at the slight cut on Logan's cheekbone.

"Don't touch me," Logan warned.

"Ajit is the only doctor you've got right now, boyo," Margaret said, kicking her wet boots off and picking them up by two fingers.

"Okay, I have no idea what's going on here, but I'm pretty sure you can cut the 'boyo' crap, magically delicious, because you look like you're about twelve," I bit out.

She looked to Ajit before jerking her head toward the door. He nodded.

"He wants to see them," Ajit said lowly.

"Who wants to see us? Who are you?" I asked.

Margaret adjusted the collar of her jacket, and everything in me seized up with fear. An emblem was pressed onto her collar, just small enough that I would've missed it in different lighting. A skeleton, from the shoulders up. Not like the Gravediggers, which had only the classic skull and crossbones. This emblem had the arms crossed above the head, fists clenched.

Margaret saw me notice it, and her smile widened. She motioned for Logan and me to follow.

"Let me do the talking here," I said, fighting the panic in the back of my throat.

For once, Logan listened. Because he'd seen the emblem, too, and he knew where we were.

I wanted to say it was impossible, but I knew it wasn't. The more I thought about it, the more the pit in my stomach made sense.

The Haunt for Jackals was in the middle of the nowhere woods of North Carolina.

SEVENTEEN

Margaret opened the door, and Logan followed her out.

Ajit put his hand on my shoulder, and then the door swung shut in front of my face.

"Eerie!" Logan shouted, his voice muffled through the metal.

I threw myself at the door, but Ajit pulled me backward.

"Get *off* of me!" I shouted, but Ajit held fast.

We had been captured by the Haunt for Jackals. Logan was human. The Haunt was at war with humans. I bit back the bile that shot up the back of my throat.

"What are you going to do to him?" I asked, my jaw clattering.

Ajit let go of me and leaned down, scooping another towel off the scaffolding and handing it to me. I knocked it out of his hand, and he cocked an eyebrow.

"He'll want to talk to you two separately," Ajit said, stepping back and leaning against the wall.

"He? Who the hell is *he*?" I hissed.

Ajit slid down until he was in a sitting position, his eyes locked on mine. He wasn't going to answer.

"You lied to me," I said. I stepped back until my back was against the railing.

"You never asked if I was in the Haunt for Jackals," Ajit said, tilting his head.

"And the slip pill? Is that real?" I whispered.

Ajit smiled and then pursed his lips. "The one I showed you was real. But the one you ordered?" He grimaced. "I'm afraid not. Those are getting harder and harder to come by."

I sunk down to the metal platform as my chest tightened.

"*Now* is where you can say that I lied to you," Ajit offered. He lifted his leg and rested his forearm on his knee.

I sucked in air through clenched teeth. "And my money?"

Ajit smiled. "Congratulations. You're a valued contributor to the Haunt's continued fight for freedom."

The rage broke loose in my chest, and I shoved myself to my feet. Ajit pulled a small pistol from his pocket and held it up.

"See, I thought you might react like this. Don't do anything stupid, Eerie. Just sit down."

Everything I'd done to get Fabian out had been for nothing. All the money I'd saved was gone. My mind spun, and I slipped back down to my knees. Ajit tucked the gun back in his pocket.

"You took everything from me," I said, my voice barely more than a whisper.

Ajit popped the collar of his jacket. "Let's not be dramatic. I did get you that Starbucks gift card."

I ground my teeth together and stared at the water, trying not to shiver.

I looked over at Ajit, who pulled a toothpick out of his pocket and stuck it in his teeth.

"You might want to settle in, sweetheart. Want another towel?"

I flipped him off, and he chuckled, flipping the toothpick around his tongue as he raised his eyebrows. "Suit yourself."

And with every hour, my dread grew. I asked questions, but Ajit just smirked as a response.

I must have nodded off, because the next thing I heard was the creaking of the door. I scrambled up as Margaret walked in and Ajit slipped out behind her.

She dug her fingers into my forearm as I tried to lunge through the door.

"LOGAN!" I shouted, throwing my weight forward.

"Dammit to hell," Margaret growled as I pulled my arm from her grasp.

I turned around and shoved her. She stumbled but caught herself on the railing. I whipped around, taking off toward the door.

I stopped when I saw a man standing in front of the door, his hands in his pockets as he surveyed me with a raised eyebrow. "I think the yelling is quite unnecessary," he said, and his voice sent shock waves through my system. I'd never seen him before, but I knew his voice. I'd heard it over and over, through TV and radio speakers.

Railius.

He didn't look older than thirty. His hair was a deep auburn, tucked behind his ears. The recognition halted me long enough for Margaret to regain her footing.

She wrapped around my neck from behind, and then hooked a foot around the back of my ankle, twisting and throwing me to the floor.

"You'd better stay down," she hissed.

"That's enough, Margaret," he said. My insides hummed as his voice rang throughout the chamber and the metal lacing of the scaffold cut into my cheek.

Before I could move, I felt him kneel next to me.

I jumped at the closeness of his body and twisted to squirm away, stopping when I realized he was holding his hand out to me.

I forced my thoughts to still. I couldn't let the fear take over.

Railius held his hand out further.

I stared him down.

"Fine. Stay there if it suits you," he said, standing.

Margaret walked around us and stood at the door, pulling a knife from her boot and spinning it through her fingers.

I don't know what I'd expected really. I suppose I'd always connected the voice to an older, bearded man, huddled in the corner of some abandoned outpost in the middle of the desert, broadcasting his threats. But this could be someone I sat next to in Business Admin, offering me gum or asking to swap notes. He didn't look angry enough to do the things I knew he did.

But the voice—it was the same voice that called for the thing that sounded like justice but looked like war; the one who set the trip wire that could send society into chaos.

The Haunt circled cities around its finger. It brought entire governments to their knees. What the hell was he doing in the middle of the backwoods of North Carolina?

A thousand questions bubbled up in my mind, but only one really mattered.

"Where is Logan?" I asked, my teeth chattering from both cold and fear.

The illumination in the water fragmented, spinning spiderwebs of light on the walls around us.

"Well, well. Now, what would the Internment say if they could see this? I do believe they've warned you about your particular interest in Mr. Winspeare, have they not?"

I sat up. "Shove it up your ass, you fucking terrorist," I hissed.

Margaret lunged, but Railius stopped her with a sweep of his hand.

He looked at me, his eyes narrowing as he tilted his head, like I was a puzzle he was going to figure out. "I'm not surprised you've gotten yourself into as much trouble as you have, with a mouth like that."

His words sounded harsh, but there was something else in them—something I wasn't expecting. Almost like he was impressed. He regarded me for a long moment before kneeling to face me. "Your fate, along with Mr. Winspeare's, is entirely up to you. Cooperate, and this will be rather painless. Though I have to say you are not off to a promising start, Eerie."

He saw the way I narrowed my eyes when he said my name, and he nodded. "I know more than just your name. I know that if I scanned your arm right now, it would say that you were human. And I know that, for some reason, you've started to act as though you actually are." He said the words lightly.

I sat up. "Yeah, you would need to know all that, considering how you cheated me. Is that how you finance everything? Stealing from desperate Hushed?"

"It's one of our many methods, yes."

The lighting lit him from underneath, and it made the planes of his face sharp and angular. His skin was pale, save for the soft violet shadow under his eyes. He smiled, softly, as though he was used to getting what he wanted through that simple gesture.

Sentences and barbs slipped in and out of my mind like smoke, so I resolved to meet his eyes with an unwavering stare. He lied to me, but that was far from my biggest problem.

"What do you want?" I asked.

Railius stepped closer to me. "The Internment just found the body of a Hushed in the brush near the prison. Tell me what she said."

That information was possibly the only thing keeping Logan and me alive. We were only as good as what we knew.

"Is that why you brought us here?" I asked, trying to turn the questions back on him.

He shook his head. "This is simple, and it doesn't need any complications. I'll make this easy. You don't tell me, and I go kill Logan Winspeare. And if you lie about what she said, I will find out. Then I'll kill the human and make you watch. Do you understand?" He spoke as though he'd said sentences like that a thousand times. I looked down at the water through the metal, hoping he wouldn't see the terror in my eyes. I had no way of knowing that he wasn't going to kill us anyway. After all, Logan and I had seen their secret hideout. We'd seen their faces. I didn't really believe that Railius was going to let us walk away.

"How do I know you're not just going to kill me once I tell you?" I asked.

His eyes were hard as stone. Unreadable. "How did you know they were going to save your brother once you signed yourself up with the Internment?"

My heart hammered harder as Railius took a step closer to me, leaning down so he could meet my eyes. How much more did he know about me?

"You didn't," he reminded me. "You simply ran out of other options. You're in the same situation now."

He tilted my chin with a finger, pushing the pad of his index finger into my flesh. It was everything I could do to not pull away and take a clawing swipe at his face.

"Margaret, what's your record time for skinning a deer?" he called over his shoulder.

"Three minutes and seventeen seconds," she responded, inspecting the point of her knife.

"Care to see if you can beat that?" Railius asked.

"Fine!" I cried out, the word flying from my throat like a frightened, winged thing.

Railius let go of my chin and took a step back.

I didn't think about whether or not Logan would be angry with me. I didn't really care. "The Internment was using the death row inmates as Harborers," I said, my voice echoing strangely against the stone.

I watched Railius's expression as the words hit him. His face didn't move, but his chest heaved quickly once, like his breath caught somewhere between his mouth and his lungs. He blinked and then turned to Margaret.

"Where did you stir?" he asked.

It was so blunt I had to take a moment to make sure I heard him right. I swallowed hard. "A shipyard in California. Three years ago."

His eyes were deep brown with flecks of green and gold. I shouldn't know what his eyes looked like. I didn't want to be that close.

"Are you sure?" Railius asked again, like it was something I would be confused about. He was asking if I was lying.

I made myself keep my eyes on his. "Yes." Desperation rose through my chest. "Let Logan go," I whispered.

At that, his gaze flicked to Margaret. He stood.

She grabbed my arms and pulled. I stumbled as I took my feet.

Railius motioned to the door, and Margaret shoved me toward it.

⤞⤝

I followed Railius into the dark. I knew he couldn't see me, so I gave myself over to the shivers that racked my body.

We turned a corner and walked through a narrow tunnel. Small floodlights connected by an orange cord lined one side of the tunnel, and I stared at the back of Railius's head.

Logan is okay. Logan is fine.

I kept reciting it to myself, keeping the fear down by pretending I could make it true.

After several minutes, Railius opened a door on his right, and I craned my neck around him to get a better view.

Metal stairs led from the door down into a cavernous stone room, lit by fire-filled oil drums. Ajit and Logan stood at the bottom.

Logan looked up, and his eyes widened.

Railius stepped aside when we got to the bottom of the stairs, and no one stopped Logan from launching himself forward as I threw myself into his arms, just to make sure he was really there. Not bleeding, not hurt at all.

"They wouldn't tell me anything, Eerie. Railius was there and then they pulled me into the dark. Oh my God, they wouldn't tell me anything, and I thought—" He stopped, pulling back to look at my face. He had no idea that he was the one who had been in danger. He was the one they talked about gutting, not me. My heart thudded in my chest as adrenaline crackled through my veins like electricity. He was fine.

"How do you know these people? How'd you know that guy's name?" he whispered.

"I'll explain when we're alone, okay?" I let him go and turned to face Railius, who stood at the front of the room. Ajit stood next to him, and Margaret guarded the door at the top of the metal scaffolding. Nowhere to run.

Logan and I stood in the middle of the room. His fingers found mine.

Railius eyed us with the same detached interest with which he'd looked down at me earlier. His gaze fell to our interlocked hands, and he cocked an eyebrow.

"You've got thirty seconds, you son of a bitch," Logan said, stepping forward and pulling me slightly behind him. I yanked him back and stood even with him. I didn't know what we were going to do, but I mirrored the sentiment.

Railius clicked his tongue once. "Someone has been watching too many movies. Is this the part where you expect me to reveal my evil plan in full and then leave you unsupervised to a very specific yet highly improbable death?" Railius's voice was even, though the irritation slunk over his features.

"You're the one with the evil lair. I work with what I've got," Logan shot back.

"And this is how you talk to the answer to your prayers?"

Logan froze.

Railius stepped closer to us. "We have reason to believe that Ironbark Prison might have secrets bigger than previously assumed."

Logan went rigid next to me. My skin itched. *Why are they telling us this?*

"I already told you what the Hushed said." Logan's voice wavered at the last word. They must have done the same thing to him as they did to me. Told him they'd kill me if he didn't tell and then crosschecked the information we'd given.

"That is but a fraction of what was happening there. And you know that. That's why you were looking for a hacker to confirm some of your darker suspicions," Railius replied.

Logan was still beneath my hand, and I tightened my grip.

"We're on the same side here, Winspeare. We wouldn't have brought you here if we weren't. It would have been easier to let the Internment fill you with lead." Railius's eyes fell on me.

I hated the way it felt, like he could see through my skin.

"What do you want?" Logan asked.

"We want to figure out what was happening in that prison. We want to conduct our investigation in peace. That is, however, difficult with people like you getting in the way."

"In the *way*?" Logan asked, bristling at the tone. "Your operative was on my porch. We followed her."

"Next time? Don't."

Logan laughed. I'd only known him two days, but I knew that laugh. That laugh always preceded something bad—

"I don't answer to you."

Railius stared at Logan, his face a blank mask that made him seem even more frightening.

This time, I pulled Logan back as I stepped forward. "We have just as much right to know what is going on in there as you do," I said.

"*We*," Railius said, his eyes locking on mine.

Logan nodded, and Railius's eyes slid over to him. "So. Thank you for the assistance, but we'll be going now. And I will look into happenings at Ironbark however I damn well please."

Railius cracked a slight smile, like he was trying to find the humor in dealing with someone stupid. It made Logan bristle. "Of course. And you can traipse up to the surface where you'll be unceremoniously gunned down by the Internment officers stationed near Ironbark. If you somehow manage to escape that fate, please be sure to let me know how successful you are at hacking the Internment's firewall with a hacker whose subtleties begin and end with the screen name 'HacktheBase513.'"

"If you know that much about her, you'll know that she's hacked the Department of Defense three separate times and the People's Republic of China at least once," Logan shot back.

"The fact that you think those are even comparable to the Internment shows how ill-equipped you are for this," Railius's voice pitched up slightly, as though he grew tired of their game.

Railius was right about one thing. If I knew the Internment at all, they would stay near where that Hushed's body fell for the next several days, searching for any sign of who was with her when she died.

When the Internment wanted something, they had a way of getting it.

"We will protect you until it is safe to go. And then you will stay out of our way."

Logan shook his head. "I won't agree to that," he said.

"Then we'll probably meet again. And on less-than-cordial terms."

Railius took a step toward us. "It is nothing personal, Winspeare. Believe that much at least. We want to bring the perpetrators of the Ironbark fire to justice as much as you do."

His voice was softer, and it set me on edge. Kindness didn't suit him.

Logan thought about it, and he looked to me. My expression told him what he already knew: we didn't have a choice.

He turned to Railius. "We stay until it's safe. Then we leave. And if we meet again . . ."

A hint of what looked like a genuine grin turned up the side of Railius's mouth. "Then we meet again."

I glared at him, and when he noticed, it made him smirk. He cocked an eyebrow and shifted in his seat, as though he was growing bored.

"Svenja will see to it that you are both comfortable. If either of you have cell phones, they were destroyed by the water, so we're not worried about contact with the outside world," Railius said, turning his eyes to the stairs. We looked up. Margaret still stood at the top by the door, her elbow resting on the metal railing as she looked over. Beside her, a blond with startling light eyes peered down at us.

"Delta Team One is on the line, ready when you are, Railius," Margaret said.

Railius nodded. "I'll take it in my room."

Margaret whispered something to Svenja, then, and she laughed. It was a boisterous sound, the kind that felt like it was hitting you in the ear with a club rather than reaching you through normal sound waves. I turned to look back to Railius, but he was gone.

I narrowed my eyes at the woman and gave her a once-over as we walked up the stairs. She wore a black shirt and tight tan pants that were tucked into knee-high high-heeled boots. She did a double take when she saw us, her blue eyes lighting up with excitement. Her perfectly curled locks swung around her shoulder, and I noticed that they were tied back in a black ribbon. It seemed impractical, but so were the boots. She didn't seem to care.

"I hate not doing recon, I miss all the fun parts!" she exclaimed as Ajit walked up the stairs and stood behind her.

"Recon? Is that what you call kidnapping?" Logan asked wryly.

"It's what we call saving your life," Ajit snapped.

The woman smiled, completely ignoring the edge in Logan's voice as she held out her hand. "I'm Svenja," she said, her smile deepening as Logan took her hand. Her voice had a distinctive accent and cadence, but I couldn't place it.

"I'm Logan," he replied.

"We know your name. We've been watching the trial," she said, and her smile faded. "We're really, really sorry about what happened to your mother." I recognized the accent. Russian.

"The Internment is full of butchers," Ajit said. There was none of the smirk I'd seen before. It was pure hatred.

"And we're going to make them wish they were never born, aren't we?" Svenja asked, putting her hands on her hips as she smiled.

I somehow knew she meant it.

EIGHTEEN

We followed Svenja. Logan and I hung as far back as we could, and I whispered to him about what happened with Ajit and the slip pill. I figured he'd understand, considering he'd done basically the same thing while looking for a hacker. He reached back and grabbed my hand. I took it. I almost tripped in the dark, and his hand shot out to steady me.

"We'll figure it out, okay?" he said over his shoulder. I stopped at the word. *We.*

It was stupid how much better that sentence made me feel, even when I knew how badly things were falling apart.

I kept my eyes on the back of Logan's neck and ran into him when he stopped suddenly. He reached around, both steadying me and pulling me to him in one movement. We were on a ledge, ten feet above a room at least as tall as the dunk tank we'd landed in. Ahead of us was a window that reached from floor to ceiling, overlooking the expanse of Rearden Falls. Purple fog hung outside, twisting just enough so that we could catch glimpses of city lights below. Snow-covered trees shot up on either side, like sentries in the dark. I hadn't realized how late it was. The floor was still stone, just like the other three walls, and the main sources of light were three fires burning in black metal fire pits set throughout the room.

"What is this?" Logan asked.

"An abandoned mine from the failed coal boom that we've converted into one of our many safe houses," Svenja explained. "When they couldn't find coal, they gutted this place until they found gemstones. Garnet, emerald, things like that." She turned to the wall. "The glass is one-sided with texturized pixel technology. From the outside, it looks like a rock face. You can see the main road up the mountain from here. It gives us a strategic advantage."

"How many of these places do you have?" Logan asked, his eyes wide.

"The Haunt is everywhere. We've got hundreds of cells like this in the US. Thousands worldwide, but I won't get more specific than that." Svenja smiled. Her teeth were slightly crooked in the front. She wore her smile well, as though she knew exactly what it could do to people.

We edged around the smaller fire pits that lined the walls until we came to another stone doorway cut into the left side of the room.

"Your room is in there, but I'll take you to the canteen first. There's an extra bed, but I assumed you two share one?" she asked. I coughed.

"Oh, we're not together. No. We're just . . . we're not together," I stuttered.

Logan coughed too, and I squeezed my hand into a fist.

Svenja turned around, oblivious to my mortification as she yanked open a door to reveal a ladder.

The canteen was a little smaller than the main room above and was more richly decorated. It had a kitchenette against the back wall and catwalk railing laced above, leading into small doorways high up in the corners. Christmas lights hung across the expanse of the whole thing, and oriental rugs were layered all over the floor. An octagonal poker table sat in the middle, placed underneath the square opening of the catwalk. Margaret and Ajit sat at the table.

Svenja came down after us.

"Okay," she said, squeezing past me and making her way to the kitchenette in the back. "Here's a change of clothes, a toothbrush, and some protein bars and sandwiches."

She brought two paper bags out from the other side of the counter.

"Don't forget to tell them that turndown service is from nine to ten," Margaret cracked, bringing a tin cup to her lips.

Svenja stopped, her head whipping to Margaret. "Excuse me for wanting to treat people like they're worth more than fodder for body count."

Ajit sighed. "Don't listen to her, Svenja."

"Thank you," Logan said, reaching out for the bag. I didn't reach for mine, and Logan took it for me. I crossed my arms and glared at Ajit.

"We're grateful," Logan said finally. I continued to glower at Ajit, who took a pull from his cup, unbothered.

There was a silence as Svenja clasped her hands and bounced on her toes.

"Well. It's been real weird, guys," Logan said, turning around to the ladder.

"You didn't ask them to play?" Ajit asked.

"They can't handle it, Ajit," Margaret said.

I stopped.

I knew we should keep walking.

I shouldn't ask what she was talking about. I shouldn't—

"What the hell are you talking about?" I asked.

Logan must have been thinking the same thing, because he let out a loud exhale as he turned around.

"She's talking about a game called Medusa," Ajit said, as he walked over to a cabinet against the wall and pulled cups and an amber liquor bottle from the shelves. "You look down at the table. On the count of three, you meet someone's eyes. If they're looking away, you're safe. If they're looking back at you, you both take the shot."

He came back to the table and set five glasses on the wood.

"But we make it a little more interesting," Svenja added, sitting down at the table and crossing her legs. "You take a shot, and you tell a secret."

I froze at the words. "You mean you tell *your* secret?" I asked. I regretted opening my mouth in the first place.

Svenja pursed her lips. "We tell parts. Pieces. Glimpses."

"So I'm here to . . . what, add the danger? The loaded chamber in Russian Roulette just in case telling me kills you?" Logan asked.

"It's hardly danger. The chances of you having anything to do with our Wounded is, statistically speaking, zero," Ajit chimed in.

Logan nodded, letting his head drop before looking over to me. "I think you were right, Margaret. I think that that game sounds like a bit much for us," he said, turning.

Relief flooded my limbs as I turned and followed him to the ladder. We were at the base of it when Margaret's voice rang out. "I thought you might say that. But I think I have something that could change your mind," she said. We turned.

Svenja's lips clenched down into a thin line, but she got up and disappeared through a side door.

Margaret reached back, pulling a laptop off the shelf behind her and opening it. She cocked an eyebrow at Logan and beckoned him forward with a crook of her finger.

With a wary glance at me, he walked over to the table.

I followed, the pit of my stomach clenching tighter with each step.

"You spent six weeks at Northwood Hospital four years ago, did you not?"

Logan stopped. He held his head a little higher, his face tightening. "Yes."

Margaret turned the computer to face us.

For a half second, the screen was black, with small, almost indistinguishable numbers and lime green Xs on a grid. She quickly hit a button, and a black-and-white video filled a screen.

Even through the pixels, I could see Logan in a hospital bed, wrapped and bruised, an oxygen mask on his face.

"What the hell is this?" I asked through clenched teeth.

Margaret leaned forward, resting her elbows on the table.

"Security footage," she said, meeting my eyes.

"What does this have to do with your stupid game?" I asked.

Margaret smirked and looked like she was going to say something, but Ajit set his cup down. "We had Svenja look closer at it. What was in the hospital database had been edited."

Logan went very still beside me. "Are you sure?" he asked.

"If Svenja says it was edited, then it was edited. She might be a walking glitter bomb, but there is not a better security footage analyst in this entire continent," Margaret shot back.

"Someone cut a minute and a half from the original. It wasn't hard to find the markers," Ajit explained to Logan. "This is what you saw at fourteen hundred hours," he said.

It was the hospital room, with Logan lying in the bed.

"Now watch the cabinet at the far corner."

One second it was closed. The next, it was open. There was no footage of it moving. It just wasn't, and then it was.

Logan stepped closer to the table.

Margaret reached over and hit enter.

"Luckily, we have the real version."

Logan lay in the bed.

Then someone walked into the room.

His hair was dark, and he wore a light windbreaker jacket—it was impossible to tell the color from the black-and-white footage. He stopped when he saw Logan in the bed.

The man wiped a hand over his mouth. As he walked farther into the room, I could see that he was holding a leather jacket. It looked like Logan's.

He walked around the side of the bed, and I held my breath.

Show me your face. Show me your face.

And then he did.

Sam MacDonald gently reached over and took Logan's hand in his. The quality of the video was terrible, but I could see him peer at the chart next to Logan's bed. Then he walked over to the cabinet and opened it, setting the jacket inside. His body blocked the view of the shelf, but Sam's arms moved like he was opening something. Like he was reaching deep inside the shelf.

I looked over at Logan, who watched the footage with wide eyes.

"Do you remember what was in that cabinet?" Margaret asked, closing the laptop.

"My bag. It had been beside me on the front porch when they—when I ran into the guys," Logan answered.

Margaret looked to the door, and, as if on cue, Svenja walked through.

She carried a worn red, white, and blue duffle bag, which she set gently on the table. Her expression was drawn, like she was an unwilling part of this plan.

Logan tensed when he saw it.

"I thought my uncle threw it out with my clothes. They were too . . ." He stopped, and then recommitted to his words. "Too bloody. But I had some files in there I hadn't been able to look through."

Ajit shook his head. "It was in his attic, up in Wrecks. We searched it when we found this footage. It's been in our evidence lockup."

Margaret sat back, her eyes fixed on Logan. "And it's yours, if you win Medusa. Don't you want to see what Sam thought was so important?"

"How do you know when we win?" I asked.

Svenja held her hands out. "You outlast us."

"I thought you said there wasn't any real danger," Logan said.

"It's not a fight to the death, Logan," Svenja laughed.

Margaret leaned forward. "Though I can't rule it out. I don't recommend trying to outdrink us."

Logan nodded. "Whatever's in the bag can't have been that important if you're willing to give it back," he said.

"Maybe not to us. Not for what we're doing. But you might find it interesting." Ajit locked his eyes on Logan. "Are you in?"

Logan nodded, the corner of his mouth turning up slightly as he cocked his jaw to the side. "Almost," he said, looking over at me. He turned back to Ajit. "You also have to give Eerie back the money she gave you for the slip pill."

Ajit raised his eyebrows. I couldn't tell if he was surprised I'd told Logan or amused at his nerve for bringing it up.

"With interest," Logan pushed.

"The offer is what it is, boyo. Take it or leave it," Margaret spat.

"We'll do it," I said. Whatever was in that bag could be important, and it could be his only chance to find some answers.

Logan shook his head, his eyes still locked on Ajit's. "Nope. A thousand bucks in the pot, or we don't play."

Margaret moved to say something else, but Ajit got up and disappeared through a side door. A moment later, he reappeared with two tightly bundled rolls of cash. "We have plenty of money," he explained, looking to me. "But we take it because it's a measure of how desperate a Hushed is. And when a Hushed is desperate, the Haunt considers it our business to know why. You'd be surprised by how much we learn just by walking through gas stations and talking to those looking for help."

He dropped the money in the center of the table.

"If you win, it's yours. With my apologies for wasting your time, madam."

I met his eyes with a steely glare. I didn't want his apology. The money, though. The money could help.

Logan eyed me, and I nodded. We sat down at the table.

"Don't get anywhere near anything dangerous, okay?" he said in a low voice. I understood what he meant. He didn't want me to get too close to my secret. He didn't have to warn me; I had no intention of telling the truth.

"Your boyfriend isn't as stupid as he looks," Margaret said. Of course she'd heard that.

"They're not together, Margaret," Svenja piped in cheerfully, her eyes narrowing as she looked at her friend. "And you should be the first person to stop assuming everyone is together, now. It's so old school."

"So is the phrase 'old school,'" Margaret shot back.

"Thanks, Svenja," Logan said, a hint of sarcasm riding his breathy voice.

Margaret looked between us as Ajit set my glass in front of me.

"This is going to be fun."

❧

I have always hated the taste of alcohol, and when I grabbed the glass and the smell drifted up to my nose, I was already cursing this plan.

"One! Two! Three! Medusa!" Ajit called.

We looked up.

Logan locked eyes with Margaret, and I looked at Svenja. She was looking away, and I took a deep breath. If I was going to keep up, I needed to get lucky.

Logan drank his shot, his fingers nimbly spinning the glass as he sat it back down. He held his arms out.

"Secrets, right? Just plain ol' secrets?"

"Stop stalling, Winspeare," Margaret snapped.

He leaned back in his chair, though he kept his hands spread wide over the table.

"Obviously, you know I spent six weeks in the hospital after a couple of thugs beat the shit out of me."

"Get to the point," Margaret said, her voice filled with irritation.

"But you don't know that I was cleared to leave after three and a half. The extra two and a half were because I was scared."

Silence slid over the room as Logan reached over and grabbed the bottle from the center of the table.

"I tanked the physical therapy sessions on purpose, until they threatened to call a psych ward for an evaluation."

They all looked at him. I half expected a snide comment from Margaret, but they were silent.

Ajit took a voluntary drink. "Well. To psych evals," he joked.

Logan laughed, and it sounded genuine. Svenja smiled and joined, and I found myself smiling reluctantly.

And it went on. One, two, three.

I kept mine simple.

I belong to a man . . . I had no idea.

I could ruin two or more people. Maybe, it was a safe bet.

I looked around to see if they could tell I was lying, but it didn't seem like it.

An hour later, I had bits of pieces of information that gave me glimpses and tastes of the legacies behind the strangers at the table. I tried to take in everything, from the flick of Ajit's wrist as he adjusted his sleeve to the way Svenja explained how she'd stirred in a ruined palace off the coast of the Baltic Sea.

But it was Logan I kept coming back to.

There was a flush in his cheeks, and he smiled as Ajit cracked a joke and Svenja poured another shot.

And there was nothing sharp about him, then. He'd shown the torn, crumpled part of himself, and the vulnerability suited him somehow.

Margaret drank almost every time. She was loose with her words, spilling bits of her story in her brash Irish brogue. She'd stirred in a barn in the late eighteenth century in southern Ireland, deep in a stable that had been forgotten in the stench of the all-consuming famine that covered the land. I felt a tug of reluctant respect. She was old—much older than any Hushed I had ever met.

She was all sharp edges and ends, resting her hands on the table with her nails curled against the wood.

One, two, three, Medusa.

Logan and Margaret locked eyes.

She killed the shot.

"Three men found me a minute after I stirred. I had more fat on me than they'd seen on a woman in years." She enunciated the words like they were individual tacks she loved throwing into the air. "Some of my periphery included some hand-to-hand combat, so those poor bastards had no idea what was happening until they were all on the floor, covered in decades-old shit."

One, two, three, Medusa.

Logan leaned forward.

"My father was having an affair." His words slurred, slightly. "Affairs, actually. One of the many things I found out about him during my mom's trial. I tracked one of his mistresses down once. She lived a few miles outside of town."

"Why did you track her down?" Ajit asked.

Logan smiled, like he was embarrassed about his younger hopes. The shots were finally taking effect.

"I was hoping I'd be able to . . . I don't know. Talk to her? Get her perspective. She threatened to call the police. I never told anyone about it."

One, two, three, Medusa.

Margaret and I locked eyes. She smiled as she tipped the glass into her mouth.

"No more periphery stories. They're depressing and against the rules," Svenja said loudly, only slightly slurring her words.

Margaret sighed. "Everything about me is depressing, Svenja. I'm Irish."

Svenja glared, and Margaret turned back to me. "My secret belongs to a man who has monuments built to him. He killed more people in ten years than you'd speak to in a lifetime."

She sat the bottle down and turned to me, as though I could deliver the punch line to her favorite joke. There was nothing I could say that could match her pain. The only thing worse than living with a memory that festered and haunted was this. Staring into the eyes of someone who looked at me as though I would never be strong enough to endure the hell they endured. That I, with my blond hair and wide blue eyes, could never understand a darkness so deep it felt like it breathed. She was looking at me like that now.

"Go ahead, girlie. Tell me how sad it is when your favorite conditioner is out of stock at Target," Margaret sneered.

Fabian would've seen the shift in the way I held my shoulders. He would've reached over and told me that it wasn't worth it. But Fabian wasn't there.

"My brother found me, naked. Huddled. Everything was ash. He'd been shot in the leg." My voice shook as I told the first hint of truth I'd told all night.

Margaret's lip curled.

"And you played Florence Nightingale, and everything was well. For me, the morning light only made things worse," she said.

Logan reached over, his fingers grasping my thigh. It was not the grip of a drunk. He squeezed twice, a warning.

That's when I realized he was only pretending that the shots affected him.

"The Pull is hard for everyone," Svenja said to Margaret.

"I'm not talking about the fucking Pull," Margaret hissed. "I'm talking about walking barefoot in the rain until your feet bleed, stepping over bodies in the road while checking to see if their shoes would fit and give you any relief. Eating month-old bread that's rotted black on the inside because your only other option is tree bark. Considering all that, keeping what I knew was the easiest thing in the world."

Ajit shook his head.

"What?" she snapped.

"Margaret likes to act like the rest of us stirred in a bubble bath, surrounded by an assortment of chocolates," Ajit said, looking at Logan. I was starting to see past the man I met in the gas station. Ajit was the balance between Svenja and Margaret—the one who kept the peace.

Margaret looked at me expectantly.

And maybe it was the whiskey, drifting through my veins like anchors, slowing down everything but my rage. Or maybe it was that the smell of ash floated through my nose. I leaned forward. Logan's hand grasped mine under the table and squeezed twice. *Stop*, it said. I yanked my hand from his, hard.

"Everyone died, the night I stirred. Everyone," I said. "Do not look at me like I know nothing."

It was stupid. I knew as I spoke the words that it was stupid. Then Margaret smiled.

What had I said?

Shit.

Everything was ash. Everyone died.

Logan's fake drunk act dropped for half a second, long enough for me to see the concern in his eyes. He swayed, slightly, letting the drunken persona slip back into place.

"Touchy, ain't she?" he asked, turning his glass upside down. "I think maybe I should walk her back up and make sure she gets to her quarters—"

"I'm fine," I said, cutting him off.

Margaret sipped from her shot glass and smiled at me. She'd wanted me to say it. She'd dropped my guard and I'd taken the bait, like an idiot. Then I saw him.

Up top, on the catwalk, deep in the shadow.

Railius.

He'd watched the whole thing. Even in the dark I could see his eyes, narrowing when they met mine. Stripping me, my muscles, my bones, my breath, every *fucking thing he knew everything I'd told him everything.*

I pulled my eyes downward. Ajit was saying something, but I didn't really hear him.

They'd planned this. This whole thing. It wasn't for Logan—it was for me.

Just like that, any haze I felt from the whiskey evaporated from my veins. I was clearheaded, and all there was was panic.

They knew I'd been lying, and they wanted to know what I knew.

❦

I was silent the rest of the game, and, by some miracle, I didn't have to drink again.

Svenja turned her glass over thirty minutes later and walked, wavering only slightly, to the kitchenette.

They must have gotten what they wanted from us, because Margaret eventually tipped her shot glass over less than an hour later and sat back, a catlike grin fixed on her face.

Then Ajit.

"Fair and square," Svenja said, returning and dropping Logan's gym bag onto the table as she sat in her seat, a giant glass of water in her other hand. She handed me the cash, and I clamped my fingers tightly over it.

Margaret's grin flicked up on the side of her mouth, and I shook my head.

"You have something to say, Eerie?" Margaret said, her voice mockingly soft. "Or maybe you've said it all already?" she purred. I looked down at my lap and clenched my jaw.

"You won't be happy until you've made every Hushed say everything they need to say. That's what you do. Get them to say what you want them to say, right? Send them out to die like dogs? Is that what you want from me?" I spat.

"Watch your mouth," Margaret said. Logan shifted, leaning closer to me.

"Excuse me. I suppose my hostage etiquette needs some work," I said.

I chanced a look over at him.

"Eerie," he started. His eyes were wide and filled with a meaningful glance, but I looked away.

"You think because we let you sit with us that I wouldn't be able to gut you and not even remember your face after?" Margaret asked, leaning back in her chair.

"Okay. We've all had a few, here—" Logan interjected.

"—let's just take a deep breath? We don't have to get along forever. Just for now." Svenja cut him off, holding both her hands up.

"You act like you're trying to save the Hushed but all you do is *use* them to your own ends. You're liars," I growled.

Margaret leaned forward. Her deep brown eyes looked almost black, and her cheekbones sharpened as she sucked her cheeks in, her nostrils flaring as she fought to calm herself down.

"Eerie," Logan said again, reaching for my hand. I shoved him off.

I stood, and so did she.

I wanted Margaret to come at me. She'd shred me. I didn't really care. Something reckless was knocking around my chest like a caged bird and I just wanted to *hit* something.

Logan stood next to me, but it was Ajit who spoke.

"We have a code never to harm one of our own."

Ajit stood, stepping aside and pushing the chair in. He took a step closer to me. "But I swear to you, if you want a fight, we'll give you one."

Logan stepped between us. I didn't even see him move. He wasn't there and then he was, his nose inches from Ajit's. Gone was the easygoing peacemaker. He was so tense he seemed to vibrate.

"Step away," Logan said, his voice low and ragged. It was different than when he'd fought with the cops. There had been a lit rage then. This was kindling. A promise.

Over Logan's shoulder, I saw Ajit's eye flicker, assessing the threat.

"I think we're done for the night," Svenja said quietly from behind us.

"Yes," Ajit said, taking a step back. "I think you're right."

NINETEEN

Logan didn't say anything as we walked to the rooms. Little alcoves were cut on either side, about six feet deep and eight feet high, complete with a small bed on the floor and a few candles. I pushed the white linen curtain on the right one and looked inside. I knew he was pissed at me, and the way he shook his head and shoved the curtain aside with a little too much fervor confirmed it.

I stuck the money under the mattress and listened to my heartbeat hard in my ears. This was dangerous for him. I was dangerous for him. This wasn't sitting in his living room, reading together. This wasn't even running from a Gravedigger bar. He was entirely too comfortable standing up to these Hushed, and he was going to get hurt.

Before I even knew what I was doing, I was throwing my curtain open and ripping his aside.

"So you're mad at me, now?" I barked.

He stood before the bed, his shirt braced against his forearms, the hair on the back of his head standing up. He'd just taken off his shirt, and he turned as I stepped into the room.

"Fuck, Eerie," he said, chucking the shirt at the bed. I'd startled him.

He was sinew and flesh, cut into lines that pulled and stretched as he held up the new shirt on his bed. I didn't even try to hide that

I was staring, and even though he seemed angry, he didn't try to hide the fact that he knew I was looking. His gaze darkened as he stared me down, and I waited for whatever flared up in my gut to settle down. It didn't.

How could rage and whatever the hell this was even exist in the same stomach? It shouldn't be like that. I was mad at him, and that should override any desire to touch that patch of skin above his belt, right before the indentation where his muscles kind of dipped, making a line up to his ribs. Heat bloomed up my neck, and I searched the room for a safe place to rest my eyes.

When I met his gaze, he raised his eyebrows. It took two seconds to revive the rage, and then everything distilled back into anger.

"And why wouldn't I be, Eerie? What was that, in there?" he asked, tilting his head. "You were trying to get into a knockdown, drag-out fight with Margaret, and all we need to do is lie low until it's clear on the surface."

I let out a harsh laugh. "You *believe* them? Railius is a liar, Logan."

"I know that, Eerie."

I started pacing. "Do you? Do you know that? Because this place is dangerous."

Logan sighed. "What was our other option? Because individual fist-fights didn't seem super productive."

I glared at him as I cocked my head. I didn't have another option.

But I wasn't really mad at him. I was mad he was here, in danger. I was mad Margaret got the worst of me.

"You're too okay with being here," I whispered.

"What does that mean?"

I stepped closer to him. "It means they're angry, and so are you. You're not mad we're here. Admit it."

He stepped closer to me. "I was, at first, when they pulled me away from you and used those bullshit threats. And then when you told me they'd lied to you."

"And now?" I pressed.

He shook his head.

"They saved our lives, Eerie. And they're able to find things out about Ironbark that I never would've been able to find out myself."

"They have their own agenda, Logan. People like them always do."

"Probably. But right now, we're here. And you can't use your anger toward them as an excuse to be reckless and stupid."

I was being angry and reckless, but not for the reason he thought.

I felt something snap within me. He couldn't see how reckless *he* was being.

"I don't answer to you. Isn't that what you said to Railius before you just accepted his offer?"

Logan ignored the dig. "I'm not asking for you to answer to me. We're in this together, and you didn't act like it in there."

"We're not in this together, Logan! We can't be in this together! I'm Hushed, and I shouldn't have let you forget that. I shouldn't have let *me* forget that. We are on opposite sides, and some lines *can't be crossed*, Logan."

He turned and walked to the bed. He picked up one of the boots, probably just because he wanted to do something with his hands. They shook. We were near an edge; I felt it. I knew what I was doing when I spoke. Knew I was shoving him with both hands.

I remembered the way Railius smirked when I'd called Logan and me *we*. At first, they had been interested in Logan. But I knew now that they had their sights set on me, somehow, and now Logan was in the crosshairs. I'd wanted to help, but I had only made things worse. And I couldn't tell him that, so I was just choking on rage that had nowhere to go.

"I'm not your enemy, Eerie."

"Maybe you should be. Maybe that's how it should be, if you were smart."

He threw the boot at the wall, his body exploding with movement, and I jumped. It bounced off the rock as he turned around, his eyes wild.

"Do you think this makes you brave? This attitude you put on like you don't give a shit about what happens to you?"

"You have no idea what you're talking about," I hissed through my teeth. He was walking on open wounds, and my limbs radiated with heat.

I saw my words land on his skin.

"Tell me, then."

His words were softer, and he stepped forward, his face tightening like he knew his arrow had hit right where I was soft.

I stepped back.

"Tell me what's going on."

"What are you talking about?"

"Something is wrong."

He dipped his head, trying to catch my eyes. I fought it, looking at the stone floor. I didn't move, and he stooped lower. He lifted his arm, stopping a few inches from my face. Then he seemed to find his courage and took my chin in his hand. His fingers were rough, and I closed my eyes at his touch.

I knew he'd douse all the rage in me if I looked into his eyes. I did it anyway.

They searched me, dipping into me like he wasn't afraid of whatever shadows he saw there.

For a moment, I wanted to tell him everything. I let it wash over me. I could tell him everything. Where I stirred and what I remembered and what I didn't and how glad I was for the blankness and how much it destroyed me. I wanted to tell him the truth.

"You're not telling me why you're really upset," he said.

I ripped my chin from his hands. He moved back but didn't back down.

"I'm upset that we're here," I answered.

"That's not it," he said, his eyes narrowing. "I can tell."

"Because we're so close? We barely know each other, Logan."

That hit him right where I wanted. Right in the middle of his beautiful chest. Good. It was better I hit him there. Better than falling against it.

He swallowed hard and let his hands fall to his side. He turned and reached down to grab his boot.

I backed up until I felt the sheet. And then I slipped out without a word.

TWENTY

I arched my back as it started.

At first, I saw familiar pieces. The woods, the picture of the little boy by the window. The images flitted in and out, until the strongest drift came into focus.

It was familiar.

Sounds of shouts and a cacophony of laughter peeled away from the bustling courtyard to my right, and I backed up until I was against the wall.

I looked around. It was the same street, the same warm tiles under my feet. The same light rain that fell like mist. I turned just as the scarred man pushed the green-eyed girl up against the wall, cupped her neck in his hand, and she brought his mouth to hers. She met him hungrily, and I looked away, an ache in my chest swelling.

He pulled away from her and lifted his head in my direction. I couldn't see his face, still, his hood was too low, though I felt his eyes on me. His gaze was like a pulse, beating somewhere deep beside my lungs. For a moment, I couldn't breathe.

Could he *see* me?

The scarred man took the green-eyed girl by the hand and slipped back out of the alleyway.

The sound of shouts rose from somewhere beyond, and another scene took its place.

I was back by the fire in the cave several years before. Back where the green-eyed girl first uttered the words *A Haunt for Jackals.*

"We need names, then," the girl with the red lips replied, looking to the green-eyed girl. "You should be Samira."

The girl with the green eyes smiled, saying the name to herself and nodding.

"I'll be Adelaide," the girl with the red lips said, pulling a piece of meat off the stick and setting it gently on her tongue. She handed the stick to the man with the scar.

"And who am I?" he asked, his eyes on Samira.

Samira drew a breath.

I snapped back to the alleyway before Samira could respond.

Samira. The green-eyed girl was named Samira. Her hair was long, her eyes heavier in this drift, but it was her.

The girl with the red lips was Adelaide. Finally, I had names.

Shouts sounded again, and I ran down the alley, following the same path I did before. My feet were silent on the street.

I peered out of the mouth of the alley just as the first shout ripped across the high-walled courtyard.

The sound of metal against metal rang out, and everything erupted. Soldiers were running through the courtyard, their swords drawn.

I saw the man look over his shoulder.

He lowered his hood.

Railius.

My heart stammered in my chest as I watched him turn and look up, his eyes raking over the high walls that surrounded the courtyard, as though he was expecting to see someone there.

"What happened?" Samira screamed. Her foot slipped on the stone, and Railius caught her.

Samira pulled at his arm. Before he turned back to her, his eyes shifted once more, meeting mine.

He saw me.

Crowds spilled out of the alley around me, drawn by the noise.

I couldn't see anymore. I turned, running the opposite way, sprinting to the end of the alleyway before skidding to a stop and banking a hard right. This pathway was wider, though I was still unsure where I was going. I followed the sounds of shouts and metal, following the flow of the street's twists and turns until it abruptly ended, throwing me out into the courtyard once more.

Hundreds of people scrambled, though their frenzy seemed centered on something in the middle of the marketplace—something just under an ornate stone statue. Just when I thought he'd disappeared, I found him.

He stood in the middle of the courtyard, his hand still tight around Samira's grip as they parted through a crowd toward a group of well-dressed officials that stood on the stairs of a marble building on the far side of the courtyard.

I saw Samira, looking around as though she hoped to find kindness in the mob. She grabbed Railius's forearm as she brought her lips to his ear. She was saying something quickly; I could see the desperation in the way she moved.

She was afraid. Terrified.

Railius said something back as a strange hush fell over the crowd. A man spoke from the steps, his voice muffled and deep.

Samira didn't stop whispering. Another hand went to her chest. Even from this far away, I could see the panic in her eyes.

Railius looked up, again, and I followed his gaze to the top of the white stone outcropping.

Another figure stood, staring back down at him. It was so still, silhouetted against the moonlight, that I thought it might be made of marble.

But it moved. It raised a slender hand and waved, moving its fingers individually. Teasing. Hateful.

Rage tightened Railius's face against his skull as he brought his eyes back down to focus on the crowd, and then to the man waiting on the steps.

Samira whispered, pulling on his arm, and Railius stopped.

Before she could take another step, Railius turned.

The movement was so quick Samira didn't even have time to scream. She reached out, putting her hand over his, but she was no match for him.

Railius pulled a dagger from his sleeve and buried it in her chest, a scream tearing from him, ripping through the night and tearing it to pieces.

The crowd exploded in screams. A woman on the marble steps fainted.

The screams shook the world around me, vibrating the air as I leaned back, trying to escape the horror of what I'd just seen. Everything felt suspended, and the scene shattered in front of me like stained glass, the screams still rattling my teeth.

❧

I was out of my bed before I'd even opened my eyes, the terror chasing me from the drift.

I stood in the middle of my alcove, my breathing staggered and shaky as I tried to process what I'd just seen.

Sweat dripped off my chin and landed on the top of my feet as I ran a hand through my soaking hair. I'd never been that deep in a drift before.

Suddenly, the air felt too thick. I couldn't breathe.

With one lunging movement, I pulled the sheet aside and took three steps in the darkness. I moved too quickly, and I slammed into the low-hanging rock. Pain shot across my forehead, and I felt a small trickle of blood drip into my eyes. I brushed it back and stepped out into the cold embrace of the mine.

A shadow stood in front of me, his eyes wild in the dark.

His bare chest glistened, the jagged scar across his neck glittering in the low light.

"What did you see?" Railius demanded.

TWENTY-ONE

"You," I breathed, swallowing hard. "I saw you."

He was the one I'd been drifting with. He was the one who'd let me in.

And from the look on his face, he hadn't realized it until now.

He stepped toward me, towering over me as his eyes searched mine. I stood still. I couldn't let him see me afraid, but every time I blinked, I saw him burying a knife in Samira's chest.

He's the scarred man.

The thought ran on a loop as I struggled to understand.

I made myself meet his eyes. I saw flickers of a thousand things, and he looked almost too surprised to be angry.

He reached out and wrapped his hand around my forearm.

"Come on." He started pulling me down the hallway.

I yanked back with all my might, throwing him off balance. "Don't *touch* me."

He spun around, his face inches from mine.

"Fight me and I will slit Winspeare's throat in his sleep."

I sucked in a sharp breath. "You don't need to drag me," I snarled.

He let me go, then, and I followed him, squeezing my hands against the tremors that threatened to unwind me.

Nothing. I should've said "nothing."

What did I see? Nothing, Railius. Certainly not you, two thousand years ago, stabbing a girl in the chest. Why the hell would I admit that?

Too late now.

He was silent as he led me through the main hall and into a dark alcove on the opposite side.

I stopped.

"If you're going to kill me, then just do it. Adding a hike feels like insult to injury, don't you think?"

He looked over his shoulder.

"I don't know if I should be flattered that you fear me so much or disappointed at your lack of regard for my imagination."

A chill sped down my limbs.

"I'm not going to kill you," he said, finally, as though he'd grown bored with my terrified silence.

I followed him down a winding metal staircase, wrestling with the fear and hatred that fought for control of my mind. I knew he was a murderer. No amount of justification or oppression could rationalize what he'd done as the leader of the Haunt. Now I'd seen that he'd done much worse. They'd been friends—maybe even more than friends, by the looks of it—and he'd still killed the green-eyed girl. My mouth tasted like bile, and I spat into the darkness.

Soon we were before a wooden door, and he was opening it, gesturing me inside.

It was a simple room. A fire burned in a metal pit near an unmade bed. Shelves of dark wood lined the walls, though they were mostly empty.

The door closed and locked. I turned to face him.

He took three measured steps toward me. His muscles coiled and stretched as he stalked closer, hands balled at his sides. The scar ran from the center of his throat and along his left collarbone, its flesh thick, white, and coiled.

"How did you do it?" he asked quietly.

"Do what?"

"Drift. With me."

"Well, you better get a pen and paper, 'cause this gets pretty complicated. I fell asleep."

"Your attitude is not appropriate in this setting, I assure you," he snapped.

"We're both covered in sweat in the middle of a cave. I can *assure* you, we're past curtsies and pleasantries."

My voice shook, and I coughed, trying to cover it up.

He stared down at me. "You lied to me about where you stirred."

I remembered him on the catwalk outcropping, watching as I fell for Margaret's trap.

"And you're here to what? Threaten me?"

"I want to talk to you."

I swallowed hard. "About what I saw?" I pushed back.

"And about what *I* saw," he said, cocking an eyebrow.

I hadn't realized he'd seen glimpses of me, too. I crossed my arms over my chest, feeling exposed.

If he wanted me to talk first, to ask panicked questions about what he'd seen in my drift, he had another thing coming. I clenched my teeth together.

"How much did you see?" Railius asked finally. His voice was tight.

Lie. That was my first instinct, but the words caught in my throat.

I told the truth, just because I knew it wasn't what he wanted to hear. He was trying to scare me, so I said what I knew would scare him.

"All of it. You, Samira, and a girl named Adelaide. I saw you on the Adrenian Pass, and in the cave after. And I saw you kill Samira years later."

Railius turned away, walking to the desk. His shoulders drooped. The movement almost made him look defeated, and a silence stretched between us. If he was going to kill me, he would have done it after I told him the truth. He took a deep breath, like he was trying to absorb the pain my words caused.

"What happened?" I pressed, my curiosity overriding my need for self-preservation.

He set both palms on the wood. "I was careless, I suppose. Fifteen hundred years will do that."

He reached up and pulled a glass bottle and two tumblers off a shelf.

Fifteen hundred years.

If he was telling the truth, he was one of the oldest. He was one of the first. I couldn't wrap my mind around it, no matter how many times I repeated the words in my mind.

I eyed him warily as he filled two glasses with an amber liquid before snatching a shirt off the back of his chair. His body looked like the statues I'd seen in museums, like he was hewn from marble. It was almost unreal, but everything about Railius seemed to hover just above reality. He seemed too big for the room, his presence almost suffocating. He was a voice over the radio that threatened war, the blade above humanity's neck, and he was also here, in front of me. I could see the freckles on his collarbone and the blue veins on his arms. I'd seen him where he belonged—where he made sense. Dark purple cape draped over his shoulders, his dark red hair longer and loose against the back of his neck.

He pulled the shirt over his head, and his skin stretched and rippled, still glistening with sweat. I looked down, unwittingly remembering the way he'd kissed Samira—like a man starved. His jaw had worked against her, his fingers white as they bracketed her neck. I had seen him vulnerable, and maybe it was sick that it felt good to have taken that from him . . . but I couldn't deny that it made me less afraid of him. I understood that hunger, so it felt like I had some common ground with this monster, somehow. I didn't know if that was a good thing or a bad thing. He had, after all, killed her in the end.

He then squared his stance, like he was hoping I would gape or shrink back. I did neither. He met my eyes again, but I made myself cock an eyebrow, trying to seem unimpressed.

"Are you going to tell me *what* I saw?" I asked.

I knew I should stay quiet. I knew I should say the bare minimum and just try and get out of the room alive. But I couldn't help it. I wanted answers. I'd seen those drifts for weeks, and I knew this might be my only chance to ask questions.

He turned around, a look of mild surprise on his face. "You question me freely. Most would be more cautious, especially given what you've just witnessed."

He stood across from me, the glass loose in his hand.

I pushed onward. "I saw the start, and I saw the end. From the look of it, it had been years in between."

He narrowed his eyes at me, and then pushed off his desk. "Your turn," he said, walking forward and holding a drink out for me as he gestured for me to sit on the end of the bed.

"My *turn*? Is this show-and-tell?"

I took the drink but stayed standing. I was not sitting on his bed. That felt too intimate.

"Seems only fair, right? I show you mine, you show me yours, and all that?" he asked, and I didn't miss the derisive tone that felt thick with a double-meaning.

I met his level gaze, and he inclined his head. "You want to know the truth? You've got to give some truth of your own."

I looked at him, taking him in. Almost two months of seeing him in my dreams, and here he was. His voice sounded the same, though there was harshness to it where there once was vulnerability. He'd hardened.

I started to take a sip of the whiskey, but I stopped. Nope. My stomach churned. Still not over Medusa yet.

"Fine."

"You stirred in Ironbark," Railius said, not skipping a beat. "I saw it."

It was like a punch to the gut, and I felt myself blink too many times.

"Yes," I swallowed. It felt pointless to try and lie if he'd seen it.

"But you don't want Winspeare to know that."

I squared my shoulders. "No."

He took a sip of his drink. "That will be interesting," he said with a snort.

Rage flickered in my chest at the sound of his amusement.

"What will?"

He swallowed his whiskey and smacked his lips. "Watching this tragedy play out. I'm truly disappointed that I won't be able to stay in

Rearden Falls to watch everything fall apart. I have no idea why you think the rules don't apply to you. Hushed and humans have no place with each other."

I glowered at him, and he tilted his head, amusement only increasing as he picked up on my anger. His eyes widened then, as his searching gaze finally landed on something. "You can't remember your Wounded."

"How do you know that?" I asked before I could stop myself.

I wanted to be aloof, withdrawn. To cross my arms and let him try and figure me out, but the questions slipped past my lips before I could stop them. No one had ever been able to give me answers. And if anyone could, it would be him. I hated that, but not as much as I hated knowing nothing.

"I've seen it before," he answered. "Hushed born under extreme duress have trouble remembering. It's rare, though, and tends to make them more open to drifts, since they have nothing of their own to hold on to. I'm guessing you've probably sleepwalked, too."

I tried to keep my face blank as I thought about waking up outside the Yard.

Railius continued. "I've just never met a Hushed this . . ." He searched for the word, but we both knew what he was going to say.

Empty.

I sat straighter and looked up. *His turn.*

"When did you fall in love with Samira?" I asked.

I saw him flinch at my blunt delivery. He lowered his glass.

"Pass," he said, his eyes glinting.

"That's not how this works—"

"It works how I say it works," he growled. "Pass."

"What happened to Adelaide? Where was she in the last drift?"

"*Pass.* I won't say it again." His tone was sharp.

"You're the one that wanted to play. Or I could ask for help, elsewhere. I'm sure Ajit and Margaret would love to help me sort through this interesting bit of history," I crooned. From the way his eyes narrowed, I'd hit a nerve.

He watched me as he parted his lips and drained the rest of his glass into his mouth. He closed his eyes as he swallowed, savoring for a moment before he lowered his glass.

"You know how to get in and out of Ironbark, don't you?" he asked finally.

The memories flashed in my mind—the way I'd stumbled through the dark, over still bodies. I remembered twists and turns, but not in detail.

Alarm bells sounded in my mind. I struggled to keep my face blank.

"The entire prison is almost completely rotted. It's rubble and ash, fire-damaged beyond all recognition. It wouldn't make a difference, even if I could remember." I was admitting it without actually admitting it.

He was going to say something more, but I cut him off. I'd answered too many questions without enough answers.

"Why did you kill Samira?" I whispered.

He paused. Just when I thought he wasn't going to answer, he spoke. "Because it needed to be done."

"And will you need to kill me, too?"

I didn't realize how afraid of him I was until he smirked. Adrenaline spun in my veins, and I took a deep breath through my nose. He slowly sauntered forward until he loomed over me. His eyes bored into mine.

"I can't kill you, Eerie. I need you to get us into Ironbark Prison."

The breath left my lungs.

"The only way to get the answers to what happened there is to take the prison. Forcing death row inmates to become Harborers and then denying appeals based on false protocol was far from the worst thing the Internment did there."

"It's crawling with Internment officers. There can't be anything worth that risk."

"Not yet. But there will be if we can kill Connelly Stewart."

I froze, and my mind filled in the blanks as he continued.

"He used the Ironbark Harborers, so his Hushed will show up there. Haunt forces will be there, ready to get all his Hushed out. To do that effectively, we need to secure the entire building, especially 3B, where Dr. Davie's lab was."

"It's not possible," I said. It was insane. I remember the team of Internment officers combing the woods. "3B doesn't even exist; I've seen the floor plans." That was a lie. I remembered 3B, but I wasn't going to volunteer any more information.

Railius leaned closer, dropping his voice.

"True, level 3B is not on any of the databases. It was off the books, a place where Dr. Davie could conduct his experiments without interruption. The only two people that know it well enough to get in without detection are Connelly Stewart and Walter Davie. Davie's dead, but if you stirred in Ironbark, you're the next best thing. It's the one place they won't be expecting intruders." I shook my head, but he kept talking. "Join us. Help us do this."

I laughed, because it was the only thing I could do. I shook my head harder, and panic rang through me. I couldn't walk into Ironbark Prison. If I survived the Internment, there was no telling what I could remember. Looking through the files was one thing—walking those halls was another, and that was *if* I wasn't completely incapacitated by panic.

"No," I said, walking over to his door.

I should have lied and said I didn't see anything. I should never have opened myself to this in the first place. I should've asked Rory how to control drifts a long time ago. This was all a mistake.

Railius's voice stopped me. "They were torturing them, Eerie. Those women were being used as Harborers by every high-ranking official in the United States government, but that wasn't all. Dr. Davie was on the brink of something—and Connelly Stewart wanted it, badly. He didn't care who got hurt."

I spun around. "I said *no*. Why are you telling me this?"

Railius walked toward me, backing me up against the door.

"I want you to have a taste of how it will sound when I say all of this to Winspeare, since I'm going to ask him to kill Connelly Stewart once the trial resumes."

His words took a moment to sink in, and then they burned.

"He won't do that. It'd be suicide."

"Oh, yes he will. I have more proof than I'm telling you, Eerie. Lab reports. Security footage of Madeline crying as she was escorted out of level 3B. Close-up screenshots of the bruises on her wrists from being tied down—"

It was instinct. My hand flew up and raked across his face before I even had time to process that I'd moved. The rage was so pure, so white-hot, that it struck from me like a viper.

Railius's head turned to the side, and then he looked back to me.

I moved to hit him again, but he caught my wrist. "You're just proving my point. Imagine what Winspeare will do when he hears this. You look me in the eye and tell me that he won't volunteer without a second thought, if it means avenging his mother? You tell me I can't stir up enough rage in thirty seconds to get him to do whatever I want?"

"He won't," I said, though it sounded feeble even to my own ears.

Yes, he would. Logan would.

My breath was staggered as I ran my fingers through my hair and stepped back.

"But you could stop this, Eerie. I don't need any of his help if you offer yours."

I fought to steady my breathing, and he read the question in my eyes.

"Help us find the back entrance, the one you escaped from. If we find it, I will find a different way to kill Connelly Stewart."

I knew those two parts of his plan had nothing to do with each other. That didn't matter. Railius would do whatever he could to get what he wanted. I fell to the ground. I don't remember my knees giving out. They worked, and then they didn't. Then I was staring at stone.

Railius sunk down beside me, one knee on the floor while his elbows were braced across the other. I looked up.

"I don't remember it all. I don't remember enough to help you," I whispered.

"You can. I can help you," he said, his voice softer. Kinder? Was it kindness? I pulled back from him at the thought. I didn't want it. Kindness wasn't something I needed from a murderer. And if he helped, what then? I'd know the truth. The truth I could never un-know. The truth that could kill me.

"If I want? Like I have a choice in this?"

"You always have a choice. I can't make you do anything." I looked at him. His face was sincere, as though he really couldn't understand how absurd his words were. He leaned closer. "I can't take life that isn't mine to take."

"But you'll take the joy from someone's life and push them to sign their own death warrant," I spat.

He nodded, like it was obvious. "Yes. I don't believe in using force to make anyone do anything. Coercion, however, is just as powerful a motivator. It's not ideal, but it's fair. This world is ugly, Eerie."

"Because people like you exist in it." I let the words rip from me in a growl. I hadn't felt this helpless since I was in the hospital, watching Fabian die. He offered his hand to help me up, but I ignored it as I shoved myself to my feet and leaned against the door.

Hope flared within me as I remembered something. I met his eyes.

"I'll tell. I'll tell everyone what you are and what you did if you try and get Logan to work with you. I've been watching your drifts for two months. I've seen more than you know."

Railius leaned forward, his hair falling over his eyes as he wrapped a hand around the back of my neck. His touch was firm but gentle, and it did not match the lit energy of his gaze. I'd hit something raw. I'd untethered something. I saw him then, as he was. The real Railius—the one from the last drift. Feral.

"Then I will skip my offer regarding Winspeare and just leave him in tattered, bloody shreds. The kind you have to identify through dental records."

I yanked back, but he tightened his grip. His eyes widened as something registered.

"Two months?" he asked.

"Yes."

He let me go and took a step back.

"I've only been here for a week," he said, going very still.

"So what?" I pressed.

He opened his eyes. "It means Adelaide is here," he said, looking around the room like he might catch her in a corner.

"Adelaide? Like . . . *Adelaide*? From the drifts? Why would she be in Rearden Falls?" I asked, remembering the glint of her red lips in the firelight.

"The same reason I am. She wants what the Internment is protecting in Ironbark."

He ran a hand down his face, and I stepped back.

"You're lying."

He laughed, a frightening, hollow sound. "You have no idea what you've just walked into, Eerie. How dangerous this all just became. I *wish* I was lying."

There was only one thought I could grab onto, the last card I had. "This isn't what Samira wanted, Railius."

He gritted his teeth. "Do not speak her name," he growled.

"But that's what this is about, isn't it? All of this? It's about her. The girl you murdered."

He reached back and ran a hand through his hair, but I could see his fingers shaking.

"This goes however you want it to go, Eerie. You or Logan. Decide."

I bit down hard on the inside of my cheek. There wasn't another option. It was this, or Logan would die. I knew it.

I looked down at the floor and nodded.

"What was that?" Railius asked, and I looked up.

"Fine. I'll do it," I said, my voice cracking. I swallowed hard against the tears at the back of my throat.

I would not let him see me cry.

Railius nodded and walked to his door. He wasn't surprised by my answer. If he knew what I'd done for Fabian in the hospital, then he had to know all along what my answer would be.

From the moment he saw Logan and me together, he'd known he'd found my weakness.

"You'd better get some rest. The Internment left Ironbark. You and

Logan will be released in the morning." He opened the door and motioned for me to follow him.

My feet moved, but I didn't feel it.

I couldn't feel anything. My mind was still trying to catch up and understand what had just happened.

Railius walked me back to the main hall, stopping just past the first fire pit.

I moved to keep walking, but he grabbed my hand. I turned and looked at him.

He brushed a stray strand of hair off my forehead and leaned close to my ear.

"Please do not think that just because I let you speak to me like that once means I will allow it again."

He pulled back and looked into my eyes. "You mean nothing to me, and you can be disposed of without a trace. Do not mistake my curiosity for compassion, and do not test my patience."

There was no malice in his eyes, that made it worse. Malice, I could work with. Malice, I understood. This was pure. Calculating. He was as hard as the stone beneath my feet.

And I knew, if I had the chance, I would kill him myself.

ᥱᚷᚥᚲ

I walked back toward the alcove, my chest heaving as I let the sobs come.

I needed the world to just *stop* for a minute. I needed everything to slow down. I couldn't catch my breath.

How the hell did everything just fall apart like this? How did everything lace up this way, before I could even blink, tying me against a pyre I couldn't get free from?

He knew me. I'd been the one watching him for weeks, but he knew exactly where to hit to make me crumble. I raked my hands through my hair, pulling hard on my roots as I sucked a breath through my teeth. I stopped suddenly when I realized Logan's light was on.

"Eerie?" His voice sounded from the other side of the curtain. It shot across my chest like an electrical charge. I wiped the tears from my cheeks with the back of my hand.

He pulled his curtain aside. He was still shirtless, and rubbed a hand over his face.

When he saw the cut above my eye, he rushed toward me.

"What happened to your head?" he asked.

I reached up and winced. I'd forgotten about that.

"We're hiding in a mine full of low-hanging caves. I was bound to hit my head sometime. It's fine," I said.

"We should get Ajit to—"

"It's fine. Please."

Logan looked doubtful. "I thought you were asleep."

"Nightmares. Thought I'd walk them off." I said, gesturing to my head. That was half true, at least.

"Does that work? 'Cause if so, I need to try it." He smiled softly.

I just couldn't handle the way his smile made my heart tighten. Not right now. Right now, I needed to be alone so I could fall apart. I wanted him as close as he could be, and I never wanted to see him again. I wanted to know how the hell he got under my skin so hard and fast.

I walked back into my alcove.

He followed, and I turned around.

"Look, I just can't talk right now, okay? I can't fight anymore."

"I wasn't looking for round two," Logan explained, holding his hands up.

"Then what do you want?" I asked, sitting down on my bed. I could see the hurt on his face, but I didn't trust myself to say anything. If I opened my mouth to apologize, I couldn't guarantee what else I'd say.

"To make sure you're okay. After today, after us, after . . . everything."

I shook my head, and tears rolled up onto my eyelashes. "Not even close," I whispered. I blinked, and one of them rolled over, down my cheek. It felt so good to say something true.

He came and sat down next to me, and I didn't pull away as he wrapped his arm around me. I sank against his shoulder, tucking my feet up under me as my cheek found his collarbone.

Logan brought his other hand up and laced it through my hair at the back of my neck, and I closed my eyes. He held me tight. "We'll get out of here, Eerie. Don't worry. We'll be fine."

The memory of Railius's sneer slid before my memory.

Hushed and humans have no business together.

I took a deep, shaky breath.

"Was there anything important in the bag?" I whispered, desperate to get my mind on something else. Anything else.

Logan let out a soft exhale.

"Not really. Just a little note that told me that one day, I wouldn't have to bear the weight of this on my own anymore. Just poetry. Nothing useful."

I pulled back and looked at him. He tucked a loose strand of hair behind my ear.

"Maybe he meant it. Maybe he just wanted you to have some peace, Logan."

Logan stopped. He shrugged, a half-meant, broken little movement that tugged on my heart. "There isn't any peace until I find what I'm looking for."

"And what are you looking for?"

"Answers. Why she was out of her cell when she died. *Why* she died."

"And what would that change for you?" Something broke free in me. I fought to pull it back in.

Logan narrowed his eyes. "I can find out what happened. And then—"

"And then *what*? Throw your life away on some vengeance trip? That's not what she wanted, Logan. You read that letter in your file, but did you *read* it? She wanted you to have a life. She would *not* have wanted *this*." I motioned around the alcove.

Logan pressed his lips together. "You don't know that, Eerie."

I felt the warning in his voice, and I pulled back.

"I know that she wanted good things for you. But this isn't good. What you're doing would've broken her heart."

Logan shook his head, and I wondered if I'd finally crossed a line.

"I can't just let this go, okay? I can't," he said. "You can't know what I've lost. You didn't watch the hope drain from her after years of being in a cage. You didn't have to witness her trying to keep her spirits up even though she lost her appeals. I cannot, *I cannot*, walk away from that."

His voice cracked, and my heart was a small ruby dashed against the rocks, because I saw it. I saw what Railius would take and unleash. I knew he would pull a trigger.

"Because you don't know who you'd be without it, Logan. I get that. This one thing defines you, and the thought of walking away from it . . . it is too much. But I have to believe it's worth it. That you can live without it." I took a deep, shuddering breath.

"Please," he said, leaning down to meet my eyes, "I don't want to fight. Not right now. We don't need to talk about this right now."

"We should go to bed," I said, looking down at the bedspread. It was a soft cream color with dark, coffee-colored flowers embroidered across it. I could almost picture Svenja walking around a department store, picking it out and inquiring about thread count. It was so out of place against the stone wall that it made me want to laugh.

I looked up when Logan didn't move.

"What?" I asked.

He exhaled sharply and shrugged, a sad smile stealing up the side of his mouth, almost like he was embarrassed.

"Never mind," he said, getting up.

"Do you want to stay in here?" I asked suddenly.

I was already paying for this. I was already suffering for how much I cared about him. The least I could do was enjoy it.

He looked down at me, his smile deepening.

We crawled to the middle of the bed, and I tucked my ear against his chest, loving the sound of his heartbeat vibrating through my eardrum.

I looked up at him, and everything went still. His eyes searched mine, and then dropped to my lips.

His eyes were so hungry and hopeful, and I knew I could shatter him if I pressed my lips to his, and I could shatter him if I didn't.

It stopped my heart, and I knew I couldn't. I couldn't do it to him or to me.

I put my head back down, and his heart beat rapidly under me. I shut my eyes tight.

Maybe I'd survive Ironbark. Maybe it wouldn't trip my memories, or, if it did, it would have nothing to do with Logan. Maybe I'd get Fabian out and Logan would come with us.

Maybe everything could still be fine. We'd face the years ahead, him aging, me not. Him human, me anything but. Maybe this would end without shattering me into a thousand pieces.

I could hold on to maybe. Maybe kept the tears at bay.

He turned off the light.

"You keep my nightmares away, too," he whispered.

TWENTY-TWO

I squinted hard against the daylight as Svenja opened the safety door. It was early, about seven. Logan had woken up before me.

"They're letting us go," he'd said.

I pretended to be surprised.

I shot Svenja a look over my shoulder, and she nodded once. *See you soon*, it said. I knew I was in this now. Railius had made it clear that he knew how and where to find me. If I changed my mind, Logan would pay the price.

The exit was about a mile away from where Margaret dropped us in, but it was a pleasant walk. We were wearing the clothes they'd found us in, but they were dry now. The money filled both my pockets. I still had to figure out a whole new escape plan, but at least I had resources if I survived long enough to use them.

The clouds in the sky were thick and fluffy, with smears of gray and charcoal. The daylight was soft and warm against the cold air, and the snow crunched under our boots. The tattered gym bag hung across Logan's shoulders.

"You're in a good mood," I said.

"Well. I know it won't please you too much, but Svenja pulled a stack of copies of my mom's letters from the archives and gave them to me."

I looked down.

Of course. It was a threat. Railius allowed all of this to remind me that he could reach out and tighten the noose on Logan whenever he wanted.

I clenched my jaw.

It wouldn't matter. I wouldn't let it come to that.

"So. Where have we been for the past day?" he asked, stepping over a fallen log.

I laughed. "That will be an interesting one to try to explain."

"Have I thoroughly ruined your reputation?" he asked, grinning at me over the collar of his jacket. I let out a soft laugh, even as my stomach clenched and I felt a rush of heat bloom up my neck.

The sunlight was in his hair and the steam of his breath rolled out from his perfect lips, and I didn't know what else to do, so I shrugged. He would do more than ruin my reputation if I let him, and I let myself wonder what would happen if I told him yes. When I'd talked to Rory in the diner, the remote possibility of being with a human felt almost laughable—safe in its absolute improbability. But with every sound of his laugh, it felt closer. The thought was dangerous and thrilling.

"Nah," I said, because I could only manage one syllable.

I heard a twig snap and I stopped, reaching an arm out to grab Logan. We both froze, and I heard it again.

He pulled me to the side, pressing me up against a tree as he shielded me with his body.

The footsteps grew louder. Two pairs of them, from their pace. Just behind us. I looked up, meeting Logan's eyes.

I motioned with my head, and he understood.

Run.

One, he mouthed.

Two, I replied.

"Three," he whispered, and we both took off.

I'd taken three feet before I skidded to a crouching stop, frozen at the sight in front of me.

"Eerie?" Rory gasped. She had her navy windbreaker on, and her hair was up in a high ponytail.

I pushed myself upright just as she launched herself into my arms.

"What the *hell*?" she breathed, pulling back to put her hands on either side of my face. "That text was all we got? You could've texted that you were staying longer. *Hey, not dead. Boning Logan.* It wouldn't have been that hard."

"I was not boning Logan," I said.

She looked over at Logan, her face tight.

He cleared his throat. "It's true."

"I wouldn't say anything if I were you. Zero words if you'd like to remain intact," Rory snapped.

"It's not his fault, Rory. It was just—" I stopped. What could I tell her?

She saw me swallow my words, and her eyes narrowed. The sunlight drifted through the leaves, casting shadows on her face. She knew I wasn't telling her everything.

Over her shoulder, Fabian came through the trees.

"Ror? Anything?"

He stopped when he saw me and rested his hand against a tree trunk, sagging in relief. He looked like he hadn't slept since I left. His eyes were ringed with purple, his beard was longer than I'd seen it since we'd been on the road. All that, mixed with his down vest and plaid shirt plus my slight delirium, made him look like a strung-out lumberjack.

"Where *were you*," he asked, crossing between the trees. His eyes were wide, his nostrils slightly flared. "What happened to your eye?" I saw Fabian's gaze flick to where Logan was, understanding washing over him.

"We might want to rethink that running plan," I hissed frantically to Logan.

"What?" Logan shot back, as my brother, roughly the size of a tree, barreled toward us. Then Fabian reached for me, his face breaking as he pulled me in to a hug. I fell into him, stiff.

"You scared me to death, Eerie."

He wrapped his arms around me, and my hands moved to his back. I didn't realize how much I needed Rory and Fabian until that moment, and then I wanted to cry and tell them everything.

"I'm so sorry. I'm so sorry, Eerie-girl. I was so out of line."

I had to be done with crying. The decision was made, and there was no use sitting around feeling sorry for myself.

"We should get out of here," Logan said, looking over his shoulder. "My aunt's cabin's is up that ridge," he said, pointing to an upward slope to the north.

I pulled away from Fabian.

Wind rustled through the trees, and prickles raced up my back.

It felt like a thousand eyes searching. Anyone could be watching, fixing crosshairs on any one of us.

Logan led the way, Fabian following.

Rory reached for my hand. She squeezed three times. I squeezed back four.

TWENTY-THREE

Watson purred and brushed against Fabian's legs as he sat at the kitchen table. His legs were too long, and his combat boots almost reached out the other side of the table. The shadows under his eyes looked so much darker inside.

Logan set a cup of coffee in front of him and stood opposite.

"So you tracked us into these woods? That's how you found us?" Logan asked.

Fabian just stared at him. Watson meowed for attention, but Fabian didn't blink. He tightened his fists, curling his fingers against the white lace tablecloth.

Rory and I stood at the counter. She insisted on inspecting the cut above my eyebrow.

"I *was* tracking you, and then your trail just dropped off. It's like you just disappeared," she said over her shoulder.

I fought to keep my face blank as Rory pulled a Q-tip from her bag and brushed against the gash.

I'd told Logan I didn't want my family knowing anything about this. They were going to stay as far back from this as I could get them.

"I met up with Logan. We went for a walk in the woods, but then we doubled back. Mystery solved," I said, gasping as Rory cleaned the cut.

"You took her out in the woods at night? Is that how she busted her eye?" Fabian asked, his voice low.

"Fabe. I told you. Low-hanging branch."

"Fabian," Logan started, and my brother glared up at him. Logan raised the coffee to his lips, but stopped and set it back down. He reached in the refrigerator and pulled out two beers instead.

He popped the caps on his belt buckle and set one in front of my brother. Logan took a swig from the other.

"I think you're the only other person on this planet that knows that *that* girl"—he pointed at me—"doesn't do anything she doesn't want to do. So if you really think that I *took* her anywhere, then feel free to carve me up with my aunt's thirty-year-old blunt butter knives, stick me in dozens of my infuriatingly mismatched Tupperware containers, and slowly feed me to that attention-deprived cat."

Watson meowed again and threw himself against Fabian's shin.

Rory snorted but covered it up with a cough as she looked back and saw Fabian's stony expression.

"You talk a lot, Winspeare," Fabian said.

"But I don't lie."

Fabian sat back in the chair. After a moment of assessing Logan, he reached out and grabbed the beer. That was a good sign.

Rory looked in her bag.

"Shoot. Logan, do you have butterfly bandages?" Rory asked.

Logan nodded. "Bathroom. Down the hall. Third door on the left."

Rory pulled me by the hand, and I turned at the doorway.

Fabian didn't take his eyes off of Logan but reached down to pet Watson.

A very good sign.

As Rory looked through the medicine cabinet, I poked my head into the guest bedroom next door. It was clean, with dark wood floors and a white duvet cover on the bed. A worn dresser sat against the opposite wall, a mirror hanging above. Pictures lined the glass, and I smiled as I took a step closer.

Rory followed me in, peeling the cover off the bandage.

"Will you stop wandering off?" she asked. I turned around.

"It happened yesterday, and I haven't bled out yet, doctor," I joked. She stepped close as she secured the bandage over my eyebrow. Her breath smelled like wintergreen.

"Good," she said, pushing a little too hard to make sure the bandage stuck.

She met my eyes. "He was really scared, Eerie. I was too."

"I'm sorry. I just . . . lost track of time."

Rory cocked her eyebrow. "I don't buy that for a moment."

I sucked on my lower lip, and Rory nodded. She wouldn't push.

She crumpled the Band-Aid trash in one hand. "Any more than I believe there was no boning."

I rolled my eyes. "Like you wouldn't be the first person I would tell if something like that happened."

Rory snorted. "True. I'd expect a full report."

I was quiet for a moment. "What if I'm bad at it?"

Rory put pressure on the Band-Aid again, and I winced.

"There is no 'bad at it,' Eerie. Love is the easiest thing in the world."

"Please. You thought I slept with him and came out looking like this. You believe I could be bad at it," I joked, and Rory's smile bloomed into a laugh.

"Might explain the busted eye," she said, snort-laughing.

"Give me a break."

Rory put the back of her hand to her mouth to stifle her giggles.

"You're the worst," I laughed, turning to the mirror to inspect the damage.

An eclectic collection of color-faded pictures lined the mirror. An older woman in a garden. Two little girls on a porch swing.

My eyes fell on a picture stuck in the corner of the mirror.

Everything inside of me stopped, like I was suspended.

A picture of a boy, sitting on a windowsill.

Peanut butter on his face, paint smeared on his cheekbone.

Just out of the frame, a blond woman stood, her arms wide, smiling.

The boy from my dreams.

The boy from my memory.

I reached up and snatched the picture from the mirror. On the other side was a caption.

Logan (2) and Madeline.

I leaned against the dresser.

"Eerie? What is going on?" Rory's voice sounded far away.

"This. I've seen this," I breathed, looking down at the picture again.

Bits and pieces ran into my mind, trickling like water through a crack. I remembered pieces.

That picture was taped to a mirror. A mirror that reflected Madeline Winspeare's face. She was saying something to a man that stood beside her, her eyes resolute.

It was Sam. Sam was talking to Madeline, and I remembered it.

I was Madeline Winspeare's Hushed.

I remembered.

I couldn't feel myself breathing, and I couldn't feel Rory's grip over mine.

"I'm Madeline's," I choked out, handing her the picture. Rory looked down, her eyes roving over the image. She jumped up and put it back on the mirror, and then wrapped her arms around me.

"Ror? Eerie?" Fabian called from the kitchen.

"We have to get you out of here," she said. I was shaking.

I didn't feel the Pull yet. The secret wasn't clear. But I knew it had something to do with Madeline, and that I needed to be away from Logan.

But I had to tell him. I had to tell him that I couldn't see him anymore.

I stepped forward, but Rory shoved me back.

"No," she growled. "You stay back, Eerie. Do you hear me? Keep your hands on that windowsill, and don't take another step forward."

I don't know how Rory got the side window open, but she did. It was only about six feet to the frozen ground, and then a straight shot to Fabian's Jeep.

"Go. I'll make an excuse. I'll tell him something," Rory said, helping me onto the sill.

"Please. Don't tell Fabian. Please."

I fell, losing my balance for a moment before turning quickly and catching the side of the windowsill. I fell to the ground, rolling to minimize the destruction of my ankles.

I ran to the Jeep as fast as I could.

Reed was right. Railius was right. Hushed and humans couldn't be together. I couldn't be around Logan, especially since I didn't know the secret. It could be about any of the dozens of torturous things they did to her in the name of science that Railius had mentioned. If I told Logan that, his need for vengeance would never go away. I might as well be killing him myself.

He needed to be away from me, and I from him.

I was so stupid.

Stupid to think this would work. Stupid to think this wouldn't completely wreck us both.

I hadn't realized I'd fooled myself into thinking that working with the Haunt wouldn't kill me. I'd fooled myself into thinking that I'd never remember everything. I'd let myself believe that I could play human forever. I climbed in the back seat and pressed my face against the fabric, wrapping my arms around my stomach and trying to make myself as small as I could.

Everything was a blur. Somehow, Fabian came to the driver's seat, and Rory jumped in the passenger seat.

They were talking, but I didn't hear them. Logan called my name, and then I heard Fabian's voice.

What were they telling Logan?

It didn't matter.

We were almost home when Rory handed me her phone.

"Type something. I'll make sure he gets it. I don't think he'll believe it unless it's in your words."

So I did.

Logan. Don't follow me.

I knew he probably wouldn't listen.

TWENTY-FOUR

No one had said anything when I got back. I didn't know what Fabian and Rory told them, but even Eva didn't push me for answers. I'd walked up to my room and slept the rest of the day.

The next day, I went to Our Shepherd of the Faith Church after school to meet Fabian. Rory had a shift at Mal's but I was off and Fabian was going to take me home.

He was already sitting there, in the back pew, one AirPod in his ear as he looked up at the altar. Dozens of lit candles flickered just in front of the cross mounted on the wall. I hadn't really thought about how I was going to get him out of Rearden Falls, or *if* I would be able to get him out at all. I realized, as I walked in, that I needed to tell Rory what I was planning, so she could do it if I couldn't.

"You here for confession?" I asked as I slid into the pew.

He looked at me from the corner of his eyes, and I leaned into his shoulder.

"Seph told me you and Rory are spending a lot of time together. She even said she saw her leave your room in one of your shirts early in the morning."

Fabian exhaled. "She said she wouldn't say anything about that."

"Yeah, well. She's three. What do you want?"

Fabian laughed.

"It's not what you think. We just . . . fall asleep together. It happened by accident, one night, and it was just . . ." He struggled for words. "It feels good to have someone next to you, you know?" he asked.

I did. The nights with Logan came flooding into my mind, and I managed a slight nod. Fabian realized what he said.

"I'm an asshole. I'm sorry, Eerie. I didn't even realize—"

I shook my head and looked at him.

"I want you to be able to tell me that you're in love. I want to hear about it, Fabe, because I'm happy for you. I understand better now. I get how you feel—" I looked at him and noticed how much light there was in his eyes. "You feel . . . happy. You're happy here?"

He thought about it for a moment, and then nodded.

It was what I wanted for him. I wanted him to be happy.

I was gone for a day, but it felt like everything changed.

He put his arm around me. "You can tell me what happened, you know. I promise not to kill him."

I sighed. "It wasn't him, Fabe. I'll explain one day."

He let it go, and I was so thankful. I didn't have it in me to dredge it up, but if there was one person who could have made me tell the whole story, it would be Fabian. I just wasn't ready.

I craned my neck to look up at him. "What are you listening to?" I asked.

Fabian looked at me like he was trying to decide if he should tell me or not.

"Um. Portuguese."

"What?" I asked.

Fabian straightened.

"I've started to kind of remember . . . Portuguese."

I stopped. "Since when?"

"Since a few days ago. I didn't want to tell you because I didn't want you to give me this exact panicked look you're giving me now," he said, eyeing the hand I'd clamped over the back of the pew. I let it go, and Fabian took my hand.

"It's okay. Nothing is going to happen, Eerie," he said.

I didn't believe him. I don't think he believed it himself.

☙

I went to sleep early that night. I wasn't especially tired, but I didn't feel like talking.

It felt like I had been out for fifteen minutes when I heard something against my window.

Crack.

I sat up and grabbed the gun from my bedside table.

Click.

I looked outside.

Logan was throwing rocks at my window. I ducked down, looking quickly to Rory and Seph's beds to make sure it hadn't woken them. It hadn't.

Crack.

No. No. This couldn't be happening.

"Eerie?" I heard him whisper-shout, and I took off. Out of the room, down the stairs until I was in the kitchen, directly below the window.

Reed stood in the dark, wearing a white tank top and gray sweatpants, his hair still wet from the shower. A lit cigarette hung lazily between his fingers. He looked out through the kitchen window, watching Logan.

"Throwing rocks at the window. Didn't fall for his originality, did you?" he asked. He put the cigarette to his lips, and the end lit up the dark.

I shoved him to the side, so he was hidden behind the refrigerator. I snatched the cigarette out of his hand and threw it into the sink.

Logan threw another rock.

Reed lifted his hands in irritation but let them fall to his sides without a word.

"Just go tell him to stop," Reed said.

"I can't," I whispered.

I couldn't go out there. I couldn't look at him. I had no way to explain. And if I heard his voice, if he walked up to me . . . I'd fall apart, and I'd already pieced myself together enough.

Logan threw another rock, and I winced.

"Wow. And just like that. Unraveled by some good hair and pretty eyes," Reed said.

"Well. You should know," I shot back. I knew it was a low blow. No one had ever mentioned his unrequited feelings for Rory out loud, and it felt like I'd broken a very important unspoken rule.

He stiffened, and I braced myself for fallout. I waited for him to run upstairs and wake everyone to watch the spectacle. Or for him to invite Logan inside.

Instead, he shrugged. "I'll get rid of him."

"What?"

"I'll get him to go away."

I couldn't see well in the dark, but his voice sounded sincere enough.

"Just tell him to go away. Tell him I'm not here."

"Hey. My methods are my methods."

"Don't be a dick, Reed."

He held his hands up again. "You could go wake Fabian. Take my help or leave it, sweet cheeks."

Logan threw another rock. I couldn't risk Logan saying something to Fabian about the Haunt or Railius.

"Fine," I said through gritted teeth.

Reed smiled and walked out into the cold. No shoes, no jacket.

I ducked deeper into the darkness, watching from the shadows as Logan noticed Reed.

I couldn't hear what Reed said, but Logan glanced up at my window.

Logan shook his head and got closer to Reed, his face earnest.

I had to look away. Seeing him was just too much.

I looked up just in time to see Reed shove Logan hard in the chest. I braced myself, getting ready to run into the snow and stop a fight.

But Logan didn't move. Didn't shove back. In the porch light, his eyes were drawn. His breath came out in slow, sad puffs against the cold night.

Reed pointed toward the driveway. With one last look at my window, Logan backed off. My heart wrenched.

It's for the best.

The best for him couldn't include me. It wasn't meant to.

Reed came back inside, shivering. Logan disappeared down the driveway.

"What did he say?" I asked.

"Isn't this counterproductive?"

"Please."

Reed rubbed his hands together. "He told me to tell you that he is going to have a really good time having sex with every girl he can get his paws on. Also that he is in possession of not one, not two, but six different venereal diseases. Also that rock thing wasn't romantic. He was just trying to break your window because he hates you."

I gave Reed a flat look as he blew breath into his hands trying to warm them up. He lit his cigarette.

It was probably best I didn't know what he really said.

"Thanks, Reed," I said quietly.

He stuck his hands in his pockets. "Don't mention it. And I mean really, don't say anything. 'Cause I'll just turn this whole scenario into some weird sexual encounter involving Eva's cooking utensils and you'll regret it."

"Gross," I said, turning around.

And even though my heart was broken, I smiled. Because it was as close to "you're welcome" as he was ever gonna get.

❧

It was quick. One minute I was drifting with Rory, looking into a campfire, and then the next I was there.

Ironbark.

Madeline Winspeare stood in front of the mirror, looking at a picture of Logan on the windowsill. Her blond hair was pulled back into a ponytail. Her orange jumpsuit was a harsh color against her pale skin.

I took it in. Everything from the bunk bed in the reflection to the tiny smudges on the glass.

She looked up and spoke. I couldn't hear her words.

Sam MacDonald stepped up behind her, his navy uniform stark against the white walls. His dark hair was pushed back, and his face was pained. His voice was clear. "I know you don't want to hear it, Madeline, but that doesn't change anything. I love you, and I won't let you give up without a fight."

Madeline's eyes hardened. "Well. I don't love you, Sam. I don't. Do you understand?"

Sam stopped, looking past Madeline, past where I could see from my vantage point.

"Why are you doing this?" he asked, looking back to Madeline in the reflection. She wouldn't turn and look at him, but she met his eyes through the mirrored glass.

She shook her head, but her strained expression didn't change.

Sam walked to the door. "I don't believe you."

"You have no choice," she said.

Sam opened the door, slipped out, and then let it close behind him.

Madeline's face crumpled, and she brought her hands to her face. Deep sobs pulled from her, and the muscles in her neck bulged.

"Why would you do that?" a muffled voice behind me asked. "You know what happens tonight. Why would you turn him away?"

I tried to turn to see who it was, but I couldn't.

Madeline lowered the hands from her face.

"Because he will destroy himself trying to save me. I can't let him do that."

"Because you love him?" the voice asked. She didn't argue. I could see the pain in her eyes.

And then I was falling.

Down past the tile floor of the cell, deep into darkness.

I landed hard in my bed, sitting up in a panic.

Madeline loved Sam.

Sam loved Madeline.

Nausea stirred in my chest, and I closed my eyes hard against it.

I took a deep breath, closing my eyes and trying to think.

Three people in the room, but I could only see two.

Fabian and I were the only Hushed to survive Ironbark. Every other Hushed died in that place. We were the only ones who would know the truth. I knew Sam loved Madeline.

"Eerie?"

I opened my eyes. Rory sat on my bed.

"Did you see it?" I asked.

"See what?" she asked, and I fell backward against my pillow in relief.

"My secret," I replied.

"No."

I put my hand on my forehead. At least not everyone had seen it. I'd broken loose from the drift before it showed. I had a little more time, then, before Fabian found out everything.

Madeline loved Sam, but she wanted him to be free.

The sentence weighed heavy on my chest.

This was it.

This was my secret. I felt sick with it. The Pull had finally arrived.

Rory moved closer.

"Do you want to talk about it?" she asked, lifting the covers and sliding in next to me.

For the first time since this whole thing started, I realized that I did want to talk about it. Rory lay on her side and took my hand. She squeezed it three times. I squeezed hers four and told her everything.

TWENTY-FIVE

When I reached into my work locker, I found a small note written in clean handwriting.

> Tomorrow night. Ten o'clock. Debrief. Two miles south of your window.
>
> —R

I would never be ready to go back to Ironbark, but this was all happening so fast.

Not to mention the feeling in my chest that wasn't going away.

Madeline loved Sam. The words ran through my mind on a constant loop, and they stuck in my throat like a pill I couldn't swallow all the way. That was why she was out of her cell. Sam let her out because he was trying to save her. I thought I was feeling something like the Pull—something starting in my chest, but all I had to compare it to was what I felt from Samira in the drift. This was not quite that, but still a dull ache that got worse when I thought about Logan.

There was a thought in my mind. Something I was thinking but didn't tell anyone, not even Rory. And she'd listened to the whole story, even though it took me about an hour to tell it, start to finish. She was calm. Didn't completely freak when I told her about the Haunt, though she looked scared.

The only thing I left out was the deal I'd made. I just told her that Railius let us go.

I kept the deal I'd made to myself. I didn't want her to carry that burden. It wasn't hers to bear.

But there was a way out of this mess, and I nursed the beginnings of a plan throughout the day. It grew stronger, and by last class, I'd decided to do it. I couldn't ask anyone for advice because no one else would understand.

Mal's went by fast, but my eyes kept jerking up every time the bell above the front door rang. It was a slow night, but every time I walked past the booth where Logan had sat, I felt like I was going to throw up. Not because of the Pull or anything. But because it was hard to believe that life could be that good three days ago and like this now.

It was empty an hour before closing, so Rory and I broke off bits of the last of the muffins in the glass pastry case and threw them across the counter, trying to catch them in each other's mouths.

Mal chastised us, but then Rory held up a piece of one of our blueberry streusel muffins, and he opened his mouth. She nailed it on the first try.

We talked about next week's shift, and I fought with Rory over the best ones.

I don't know why I did that. Old time's sake, I guess.

I wouldn't be there next week.

TWENTY-SIX

The whole way up the mountain was dark, save for the moonlight, which peeked out from behind clouds every few minutes. The gravel cracked and popped under the tires of Fabian's Jeep as I rounded the switchbacks up toward Logan's cabin.

I drove with the windows down and the heater cranked as high as it would go. I breathed in the frigid air, loving how it smelled like hickory and evergreen and woodsmoke. It was too morbid to think that it was the perfect night to die.

Luckily, I didn't think of it like that, but it was a good night to save Logan's life. It was a good night to tell him the answers he needed. It was a good night to tell him everything.

Madeline loved Sam, but she didn't tell him. She had a chance, and she chose Sam's life over hers. Even in her final hours, she tried to choose someone else over herself. If Logan knew that, he would understand that she would want him to leave this place, go far away, and live his life.

That's what I wanted too.

I was probably not going to survive Railius's crazy plan, anyway. I'd accepted that much. The very least I could do was decide my own fate. And for the first time, fear couldn't get me. If there was any time to have a panic attack, this was it. But this was how fear dies. I stood at the threshold of the most terrifying moment of my life, and I finally felt in control.

And honestly, I relished the idea of Railius waiting in the woods and realizing I wasn't going to show up.

When I first pulled up, I thought Logan wasn't home. The blinds were pulled and the string lights were off. I craned my neck as I killed the headlights and rolled to a stop by the front steps.

"Seriously?" I whispered, looking at the night sky. "I'm trying to do the right thing, here," I said, pleading to the heavens.

Then I saw it. Just a flicker, but it was there. Firelight. He was in the living room.

My hands shook as I opened the Jeep's door. I threw my coat and scarf on the front seat, along with the keys. There was a note to Fabian in the front pocket. It explained everything. I'd left one for Rory in my bed, along with instructions on how to find the money. If she and Fabian wanted to run away, they could. It was all I could do. I closed the door behind me as quietly as I could, and then walked up the front steps. My breath came in foggy gasps, and I shut my eyes tight. I felt the falling feeling—the burning at the back of my throat. Panic was right there, ready to swallow me whole. I opened my eyes wide, and then took one step. Then another.

You can do this.

I grabbed Fabian's cross with one hand and then opened the door with the other. I'd stolen it from his dresser before I left.

The door was unlocked, and I walked in. I closed it behind me and turned the corner into the living room.

Logan sat by the fire, a book open in front of him. A half-empty drink rested on the brick next to him. A throw blanket was draped over his shoulders. His eyebrows drew together in confusion, and then he looked relieved as he realized it was me.

"Eerie," he whispered, and I shut my eyes again. If he talked, this was going to be harder.

With one movement, he stood, letting the blanket and book fall to the floor. He was shirtless and barefoot, his plaid pajama pants low on his hips.

"What the hell happened? I've been calling you; I've been to your house—Reed—" he started, but I shook my head, stepping closer. It would be hard to find the line between breathing him in enough to build the courage to die and being so enrapt by him that I didn't want to leave.

"I know. I sent him out," I said, tears filling my eyes. My voice was thick, and the sound of it stopped him.

"What?" he whispered.

"I sent him out to send you away."

"Why would you do that?" he asked, his voice low. It cracked. "What happened? You just left, and I had no idea."

His voice fractured me in the deepest places. I could almost feel myself cracking, my heart snapping like a branch under the weight of too much snow.

Do it. Do it now, or you won't be able to.

He was so splintered in front of me, it took everything I had to not rush forward and try and piece him back together. *I am putting him back together*, I reminded myself. *I'm saving us both.*

The silence that surrounded us was thick with heat. I exhaled, and it was a sticky, punctuated sound through the tears.

He stepped closer, and I stepped back, holding out my hand.

"Listen."

"What are you doing?" His voice shifted, filling with something like fear, and a sob pulled from me.

"You need to listen, okay?" I took an uneven breath.

"What are you doing, Eerie?" His voice shook, and his eyes were shining more, now.

"What I should've done when we met. But I couldn't, because—"

"Stop," he said, a warning edge in his tone. It was like he knew what I was going to say. *It doesn't matter.*

I squeezed my eyes shut. It didn't matter, and it didn't help. I could feel him near me. I needed to speak now, or I never would.

"I didn't stir in a shipyard in California, okay?"

"Eerie." His voice was getting more frantic. He rushed toward me, pushing his body flush with mine, and I pressed my hands against his chest. His skin was hot from the fire, and I tried to keep him from getting too close.

"I didn't—"

"EERIE! STOP!" he shouted from the bottom of his chest. It scared me, and my eyes flew open as he dug his hand into the back of my neck and pressed me against him, yanking my hair back softly so that I had to look him in the eye. His other arm snaked around my waist, pinning me.

"Stop," he begged, releasing my hair and hauling me close so that he was hugging me tightly, my face pressed to his chest. I let out a small sob, turning to press my open mouth between his pecs as I took a deep breath. The salt from his skin mixed with my tears, and I savored the bite of it on my tongue. He pressed his lips to the top of my head and tightened his grip on me like he could keep me from falling apart.

"I know. I know you lied. I know you stirred in Ironbark. I figured it out in the mines. I couldn't be angry, Eerie. I tried. That night, when I came to check on you, I was going to confront you about it. But I saw you, and—I couldn't. If gaining answers means losing you, *I don't want answers*. Not like that."

My fingers curled against him, and, with every bit of strength I had, I shoved him back. "You can't stop me from saying what I came here to say," I cried.

"The hell I can't," he snarled, his expression tight and furious. He knocked my arms away and brought his mouth to mine with a startling and unwinding fury, his lips parting mine like he was trying to drink the poison from my veins. One hand braced the bottom of my jaw as the other wrapped around my hip with a punishing grip. He pushed me back against the wall, and his tongue met mine. I dissolved, melting into him, pressing my tongue against his and bringing my hands up around him. A small, strangled sound escaped his throat, and it was the match on the gasoline.

This was it. The moment I was dreading and aching for. It was everything and I was on fire and flying and I wanted to be closer.

I wrapped my legs around his waist, and he reached down and put a hand under me, while the other hand braced the wall on the other side of my head. My hands were in his hair, and the scruff on his face was rasping so hard against my lips I was sure I was bleeding, but I only wanted more. I wanted everything he could give me. I could drown in the electrical feeling lighting my bones up like I'd been struck by lightning . . .

I need to stop.

I pulled him as deep as I could, tasting him as much as possible. I wanted the feel of him on my tongue as I spoke my last words. *One more second. Just one more.*

But it would never be enough, and the deepest part of me knew that truth.

Stop, Eerie.

He pulled back and softly bit my bottom lip, his gasping breath hot on my tongue. I untangled myself from him and set my feet back on the floor, though I didn't let go of him. He leaned down, still bracing his arm by my right ear as he pressed his forehead to mine and pushed our bodies together.

"Do not say it. Do you hear me? I'm choosing you. I'm *choosing you.* I want answers, but not like this."

He kissed me again, softly, and another soft sob left me as I tried to memorize the taste of his lips. The curve of his jaw. The light in his eyes.

Easiest thing in the world.

It was.

I pulled my face from his, keeping my fingers tight in his hair.

A tear slipped down his cheek, and he closed his eyes, breathing me in.

"I want you. I need you, Eerie."

Now.

I closed mine.

"Sam and your mother were in love, Logan. He offered her a way out, but she refused because she wanted him to live his life. That's why she was out of her cell. He tried to save her."

Logan's eyes opened, and I hated that the last thing I would see would be the terror there.

My knees gave out, and I sank to the floor.

"No. No. No, no, no," Logan cried, falling to the floor in front of me. "Dammit! *No!*" he screamed, cupping my face in his hands.

"It's okay," I whispered.

Tears streamed down his face.

"No, no," he cried, his voice hitching in the saddest sound I'd ever heard. "Dammit. *Dammit.*" He was panicking, his breathing short and shallow. His face twisted up in sorrow.

"It's okay. Logan. It's okay. Just kiss me, okay?"

He sagged, like I'd just ripped his heart out of his chest, but he reached out and pulled me to him. He pressed his lips to mine, gently, between sobs.

I waited for the fade.

I didn't know what it felt like. I hoped it didn't hurt, but I didn't really care. If I was with Logan, nothing could hurt that bad.

"I'm sorry," I whispered, and nothing had been more true.

I took a deep breath, and then, nothing.

I took another deep breath.

Nothing.

Logan pulled back and looked at me.

"What?" he breathed.

"That wasn't it?" I whispered.

"What?" Logan asked, meeting my eyes, a wild hope ravaging his features.

I pulled the buttons open on my flannel shirt and looked down.

No black spread. No inky mark.

My thoughts were a swirling storm in my mind, and I fought to keep up.

I'm not dead.

Logan ran his hand over my chest, goosebumps pebbling under his rough fingers as he ran them over my soft skin, searching for a sign of death to appear.

"Nothing. Eerie. You're alive. You're alive?"

He let out a wild, untethered yell that was somewhere between a shout and laugh and pulled me to him, crushing me in a hug. I returned it, and the sobs I'd held back so poorly ripped from me.

He wrapped a hand in my hair.

That wasn't my secret. Then what was it? I'd been so sure. The picture. I'd felt it so strongly.

I'd wanted to give my life for Logan's. That was the Pull, right?

I stopped as a thought hit me. It was so strong it nearly knocked the breath out of me.

The memory was periphery. From whom, I didn't know. But it wasn't the Pull I was feeling then.

Wanting to give my life for Logan's? That was something else. Something too raw and terrifying to name.

I squeezed tighter, and Logan lost his balance, toppling backward. I landed on top of him. I put my hands on either side of his head, and tears slipped out the sides of his lashes.

I kissed him hungrily, and he rolled over, bringing us closer to the fire. He pressed his hard body against mine as his eyes darkened with rage and something I couldn't quite place. His hands wrapped around my wrists, and he pinned them on either side of my head as he tilted his head and glared at me, his body shaking.

"How *dare* you," he growled. "How *dare* you, Eerie? Just give up like that?"

I shook my head, and he took a deep, steadying breath. "No. It wasn't giving up, Logan." He loosed his grip on my wrists, and I sat up, finally able to put what I was feeling into words. "I've spent my entire existence being afraid. Running and avoiding and lying. Hoping no one found me out and hoping *I* didn't find myself out. It was exhausting. I looked my deepest fear in the face, and it didn't consume me."

Logan ran his finger over my lip, and I smiled. "That fear is gone. I walked right through it."

I wanted to cry with the realization. I stared down at my hands. I'd clenched them and walked up the steps. They'd opened the door when I was convinced I'd never walk back out again.

And I'd survived.

This is what Fabian was talking about. This is what he wanted. This is why he searched. This was the choice he was talking about.

It made so much more sense, now. I'd thought he'd given up hope. I'd been so wrong.

"Just please, don't ever do it again," his voice breaking as he whispered his plea.

I stopped, realizing that if I was still alive, I would still be expected to meet Railius tomorrow night. I took a deep breath, and Logan raised his eyebrows.

"Were you serious about not wanting answers?" I asked.

The fire illuminated half his face as he studied me.

"Yeah. I'm not done searching. I won't be done until there's justice. But justice at any price . . . that's not the life my mom would've wanted for me. The life I want. I see that now. I don't think I understood what I was losing, before. I didn't have anything to lose."

He brought his finger up and cupped my cheek with his hand.

"So even if Railius tried to get you to help with the Haunt . . . you'd say no?" I asked, pressing my hand against his and leaning into his touch even more.

Logan made a face, but I shook my head. "Please. I can't explain further than that. Maybe at some point, but not right now. But I need to know your answer. You'll leave this alone?"

After a moment, Logan nodded. "I want a life, Eerie. And I want it with you. Just . . ."

He leaned forward, meeting my eye.

"If this is going to work, you have to stop trying to protect me, okay? We're partners in this. That wasn't your secret. When it does come, *if* it comes, we'll deal with it together."

"There's not supposed to be a *together*, Logan. Not with us."

"Do you want there to be?"

I stopped. I couldn't take this back. I didn't want to.

I nodded.

"Then I'm with you," he said. "Whatever it takes, I'm going to be right here."

My heart swelled so much I thought my chest would burst. I pulled him in for a deep kiss, which he returned through a smile.

I quickly pulled back and looked him in the eye.

"Okay. But there is one more thing I have to do. Tomorrow night, I have to end something. I can't tell you any more than that. You just have to trust me. Can you trust me?"

Logan was still as he met my eyes. Then he nodded before pulling me down to the floor again, covering my mouth with his.

And in that moment, I let every human thing I'd ever felt but pushed down come to the surface. His hands came to my ribs, and I let out a breath that sounded unlike any sound I'd ever made. I wanted to be human, as much as I could. I wanted to be alive, and I told him that. He smiled against my lips, and I knew he understood.

We stayed like that until the fire was nothing but embers, my skin lit with his touch.

At 169 days, I stopped counting.

TWENTY-SEVEN

"Someone got in late last night," Rory teased as I threw my bag over my shoulder. I'd ripped up the note I'd left her and flushed it down the toilet. I wouldn't need it anymore.

Fabian looked up, eyebrow cocked as he took a deep pull from his coffee.

I smiled through chapped lips and stared at my family gathered around the breakfast table.

"Logan and I are together. If Officer Waybourne wants to revoke my stipend, then I have some savings. But I've never said anything when there are strange women sneaking out in the pre-dawn hours, Eva. Or when whatever the hell stranger you find at last call raids our kitchen in the middle of the night and eats all our shredded cheese, Reed."

Eva cocked her eyebrow at me. Reed shrugged—he had no rebuttal.

"You can kick me out if you like, but otherwise, I'm not going anywhere. I . . . ." I stumbled over my words, but then took a deep breath. "Yeah. That's how it is."

Seph slow-clapped, and Reed tried to hide a smirk over his coffee cup. Eva looked out from the refrigerator door, her eyes narrowed but not angry. I nodded once as I turned around and walked out, fighting the smile on my lips.

❧

Logan picked me up from work later. *Together.*

I loved how it sounded.

I loved the way Logan's face lit up when he walked into the diner, his cheeks red from the cold. The feeling was so overwhelming that it almost hurt, but I still wanted more of it. I loved when he stopped what he was doing to look at me, like he wanted to double-check that I was real, that I was there, and that I wanted him as much as he wanted me. I loved how he kissed, like he couldn't get enough of me, and how he'd move to walk away and whip around to pull me back to him. I loved how his body fit perfectly with mine, and how the next day was a blur of time in the cabin, my skin raw from kissing and face hurting from smiling. I loved how I told him I was nervous about sex, so he told me we'd go as slow as I wanted. Because we could. Because we had all the time we needed. He was right.

On the way back from the cabin later that day, Logan stopped to grab us coffee, and I sat in the truck as a slight rain fell, pelting the cab.

He ran inside, and my eyes drifted to the center console.

It wasn't that I was snooping. It was just sitting there, in one of the cup holders.

A piece of lined paper, folded in two. Torn and crinkled around the edges.

The words were faded.

Um dia você vai saber onde pesam os fardos e então não vai mais se sentir solitário.

I looked over it a couple of times, as if I could will myself to understand the language it was written in. I looked up just in time to see Logan running back toward the truck. I could have set it down and pretended I never saw it. But something in me felt dirty at the thought.

Logan slid inside. His hair was wet. He handed me my coffee and I wanted the moment to freeze, right there. Just to let me sit in it for a while longer.

Instead, I held up the paper. He looked at it and then to me, but he didn't look angry.

"I didn't mean to pry, I just . . ." I took a deep breath. "What is this?"

"I figured you wouldn't want to see it. It's the note Sam left in my bag. *One day, you'll know where the burdens are laid and you won't feel so alone.* I forgot I still had it in my pocket that night I came to your house."

"What language is it?"

Logan smiled as he stuck the key in the ignition and the Jeep roared to life.

"Portuguese. Remember? I told you Sam lived in a bunch of different places? One was Brazil. His parents were missionaries."

"Portuguese," I whispered, piecing something together.

"Can I take this?" I asked quietly. "I'll bring it back, I just—"

I looked up, stopping at Logan's concerned expression. I made myself continue.

"I just know someone who might want to see it."

Logan shifted into reverse, his eyes glued to the mirror. If he understood what I was saying, he didn't let on.

"Go ahead. It's a dead end for me anyway."

That would have to wait, for now. I couldn't think about it too much or I'd talk myself out of it.

I reached down and grabbed my coffee, taking a deep sip.

Something sweet and spicy invaded my senses, and it took everything I had not to spit it out.

"What was *that*?" I asked when I'd swallowed it.

Logan glanced down at the center console. "My coffee?" he asked.

"Logan Winspeare, is this a *pumpkin spice latte*?" I asked. I couldn't even ask the question without laughing.

He reached over and snatched it. "Yes. Yes, it is, Eerie. Because it's delicious and only available for a few months each year and I'm not a snob."

"I'm going to get you some Ugg boots," I whispered playfully.

"I'll get some highlights," he shot back. "Really lean into it."

I doubled over, cracking up until tears came out of my eyes.

Logan tried to take a drink but couldn't through his laughter.

I didn't even worry about what I had to do that night. I didn't let Railius into my mind at all. We laughed until our sides hurt, our happiness seeming like some great defiance that couldn't be matched.

⟡

Later, I walked up to Fabian's room. Rory sat on the bed, but she held her hands up when I moved to leave. "No. Stay. I was going to go check on Reed, anyway," she said.

Fabian was sitting at his desk, absorbed in a book with thick leather binding.

"Fabe?" I asked. He turned around.

My breath shook as I forced myself to breathe.

"I found something for you," I said, sticking my hand in my pocket.

I could still turn away. I could book it down the stairs and later be like *just kidding* or *sorry I was about to pee my pants* or something equally lame.

But instead, I held the paper out to him.

He looked at me and then to the paper. Then to me again.

"Part of me still does not want to give this to you," I said.

He took it. His eyes flitted over the paper, and he looked up at me. "Where did you get this?"

"It was a note to Logan from Sam MacDonald."

Fabian was quiet for a moment. "And you're giving it to me?"

"A week ago, I wouldn't have."

"What changed? You hate anything having to do with looking for answers."

I shrugged. "I want you to find what you're looking for, because I think you deserve a choice. I guess."

I wanted to rip it up. I'm scared you'll remember. I'm scared that you'll feel the Pull and be powerless against it.

He had to make his own choice, as I had made mine. It was the decision I made when I was driving to Logan's. I couldn't force Fabian to do anything. He chose to be in Rearden Falls. He chose not to take the slip pill. No amount of scheming on my part could change that. I had to stop living in fear, and that included the fear I carried for him.

Fabian ran a hand over his face. I tried to read his expression, tried to see if I could tell if he was remembering anything.

"Do you . . . You know what? I don't want to know," I said, half laughing, half trying to keep my voice steady. "I'm going to bed."

I turned to leave.

"Eerie?" Fabian called. I turned around, my hand on the doorframe.

I turned, and Fabian's expression had changed. He moved his jaw back and forth for a moment. "There is something."

He shoved himself up when he saw the look of fear on my face. "Not from this. Listen."

He pulled my hand, and we sat on his bed. He took a deep breath through his nose.

"You weren't the first person I found at Ironbark. The first . . . alive person."

I felt everything go still as I looked at my brother. My brother, who had told me everything. A familiar anger threatened to break loose, but the look on his face kept it at bay.

"It wasn't even someone who worked at the prison. It was some teenaged kid who was restocking the vending machines in the visitor wing when the whole thing happened. He was . . ."

I realized then, in the look on Fabian's face, that this wasn't something he was trying to hide from me, not in the way he had with the slip pill. This was something he wished he could forget himself. Suddenly, I wanted to stop him. I didn't want to know.

"He didn't make it out," I finished, and Fabian shook his head as he closed his eyes. A tear streaked down his cheek.

"Fabe—"

"He tried to help. He was no bigger than you. The sleeves on his work shirt were . . ." Fabian held his fingers in a loose cuff around his arm. "They were massive on his arms. Like it was a hand-me-down from his big brother or something. I don't even know what he thought he was doing. So stupid. But I was trying to get out of the stairwell, and the door was stuck. Everything was falling apart, Eerie. The walls were coming down. But the door was still locked. And he saw me through the little window and ran to me. He ran through the hallway that was collapsing. He opened the door. I ran out, but he wanted to go in. I told him there was no one else alive down there."

Fabian took a breath, finding the thread of the story again. "As we ran, a beam fell. It hit him in the head, and . . . he was holding himself together with his hand. I helped him outside. He went down, and I knew it was too late. There was so much blood. I asked him why he did that, why he helped me. Why was he that stupid. And he told me that it was what he was supposed to do. And he asked if I knew any prayers, and I said I didn't. And then . . . then he was gone."

I looked at my brother. He wiped his nose with the back of his hand, and I could see what he was doing. Picking up the memory, wrapping it back up, and putting it somewhere safe. Somewhere in the back of his mind.

"That's not why I believe in God, if that's what you're wondering."

"I wasn't thinking that," I said, realizing I believed him.

"But it's why I wanted to. That kid. That kid who is mentioned in passing in all the articles. It turned out he really was filling in for his older brother. I wanted to be like him. I still want to be like him."

Fabian looked down at the scrap I'd just given him. "Are you mad at me?"

I let the question sit, but only because I thought it needed a pause. "No," I said.

That was true.

He nodded and lifted the paper. "So . . . thank you. I know how hard this was."

"No you don't," I half-joked, and he smiled as I kissed his head.

He was still studying the words as I walked away.

Later, in my room, an image flitted across my mind. I couldn't place it, but I grabbed a pen and an old receipt and started sketching it from memory. I realized what I was drawing when I was about halfway done. It was my way out.

I sketched faster.

TWENTY-EIGHT

The moon was hidden behind clouds, and the woods were darker than usual. A dense gray covered everything. I carried my Beretta with me in the waist of my jeans.

Rory wanted to go with me, but I'd told her it was something I needed to do alone.

Which, by the way, always sounds better in a warm, lit living room than it does deep into thick woods.

The GPS tracker on my phone said I'd walked two miles, and I stopped.

For just a split second, I thought he wasn't going to show.

But then he stepped out from behind a tree. I didn't realize until I saw his face that I didn't really think it was going to be him. Svenja, maybe. Or Ajit.

"My connections tell me that you and Mr. Winspeare have been seeing a lot of each other," he said.

"Connections? You mean spies?"

Railius walked toward me, his eyes locked on mine.

"We know our window, and we're going to have one chance. I need you to be ready at a moment's notice—"

"I'm not doing this," I said, inserting a sharp edge to my voice.

Railius was still.

I took a step forward. My muscles sang with tension as the words revved in my chest. I savored them as they slipped past my lips. I showed him the sketch. He recognized it.

"Where did you get that?"

"On the computer, before Margaret showed us the hospital footage. It was only up for half a second, but that's all I need."

He stared at me.

"I ran the numbers. They're GPS coordinates. And based on their placement on this grid, I'm guessing they're the locations to the Haunt's safe houses."

Safe houses. Agents. I knew exactly where the Haunt had informants—and that was information humans would pay big money for. Svenja had said there were hundreds of different cells. The Haunt always had several different missions going on at once, and with this information, I could ruin almost all of them.

"That's enough," Railius warned, but I shook my head.

"And those other numbers? The ones in the left-hand corner? Those are Internment-issued Hushed IDs. I'm guessing they're either people of interest or members of the Haunt. The Feds would love these. Can you imagine the headlines—*Haunt for Jackals affiliates discovered.* The humans have waited years for a break like this. Sure, you can change all of them. But not before they would find you."

Railius narrowed his eyes, but I took a step forward. I knew I had him just where I wanted him.

"I told Logan everything. He's not your pawn anymore."

Railius looked at me, and I knew my strength had caught him off guard.

"You're playing a dangerous game," he said, his voice low and taut.

"I was already playing. I was just losing. Now I'm winning."

"And the game has changed, Eerie. It is more dangerous than you realize."

"Because of Adelaide? The fearsome creature? She hasn't bothered me. You're the only Hushed who has threatened me lately. I'm out." I turned around.

"This is not something you can step out of, Eerie. This is something that will knock down your front door. It will spill into your life, bringing death."

I looked at him over my shoulder.

He didn't lash out. Didn't make threats. Nothing. He looked . . . defeated.

Good.

"I wouldn't remember the way in, anyway. I thought I'd remembered something, but it was . . . nothing. I wouldn't want me as an Ironbark guide."

Why are you talking? Why are you trying to make him feel better?

Railius looked up at me. "It's because you don't want to remember."

I stared at him.

"What I could teach you? It was simple. It starts with *wanting* to remember. But you don't."

I shook my head, bringing the day's memories back to mind.

I met his eyes in the darkness. "You're right. I don't. Good luck, Railius," I said, turning around and walking resolutely back into the dark.

And I fought, with everything I had, to shake his words from my mind.

⚬✖⚬

I woke up again with a sound at my window. Not a crack, this time. A squeak.

My eyes were still closed as the sound fully registered in my senses. Someone was opening the window.

Someone was opening the window.

I sat up and found Margaret sitting on my bed.

I bit back a scream and put the back of my hand to my mouth.

"You guys have *got* to start using doors," I whispered.

There was no smirk on her face. In fact, in the glowing reflection of the night, she looked almost scared. Young, even.

She started to speak, but I shushed her and slipped out of bed, motioning for her to follow me to the hallway. It was empty.

I closed the door behind us, and the only light coming through was from the thin window above the stairs.

"I know you talked to Railius," she whispered.

"If you're here to beg on his behalf," I started, but she shook her head, loosing her fiery hair around her shoulders.

"He doesn't know I'm here. None of them do." Her accent was thicker as she whispered.

"They are going to try and take Ironbark without you," she explained. "Without what you know in your periphery, it's never going to work."

"I don't even know how to access my periphery," I clarified, and she shook her head again.

"But you could if you tried. If you really, really tried. If you weren't so busy pretending to be human," she said, the rage slipping back onto her features. I moved to turn away, and she reined it in quickly, reaching to wrap her fingers around my forearm. "I'm sorry. Listen. It's not just that, Eerie. It's not just that they will all die—*all* of them—if they run into this blind. It's that they're going up against *her*."

The inflection in her voice told me who she was talking about.

"Adelaide?" I asked, thinking of Red Lips from the drift. If there was a Hushed to fear, it was her. "Railius found her?"

"No. But she's close. Please, Eerie. We need your help tomorrow night."

My skin crawled at the sound of her plea. It was easier to dismiss her when she was being awful. I took a deep breath. I was not going to be pulled into this. Not for anything. *Tomorrow night.* She'd accidentally given the timing away.

"Why don't you just postpone the mission?"

Her eyes widened, like she could not believe how stupid I sounded.

"Because then, if Railius is right and she's looking for something about Ironbark, she gets it first." She stood up. "I thought I could reason with you. You're a bitch, but at least you understand what it's like to not want to lose someone you love."

"I'm sorry, Margaret. I just . . . I can't. I don't remember, and I am not going to risk remembering too much. Not now that I'm finally living. I can't."

Margaret's features hardened. "You're not sorry. If you were, you'd understand what you're sentencing us to—and *sorry* means nothing in the face of that."

She took off, ripping the bedroom door open.

I chased her, but by the time I'd reached the doorway, she was gone, my curtain blowing gently in the freezing night air.

TWENTY-NINE

"You're going to wear holes in that countertop, sweetie," Dee warned.

I pulled back, realizing I'd been lost in thought for the past ten minutes, scrubbing the same space of counter with a dishrag.

"Oh. Sorry," I said, pulling back and throwing the dish towel over my shoulder.

"Penny for your thoughts?" she asked. "Or is it one of them special thoughts, the kind you kids die if you tell?"

I laughed. "No. Nothing special. Just normal stuff."

I thought I'd feel better when I woke up. I'd severed myself from the Haunt, and I'd actually got seven hours of sleep. The world was my oyster, even if it was just going to be Dee and I during the late afternoon rush because Rory was going to be late to her shift. She had to meet with her adviser about transfer credits.

But something about Margaret's desperation sat in my stomach. I'd spent the whole day trying not to think about it.

Not my problem, I reminded myself.

The bell rang above the door, and I was surprised to see Reed walk in.

His eyes were clearer than I'd ever seen them, and he actually smiled as he walked up to the counter.

"Well hey there, puddin'," I said, using my best small-town waitress voice. Dee looked at me over the cash register.

"Come on, Dee. Copying is the sincerest form of flattery."

"I'll show you the sincerest form of flattery," she threatened.

I smiled and looked back to Reed. He was smiling, too, and I realized how long it had been since I'd seen him smile. Months, at least. It looked good on him. He was quite handsome when he wanted to be. "You seem . . . well. Different? I guess? And why are you off work so early?"

"Okay, Inquisitor General. How about a piece of apple pie before the questions?"

I got him a piece of pie from the case and slid open the low freezer, scooping out two huge globs of vanilla ice cream.

"Whoa. I didn't ask for all that," he said, sliding a cigarette behind his ear.

"Shhhhh," I said, sliding the plate toward him. "This is for helping me out. Also it's 'dress like a greaser day,' so you're in luck," I joked, circling an outward-facing palm in his general direction.

"I warned you not to talk about helping you. Now I'm going to have to tell everyone that we made sweet, nasty love with Eva's electrical whisk."

I laughed and grabbed a tray of utensils, setting it in front of me on the counter.

"How would that even work?" I asked, snagging a stack of napkins and starting to roll bundles.

"Carefully," he said through a mouth of pie.

I laughed.

He swallowed. "You seem different, too. The Winspeare lad working some of that old pelvic magic?"

I rolled my eyes and turned away, setting the crate of utensils on a shelf. I shot him a withering look over my shoulder.

"Hey, hey. Okay. I'm sorry," Reed said, lifting himself off the stool to reach out to me. "I just meant . . ." he took a deep breath and looked down at his plate for answers. "It looks like love has made you happy."

I turned back to him. The word felt strange in the air. The word I hadn't said, because it was too weird still. Too new. "It wasn't just that, exactly."

"What was it, then?" he asked, his face open and eager as he looked up. His eyes searched mine.

"I bared myself to someone, I guess," I caught my words and tried to preemptively cut him off, but he wasn't making a nasty joke out of it. He was listening. "I showed him all of me, all the good parts and the bad, and he still wanted them. I walked through fire to get there, and then there was worth it."

Reed smiled and looked down. "Sounds just peachy, kid," he said in his best greaser voice.

"Well. You'll figure it out one day."

He smiled, but it didn't reach his eyes. "I don't think so."

I nodded, looking around the diner. "She—or he—could be in here right now, admiring you from afar. You'll share a pop. Chaperoned sparks will fly."

Reed shook his head. "I don't think so. I'm a shard of a monster, aren't I? I can't be that different than my human. No one wants that on its best day."

My smile slipped off my face, and I shook my head. "What? No. Reed, that's not true."

He pushed the apple pie around his plate. "Come on," he said, shaking his head.

"No! Really! Think about it! She—"

"—what the fuck would you know, Eerie?" he said, glancing up but not meeting my eye.

I stepped back from the counter like I'd been slapped.

He shook his head and laughed, but it was a sad sound, like he was trying to use it to pave all the fissures he'd just shown.

"I'm just kidding," he said, his voice tight.

I stayed back.

He looked up, and his eyes were shining.

"Sorry," he said, smiling sadly. Almost like he was embarrassed.

He pulled out his wallet, but I shook my head.

"It's okay. On the house." I chanced a smile, but I knew whatever had just happened, whatever we'd just shared, was shattered.

I stepped back up to the counter.

He threw a five-dollar bill into the tip jar.

"Get you and that fella somethin' nice," he said.

I nodded, and he looked at me for a moment.

"Thank you, Eerie."

I inclined my head. He turned to go, and I grabbed his plate and set it on the dish rack, stealing a bite of the apple pie crust.

Reed stopped at the door. He looked back at me and popped the collar of his black jacket.

I laughed, and he left.

I turned around and snatched another piece of crust.

When I turned back, I froze.

Through the front window, I saw Reed, frozen as he looked to his right.

He looked at a group of three women. They all wore chunky sweaters, all with perfectly dyed and styled hair, all carrying shopping bags. Mrs. Bell, Jason's mother, was in the middle. I froze. The Bells never came this close to the diner. They hated this part of town.

I felt the earth tilt, and everything slowed. All sounds stopped.

No.

I shoved off the counter, and my shoes slipped against the wet tile. Reed turned his head.

"Reed! NO! REED!" I screamed, not caring if it startled anyone.

I saw his lips move.

Saw Mrs. Bell look up.

Saw her smile fall.

Saw her perfectly manicured hand fly to her mouth.

I jumped over the counter, spinning my legs around and launching myself toward the floor. I hurtled toward the glass door.

Reed's lips stopped moving.

He looked back through the window just as I reached the door.

I yanked it open against the freezing air just as he fell to his knees, and then tipped sideways.

"Reed! No. Reed, oh, God. Reed."

I slid, catching his head before it could crack against the street. The wet sludge soaked through my jeans.

Cars honked and swerved around me as I fought to shift Reed's body back onto the sidewalk.

I put my hands on either side of his face.

"Please. Reed, please," I whispered, my tears hitting his cheeks. His eyes were still wide open. His collar was still popped.

Dark tendrils spread up over the top of his tattered gray T-shirt.

I screamed. It shredded my throat, but I screamed until my breath was gone.

When I finally sucked in another breath, all I heard was Mrs. Bell's voice muttering, "What? What?! *What*?! Jason? What?" as one of her friends put an arm around her shoulders and the other snapped, "I am calling a cab, Debra! I can't hear a damn thing."

They stepped aside, and Rory turned the corner.

She stopped in her tracks when she saw us. The books fell from her hands and landed in the slush.

I screamed again, bringing Reed's head to my chest as I rocked back and forth on the ice.

THIRTY

Fabian and I sat in the front pew of the church. It was raining outside, and the parishioners who came in all had umbrellas and water-soaked coats.

Rory, Seph, and Eva had all left an hour earlier, but Fabian said he needed a little more time. I did, too. Rory had offered to bring me dry clothes, since my pants were still wet, but I didn't really want to change. It was stupid, but somehow, they helped me remember that the whole thing had happened. That Reed really had walked into the diner, ordered a piece of pie, and then died.

"Seven years. He didn't care about it for seven years and then he just gives in?" I asked quietly.

"Mrs. Bell wasn't in town that much, Eerie. Maybe he *did* care about it for seven years. Maybe that entire time he fought to make us believe he couldn't care less about that kid, when really it ate him alive," Fabian answered.

A woman in a light pink poncho lit one of the dozens of candles that sat at the base of the altar. She bowed her head and then stood, smiling at us as she walked down the center aisle. I inclined my head to her. When she opened the door at the back of the church, the sound of rain flooded the sanctuary. Then it closed, and we were the only two souls in the building. If you believed we had souls. I still wasn't so sure.

I thought about what Reed had said about Exhumed. That Hushed could have a second chance. I got why people would want hope in moments like this. Why Sarah thought we were just hijacked souls, taken from our place and forced to carry a secret that wasn't ours. It was tempting to think that Reed could come back somehow. That even now, maybe in death, he'd gone back to where he'd come from. Today, I imagined him somewhere better than I ever had before, and it suited him. I hoped he was there, now. That he was in a 1950s malt shop, living with his slick hair and a cigarette behind his ear in his own time, and the only secret he had was his crush on the town goodie-goodie.

I'd called Logan to tell him what happened and told him I'd call him later. I needed some time to detangle the threads of my mind.

Something in me had shifted as I'd held Reed's head in my lap, and I was reminded of it every time I swallowed and felt the sharp pain in the back of my throat where I was still raw from screaming.

You don't know because you don't want to know.

Margaret's words rang through my head, and I saw the image replay in my mind. Reed walking out of the door. Turning right. His eyes locking on Mrs. Bell.

You don't know because you don't want to know.

I could get up and leave this church and never come back. Go to Logan's cabin and kiss and pretend I was human. But I was Hushed. And if I didn't start acting like it, more would die. Svenja, Ajit, even Margaret . . . they would all be like Reed. They'd be cold, their eyes unseeing.

I had ignored it and shoved it down, somehow managing to convince myself that I was being brave by avoiding the truth. But I felt it the moment I saw Reed through that glass.

"Do you think your God hears us, Fabian?" I asked.

Reed had told him he was running to grab a coffee and that he'd be right back. He'd patted Fabian on the shoulder as he walked out of the garage. I still didn't know when Reed decided to do it. Or if he'd decided at all.

Fabian took a deep breath. "Yes."

"And you think we have a purpose? That we're not some weird accident or a punishment?"

"You know what I think."

"Yeah, but right now I need to hear it."

Fabian reached for my hand. "I think God once said that what was done in the dark will be brought to the light. He never said how."

I nodded, biting hard on the inside of my cheek.

"That book has some catchy lines," I said.

Fabian squeezed my hand as we gazed up at the facade of deep, polished wood and stained glass.

"I mean, yeah. That's one way to put it," he said.

"What's another good one?"

Fabian sighed. I leaned my head on his shoulder.

"Love is patient. Love is kind; love does not envy or boast; it is not arrogant or rude. It does not insist on its own way; it is not irritable or resentful; it does not rejoice at wrongdoing, but rejoices with the truth. Love bears all things, believes all things, hopes all things, endures all things."

I loved the sound of Fabian's voice echoing in his chest. It reminded me of being huddled up in a garage with him while he read a beat-up copy of *The Brothers Karamazov* until I fell asleep.

"Kind of an impossible standard. But I like it," I whispered.

"Hmmm. Reed liked that one, too."

I lifted my head. "Reed? Our Reed?"

Fabian smiled. "I'd say it sometimes at work when something wasn't going right. It helped me keep perspective. I would also say it when Reed was getting pissed at someone."

"Would it calm him down?"

"Not at all, but it made him more irritated at me, which was better than getting fired."

I laid my head back on his shoulder.

He took a deep, slow breath. "Sam's favorite is the one inscribed on the wall there," he said, pointing to our left, just above the bottom stair.

I sat up suddenly, looking over at him.

"What?" I asked.

Fabian met my eyes. "I was going to tell you sooner, but there wasn't really a good time."

"You remember?" I asked.

Fabian nodded. "Not everything. Not the secret."

I pushed myself up off the pew. "What do you remember?"

"Bits and pieces. That I belonged to Sam. That he used to come here after work sometimes. It was peaceful. And that he loved Madeline Winspeare."

I couldn't explain that I knew that already without telling him the whole story of my time with the Haunt.

"Sounds messy," I said, walking toward the spot on the wall Fabian had pointed to.

"I'm pretty sure it got them both killed."

I stared at the spot on the wall that he'd pointed to. The part with the scripture.

"Which verse was Sam's favorite?" I asked, just as my eyes found the words in the wood.

Fabian spoke. "Come to Me, all who are weary and heavy-laden, and I will give you rest."

And the ground fell out from under me.

One moment, I was there, sitting by the wall, and the next, I was back in the cell, with Madeline's reflection looking back at me, her face crumpled.

"Because he will destroy himself to save me, and I can't let him do that," Madeline said, her voice thick with tears.

"You know what happens tonight. Why would you try to turn him away?"

And then the perspective moved, like my line of sight was shifting. I could finally see who had been speaking in the corner of the cell after Sam left.

Because you love him?

Behind Madeline, a young man stood, his face pained as he met her gaze in the mirror.

Dr. Davie.

His eyes flicked up, meeting mine.

Ours.

I wasn't Madeline's Hushed.

I was his.

I saw everything. His lab, lit by a small desk lamp that sat directly above where I stirred.

Everything smudged.

Then he was in the woods, wearing a dark sweatshirt and carrying a backpack.

He stopped, kicking up a layer of leaves and reaching down to punch in a code.

The trapdoor opened and he slid down a ladder, landing at the top of a rickety, winding staircase.

At the bottom, he pulled a lab coat off a hook and punched in another code.

A wide white hallway. On the wall, lit in green, read, "Level 3B."

The level of Ironbark that wasn't supposed to exist.

The memory swirled and settled again.

Madeline was in the lab, a needle in her arm. Dr. Davie moved it, and she winced.

"Sorry," he said, and she smiled.

I felt the way his chest constricted at the sight, felt the way the surprise registered on my skin.

She doesn't deserve this.

It wasn't a new feeling. It slid through his chest easily, like it had worn grooves.

Whatever he had been doing, it had started to make him sick.

It flashed to the keypad at the base of the stairs again, and I saw his hand pull back before recommitting and punching in the numbers.

She doesn't deserve this.

Then we were back in Madeline's cell, Dr. Davie behind her. He looked at the picture of Logan, the sweet boy she left behind, the one who would never know how strong his mother was.

"I have to take your vitals now," he said, and she nodded.

"Of course. Have to do this by the books, right?" she asked.

The memory tilted, and when it righted itself, I saw from Dr. Davie's eyes once more.

The words taped up by Madeline's cell door, written by Sam:

Come to me, all who are weary and with heavy burden, and I will give you rest.

And then I was back in the church, staring at the words as my mind spun and my blood boiled. I'd fallen to my knees, and Fabian was beside me, rubbing my back.

"What happened?" he asked.

I didn't feel anything in my chest. I'd seen Dr. Davie, and I'd seen him walk in and out of the prison without officially signing in, but none of it tugged deep in my bones. I'd seen so much I felt like I would burst, but nothing stood out.

I still didn't know my secret.

"I belong to Dr. Davie," I whispered.

Fabian sat back.

"What else?" he pressed.

I shook my head. "I don't know. I saw weird fragments, kind of like you. Images."

"Do you feel the Pull?"

I shook my head and looked up at the words.

The words had triggered the memory. Madeline kept them in her cell.

I stopped.

The words pulled at my mind, and suddenly, Madeline's handwriting slid across my memory.

There are so many people here willing to shoulder the burden of the pain we all feel.

Then Sam's.

Um dia você vai saber onde pesam os fardos e então não vai mais se sentir solitário.

Burdens.

They were trying to tell us something.

"Wait," Fabian said. I followed his gaze to the candle that rested below the scripture.

It was high up, barely used. He reached up and pulled it out of the sconce. Carefully, he tipped it, pouring the wax out onto the railing, and we both saw something rested at the bottom.

A necklace.

Fabian looked up at me, and then pulled the necklace out of the candle, blowing to try and cool the wax.

I knew what was happening, though I don't really know how I knew. It was the crash I always waited for—the moment when a Hushed remembered. Whatever this necklace was, it triggered his memories. I'd never seen it before. But his eyes were darting rapidly under his closed eyelids, and his hand clasped tight over the chain of the necklace. Half of me waited for the fear, for the part of me that would reach out and grab Fabian's face and scream to shake him loose. But that didn't come.

He wanted to know, and I had to let him.

I had to trust him. I had to watch this weird transformation and know that he would still be my brother at the end of it, no matter what.

He opened his eyes and let out a sharp exhale.

"It was for me to give to Logan," he said, smiling softly as he closed his eyes. "Sam left it here the night he died."

I clenched and unclenched my teeth as the words settled in.

Logan was Fabian's Wounded.

Fabian looked up at me. "It's okay, Eerie."

"It's far from 'okay,'" I said, and Fabian took my hand. I knelt down next to him. My heart hammered in my chest.

He brushed the wax away. It was a pewter cross, just like Logan's. Fabian turned it over. Numbers were etched into the back. He remembered.

"GPS coordinates to a lockbox. Madeline would've flipped if she knew, but Sam knew that if something went wrong, if they didn't make it out, Logan wouldn't stop looking until he found answers."

That was true. I hated that it was true.

"What's in it?" I asked.

Fabian looked up from the necklace.

"It's filled with almost every secret given to a Harborer at Ironbark.

The Harborers gave them to Madeline, and she gave them to Sam. He never read them, that's why they never became attached to him."

My chest hollowed.

"So . . . so all the other Hushed died that night—"

"—but they didn't take the secrets with them, like the Internment wanted," Fabian finished, a smile turning up the corners of his mouth.

"Did you see how the fire started?" He shook his head.

My head was swimming, and I shut my eyes tight.

"And where is the lockbox?" I asked.

"Um. Well."

I opened my eyes.

"Fabian."

"Ironbark. Beneath Sam's locker on level 2B. He built it deep beneath the base."

"But you can't get close to Ironbark," I reminded him. "It's not safe."

"No. I've never *chosen* to get close because it wasn't worth the risk. Now there's a reason."

"Fabian," I said, swallowing down the words I wanted to shout at him. I took a deep breath. We couldn't get in a fight right now. I stood, ignoring the way the world tilted as I walked over to the first pew.

"Fabian, Logan just got his life back. If you bring this up, if you give him this . . . I'll lose both of you, and I can't."

Fabian touched my cheek.

"What did I say? What have I said all along? I need to know the truth in order to figure out what to do with it, Eerie. I know how far Logan's come, and I wouldn't take that from either of you. But I still have to find it. The box was Sam's, and I need to protect it. I need to find a way into Ironbark as soon as possible."

Ironbark. Where the box of written secrets was waiting—the box that Fabian alone could find. Ironbark, which was going to be attacked by the Haunt, tonight.

"No. Don't get anywhere near Ironbark tonight," I said, looking up into Fabian's eyes. "We need to get home. Now."

THIRTY-ONE

I ran into my room. I could tell from Rory's untouched bed that she hadn't been home yet.

My mind was far away as I reached under my bed and pulled out my boots.

My cell phone rang again, and I picked it up.

"Hey," Logan's voice said on the other end.

"Hey," I answered back, pressing the cell phone between my shoulder and ear as I yanked the laces on my boots.

"Are you okay?" he asked. "Do you need to get out? Want me to come get you?"

"No. Fabe and I just got back from the church. I just need to rest, I think."

I stared out the window, looking down the street into the darkness. Wet, icy slush reflected on the pavement, and my mind remembered the sickening way Reed's knees gave way. The way the ice bit through my jeans as I slid to catch him.

I looked up at the ceiling.

"Can I come get you for breakfast tomorrow?" Logan asked, and I smiled despite the tightness in my chest.

"Absolutely," I whispered.

I wanted to tell him. I hated keeping secrets. But I knew he'd tell me not to go if I did, or worse—he'd want to come. Fabian had promised to leave it be for the night, but I knew I couldn't keep him from answers for long. If I could find the box first, I could bring it to him and keep him safe.

My eyes darted down, taking in the dark street once more, and something caught my eye.

Lights at the end of the street.

Three. Then five. Then six.

"I'm gonna go, okay, Logan? I'm really tired."

"I'll text you in the morning."

"Okay. Love you. Bye," I said, hanging up.

I looked down at the phone in panic.

I just told Logan I loved him, and the fear that bit up the back of my throat felt new and terrifying and . . . good, somehow. I didn't mean to say it. But that didn't make it untrue. I let out a small laugh.

I loved him.

Seph appeared in the doorway.

"Eerie? There's someone here to see you." Her voice was strained.

"Who?" I asked.

She shrugged and disappeared.

I followed her down the hallway and glanced into Fabian's room. It was empty.

"Seph? Where is Fabian?"

She stopped at the top of the stairs.

"He went out, I think."

I froze.

Fire ripped up through my limbs. He was going to Ironbark. He was going to do exactly what I'd asked him not to do, and he was going to get killed in the process.

I stopped at the window above the stairs and looked out.

The lights were getting closer, and I could see their sources now.

Flashlights, cell phones, and . . . a literal torch. I cranked open the window, and the frozen air slipped over the sill. I shivered but didn't move until I was sure of what I was seeing. Then, I heard a hint of words. A melody.

What's in a man should stay with him
What's his should never walk . . .

Gravediggers. A dozen of them. And I knew where they were headed.

It couldn't be. Gravediggers kept their violence under the radar. They didn't do *this*.

I stepped back from the window. I had my gun, but it would do nothing against a mob.

"Eerie!" Seph called from downstairs.

I had to get Eva and Seph out of the Boneyard.

My phone buzzed in my pocket, and I shut it off as I jumped the last six stairs.

I landed at the bottom, and Seph stood by the open front door.

Standing there in an immaculate navy suit, her coral lipstick bright and perfectly lined, was Officer Waybourne from the Internment.

"Oh, this isn't a great time," I said. I laughed and turned around, leaving Waybourne in the doorway. "Eva!" I looked to Seph. "Get Eva. *Now.*"

Seph nodded and ran up the stairs. I shoved what I deemed to be important into a reusable grocery bag.

"I trust I'm not interrupting?" she said, though I could tell she didn't care. "We have come across some disturbing information, Ms. . . ." She looked down at her notes.

"Ashwood," I said, half-listening as I chucked bottles of water into the bag.

She continued as though I hadn't said anything.

". . . 900628. Regarding your very public relationship with a certain Logan Winspeare."

I stopped then, giving her a withering stare.

"You hear that, right? The people *marching* this way? I trust you saw the Gravediggers when you drove up here. SEPH! HURRY UP!" I yelled.

"Gravedigging is illegal. We are here to discuss your actions, so please stop trying to deflect."

My phone buzzed. I ignored it and pushed Waybourne as I moved to the place where Eva kept cash tucked under a fruit bowl.

"Logan Winspeare and I are together. Either help me right now or shove your stipend up your ass and get the fuck out of my house."

Waybourne narrowed her eyes, and I could see her biting back her own similarly colorful reply. "I'm going to have to have you fill out this paperwork and sign at the bottom, acknowledging your confession."

"*Confession*? You have a scarlet letter you'd like me to pin to my shirt, too?"

The sound of the chant wafted in, and Officer Waybourne finally turned, like it just dawned on her that she might be in danger too.

Eva and Seph ran down the stairs, rucksacks over their shoulders. Eva shoved past Officer Waybourne, and Seph and I followed. I handed Seph the bag I'd packed.

The chant sounded like a roar coming up the street. Once we cleared the high hedges at the end of the driveway, my heart clenched in my throat.

I'd thought there were a dozen, but there were at least fifty, with Jason Bell leading the group. I saw the hatred in his eyes, the rage etched on his features as he shouted the words. *No deed nor look should crawl back up and sure as hell should never talk.* Tansy walked next to him, her lower jaw jutted forward, her glittering purple leggings throwing fragments of light like a disco ball.

He started this. Jason started this because Reed told his darkest, most painful thing.

Officer Waybourne unlocked her silver Camry with a click of her keychain.

I pushed Seph toward the car, but Officer Waybourne held up her hand. "It's *really* against protocol to have any civilians in an official vehicle," she said, her voice sticky sweet.

My stomach dropped. "Are you serious?"

"They're going to rip us apart," Eva explained.

"Gravedigging is illegal," she repeated as the chant grew louder. "I'm really sorry," she said, opening the door and sliding inside. I yanked on the passenger door, but she locked it just in time.

"They are going to *kill* us!" I shrieked, climbing on top of her hood.

The lights of the torches washed the street in an orange glow. "Take my family!" I yelled into the windshield.

Officer Waybourne ignored me, shooting backward. I jumped off the hood just in time, scooping down to grab a clump of snow and hurtling it at her windshield as she pulled on to the street.

There was nowhere to go in the snow, no help for miles in any direction but the one the Gravediggers were coming from.

They were just past Mr. Cauly's, making a path for Officer Waybourne's vehicle, and I immediately understood why they were marching, even with the cold. They wanted this to be public. The crowd had grown as they got closer. They were counting on supporters joining them . . . and they had.

I took a deep breath, looking from Seph to Eva.

"What are you doing?" Eva asked as I took several steps toward the street.

"Protecting our family," I replied, turning. Then I walked out of the mouth of our driveway. "Looking for me, dickwads?" I shouted into the night.

Jason signaled for the group to stop walking, and they did.

His eyes glittered like two pools of rotten blood in the firelight.

My phone buzzed in my pocket.

"Eerie!" Seph called, but Eva covered her mouth and pulled her up the driveway. I kept talking, hoping my voice would cover Seph's.

"Well, you found me, and I have to tell you, *I am in no mood*. Also, *huge* waste of manpower, with only one Hushed home to scare," I said, throwing my arms out. "By the way, Tansy, sweetie. Your leggings shrunk in the wash, so sorry."

"We should've done this a long time ago," Jason said through his teeth. Even in the firelight, with a whole house distance separating us, I could see his face was swollen from crying.

He pulled out a knife, and fear unraveled in my limbs.

I don't know what I'd been expecting. A pitchfork, or something? But the sight of the blade glinting in the firelight made it real.

The horn was so loud I thought the sky was falling.

It came out of nowhere, splitting the night with its odd little jingle. *Da-da-da-da-duuuuummm da-da-da-da-duuummmm* . . . the

"La Cucaracha" melody I was used to hearing every Sunday morning.

Then Mr. Cauly backed his tank of a truck out of his driveway. He careened right between the mob and me, the exhaust from his ancient muffler clouding the air. He slammed on the brakes and still slid three feet back.

His Vietnam veteran flags were flying from both windows, and when he rolled down the passenger glass to yell at me, I saw that he was wearing an American flag bandana around his head. "Get in!" he shouted.

I motioned for Eva and Seph to come, and they ran toward us.

I heard things hitting the opposite side of the truck as I opened the door and helped Eva and Seph inside. Shouts rose into the night.

"Dammit to hell in a fiery sin wagon," Mr. Cauly mumbled, pulling an old revolver from his glove compartment and cranking a hand lever that opened a sunroof.

He stood up through it—he was very nimble for a man pushing ninety—and fired three shots into the night. Several members of the crowd screamed, and they all backed up.

"Hey! HEY! This is *my* neighborhood, and *I* get to decide who dies on this street! And *I* say it's the first person that throws another dagnab thing at my truck! Got it!?"

I jumped up onto the footrest outside the passenger door, and a hand grabbed my arm. I yelped and looked back.

It was Railius, wearing a black baseball cap and jeans. He carried a hockey stick.

"What the hell?" I asked, stepping down from the truck.

"I saw them on Main and heard them talking. I followed. My car is just behind those houses," he said with a jerk of his head.

Mr. Cauly turned his gun on to Railius, but I held my hands up. "He's cool!"

"What?" Mr. Cauly barked.

"It means don't shoot!" Seph yelled over the back seat.

"Who is this?" Eva asked.

"A friend. Look. I'll meet you at Our Shepherd of the Faith. Go there and wait. I'll be fine! Go!"

I slammed the door, and Mr. Cauly's truck sputtered and popped.

Railius and I ran across the street, disappearing in a cloud of fumes.

When I could breathe, I stopped. We were in my neighbor's back-yard, hiding behind their swing set.

He threw the hockey stick into the bushes.

"A hockey stick?" I asked.

"Just trying to fit in with the mob."

Thunder clapped overhead, and raindrops fell. Soft at first, and then faster.

My phone buzzed again.

I pulled it out of my pocket, thought better of it, and stuck it back inside.

"How did you know I was going to come help you?" I asked.

Railius put his hands on his knees. "I didn't. I was going to come beg you. What made you change your mind?"

I stood upright. I couldn't afford any more detours, but I was start-ing to realize that I would probably never trust Railius.

"You're not the begging type," I said. I narrowed my eyes at him. The sight of him—from his dark shirt to the way his hair fell in his eyes—brought back the memory of that night. The threats he made. The way I'd watched him kiss Samira. I hated the way he held my eyes, hated that it took effort to look away.

I wanted to help, but that didn't mean I had to like him.

He took the baseball cap off and tossed it into the darkness.

"Not usually. But this is a special occasion. We don't have much time to try to figure out how to make you recall a little bit of the floor plan—"

"You don't have to worry about that," I said, my voice clipped.

Railius's eyes searched mine, and he nodded. He understood. I'd remembered. Some, anyway. Enough to be of use.

"Is that why you came with me?" Railius asked.

I didn't want him to know that I wanted to help them. He didn't deserve to know that. That the thought of Svenja or Ajit or even Mar-garet dying felt too much like losing Sarah or Reed. It would just give him more to exploit.

I took another deep breath and started walking toward the car.

"I came because I think my brother is going to get himself killed."

THIRTY-TWO

Railius took the entire mountain road at eighty miles per hour, and it was everything I could do to not throw up as he told me the plan in clipped, quiet tones. They were tracking Connelly Stewart, and a Haunt operative would kill him at midnight. We had to be on level 3B, ready to gather whatever Hushed may show up and get them into the woods. It was 11:05.

I agreed to help, with one condition—we check level 2B for Fabian. I hoped he wasn't there. I hoped that he wasn't that stupid. Railius agreed, no contingencies. It wasn't like him.

"You weren't lying about Adelaide?" I asked.

"No, I wasn't." It scared me to hear his voice come out so small.

"Are you going to tell me what happened?"

"There is no time, and it doesn't matter now."

"Can you at least tell me what she wants?" I asked.

"Darkness and death. The unraveling of everything. War between humans and Hushed."

"So, the same thing she's always wanted," I replied.

Railius looked at me strangely. He wasn't used to someone knowing Adelaide like I did.

He nodded.

"How much backup did you call?"

Railius kept his eyes on the road. "None. There's a chance the other cells are being watched, and I couldn't risk blowing our cover for this mission. We might have cover from a nearby cell for our exit, but that's it."

"So we are the only hope," I clarified, trying not to sound frightened.

Railius nodded.

The ravine was dark, but I was sure-footed. I stepped over fallen trees and avoided low-hanging branches. I even counted steps like I'd done the walk hundreds of times before. I hadn't, but Dr. Davie had. And I remembered every time.

"You sure know where you're going," Railius whispered, tripping over a branch. It gave me more satisfaction than I wanted to admit.

"Yes," I answered as he got up. Short and sweet. I liked that he started talking first. For the first time since I'd met him, I felt like I had the upper hand.

Then, we were there.

Ironbark sat on the bottom of the ravine, its great stone face dark and foreboding in the gray haze and rain.

I'd never wanted to be here again. If it were up to me, I'd spend the rest of my life on the opposite side of the earth from this hideous thing.

Yet here I am. Again.

I felt the familiar burn of fear release from the back of my neck and spread over my jaw. I clenched my teeth and curled my fingers up in a ball. *Not now.*

The adrenaline raged, but I managed to keep my mind clear enough to keep my wits.

Railius let out a low whistle, and someone dropped down from the tree next to us.

"Fuck," I breathed, throwing my hand over my heart.

Svenja smiled. "I knew you'd come around," she said, hugging me. She smelled like peonies. Peonies. In the middle of a bloody war zone.

My phone buzzed again. It was Logan, but it stopped after two rings.

"Have you seen my brother around here?" I whispered to Svenja.

She shook her head. "Sorry, love. I haven't been looking."

"He's kind of hard to miss," I mumbled. I looked around.

"Wait. Where are Ajit and Margaret?"

"On the other side of the ravine. They'll cover us when we need to get out."

I nodded.

"Lead the way, Eerie," Railius said, a strange respect in his voice.

I stepped forward, slipping in mud.

A bullet whizzed past my head and buried itself into the tree trunk just inches from my face.

"What the hell?" I hissed.

Svenja put a finger to her ear. "Um. Yes. That was Margaret. She says 'Hi.'"

It was now or never, and I pushed through the trees. Dr. Davie had walked that path almost every day. He wasn't just in Ironbark for monthly checkups or to oversee executions. He was there every day, taking the secret way in, and working on the floor that wasn't supposed to exist.

I hadn't stopped long enough to hate him. I hadn't had time. But there, in the dark, walking the path he'd walked, I started to. He had growing dread and reservations—I got that much from my periphery. But it wasn't enough to stop him.

Svenja came up beside me.

"Thank you," she whispered, and I was grateful for the distraction. I could hate Dr. Davie all I wanted, but I was still part of him. My worst fears were true. For the first time in my life, I started to understand Reed, and it made the weight in my chest over losing him that much heavier.

"Don't thank me yet. Let's just not get killed."

The trapdoor was halfway down the hill, and we were soaked by the time we reached it.

I kicked the debris sideways and leaned down, my fingers hovering over the keypad as I took a deep breath. I followed where my fingers led, trying to ignore the raindrops pelting the back of my head.

11. 4. 17. 28. 21. 21. 15. 5.

Nothing happened.

"Does it even still work?"

A hand scanner lit up, though the light was dim enough that those on the hillside would never be able to see it.

I stopped for a moment, and then put my hand against it.

It's making sure I'm not Hushed.

Of course. They would've made provisions in case he was killed.

They hadn't counted on the slip pill. It read that I was human.

A little green light in the corner of the door lit up, flashing twice.

Beep beep. It popped open.

The light turned red, and for a moment I worried that I'd just sent a signal. Somewhere, someone knew that this door was open.

Then I remembered. Nothing about 3B was in the records. Even most of the security detail on the main floor didn't know it existed.

The winding stairs were just as I remembered them. Out of instinct, I skipped the third to last step and told Railius and Svenja to do the same. When I got to the bottom, I looked back. It was rusted out. It looked like it had been out for some time. Dr. Davie always avoided that step.

I punched in a different set of numbers at the door.

13. 6. 29. 26.

With a thick hiss, the sliding door opened.

The hallway was massive, with the white tiles reflecting the fluorescents, making the whole place almost too bright. I had to squint until my eyes adjusted.

"There's a patrol that goes into the stairwell above every fifteen minutes," Railius explained, pulling two guns from a holster over his shoulders and handing me one. Svenja re-laced a boot as Railius spoke.

My eyes were pulled to a doorway on my left.

Railius was still talking when I walked over and punched in another code that came to my mind, unbidden.

"Eerie? This is important," he warned.

"So is this," I whispered to myself.

The door popped open.

The room still smelled like bleach and lemon-scented cleaner, though someone had turned all the furniture upright.

I felt someone behind me as I walked toward the familiar desk.

"Eerie?" Svenja whispered.

I stepped closer to it, craning my head to look below. I knelt on the ground where I had stirred.

My phone buzzed again, but I didn't even feel it, really. The memory of that night rushed through me like a fed flame, and I saw everything.

Dr. Davie, who was supposed to check Madeline Winspeare out of her cell and lead her to the lab for the first trial run of his new procedure, decided that he couldn't go through with it.

Instead, he decided to help Sam MacDonald get Madeline out. Together, they were going to expose what the Internment was doing to the inmates, as well as the experiments they were financing. They were going to tell the world about the war the Internment was planning to start.

I saw glimpses.

Dr. Davie meeting Sam in the break room. Both of them walking toward Madeline's cell. They escorted her down to level 3B, but there were more guards on the bottom level than they expected. Dr. Davie shouted at Madeline and Sam, telling them to *run*. But he didn't know about the fail-safe.

The kill-switch the Internment had installed in case anyone tried to escape.

It went off seconds after the guards found Sam and Madeline, setting dozens of fires throughout the prison in a matter of seconds and locking all the doors.

The Internment would rather kill everyone inside than let one person escape to tell their secrets.

Some of the other guards realized what was happening and tried to fight their way out, but several Internment loyalists shot all those trying to escape. Dr. Davie was reaching for a fire extinguisher when a guard shot him from behind. Madeline and Sam locked themselves in a stairwell, where they died from smoke inhalation ten minutes later.

I saw flames and blood. I saw Madeline and Sam holding each other as they took their final breaths.

The screams grew louder in my memory until a sob wrenched from my chest, pulling me back into the present. I was standing in the lab, tears streaming down my cheeks.

I lurched forward, reaching for the bottom of the desk, pulled by the edges of a memory. My fingers searched the bottom of the underside of the desk, stopping when they hit the fraying, cracked paper taped there.

Carefully, I pulled the paper loose. With shaking fingers, I opened it.

If you are reading this, I am sorry. It means you exist, and I do not. I leave you with a terrible legacy. When Connelly contracted me to develop this procedure, I knew I should have said no, should have turned down this post and moved back to New York. But I couldn't pass up this chance for unlimited funding, and for that I am deeply ashamed. Now you exist, my Hushed, and you know what damage this horrible knowledge can do. I beg you, please. Do not give in to what your very essence asks you to do. Fight to right this devastating wrong I have committed. I hope you will find this note, along with the coat and boots I left for you. You must run, and never stop. Connelly was not the only one who knew what I was trying to accomplish here. There are bigger threats, and they will be hunting you.

I'm so deeply sorry. Only now, hours from committing professional and possibly quite literal suicide, do I understand what Oppenheimer meant when he said: "I am become death, the destroyer of worlds."

I am become death, so you must become more.

—W. Davie

I wiped tears from my face with the back of my hand.

This room was so full of sadness. I knew what he was doing there. The procedure he intended to practice on Madeline. I knew what kind of hell it could raise.

I'd thought this knowledge would consume me, tear me up with its terrible teeth and spit me out, leaving a gaping wound in my chest that would shred my mind and send me running for my Wounded.

But for the first time, I felt purpose, and it filled me with a fire I had never felt before.

I am become death, so you must become more.

The procedure he'd discovered was going to be used to extract Hushed from living people. And while the Internment vowed that it would only be used in the direst situations, Dr. Davie knew better. That's why he was quoting Oppenheimer, the father of the atomic bomb.

He had created something that was going to be theoretical. Rare. But weapons never stay rare.

I am become death, Oppenheimer had said.

And Dr. Davie knew his procedure would be just as dangerous. The Internment would give the procedure to the military, who would use it to extract whatever they wanted from whoever they wanted. And that wasn't even considering what atrocities would be visited upon innocent Hushed that were pulled into existence.

No secret would be safe. It would be the beginning of the death of free will. My mind spun as I thought about how many secrets were kept to keep people safe. How many secrets were kept to keep lives together.

"Eerie," Railius said, his voice strong enough to make me jump.

I spun around, and Railius motioned for me to follow. This would have to wait. We had to go get Fabian. I stuffed the note in my pocket.

"Are you okay?"

I nodded and wiped away the last of my tears.

I looked down at my watch. 11:35.

We moved soundlessly up the stairs to level 2B. Svenja stood behind me and pulled out two small, curved blades. The handles were bent inward and wrapped with leather binding. I looked at her over my shoulder.

"You brought knives to a gunfight?" I hissed.

"They're called falcatas," she whispered, spreading her fingers wide and redoubling her grip, "and believe me. The Internment made a mistake bringing guns to my knife fight."

When I didn't say anything, she winked.

Level 2B looked nothing like the one below. Where there had been tile and well-lit hallways, there was now rough concrete and open bulbs. The fire damage was more evident up here.

Three guards were headed our way from the other direction, one wearing a hat that said "security." I held up three fingers over my shoulder to Railius and Svenja as I looked around the corner. When they were ten feet away from us, the guard in the hat stopped. Without a word, he reached up and hit the guard over the head, knocking him out. When the second guard turned back, the one in the hat punched him in the face.

"What the—"

The guard took the hat off and turned to face us.

Logan.

"What the hell?" I hissed, stepping out from behind the corner. Railius and Svenja followed.

"I ran to your house when I heard about the mob and saw Seph and Eva in that guy's truck. They told me what happened and that you'd run off with 'a friend.'"

"How did you get that?" I gestured to the guard's uniform.

"Felony record? I'm good at this sort of thing." Logan shrugged, as though that explained everything. He pulled a gun from one of the passed-out guards and handed it to me.

"We don't have time for twenty questions," Railius said brusquely, pushing past us with his gun braced in his hands. "Stay with us, Winspeare. We'll get Fabian, and then you two are getting out of here."

My face burned as Logan looked at me, his expression puzzled.

"What is this, Eerie? I thought we were done with the Haunt."

"Let's survive this, and I'll tell you everything. At least, what I can without, you know. Dying. Okay?" I said.

He kissed me quickly. An agreement.

The locker room was a wide space with metal rafters running across the ceiling and lockers lining all the walls. A small closet with a mesh door was tucked in the far-right corner.

Fabian was kneeling at the base of an open locker that sat in a corner. He looked up, startled, when we walked in. "What is this?"

"What is *this?*" I snapped, pushing forward. "I told you to not do anything tonight!"

"Yeah, 'cause we always listen to each other," he quipped.

His eyes went from me to Railius, to Logan in the guard's uniform, and then to Svenja. My breath stilled in my throat as I remembered . . . Fabian belonged to Sam.

I could see the tension on Fabian's face, but before I could tell Logan to leave, Fabian shook his head. "It's fine, Eerie," he said, answering my unasked question. "I feel the Pull, but it's not bad. Probably because there is something else I need to get to. Something bigger than just one secret."

Logan's eyes widened, but he took it in stride as he looked at my brother and nodded once.

"If you feel it getting stronger, tell me," Logan said, and Fabian returned the nod.

Fabian turned back to the locker, and Svenja closed the door before standing in front of it. Logan stood next to her, pulling the hat lower and keeping his eyes fixed out the narrow window into the hallway.

"Whatever this is, it's important, Eerie," Fabian explained.

"11:42. You have thirty seconds," Railius warned. I looked over Fabian's shoulder. Deep inside, at least a foot down, was a metal box. It fit just inside, with its edges wedged in.

Fabian grunted, trying to pull it out again and failing. "We can fight later. It's wedged." He looked back at Railius. "Who is this guy?"

"Railius," I answered.

Fabian paused.

"Like . . . *Railius* Railius?"

I nodded, purposefully keeping my eyes from his. "And he says you have thirty seconds, and you'd better believe him."

"Fabe, will this work?" Rory called out, walking out of the closet with some WD-40 in hand.

Railius looked up at the sound of her voice and his face tightened, turning the color of ash.

Fabian yanked the box one more time, and it wrenched free.

"Got it," he said, triumph in his voice.

Railius spoke, and it was so low I almost didn't hear him. "Adelaide."

"What?" Rory asked.

There was just enough moment for a breath, and then all hell broke loose.

Railius lifted his gun at Rory, and she dropped the can she'd been holding.

Svenja stepped away from the door, her blades ready for a fight.

"Whoa, what the hell?" Rory asked, her voice high-pitched and panicked. Fabian stood up, and Railius pulled another gun from the back of his holster and pointed it at Fabian's chest. Logan whipped out his gun and pointed it at Railius's chest just as I pointed my gun at Railius' head.

Then Svenja took a step forward and wrapped her blade tight around Logan's neck.

"Don't move," Railius said, his eyes fixed on Rory.

"Railius! This is a mistake," I hissed. "A mistake we don't have time for."

Railius shook his head. "The whole time. You were right with her the whole time," Railius said, a manic, breathy laugh escaping from him.

Rory's eyes filled with tears, and she looked at me.

"Eerie. What's he talking about?" she whispered.

"Railius. She's my best friend. I've known her for years. She's not Adelaide. You're imagining things, and it's 11:45. We don't have time for this."

I met Logan's eyes. His hand worked its way slowly to Svenja's arm, and he squinted at me.

I understood.

Now.

Logan yanked free of Svenja, and it seemed like everything slowed down. Fabian knocked the gun out of Railius's hand, and Railius knocked Fabian back against the lockers before turning back to Rory, his eyes filled with a wild hatred.

The gun clattered to the floor, and I lunged at him.

Without skipping a beat, he pulled a knife from his boot and held it out, and I stopped just in time so that the tip of the blade touched my chest.

I looked up and met Railius's eyes, and everything went black.

THIRTY-THREE

The drift was sudden and urgent. I was back in the streets again, with the tile hot against my feet, the smell of roasting meat and woodsmoke filling my senses. I was deeper than I'd ever been in a drift.

I was seeing it through Samira's eyes, and I knew what she knew. I felt what she felt, and the line between our thoughts blurred.

Salernum. I knew the name of the city. The air was heavy with rain that beckoned steam from the torches.

Railius was next to me then, as I'd seen him before. His hair was damp. His cloak was thick and deep purple, his steps decisive as we wound through the streets. He reached out and took my hand in his. We walked faster, keeping close to vendors selling eel fried in olive oil and *mulsum*—honeyed wine. They shouted at us as we passed, but I kept my head down. I was wearing silk lined with gold trim, my feet laced in sandals.

I knew we were supposed to meet Adelaide in the square to go to the docks. Adelaide, who'd taught me how to skin a rabbit and paint my lips with berry juice.

Railius stopped, pulling me to the side so a merchant with a wide cart of dates piled high in red clay jugs could pass through.

I looked over at him.

There was hope on his face, and I understood the weird feeling in my chest when he met my eyes.

Railius, who'd become Samira's best friend over the five years. While Adelaide had taught her how to sharpen a blade, Railius had taught her how to stitch a wound and tell a joke.

She trusted him. When he said they would get through the town undetected, meet Adelaide at the docks, and leave the peninsula forever, she trusted him. Even though this is where her Wounded lived, if he said she would be fine, then she would be fine.

We kept the hoods over our heads.

The worry was thick and real in my chest.

We would only be there for a few more minutes. We'd meet Adelaide in the square and we'd be free.

Men with leather-plated armor walked past us, and one with a skinny face and thick lips looked twice at me. Shouts sounded from somewhere deep in the square, and Railius stopped as three more soldiers turned the corner and walked toward us.

Railius pulled me into a thin walkway, barely enough to walk through, and I pressed my back to the wall. He covered me, and I ducked my head against his shoulder.

It will be over soon, he said.

I wanted to agree, but the Pull was like someone had flipped a switch in my chest. It was like wires were in between my skin and muscle, bending in the direction I was supposed to go. Samira's Wounded was an alchemist. She was to tell him what the emperor had learned before he died. The Pull *hurt*. It burned and bent, like someone was brushing a torch against my chest.

I sucked air through my teeth. My hands found the side of his head.

Think of something else, he told me, his voice tightening at the sight of my pain.

Maybe it was fear. Maybe adrenaline. Or maybe just five years' worth of looks and laughs and firelight talks. Either way, the kiss happened.

I lifted my head. My lips brushed against his chin and then found his mouth.

He leaned his head down and met my lips, and it was like I'd opened a furnace.

It was the kiss I'd seen in the drift before, and it was as deep, as disarming, and as exposing as it seemed.

This was a cutout of a time and place, a memory that stained deep into the paper but didn't roll over the edges, so I surrendered to it. I fell further into the drift as I fell deeper into the kiss, as though it was grounding me.

It was holding me to the earth. Anchoring me.

The shouts grew louder, and I pulled away, looking over his shoulder. I took him by the hand and followed the alleyway.

I didn't know what the commotion was, but we needed to find Adelaide. Quickly.

We turned a corner, pushing past a woman who was dying fabric with deep, black berries, and found ourselves staring into a line of soldiers.

"Come with us. The council would like to have a word with you both," a portly guard with a sweaty upper lip said.

I looked back at Railius, but I knew there was no way around it.

He nodded.

"We're just travelers. They take people aside and question them all the time. It is routine," he whispered in my ear as we walked.

He came up alongside me, lacing his fingers through mine.

As we emptied out onto the main courtyard, I knew he was wrong.

"What happened?" I yelled as I looked out at the crowd gathering in front of the council steps.

My foot slipped on a stone step, and he caught me with one arm.

There were hundreds of people, and they parted as we passed through them, led by guards.

Monster, someone hissed. Another person spat, just missing my foot.

Railius was confused now, too, and he rested his hand close to his hip, where I knew he kept a blade. Not that it would do us any good here, with hundreds of people and dozens of soldiers surrounding us.

The Ghost of Adrenian Pass, someone else whispered.

We passed the center of the courtyard where a bronze statue stood, its shoulders back, arms raised aloft.

As we passed it, I froze.

Several men and women, dressed in the finest silk, stood on the steps leading into the bathhouse. One stood in the very back, his mouth twisted in a sneer.

The alchemist. Samira's Wounded. The Pull buckled within me, searing my bones.

I stopped, and Railius stopped with me. He saw the man on the steps and understood.

"Keep moving," the soldier behind me said.

"Railius," I whispered, and my voice was hers, lower and filled with panic.

I'd never told him what the secret was. I never needed to, until now.

Panic rose in my chest as the words floated into my mouth like bile. They filled my nose and mouth, and it was like I was going to choke on the absolute destruction they could bring.

I was going to tell him. This evil man who was in my periphery as a boy, drowning a childhood rival in a creek after a ball game had turned sour.

The words rose in my throat.

I pulled on Railius's hand.

The closer I got, the stronger it became.

Samira was going to tell this man how to ruin the world, and I could feel her panic, because I'd just felt it minutes before in Dr. Davie's lab.

"Please," I said, and Railius stopped. I pulled him close and whispered into his ear.

"If I tell him, he will know how to pull secrets out of people while they still live. It's what the emperor did not live long enough to accomplish."

Railius pulled back and looked at me, and his eyes reflected my terror.

That's what Samira knew. How to pull Hushed out of people while they were still alive.

"Freedom will die, and terror will reign for our kind and theirs," I finished.

Fear stretched across Railius's face.

"Keep moving," the soldier ordered.

I reached down and grabbed Railius's blade.

"Please," Samira's voice begged.

The alchemist started walking down the steps.

Railius shook his head, a resolute *no*. "Adelaide will be here," he said, but I shook my head and pulled the knife closer.

"Please. I'm going to die anyway. Please don't let him win like this."

Railius was horrified, but I wrapped my hand around his hand lifted the blade.

I whispered *please please please* and took a deep breath as the last of her resistance failed. The alchemist was within earshot.

"He knew how to—" I started, and Railius pulled the blade above his head.

He screamed and brought the blade down as hard as he could.

It sunk into my chest, and everything shattered.

I screamed. It was raw, and Samira's voice mixed with mine, reverberating until they sounded like one.

Until they were one.

Railius pulled the knife from my chest, but something else ran me through.

The pain was unbearable. It was an epicenter, and little fissures and cracks ran from it, slipping under my skin.

Because this wasn't a drift. It was a memory.

I saw everything unfolding before me like a map, finally making connections on roads that could never have been reached before. Ink writhed into the corners, filling things in. Terror and understanding bloomed in my chest where the knife had been buried. I fell to the ground, my vision flickering.

One of the last things I saw was a silhouette on the ledge of the wall surrounding the courtyard.

The woman in a white cloak.

Adelaide.

I could finally see her face.

It was Rory.

As my vision whited out, I saw her smile and wave.

Everything went black, and I felt the prison floor under me as I wavered between the drift and reality.

I knew what the emperor wanted the alchemist to know: the same thing Dr. Davie had discovered in the lab on 3B. The emperor had brought us forth through magic. Dr. Davie used what he called science, but the result was the same.

It was crazy, and my mind clawed at it, biting and pulling back as hard as it could as the realization bubbled to my mind.

It was the same secret. Born once of alchemy, and reborn through science centuries later.

I was Samira. I was the green-eyed girl, and I know how to create Hushed. I know how we all came to be.

I had a new body and a new name, but I was her.

I was Exhumed.

THIRTY-FOUR

I didn't land so much as crash back into my body, which felt too small for me. For the pain I carried. For what I knew.

Logan was leaning over me. His mouth was moving but I couldn't hear words.

I shoved myself upright. Rory was against the door of the storage room, her eyes wide, and Railius was on all fours. Svenja helped him up.

We'd all drifted. Something about the knife against my chest had brought the memory back so strongly that we were all pulled in.

I was against the lockers, sweat dripping down the back of my neck as Logan shouted my name again and again. Eventually, I heard him.

"Are you okay? Eerie?"

I looked at him.

"Yes," I breathed. I was and I wasn't. All at once, I was destroyed and put back together.

I turned.

Adelaide.

I am Samira, and Rory is Adelaide.

Railius.

I was remembering when I died in Salernum, when I'd stopped

breathing after I begged Railius to stab me in the chest because it was better than revealing what I knew.

What I know again.

It is what Dr. Davie had discovered only days before the fire. It was the procedure he was planning on practicing on Madeline that night. He had figured out how to extract secrets from living specimens. And now I knew how. I knew the process—all the mechanics, like an equation I could recite even if I didn't really understand it.

The Pull was finally there, but vague. Like a dull pulse at the base of my ribs.

It was everything I had to pull myself up. I looked at Logan and forced myself to actually see him. I looked to Rory. She was breathing hard as she pushed herself up. "Shit," she muttered, meeting my eyes as understanding washed over her. "*Shit.*"

Railius's eyes were wide as he struggled to get to his feet.

"What was that?" Fabian asked, reaching out to Rory.

Rory was reaching out to Fabian, and he was walking over to her, the box clenched in his loose fist.

"Fabian, wait," I said.

It was too late.

Rory's eyes flicked to mine, and then she lurched forward, snatching the box and running out of the room faster than I could yell.

I shoved myself off the lockers and sprinted after her, stooping to grab the gun and catching the last glimpse of her before she ran down the stairs.

"Rory! Wait!" I wanted to cower in a corner until I understood what I'd just learned. But there wasn't time. I had to keep moving.

I ran back down to 3B, the white tiles almost blinding me. I looked in every direction. Nothing. It was 11:57.

A splintering noise ripped from the speakers on the walls, a wailing that felt like it was trying to knock me over.

"What is that?" I yelled. The hair on my arms stood up. The sound was familiar.

"They know we're here," Railius shouted back as he reached the bottom of the stairs.

Logan was there, then, followed by Fabian and Svenja.

"What the hell is going *on*?" Fabian said, and I spun around.

It was 11:58.

The noise stopped. It started, and then stopped again, the sound like an electric charge ripping through my eardrum. It came and went in intervals.

"Eerie, what was that?" Fabian was unfocused, now, and too concerned about what he'd just seen to understand, and I didn't have time to explain.

"They're on their way. The Internment."

Fabian was always focused in a crisis. He'd carried me out of the forest and saved my life.

Now I had to save his.

Logan grabbed my hand, and I looked at him. He had no idea what had just happened, but he was there. He nodded resolutely.

"We have to go, Railius," I turned and screamed in between siren blares.

"Not yet!" he yelled back.

It was 11:59.

The sound of helicopters above us beat down, the cacophonous sound clashing with the pitch of the siren. "They're here," Railius said.

"We have to abandon this!" I said, holding his gaze for the first time since the drift. His eyes bored into mine, and I didn't look away.

"If we leave, any Hushed in here die," he said.

"If we don't, *we* die," I shouted back. They burned this place down once to keep its secrets. They killed their own. They'd do it again. But Railius was right. If we left, any Hushed that appeared at midnight would be killed.

I looked down.

12:00.

The siren stopped.

The hall was the kind of silent that feels too loud. The kind of silent that stirs up a unique kind of panic. Something was wrong.

I looked down the pristine hallway. Nothing.

Then an explosion ripped through the left side of the building, shaking the floor and rattling debris from the ceiling.

Smoke slid from under the stairwell door, its tendrils reaching out like a living thing.

Another explosion shook the prison, somewhere farther down the hall.

Railius looked up.

"They're pulling a Lit November." He dropped his eyes to mine. "They're dropping bombs from those helicopters, Eerie. They'll level the whole place."

Then we heard the first scream. It was shrill and full of terror.

I stopped when I heard it. I turned, looking down the long hallway, still reeling from the blast. Then the first Hushed walked out of the room the farthest down the hall, her bronzed skin a shock against the fluorescents. She was naked, shaking as she stumbled forward through the debris.

Another scream sounded just before another explosion, just two doors down. Railius ran after it. A man about Fabian's age walked out of the room next to Svenja. She took off her jacket and handed it to him.

One by one, Hushed stepped out of rooms.

Smoke filled the air, and I felt my vision tunnel. The Internment dropped another bomb, and the whole building shook.

I was right back where I started. Right back at the place of my nightmares.

Clear the rest. That's what the voice had said over the walkie-talkie the night I stirred. Kill the Harborers. They were doing the same thing, knowing Connelly was dead and that his Hushed would be here.

I clenched my fists.

Not this time. Not this fucking time.

I whipped around. Logan was there, tucking his gun into his pants.

"We have to help them," he said, but I grabbed his shoulders and forced him to meet my eyes.

"Logan. Get Fabian out of here." I stopped, realizing that he couldn't. Fabian couldn't be alone with Logan.

"I'm not leaving you here," he said.

"You could be their Wounded. Your presence could kill them," I explained, and his expression fell as he looked over my shoulder. "Svenja!" I shouted. She looked over her shoulder and then ran down the hallway toward me.

"Please," I said to Svenja, "get my brother out. And make sure Logan doesn't say a word to Fabian. Can you do that?" Svenja nodded. I looked back to Logan.

"Please. Just get out and be safe and just . . . be safe, okay?" I asked Logan as he reached out and took my hand.

He nodded. He knew I couldn't explain anything.

Not until I found Rory.

Logan grabbed Fabian, and they disappeared with Svenja down the smoky hall.

I turned back just in time to see a figure slip back up the stairwell. Rory.

My feet were moving before I could yell after her. The stairwell was filled with smoke, but I didn't even notice until I had to stop to cough up a lung.

There was something missing, here. A piece I didn't understand. I had to find her. Rory was my best friend. She was the hand I held in the dark. She wasn't my enemy, no matter what this weird effed-up history said.

Level 2B was destroyed. The ceiling was caved in, revealing slivers of night sky two levels up. Rubble covered the floor, and fires burned along the walls.

I peered into what looked like an old break room. The vending machine was on fire, and cellophane-covered snacks popped and hissed. Tables were overturned, and rock and dust covered the leather couches.

From behind the doorway, someone swung a box at my head.

I ducked, but Rory swung the box again wildly.

I launched myself at her, hitting her in the forearm. The box fell to the ground with a clatter, and she sidestepped me, swinging a leg around and catching me in the chest, sending me back into the tables. I rolled backward, ignoring the exploding pain in my shoulder and lower back.

I grabbed my gun and pointed it at her chest as she leaned down to grab the box off the floor by her foot.

"Rory! Stop!" I shouted, straightening. We were on opposite sides of the room.

She eyed me and then stood upright. Her hair was loose around her face, and she breathed heavily. Her lip was cut, making her mouth glisten red in the firelight. She looked just like the Adelaide from my memory.

"What the hell? What the hell is this?" I gasped. "Rory—"

"You saw what I saw, Samira," she spat out. "Eerie. Whatever the hell you are."

"If it's all true, then we were friends. If I'm Samira and you're Adelaide, then we're *friends*. We weren't at first, but—"

Rory took a step, and so did I, keeping my gun on her chest because the feral look in her eyes wasn't like Rory. It was something else, and it scared me.

"You really don't remember, do you?" she whispered.

"Is this about Railius?" I asked, remembering the kiss. "Because Samira might have loved him, I don't know. She's like a book I read a long time ago, Ror, and I'm just piecing it together. Please. If she did— if *I* loved him, I don't now."

She laughed, and it made me tighten my grip on the gun.

"You think this is about a *boy*? No. This is about us and the steps he never took to ensure our survival. *I* did what needed to be done. *I* tracked down Dr. Davie's research and followed him to Rearden Falls. I found the only two Hushed to survive Ironbark, hoping there would be scraps of something I could use. Even as you were explaining your drifts, I thought they were from Railius. Or that you were maybe seeing mine. I never thought it was your own memory. I just thought . . ." she shook her head. Her words were thick.

"I just never thought you would be back. Exhumed are a myth. Either way, I'd written you off. You were so fucking *helpless*. Scared of *everything*. That's why I focused on Fabian."

Tears welled up in my eyes.

I didn't want to believe anything she was saying, but her face was so full of something I had never seen before. Her bloody lips curled in hatred. Her eyes were lit by the room crumbling around us. It was like Rory was fading away. She looked like Adelaide. Suddenly, all her knowledge about everything made sense. She knew how to control drifting. She knew our history because she was *there*.

"What are you going to do?" I asked. "What good could possibly come from anything in that box? Anything Dr. Davie was doing? Even *he* knew it was evil, Rory!"

She smirked. "We could outnumber humans. We could pull Hushed out before humans are dead—before they can get rid of them themselves—and then we could fight back. That's what needs to happen if we're going to survive. Without humans, there won't be a Pull. And there are other horrors in this box, things that can help in the coming war. Secrets and discoveries even I can't imagine."

She smiled at the thought.

I shook my head. Rory loved waffles and hated polka dots and cried with me when Sarah died. She wasn't capable of this.

I threw the gun to the side, and Rory cocked an eyebrow.

I took a step toward her.

"We don't have to do this. Whatever happened, way back when, it doesn't have to matter now. I love you, Rory—"

"MY NAME ISN'T RORY! AND YOUR NAME ISN'T EERIE!" The words splintered from her as she rushed forward, her face inches from mine. She breathed hard as her skin tightened against her skull. She shook her head. "And when the day comes, you'll make the same choice. You'll betray me again."

My heart sputtered, and I reached for her. "What did I do? I don't even remember! Talk to me, Rory. Please. Give me the box, and we'll stop this. We'll leave Rearden Falls. You, me, Fabe—"

She yanked back.

"There's no escaping this, Eerie. You've run from everything, until now. Found the loophole in every situation. But now your past has found you. And you will carry it."

"You're the one that told me I was more than my secret. I believed you. Believe me, now."

Rory put her hands to her head. "I WAS HOPING YOU WOULD DIE. Don't you get it?"

I froze, and she held her arms out to her sides.

"It was a win-win for me. Either you would be out with Winspeare, which gave me time to get closer to Fabian and try and crack his ridiculous holier-than-thou act, or you would die and give him the push he needed to remember everything he could about Ironbark. *I wanted you to die. I wanted you to give in to the Pull and die.*"

Tears ripped down my cheeks as I looked at her, my eyes searching hers.

"You're lying."

"Am I? What do you think happened to Reed?"

My heart seized, and she tilted her head. She took a slinking step toward me.

"He was easy. You know how long it took me to convince him that he was better off dead? That he was just the shard of a monster?"

Shard of a monster. He'd said those exact words.

My hands curled into claws, and my breath was white-hot.

The tears were gone, and all that was left in me was rage.

"Ten minutes," she continued. "Fabian needed a recall to the righteous cause, and Reed was right there, crying like you're crying now—"

I lunged at her, screaming my throat raw as I clawed at her face and knocked her down.

She laughed as she whipped me around, reversing my momentum and throwing me across the room. I landed and rolled up to my knees.

"Eerie!" I heard Railius shout my name from down the hall.

An explosion sounded somewhere in the building.

Adelaide sneered at me as she took a step toward the metal box that lay on the floor.

The name Rory was burned through, turned to ash by the memory of Reed's last words to me. She was Adelaide, and the hatred I felt was like fire. I stood.

Another explosion sounded, closer than the others.

Everything was chaos. The roof above creaked, caving in between us. Dust and debris flew everywhere, and I heard her shriek. I couldn't tell if it was from pain or rage, and I was too angry to care about either.

"Eerie! Come on!" Railius was at the door.

I ran forward, grabbing the box from the floor and turning toward the hallway.

A fiery mess collapsed in front of the doorway in front of me, blocking me from Railius.

"Back up," he called. "I'm going to kick it through!"

Behind me, I heard a strangled scream.

Don't listen.

"Eerie!" she cried, and I saw her, trapped under a support beam, surrounded by flame and dust and debris.

"Eerie! Help! Please!"

"Do not listen to her!" Railius said as he frantically tried to clear the door.

"*Please!*" she screamed as the fire got close to her.

I hated that I stopped.

I hated that I couldn't leave her to be burned alive. I couldn't run and leave her screaming, like I'd left everyone the night I stirred.

"No!" Railius called as I bolted backward. Soot covered her face, and blood streamed down her face from a cut on her hairline.

"Thank you, Eerie," she gasped.

"Push on three! One, two—"

It took everything I had to lift it off her. I shoved the beam so it fell to the other side.

Then her leg swung around, hitting behind my ankles, and I was on my back. She was on top of me.

"Eerie!" Railius called out, kicking the last bit of drywall as hard as he could.

Adelaide lowered her bloody face to mine. She had the gun, and she cocked it with one hand, putting the barrel to my forehead.

"You think you're so *good*. And maybe you are. But that's what got a knife in your chest the first time, and it will be what kills you this time."

I kicked but hit nothing but air. I wrapped my hand around her wrist.

"Then do it," I spat at her, enjoying the look of surprise on her face. "If you're so evil, then just end it."

She pushed the barrel harder against my head. I could feel her hand shaking.

I waited for death. For the sharpness of it, for the fade out. I squeezed her wrist three times, and she snarled, pushing the barrel deeper against my forehead.

Then she was off of me. The gun clattered to the ground.

I rolled to my knees just in time to see her grab the box and jump over the fallen table to the crumbling outer wall.

She scaled it in two seconds, turning at the top to look back at Railius. She blew him a kiss and then disappeared into the night.

❧

Logan met us in the hallway. Of course he'd run back inside. I knew he would, regardless of what I told him to do. Railius had one of my arms across his shoulders, helping me limp-run down the hall, and Logan took the other.

It felt like the sky was falling. We barely made it up the rickety staircase before there was a crash loud enough to shake my ribs and the entire northern wing of Ironbark collapsed behind us.

We were out into the wet night, and my heart faltered as I looked up on the ravine.

Dozens of Internment officers ran down toward us.

Railius, Logan, and I stopped.

Gunshots sounded through the night, and I braced for the pain.

Except it didn't come. The Internment officers fell, one by one, and Railius pulled us left as we ran for the dark tree line.

"What was that?" Logan asked.

"The backup I didn't think would get here in time," Railius answered as the shadow embraced us.

THIRTY-FIVE

I laid in Logan's bed, but I couldn't sleep. The moonlight rolled in through the glass, casting weird shadows around the room.

He was still next to me, and I rolled over to look at him.

I touched his face.

We'd gone to the cabin after everything fell apart. Railius had offered us shelter at the Haunt's headquarters, but with the dozens of Hushed that had showed up from different cells to cover us in addition to the six new ones we'd saved from Ironbark, I knew it would be a tight fit as it was. Railius said it probably wasn't safe for me to be alone, but I told him I wasn't alone.

We got away before the blue-and-red police lights flooded the mountain pass, followed by the reporters. It would be interesting to see how they explained this one.

I'd meant what I'd said to Adelaide about choosing my own life, and I didn't realize how much I'd meant it until the gunshots died down and I made sure Fabian was still alive. Stunned, confused, hurt . . . but alive. Svenja took him to the church—it's where he said he wanted to be—and told me she'd stay with him until morning.

When I turned back to Logan and threw myself in his arms, I knew.

My name was Eerie, not Samira.

I was made by a man who regretted the secret he made, but who had no choice but to trust it. To trust me. That's what the letter had said.

And I wanted Logan.

Adelaide had been wrong back in the Adrenian Pass, when she'd told me that compassion would kill me. And she'd been wrong at Mal's when she told me that my secret didn't matter.

I was whole, and the choice was still mine.

I leaned down and kissed his lips, and then stood up, walking to the window.

It was snowing, and the flakes refracted the moonlight, throwing the whole night into crystal chaos.

Just outside, beyond Logan's window and past the back porch, a figure sat on a tree stump, looking up at the moon.

I threw on Logan's snow jacket and boots and crept outside without a sound.

⁌⳺⳺

"Your place a little crowded?" I asked, crossing my arms over my chest as I stepped over a tree root and crossed the clearing toward Railius. Logan's boots were huge, so I'm pretty sure I looked like I was cross-country skiing.

He shrugged. "Something like that. I hate sharing a bathroom."

The snow fell on his eyelashes, and he looked down.

"I shouldn't have helped her. It was my fault she got away," I said finally.

He looked up at me and shook his head.

"She can't do anything with the box without Fabian. She needs the key . . . and he has it. Once she burns out all her options, she'll be back."

I bristled. "You mean for Fabian?"

"We'll be ready when she does," he said.

I nodded and looked down at Logan's boots. I hadn't even thought about how I was going to navigate Logan and Fabian being near each other. I hadn't let myself fully consider that they couldn't be. It was too painful.

"I still can't believe it. I can't believe it was Rory. This whole time."

"Keep your friends close," Railius started.

"And your enemies seducing your brother while counseling you on all major love decisions and being your best friend." I joked to keep from having a complete breakdown. This was the worst night, and all I wanted to do was tell Rory about it.

He laughed. It was genuine, and I remembered it from a glimpse of the in-between years. I remember the sound of it echoing in a tavern hall or beside me as we walked along the Thames, throwing day-old bread to the ducks while Adelaide talked to a soldier, catching my eye just long enough to wink at me over his shoulder.

The memory scattered like dandelion dust.

"We used to laugh like this all the time," Railius said quietly, and I looked down.

"I don't quite remember. I hope I will," I said, looking up. "She said I'd betrayed her," I said, looking up at Railius. "I don't remember it. I don't know what she's talking about."

He leaned his head back at my words, and then licked his lips, slowly. They were chapped against the cold. He pushed himself to his feet, and I looked down.

"Did I? Did I betray her?" I pressed.

Railius stuck his hands in his pockets and brought his shoulders up to his ears.

He eyed me skeptically, and I glared at him.

"Tell me."

"Things will come back to you in time, Samira—" He stopped, and I looked down again. Calling me by that name was a slip, and he was embarrassed. It was true, but at the same time, it wasn't. I wasn't Samira. Not really. I was mismatched. A body and a soul and free will all working to try and meld together.

He sighed. "I remember where we came from. I know, in painful detail, how dark the deal was that made us. You were—and are—the next phase. The one that Adelaide thought would bring freedom, but would also bring death to everyone that touches it."

He was right. Somewhere in the back of my mind, I remembered Connelly telling Dr. Davie that it would be used only on prisoners of war. Only on murder suspects. But he knew it was a lie, even then. Humanity wouldn't use it as a precaution. It would be a weapon. It would be used to pull secrets out of anyone and everyone. It was a threat to the very existence of free will.

"And Adelaide?"

He looked down. "She knows how to end this curse."

I swallowed hard.

"What does that mean?" I asked. He shrugged, and I pushed. "Don't you know? Through drifts, or something?"

"She has always kept it closely guarded. As I had. You could access mine because of who you are. Because of our history. Our trust. I guess it was like muscle memory."

I looked at him. There was pain in his eyes, but he pushed past it.

"But I've never been able to crack Adelaide."

"She won't tell?"

"She told you that she could end it, but never told you how. She thought you'd agree that she should keep the secret to herself."

"I didn't," I filled in quietly.

He shook his head.

"You told her she should tell her Wounded."

"I told her to go die."

Railius exhaled sharply. "In your defense, you did convince me to kill you at one point, so I think that whole situation probably begs for context. I was not there, so I can't help you."

I shivered and shut my eyes tight. "I don't remember doing any of that. I don't even know what she told me."

I looked down, taking a deep breath. *The time will come again, and you will betray me.*

"So the Hush-a-Bye rhyme . . . it's about us?" I asked, thinking about the words.

Then there was one where once were few.

Railius nodded. "Adelaide convinced the humans that I'd been the one killing villagers. She used my killing you as proof of my violent nature, collected the reward for turning me in, and started a deep fear of our kind, back then. She got her revenge and the spark for war all at once."

"They arrested you?" I asked. I hadn't thought about what happened after the drift ended.

Railius smiled sadly. "That's a story for a different time, when it's a little warmer and there is more whiskey, I think."

I pressed my hand to my forehead. "I always thought Exhumed were a myth. I'm still not sure I understand how this happened."

Railius shrugged. "Last time we were created, it was through magic. It seems Dr. Davie was able to replicate the same phenomenon through science, and you came back."

"How? It doesn't seem like that would be possible."

"Magic and science aren't that far apart, Eerie."

He said it with such assurance, without a hint of hesitation in his voice. Like it was something everyone should understand.

"This is all . . ." I laughed through the tears that welled up in my eyes. "It's all a lot," I said.

"I know."

I looked up at him.

"It's so strange," he whispered, "you're here, but you're not. You have no idea how much I've missed you."

He touched my cheek, and I wanted to pull back. I wanted to gasp, but I couldn't. Because somewhere deep down, in a place that had just woken up, I missed him too. I didn't know what to do with that.

Railius smiled at me. It was genuine, but sad. "I don't mean to push you, but we have other things to talk about."

The silence was heavy around us as the snow fell. His eyes met mine through the falling ice, and I looked down. "Look. I know that . . . I know that we had, um. History, no pun intended. And I just—"

"Eerie," he started, and I shook my head harder.

"I just—"

"*Eerie.*"

"I'm with Logan. That's what I'm trying to say. Completely. Embarrassingly. It's pretty bad."

I lifted my eyes, and Railius raised his eyebrows. "Well. Okay. I was going to talk about the Haunt's next move, but glad we cleared that up too."

It was freezing, but my throat flushed horribly, and I tucked my chin to my chest.

"Right. The Haunt."

"I want you to take your rightful place, Eerie. Next to me—*not like that*," he said, when I cocked an eyebrow at him. "But if the Hushed from tonight are right, we have to move quickly. There is something coming. Something worse than what was happening at Ironbark."

I looked down and remembered Dr. Davie's note.

"Tell me," I said, glancing up at Railius.

Railius met my eyes. "We didn't get all Connelly's Hushed tonight. A man at his level didn't just have secrets in Ironbark. And we weren't the only ones tracking him."

"The Internment? Gravediggers?" I asked.

"I think there is a sort of alliance between the two, and more dangerous than both. And they are going to be looking for Connelly's Hushed. Eerie, any of those Hushed could have periphery that point to what Dr. Davie was trying to discover. They could point to you. It might have already happened. We have to find Connelly's Hushed, wherever they are, before the humans do."

"And before Adelaide," I added, because I knew it would only be a matter of time before she discovered this as well.

"But even if they figured out I existed . . . I can't tell them anything if they're not my Wounded." I put a hand to my chest. There was a dull ache in between my ribs.

Railius didn't say anything, and I felt my stomach drop. There was more, and I knew it. All of this, and there was still something worse I needed to know.

"That's just it, Eerie. We're not the same as most Hushed. We don't just have one Wounded. You, Adelaide, and I all belong to *everyone* who has been affected by Hushed."

Everything in me stilled. "What do you mean? Every human is my Wounded? I could tell anyone?"

"It means the Pull won't be as intense, because it isn't directed at one person. But yes, Eerie. The whole world is our Wounded. We're the only ones who have ever dealt with this. Other Hushed have come close, even lasted centuries. But we're the only ones who have lasted this long. I can teach you how to cope with it, but it's never going away. I need you to help me, Eerie. And you need me to help you. If you give into your Pull, no human will ever be safe again. Including the one you love."

"You know his name," I shot back.

Railius nodded and looked out over my shoulder. "Logan. Logan won't be safe. You need to stay close to me to protect him."

A week ago, I would've told him to piss off.

Two days ago, I wanted to kill him.

Tonight, I knew he was right.

There was evil in this world, and it wasn't going to wait for me to be ready. Whether I liked it or not, I was in this. I'd been in this since the beginning.

"If I go with you, I bring Logan."

"Logan is a human, Eerie. We've talked about this."

"Take it or leave it, because I'm not going anywhere without him. Also he'd probably just keep showing up in the middle of raids in various costumes until you let him join anyway."

Logan could kill me, but I wasn't doing this without him. I was stronger than I'd ever thought, and I wasn't going to run from him now. We would figure this out.

Railius rolled his eyes, but I saw the hint of a smile turn up the corner of his mouth.

"Fine," he said, reaching out to shake my almost-numb hand.

His skin was warm, and his hand swallowed mine.

He met my eyes, and I fell into his out of habit.

I didn't want to remember anything more. It would only hurt.

I tore my eyes away from his and turned around.

"Tomorrow?" I asked.

"Tomorrow," his voice rang out behind me.

⤜⊷⤛

When I went back inside, Logan was awake, reheating coffee in the microwave.

I went up behind him and wrapped my arms around him.

He turned around.

I'd told him everything by the fire earlier, before we'd fallen asleep. He'd lain next to me, twirling my hair in his fingers, and he didn't freak out once. Not even when I told him I'm technically two thousand years old. Or that I'd once kissed Railius. Whatever that had been, it died with Samira. I couldn't show him the note Dr. Davie had left me, but he understood that there were things I had to keep to myself.

He *had* been pissed that I'd lied about going to Ironbark, but I told him it wouldn't happen again. It wouldn't. I meant it when I told Railius that Logan and I were in this together.

And Logan would've let me cry about Rory, but I didn't want to.

How do you mourn someone who wasn't dead? How do you mourn someone who never really existed?

"What does Railius want?" he asked.

I took a deep breath. I'd been trying to figure out the way to phrase this as I walked back inside.

"Remember when I said we were done with the Haunt?"

Logan nodded slowly.

"What if I was second-guessing that?"

The microwave behind him beeped, and he reached up and hit the button without breaking my gaze.

"I would say it was about time."

I straightened, and he turned around and pulled his coffee out of the microwave.

"I thought you'd be fine just leaving it alone?"

He blew on his coffee and nodded. "And I was. When this was

about vengeance. But it's not. This is about right and wrong, now. And I know which side is right."

I looked down.

"It will be dangerous," I warned.

He stepped closer and slinked his arm around my waist. "Felony record, remember?"

I looked up at him.

My whole world had fallen apart, but he was still the same. He was constant. He was still Logan, and he was looking down at me. Eerie.

I kissed him, and he pulled me closer.

I pulled back, slightly.

"Are you drinking a reheated pumpkin spice latte?" I whispered against his lips.

Logan smiled and pulled me close, kissing me as the pink light of morning broke over the hills.

It broke over a world of charred, broken things. A world of bones, coming out of their corners, rising out of shadow to kick up embers and set the world on fire.

ACKNOWLEDGMENTS

I started writing this book in 2014. It has found homes at two different publishing houses before Blackstone, and both fell through. It has broken my heart and mended it back together in too many ways to count.

I've written this book in three different houses while pregnant with three different kids. I've written in my parents' kitchen in the middle of the night, coffee shops, parking lots, airport lounges, on set while filming in London. It's been edited halfway to shit, torn apart by editors who didn't like it, printed and sticking out of my bag while I taught classes and dropped kids off at daycare . . . It stuck to me like a dream I wasn't giving up on.

And I'm not strong enough to do that kind of journey alone. Stephen King says writing can be a lonely pursuit, but I wasn't lonely at all.

So, I have some people to thank for ten years of support, even if that word isn't enough to capture what they've done for me.

I want to thank Ross, my husband. The man who woke up before me to make sure the vibes were right for my 5:00 a.m. writing session, even though I know he was exhausted. The man who took me out for a cupcake when I hit worldbuilding snags and talked through them with me. Not every writer gets a Ross, but it's my deep hope that every writer finds one. I would not be here without him, and I mean that literally. I would have starved eons ago.

My parents. My mom, who would routinely take all my kids from me and wave me off to go write and has never doubted that this day would come. More than that—thank you for loving a kid who couldn't have been more different from you and not trying to change her. Thank you for your love of dark stories and for telling me it was okay to love them, too.

Dad—when I was thirteen, we went and saw *Spider-Man* at the Edwards Theater. We were standing by the pinball machine after, waiting for someone to use the bathroom, and you talked to me about the movie like I wasn't a mentally ill thirteen-year-old. You told me sometimes movies like that ask questions of life that you can't put into words, and I never forgot that. And thank you for being a steady crash-landing pad for us. I couldn't have made it this far without it—and I don't think you get paid enough for that.

Ash. This book is dedicated to the weird blond chick who walked into my classroom when I was a young adjunct and then just decided to never fucking leave. It's not often you meet one of the most important people in your life after falling off a bike and limping into a lecture hall, but God is funny, sometimes. Thank you for keeping Haunt alive, even when I thought it was dead. Thank you for the "omg this song" texts, the "is this unhinged" questions, tequila and *New Girl* sessions (and understanding why we gotta rewind the first Nick and Jess kiss three times), helping me pick the right outfits, talking me out of bad piercings but into bangs, and marrying my brother. You're such a lightweight; I feel fine.

Isaac: for having a huge brain and even bigger heart and somehow always finding time to show up and cheer for the freak who writes for a living. You're saving the world but still answer my FaceTime calls when I need someone to vent to. I'll never say this to your face but you're a wonderful person and a gifted scientist.

Sue and Ross: Thank you for every read-through, every article about writing, every "you go girl" text. I won the in-law game, and I'm so grateful for you.

To Brittany Sawrey-Coulson. For being a safe place to land, a shoulder to cry on, and the one who wipes the mascara from under my eyes and reminds me who I am. Thank you for your story heart, your words of wisdom, and your love.

Anna Bright—my mu'fuckin bes fran—for the slightly psychotic texts about our slightly psychotic children, and for being a badass writer mama who understands the stress of being on sub while dealing with hand/foot/mouth. Love you.

To Landon, Alanna, Hil, Jill, Lee, Kate . . . thank you for being on this journey with me. Michael Robin, you weirdo. Thank you for texts about pie and calling me to talk me through a mental breakdown. A deep bow to my sisters—Hannah, Rachel, and Becca, for walking through the weirdest years with me and knowing there are more to come. Marie, Stu, David, Bri, Victoria, Elaina, Jack, Remi, and Cami . . . thank you for the text hype, the hilarious reels, and the love. To my cousins who are ride-or-dies from states away: Heidi, Amber, Seth, Jesse, AJ, Sami, Mitchell—love you. The Dubach/Rutherford clan—for early reads and being the best cheerleaders a girl could ask for. Stephen and Allison, for being a safe haven. Alan and Erika, for the same reason. Dr. Arai and Luke, for keeping it weird. Kathy Gruber . . . for being the president of my Ohio pep squad. You're magic.

My Beechwoodians: You make living here feel like home. I love you all.

And to Loue, who has been with me from the start. You showed me what enduring love looks like. So many of the beautiful moments of Eerie and Rory's friendship are based on ours. Not many people get to have a ride-or-die for over half their life. Thank you for being mine. 1-2-3. 1-2-3-4.

And to my kids. Aryn Lee, Liam Robin, River Grace, and Benjamin Isaac—and for nieces and nephew who do life with us: Emilia, Sophia, and Eli. For the notes slid under the door while I'm writing, for the Post-its under my desk. For the snuggles after a long day. I love you guys.

And of course, the team who brought *The Hushed* to life, and believed in it for so long:

The inimitable Gwen Beal and the lovely team at UTA who saw the merit in this story and fought for it. Mary Pender, who has been with me since 2016 and never once doubted what this story could be. Echo Matthews, Daniel Vang, and Jonathan Rosenthal, for always having my back.

My wonderful team at Blackstone: Daniel Ehrenhaft, William Boggess, Linley Delucchi, Levi Coren, Nicole Sklitsis, Tatiana Radujkovic . . . the whole publishing journey was worth it to wind up with you guys. Thank you for loving this story and giving it the perfect home.

A special thank you to Lana Harper and Kathryn Purdie, who read the book early and gave blurbs before it was even officially sold. You are both the definition of writers helping writers, and I cannot thank you enough for helping make my dreams come true.

And finally, thank you to God. The Storyteller, the one made me to do this job that brings me untold joy. May I stay directly behind You as You cut the path before me, and may we all rest in knowing no secrets we bear could separate us from Your love.